# FAR TO SEEK

Owing to the antiquity and rarity of this book, certain pages are regrettably absent, and readability is compromised due to the blurring of the original text. If you possess any insights regarding the availability of these missing sections, kindly inform us. Your assistance is crucial in ensuring the completion of this significant work for the benefit of future generations.

# FAR TO SEEK

## A ROMANCE OF ENGLAND AND INDIA

MAUD DIVER

GYAN

*Published by*

Gyan Publishing House
5, Ansari Road
Daryaganj, New Delhi-110002
Phone: 011-47034999, 9811692060
E-mail: books@gyanbooks.com

*Distribution Network*
gyanbooks.com
India, USA, Canada, UK, Australia



ISBN: 978-93-7133-014-5 (PB)

First Published, 1921

2nd Impression 2025

*Printed at:* Gyan Press, Delhi.



**FAR TO SEEK**
Author Maud Diver

# Far to Seek

A Romance of England and India

# FAR TO SEEK

## A Romance of England and India

BY

MAUD DIVER

AUTHOR OF 'CAPTAIN DESMOND, V.C.,' 'LILÁMANI,'
'DESMOND'S DAUGHTER,' ETC.

"I am athirst for far-away things.
My soul goes out in longing to touch the skirt of the dim
distance . . .
O Far-to-Seek! O the keen call of thy flute . . . !"
—RABINDRANATH TAGORE.

"His hidden meaning dwells in our endeavours;
Our valours are our best gods."
—JOHN FLETCHER.

1921

*TO*

*MY BLUE BIRD,*

*BRINGER OF HAPPINESS TO MYSELF*
*AND OTHERS,*

*I DEDICATE THIS IDYLL OF*
*A MOTHER AND SON.*

*M. D.*

---

" *The dawn sleeps behind the shadowy hills,*
*The stars hold their breath, counting the hours. . . .*
*There is only your own pair of wings and the pathless sky,*
*Bird, oh my Bird, listen to me—do not close your wings.*"

—RABINDRANATH TAGORE.

# AUTHOR'S NOTE.

As part of my book is set in Lahore, at the time of the outbreak, in April 1919, I wish to state clearly that, while the main events are true to fact, the characters concerned, both English and Indian, are purely imaginary. At the same time, the opinions expressed by my Indian characters on the present outlook are all based on the written or spoken opinions of actual Indians—loyal or disaffected, as the case may be.

There were no serious British casualties in Lahore, though there were many elsewhere. I have imagined one locally, for purposes of my story. In all other respects I have kept close to recorded facts.

M. D.

# CONTENTS.

# PHASE I.

# THE GLORY AND THE DREAM

# CHAPTER I.

"Thou art the sky, and thou art the nest as well."

BY the shimmer of blue under the beeches Roy knew that summer—"really truly summer!"—had come back at last. And summer meant picnics and strawberries and out-of-door lessons, and the lovely hot smell of pine-needles in the pine-wood, and the lovelier cool smell of moss cushions in the beech-wood—home of squirrels and birds and bluebells; unfailing wonderland of discovery and adventure.

Roy was an imaginative creature, isolated a little by the fact of being three and a half years older than Christine, and "miles older" than Jerry and George, mere babies, for whom the magic word adventure held no meaning at all.

Luckily, there was Tara, from the black-and-white house: Tara, who shared his lessons and, in spite of the drawback of being a girl, had long ago won her way into his private world of knight-errantry and romance. Tara was eight years and five weeks old; quite a reasonable age in the eyes of Roy, whose full name was Nevil Le Roy Sinclair, and who would be nine in June. With the exception of grown-ups, who didn't count, there was no one older than nine in his immediate neighbourhood. Tara came nearest: but *she* wouldn't be nine till next year; and by that time, he would be ten. The point was, she couldn't catch him up if she tried ever so.

It was Tara's mother, Lady Despard, who had the happy idea of sharing lessons, that would otherwise be rather a lonely affair for both. But it was Roy's mother who had the still happier idea of teaching them herself. Tara's mother joined in now and then; but Roy's mother—who loved it beyond everything—secured the lion's share. And Roy was old enough by now to be proudly aware of his own good fortune. Most other children of his acquaintance were afflicted with tiresome governesses, who wore ugly jackets and hats, who said "Don't drink with your mouth full," and "Don't argue the point!"—Roy's favourite sin—and always told you to "Look in the dictionary" when you found a scrumptious new word and wanted to hear all about it. The dictionary, indeed! Roy privately regarded it as one of the many mean evasions to which grown-ups were addicted.

His ripe experience on the subject was gleaned partly from neighbouring families, partly from infrequent visits to "Aunt Jane"—whom he hated with a deep unreasoned hate—and "Uncle George," who had a kind, stupid face, but anyhow tried to be funny and made futile bids for favour with pen-knives and half-crowns. Possibly it was these uncongenial visits that quickened in him very early the consciousness that his own beautiful home was, in some special way, different from other boys' homes, and his mother—in a still more special way—different from other boys' mothers. . . .

And that proud conviction was no mere myth born of his young adoration. In all the County, perhaps in all the Kingdom, there could be found no mother in the least like Lilámani Sinclair, descendant of Rajput chiefs and wife of an English Baronet, who, in the face of formidable barriers, had dared to accept all risks and follow the promptings of his heart. One of these days there would dawn on Roy the knowledge that he was the child of a unique romance, of a mutual love and courage that had run the gauntlet of prejudices and antagonisms, of fightings without and fears within; yet, in the end, had triumphed as they triumph who will not admit defeat. All this initial blending of ecstasy and pain, of spiritual striving and mastery, had gone to the making of Roy, who in the fulness of time would realise—perhaps with pride, perhaps with secret trouble and misgiving—the high and complex heritage that was his.

Meanwhile he only knew that he was fearfully happy, especially in summer time; that his father—who had smiling eyes and loved messing with paints like a boy—was kinder than anyone else's, so long as you didn't tell bad fibs or meddle with his brushes; that his idolised mother, in her soft coloured silks and saris, her bangles and silver shoes, was the "very most beautiful" being in the whole world. And Roy's response to the appeal of beauty was abnormally quick and keen. It could hardly be otherwise with the son of these two. He loved, with a fervour beyond his years, the clear pale oval of his mother's face; the coils of her dark hair, seen always through a film of softest muslin—moon-yellow or apple-blossom pink, or deep dark blue like the sky out of his window at night spangled with stars. He loved the glimmer of her jewels, the sheen and feel of her wonderful Indian silks, that seemed to smell like the big sandalwood box in the drawing-room. And beyond everything he loved her smile and the touch of her hand, and her voice that could charm away all nightmare terrors, all questionings and rebellions, of his excitable brain.

Yet, in outward bearing, he was not a sentimental boy. The Sinclairs did not run to sentiment; and the blood of two virile races—English and Rajput—was mingled in his veins. Already his budding masculinity bade him keep the feelings of 'that other Roy' locked in the most secret corner of his heart. Only his mother, and sometimes Tara, caught a glimpse of him now and then. Lady Sinclair, herself, never guessed that, in the vivid imaginations of both children, she herself was the ever-varying incarnation of the fairy princesses and Rajputni heroines of her own tales. Their appetite for these was insatiable; and her store of them seemed never ending: folk tales of East and West; true tales of Crusaders, of Arthur and his knights; of Rajput Kings and Queens, in the far-off days when Rajasthán—a word like a trumpet call—was holding her desert cities against hordes of invaders, and heroes scorned to die in their beds. Much of it all was frankly beyond them; but the colour and the movement, the atmosphere of heroism and high endeavour quickened imagination and fellow-feeling, and left an impress on both children that would not pass with the years.

To their great good fortune, these tales and talks were

a part of her simple, individual plan of education. An even greater good fortune—in their eyes—was her instinctive response to the seasons. She shared to the full their clear conviction that schoolroom lessons and a radiant day of summer were a glaring misfit; and she trimmed her sails, or rather her time-table, accordingly.

"Sentimental folly and thoroughly demoralising," was the verdict of Aunt Jane, overheard by Roy, who was not supposed to understand. "They will grow up without an inch of moral backbone. And you can't say I didn't warn you. Lady Despard's a crank, of course; but Nevil is a fool to allow it. Goodness knows *he* was bad enough, though he was reared on the good old lines. And you are not giving his son a chance. The sooner the boy's packed off to school the better. I shall tell him so."

And his mother had answered with her dignified unruffled sweetness—that made her so beautifully different from ordinary people, who got red and excited and made foolish faces: "He will not agree. He shares my believing that children are in love with life. It is their first love. Pity to crush it too soon; putting their minds in tight boxes with no chink for Nature to creep in. If they first find knowledge by their young life-love, afterwards, they will perhaps give up their life-love to gain it."

Roy could not follow all that; but the music of the words, matched with the music of his mother's voice, convinced him that her victory over horrid interfering Aunt Jane was complete. And it was comforting to know that his father agreed about not putting their minds in tight boxes. For Aunt Jane's drastic prescription alarmed him. Of course school would have to come some day; but his was not the temperament that hankers for it at an early age. As to a moral backbone—whatever sort of an affliction that might be—if it meant growing up ugly and 'disagreeable,' like Aunt Jane or the Aunt Jane cousins, he fervently hoped he would never have one—or Tara either. . . .

But on this particular morning he feared no manner of bogey—not even school or a moral backbone—because the bluebells were alight under his beeches—hundreds and hundreds of them—and 'really truly' summer had come back at last!

Roy knew it the moment he sprang out of bed and stood barefoot on the warm patch of carpet near the window, stretching his slim shapely body, instinctively responsive to the sun's caress. No less instinctive was his profound conviction that nothing possibly could go wrong on a day like this.

In the first place it meant lessons under their favourite tree. In the second, it was history and poetry day; and Roy's delight in both made them hardly seem lessons at all. He thought it very clever of his mother, having them together. The depth of her wisdom he did not yet discern. She allowed them within reason, to choose their own poems: and Roy, exploring her bookcase, had lighted on Shelley's 'Cloud'—the musical flow of words, the more entrancing because only half understood. He had straightway learnt the first three verses for a surprise. He crooned them now, his head flung back a little, his gaze intent on a gossamer film that floated just above the pine tops—'still as a brooding dove.' . . .

Standing there, in full sunlight—the modelling of his young limbs veiled, yet not hidden, by his silk night-suit; the carriage of head and shoulders betraying innate pride of race—he looked, on every count, no unworthy heir to the House of Sinclair and its simple honourable traditions: one that might conceivably live to challenge family prejudices and qualms. The thick dark hair, ruffled from sleep, was his mother's; and hers the semi-opaque ivory tint of his skin. The clean-cut forehead and nose, the blue-grey eyes, with the lurking smile in them, were Nevil Sinclair's own. In him, at least, it would seem that love was justified of her children.

But of family features, as of family qualms, he was, as yet, radiantly unaware. Snatching his towel, he scampered barefoot down the passage to the nursery bathroom, where the tap was already running.

Fifteen minutes later, dressed, but hatless and still barefoot, he was racing over the vast dew-drenched lawn, leaving a trail of grey-green smudges on its silvered surface, chanting the opening lines of Shelley's 'Cloud' to breakfast-hunting birds.

## CHAPTER II.

"Those first affections,
Those shadowy recollections, . . .
Are yet the fountain-light of all our day;
Are yet the master-light of all our seeing."
—WORDSWORTH.

THE blue rug under Roy's beech-tree was splashed with freckles of sunshine; freckles that were never still, because a fussy little wind kept swaying the topmost branches, where the youngest beech-leaves flickered, like golden-green butterflies bewitched by some malicious fairy, so that they could never fly into the sky till summer was over, and all the leaf butterflies in the world would be free to scamper with the wind.

That was Roy's foolish fancy as he lay, *ventre à terre*—to the obvious detriment of his moral backbone—chin cupped in the hollow of his hands. Close beside him lay Prince, his golden retriever; so close that he could feel the dog's warm body through his thin shirt. At the foot of the tree, in a nest of pale cushions, sat his mother, in her apple-blossom sari and a silk dress like the lining of a shell. No jewels in the morning, except the star that fastened her sari on one shoulder and a slender gold bangle—never removed—the wedding-ring of her own land. The boy, mutely adoring, could, in some dim way, feel the harmony of those pale tones with the olive skin, faintly aglow, and the delicate arch of her eyebrows poised like outspread wings above the brown, limpid depths of her eyes. He could not tell that she was still little more than a girl; barely eight-and-twenty. For him she was ageless:—protector and playfellow, essence of all that was most real, yet most magical, in the home that was his world. Unknown to him, the

Eastern mother in her was evoking, already, the Eastern spirit of worship in her son.

Very close to her nestled Tara, a vivid, eager slip of a girl, with wild-rose petals in her cheeks and blue hyacinths in her eyes and sunbeams tangled in her hair, that rippled to her waist in a mass almost too abundant for the small head and elfin face it framed. In temperament, she suggested a flame rather than a flower, this singularly vital child. She loved and she hated, she played and she quarrelled with an intensity, a singleness of aim, surprising and a little disquieting in a creature not yet nine. She was the despair of nurses and had never crossed swords with a governess, which was a merciful escape—for the governess. Juvenile fiction and fairy tales she frankly scorned. Legends of Asgard and Arthur, the virile tales of Rajputana and her warrior chiefs, she drank in as the earth drinks dew. Roy had a secret weakness for a happy ending—in his own phrase, "a beautiful marry." Tara's rebel spirit rose to tragedy as a flame leaps to the stars; and there was no lack of high tragedy in the records of Chitor—Queen of cities—thrice sacked by Moslem invaders; deserted at last, and left in ruins—a sacred relic of great days gone by.

This morning Rajputana held the field. Lilámani, with a thrill in her low voice, was half reading, half telling the adventures of Prithvi Raj (King of the Earth) and his Amazon Princess, Tara—the Star of Bednore: verily a star among women for beauty, wisdom, and courage. Many princes were rivals for her hand; but none would she call "lord" save the man who restored to her father the Kingdom snatched from him by an Afghan marauder. "On the faith of a Rajput, *I* will restore it," said Prithvi Raj. So, in the faith of a Rajputni, she married him:—and together, by a daring device, they fulfilled her vow.

Here, indeed, was Roy's 'beautiful marry,' fit prelude for the tale of that heroic pair. For in life—Lilámani told them—marriage is the beginning, not the end. That is only for fairy tales.

And close against her shoulder, listening entranced, sat the child Tara, with her wild-flower face and the flickering star in her heart—a creature born out of time into an unromantic world; hands clasped round her upraised knees, her wide eyes gazing past the bluebells and the beech-leaves at some fanciful inner vision of it all; lost in it, as Roy was lost in contemplation of his Mother's face. . . .

And this unorthodox fashion of imbibing knowledge in the very lap of the Earth Mother, was Lilámani Sinclair's impracticable idea of 'giving lessons'! Shades of Aunt Jane! Of governess and copy-books and rulers!

Happily for all three, Lady Roscoe never desecrated their paradise in the flesh. She was aware that her very regrettable sister-in-law had 'queer notions' and had flatly refused to engage a governess of high qualifications chosen by herself; but the half was not told her. It never is told to those who condemn on principle what they cannot understand. At their coming all the little private gateways into the delectable Garden of Intimacy shut with a gentle, decisive click. So it was with Jane Roscoe, as worthy and unlikeable a woman as ever organised a household to perfection and alienated every member of her family.

The trouble was that she could not rest satisfied with this achievement. She was afflicted with a vehement desire—she called it a sense of duty—to organise the homes of her less capable relations. If they resented, they were written down ungrateful. And Nevil's ingratitude had become a byword. For Nevil Sinclair was that unaccountable, uncomfortable thing—an artist; which is to say he was no true Sinclair, but the son of his mother whose name he bore. No one, not even Jane, had succeeded in organising him—nor ever would.

So Lilámani carried on, unmolested, her miniature attempt at the forest school of an earlier day. Her simple programme included a good deal more than tales of heroism and adventure. This morning there had been rhythmical exercises, a lively interlude of 'sums without slates' and their poems—a great moment for Roy. Only by a superhuman effort he had kept his treasure locked inside him for two whole days. And his mother's surprise was genuine: not the acted surprise of grown-ups, that was so patent and so irritating and made them look so silly. The smile in her eyes as she listened had sent a warm tingly feeling all through him, as if the spring sunshine itself ran in his veins. Naturally he could not express it so; but he felt it so. And now, as he lay looking and listening, he felt it still. The wonder of her face and her voice, and all the many wonders that made her so beautiful, had hitherto been as much a part of him as the air he breathed. But this morning, in some dim way, things were different—and he could not tell why. . . .

His own puzzled thoughts and her face and her voice became entangled with the chivalrous story of Prithvi Raj holding court in his hill fortress with Tara—fit wife for a hero, since she could ride and fling a lance and bend a bow with the best of them. When Roy caught him up, he was in the midst of a great battle with his uncle, who had broken out in rebellion against the old Rana of Chitor.

"All day long they were fighting, and all night long they were lying awake beside great watch-fires, waiting till there came dawn to fight again. . . ."

His mother was telling, not reading now. He knew it at once from the change in her tone.

"And when evening came, what did Prithvi Raj? He was carelessly strolling over to the enemy's camp, carelessly walking into his Uncle's tent to ask if he is well, in spite of many wounds. And his uncle, full of surprise, made answer: 'Quite well, my child, since I have the pleasure to see you.' And when he heard that Prithvi had come even before eating any dinner, he gave orders for food: and they two, who were all day seeking each other's life, sat there together eating from one plate.

"'In the morning we will end our battle, Uncle,' said Prithvi Raj, when time came to go.

"'Very well, child, come early,' said Surájmul.

"So Prithvi Raj came early and put his Uncle's whole army to flight. But that was not enough. He must be driven from the kingdom. So when Prithvi heard that broken army was hiding in the depths of a mighty forest, there he went with his bravest horsemen, and suddenly, on a dark night, sprang into their midst. Then there was great shouting and fighting; and soon they came together, uncle and nephew, striking at each other, yet never hating, though they must make battle because of Chitor and the Kingdom of Mewar.

"To none would Suráj yield, but only to Prithvi, bravest of the brave. So suddenly in a loud voice he cried—'Stay the fight, nephew. If I am killed, no great matter. But if *you* are killed, what will become of Chitor? I would bear shame for ever.'

"By those generous words he made submission greater than victory. Uncle and nephew embraced, heart to heart, and all those who had been fighting each other sat down together in peace, because Surájmul, true Rajput, could not bring harm, even in anger, upon the sacred city of Chitor."

She paused—her eyes on Roy, who had lost his own puzzling sensations in the clash of the fight and its chivalrous climax.

"Oh, I love it," he said. "Is that all?"

"No, there is more."

"Is it sad?"

She shook her head at him—smiling.

"Yes, Roy. It is sad."

He wrinkled his forehead.

"Oh dear! I like it to end the nice way."

"But I am not making tales, Sonling. I am telling history."

Tara's head nudged her shoulder. "*Go* on—please," she murmured, resenting interruptions.

So Lilámani—still looking at Roy—told how Prithvi Raj went on his last quest to Mount Abu, to punish the chief, who had married his sister and was ill-treating her.

"In answer to her cry he went; and climbing her palace walls in the night, he gave sharp punishment to that undeserving prince. But when penance was over, his noble nature was ready, like before, to embrace and be friends. Only that mean one, not able to kill him in battle, put poison in the sweets he gave at parting and Prithvi ate them, thinking no harm. So when he came on the hill near his palace the evil work was done. Helpless he, the all-conqueror, sent word to Tara that he might see her before death. But even that could not be. And she, loyal wife, had only one thought in her heart. 'Can the blossom live when the tree is cut down?' Calm, without tears, she bade his weeping warriors build up the funeral pyre, putting the torch with her own hand. Then, before them all, she climbed on that couch of fire and went through the leaping scorching flames to meet her lord——"

The low clear voice fell silent—and the silence stayed. The vague thrill of a tragedy they could hardly grasp laid a spell upon the children. It made Roy feel as he did in Church, when the deepest notes of the organ quivered through him; and it brought a lump in his throat, which must be manfully swallowed down on account of being a boy. . . .

And suddenly the spell was broken by the voice of Roger the footman, who had approached noiselessly along the mossy track.

"If you please, m'lady, Sir Nevil sent word as Lord and Lady Roscoe 'ave arrived unexpected; and if convenient, can you come in?"

They all started visibly and their dream-world of desert and rose-red mountains and battle-fields and leaping flames shivered like a soap-bubble at the touch of a careless hand.

Lilámani rose, gentle and dignified. "Thank you, Roger. Tell Sir Nevil I am coming."

Roy suppressed a groan. The mere mention of Aunt Jane made one feel vaguely guilty. To his nimble fancy it was almost as if her very person had invaded their sanctuary, in her neat hard coat and skirt and her neat hard summer hat with its one fierce wing, that, disdaining the tenderness of curves, seemed to stab the air, as her eyes so often seemed to stab Roy's hyper-sensitive brain.

"Oh dear!" he sighed. "Will they stop for lunch?"

"I expect so."

He wrinkled his nose in a wicked grimace.

"Bad boy!" said Lilámani's lips, but her eyes said other things. He knew, and she knew that he knew how, in her heart, she shared his innate antagonism. Was it not of her own bestowing—a heritage of certain memories—ineffaceable, unforgiveable—during her early days of marriage? But in spite of that mutual knowledge, Roy was never allowed to speak disrespectfully of his formidable aunt.

"You can stay out and play till half-past twelve, not one minute later," she said—and left them to their own delectable devices.

Roy had been promoted to a silver watch on his eighth birthday, so he could be relied on; and he still enjoyed a private sense of importance when the fact was recognised.

Left alone they had only to pick up the threads of their game; a sort of interminable serial story, in which they lived and moved and had their being. But first Tara—in her own person—had a piece of news to impart. Hunching up her knees, she tilted back her head till it touched the satin-grey bole of the tree and all her hair lay shimmering against it like a stream of pale sunshine.

"What do you think?" she nodded at Roy with her elfin smile. "We've got a Boy-on-a-visit and his mother, from India. They came last night. He's rather a large boy."

"Is he nine?" Roy asked, standing up very straight and slim, a defensive gleam in his eye.

"He's ten and a half. And he looks bigger'n that. He goes to school. And he's been quite a lot in India."

"Not my India."

"I don't know. He called it 'Mballa. That letter I brought from Mummy was asking if she could bring them for tea."

"Well, I don't want him for tea. I don't like your Boy-on-a-visit. I'll tell Mummy."

"Oh, Roy—you mustn't." She made reproachful eyes at him. "Coz then *I* couldn't come. And he's quite nice—only rather lumpy. And you can't not like someb'dy you've never seen."

"*I* can, I often do." The possibility had only just occurred to him. He saw it as a distinction and made the most of it. "Course if you're going to make a fuss——"

Tara's eyes opened wider still. "Oh, Roy, you *are*——! 'Tisn't me that's making fusses."

Though Roy knew nothing as yet about woman and the last word, he instinctively took refuge in the masculine dignity that spurns descent to the dusty arena when it feels defeat in the air.

"Girls don't never fuss—do they?" he queried

suavely. "Let's get on with the Game and not bother about your Boy-of-ten."

"And a half," Tara insisted tactlessly, with her sweetest smile. But when Roy chose to be impassive pin-pricks were thrown away on him.

"Where'd we stop?" he mused, ignoring her remark. "Oh—I know. The Knight was going forth to quest the Elephant with golden tusks for the High Tower Princess who wanted them in her crown. Why *do* Princesses always want what the knights can't find?"

Tara's feminine intuition leaped at a solution.

"I 'spec it's just to show off they are Princesses and to keep the Knights from bothering round.—So away he went and the Princess climbed up to her highest tower and waved her lily hand——"

In the same breath she, Tara, sprang to her feet and swung herself astride a downward sweeping branch just above Roy's head. There she perched like a slim blue flower, dangling her tan-stockinged legs and shaking her hair at him like golden rain. She was in one of her impish moods; reaction, perhaps,—though she knew it not—from the high tragedy of that other Tara, her namesake, and the great greatest-possible grandmother of her adored 'Aunt Lila.' Suddenly a fresh impulse seized her. Clutching her bough, she leaned down and lightly ruffled his hair.

He started and looked reproachful. "Don't rumple me. I'm going."

"You needn't, if you don't want to," she cooed caressingly. "*I*'m going to the tipmost top to see out over the world. And the Princess doesn't care a bean about the Golden Tusks—truly."

"She's jolly pleased with the knight that finds them," said Roy with a deeper wisdom than he knew. "And you can't be stopped off quests that way. Come on, Prince."

At a bend in the mossy path, he looked back and she waved her lily hand.

To be alone in the deep of the wood in bluebell time was, for Roy, a sensation by itself. In a moment, you stepped through some unseen door straight into fairyland—or was it a looking-glass world? For here the sky lay all around your feet in a shimmer of bluebells: and high overhead were domes of cool green light, where the sun came flickering and filtering through millions of leaves. Always, as far as he could remember, the magical feeling had been there. But this morning it came over him in a queer way. This morning—though he could not quite make it out—there was the Roy that felt and the Roy that knew he felt, just as there had suddenly been when he was watching his mother's face. And this magical world was his kingdom. In some far-off time, it would all be his very own. That uplifting thought eclipsed every other. . . .

Lost in one of his dreaming moods, he wandered on and on, with Prince at his heels. He forgot all about Tara and his knighthood and his quest; till suddenly—where the trees fell apart—his eye was arrested by twin shafts of sunlight that struck downward through the green gloom.

He caught his breath and stood still. "I've *found* them! The Golden Tusks!" he murmured ecstatically.

The pity was he couldn't carry them back with him as trophies. He could only watch them fascinated, wondering how you could explain what you didn't understand yourself. All he knew was that they made him feel 'dazzled inside,' and he wanted to watch them more.

It was beautiful out in the open with the sunshine pouring down and a big lazy white cloud tangled in tree-tops. So he flung himself on the moss, hands under his head, and lay there, Prince beside him, looking up, up into the far blue, listening to the swish and rustle of the wind talking secrets to the leaves, and all the tiny mysterious noises that make up the silence of a wood in summer.

And again he forgot about Tara and the Game and the silver watch that made him reliable. He simply lay there in a trance-like stillness, that was not of the West, absorbing it all, with his eyes and his dazzled brain and with every sentient nerve in his body. And again—as when his mother smiled her praise—the Spring sunshine itself seemed to flow through his veins. . . .

Suddenly he came alive and sat upright. Something

was happening. The Golden Tusks had disappeared, and the domes of cool green light and the far blue sky and the lazy white cloud. Under the beeches it was almost twilight—a creepy twilight, as if a giant had blown out the sun. Was it really evening? Had he been asleep? Only his watch could answer that, and never had he loved it more dearly. No—it was daytime. Twenty past twelve—and he would be late——

A long rumbling growl, that seemed to shudder through the wood, so startled him that it set little hammers beating all over his body. Then the wind grew angrier—not whispering secrets now, but tearing at the tree-tops and lashing the branches this way and that. And every minute the wood grew darker, and the sky overhead was darkest of all—the colour of spilled ink. And there was Tara—his forgotten Princess—waiting for him in her high tower; or perhaps she had given up waiting and gone home.

"Come on, Prince," he said, "we must run!"

The sound of his own voice was vaguely comforting: but the moment he began to run, he felt as if some one—or Something—was running after him. He knew there was nothing. He knew it was babyish. But what could you do if your legs were in a fearful hurry of their own accord? Besides, Tara was waiting. Somehow Tara seemed the point of safety. He didn't believe she was ever afraid——

All in a moment the eerie darkness quivered and broke into startling light. Twigs and leaves and bluebell spears and tiny patterns of moss seemed to leap at him and vanish as he ran: and two minutes after, high above the agitated tree-tops, the thunder spoke. No mere growl now; but crash on crash that seemed to be tearing the sky in two and set the little hammers inside him beating faster than ever.

He had often watched storms from a window: but to be out in the very middle of one all alone was an adventure of the first magnitude. The grandeur and terror of it clutched at his heart and thrilled along his nerves as the thunder went rumbling and grumbling off to the other end of the world, leaving the wood so quiet and still that the little hammers inside seemed almost as loud as the plop-plop of the first big raindrops on the leaves. But, in spite of secret tremors, he wanted tremendously to hear the thunder speak again. The childish feeling of pursuit was gone. His legs that had been in such a fearful hurry, came to a sudden standstill; and he discovered, to his immense surprise, that he was back again——

There lay the rug and the cushions under the downward sweeping branches with their cascades of bright new leaves. No sign of Tara—and the heavy drops came faster, though they hardly amounted to a shower.

Flinging down bow and arrows, he ran under the tree and peered up into a maze of silver grey and young green. Still no sign.

"Tara!" he called. "Are you there?"

"'Course I am." Her disembodied voice had a ring of triumph. "I'm at the tipmost top. It's rather shaky, but scrumshous. Come up—quick!"

Craning his neck he could just see one leg and the edge of her frock. Temptation tugged at him; but he could not bear to disobey his mother—not because it was naughty, but it was her.

"I can't—now," he called back. "It's late and it's raining. You *must* come down."

"I will—if you come up."

"I tell you, I can't!"

"Only one little minute, Roy. The storm's rolling away. I can see miles and miles—to Farthest End."

Temptation tugged harder. You couldn't carry on an argument with one tan shoe and stocking and a flutter of blue frock, and he wanted badly to tell about the Golden Tusks. Should he go on alone, or should he climb up and fetch her——?

The answer to that came from the top of the tree. A crack, a rustle and a shriek from Tara, who seemed to be coming down faster than she cared about.

Another shriek. "Oh, Roy! I'm stuck! Do come!"

Stuck! She was dangling from the end of a jagged bough that had caught in her skirt as she fell. There she hung ignominiously—his High Tower Princess—her hair floating like seaweed, her hands clutching at the nearest branches that were too pliable for support. If her skirt should tear, or the bough should break——

"*Keep* stuck!" he commanded superfluously; and

like a squirrel he sped up the great beech, its every foothold as familiar to him as the ground he walked on.

But to release her skirt and give her a hand he must trust himself on the jagged bough, hoping it would bear the double weight. It looked rather a dead one, and its sharp end was sticking through a hole in Tara's frock. He set foot on it cautiously and proffered a hand.

"Now—catch hold!" he said.

Agile as he, she swung herself up somehow and clutched at him with both hands. The half-dead bough, resenting these gymnastics, cracked ominously. There was a gasp, a scuffle. Roy hung on valiantly, dragging her nearer for a firmer foothold.

And suddenly down below Prince began to bark—a deep, booming note of welcome.

"Hullo, Roy!" It was his father's voice. "Are you murdering Tara up there? Come out of it!"

Roy, having lost his footing, was in no position to look down—or to disobey: and they proceeded to come out of it, with rather more haste than dignity.

Roy, swinging from a high branch for his final jump—a bit of pure bravado because he felt nervous inside—discovered, with mingled terror and joy, that his vagrant foot had narrowly shaved Aunt Jane's neat hard summer hat: Aunt Jane—of all people—at such a moment, when you couldn't properly explain. He half wished he *had* kicked the fierce little feather and broken its back——

He was on the ground now, shaking hands with her, his sensitive clean-cut face a mask of mere politeness: and Tara was standing by him—a jagged hole in her blue frock, a scratch across her cheek, and her hair ribbon gone—looking suspiciously as if he had been trying to murder her instead of doing her a knightly service.

She couldn't help it, of course. But still—it was a distinct score for Aunt Jane, who, as usual, went straight to the point.

"You nearly kicked my head just now. A little gentleman would apologise."

He did apologise—not with the best grace.

"My turn next," his father struck in. "What the dickens were you up to—tearing slices out of my finest tree?" His twinkly eyes were almost grave and his voice was almost stern. ("Just because of Aunt Jane!" thought Roy.)

Aloud he said: "I'm awfully sorry, Daddy. It was only . . . Tara got in a muddle. I had to help her."

The twinkle came back to his father's eyes.

"The woman tempted me!" was all he said; and Roy, hopelessly mystified, wondered how he could possibly know. It was very clever of him. But Aunt Jane seemed shocked.

"Nevil, be quiet!" she commanded in a crisp undertone; and Roy, simply hating her, pulled out his watch.

"We've got to hurry, Daddy. Mother said 'not later than half-past.' And it is later."

"Scoot, then. She'll be anxious because of the storm."

But though Roy, grasping Tara's hand, faithfully hurried ahead because of mother, he managed to keep just within earshot; and he listened shamelessly, because of Aunt Jane. You couldn't trust her. She didn't play fair. She would bite you behind your back. That's the kind of woman she was.

And this is what he heard.

"Nevil, it's perfectly disgraceful. Letting them run wild like that; damaging the trees and scaring the birds."

She meant the pheasants of course. No other winged beings were sacred in her eyes.

"Sorry, old girl. But they appear to survive it." (The cool good-humour of his father's tone was balm to Roy's heart.) "And frankly, with *us*, if it's a case of the children or the birds, the children win, hands down."

Aunt Jane snorted. You could call it nothing else. It was a sound peculiarly her own, and it implied unutterable things. Roy would have gloried had he known what a score for his father was that delicately implied identity with his wife.

But the snort was no admission of defeat.

"In *my* opinion—if it counts for anything," she persisted, "this harum-scarum state of things is quite as bad for the children as for the birds. I suppose you *have* a glimmering concern for the boy's future, as heir to the old place?"

Nevil Sinclair chuckled.

"By Jove! That's quite a bright idea. Really, Jane, you've a positive flair for the obvious."

(Roy hugely wanted to know what a "flair for the obvious" might be. His eager brain pounced on new words as a dog pounces on a bone.)

"I wish I could say the same for you," Lady Roscoe retorted unabashed. "The obvious, in this case—though you can't or won't see it—is that the boy is thoroughly spoilt, and in September he ought to go to school. You couldn't do better than Coombe Friars."

His father said something quickly in a low tone and he couldn't catch Aunt Jane's next remark. Evidently he was to hear no more. What he had heard was bad enough.

"I don't care. I jolly well won't," he said between his teeth—which looked as if Aunt Jane was not quite wrong about the spoiling.

"No, don't," said Tara, who had also listened without shame. And they hurried on in earnest.

"Tara," Roy whispered, suddenly recalling his quest. "I *found* the Golden Tusks. I'll tell it you after."

"Oh, Roy, you are a wonder!" She gave his hand a convulsive squeeze and they broke into a run.

The "bits of blue" had spread half over the sky. The thunder still grumbled to itself at intervals and a sharp little shower whipped out of a passing cloud. Then the sun flashed through it and the shadows crept round the great twin beeches on the lawn—and the day was as lovely as ever again.

And yet—for Roy, it was not the same loveliness. Aunt Jane's repeated threat of school brooded over his sensitive spirit, like the thundercloud in the wood that was the colour of spilled ink. And the Boy-of-ten—a potential enemy—was coming to tea. . . .

Yet this morning he had felt so beautifully sure that nothing could go wrong on a day like this! It was his first lesson, and not by any means his last, that Fate—unmoved by 'light of smiles or tears'—is no respecter of profound convictions or of beautiful days.

## CHAPTER III.

"Man am I grown ; a man's work I must do."
—TENNYSON.

TARA was right. The Boy-of-ten (Roy persistently ignored the half) was rather a large boy: also rather lumpy. He had little eyes and freckles and what Christine called a "turnip nose." He wore a very new school blazer and real cricket trousers, with a flannel shirt and school tie that gave Roy's tussore shirt and soft brown bow almost a girlish air. Something in his manner and the way he aired his school slang, made Roy—who never shone with strangers—feel "miles younger," which did not help to put him at ease.

His name was Joe Bradley. He had been in India till he was nearly eight; and he talked about India, as he talked about school, in a rather important voice, as befitted the only person present who knew anything of either.

Roy was quite convinced he knew nothing at all about Rajputana or Chitor or Prithvi Raj or the sacred peacocks of Jaipur. But somehow he could not make himself talk about these things simply for "show off," because a strange boy, with bad manners, was putting on airs.

Besides, he never much wanted to talk when he was eating, though he could not have explained why. So he devoted his attention chiefly to a plate of chocolate cakes, leaving the Boy-of-ten conversationally in command of the field.

He was full of a recent cricket match, and his talk bristled with such unknown phrases as "square leg," "cover point" and "caught out." But for some reason—pure perversity perhaps—they stirred in Roy no flicker of curiosity, like his father's "flair for the obvious." He didn't know what they meant—and he didn't care, which was not the least like Roy. Tara, who owned big brothers, seemed to know all about it, or looked as if she did; and to show you didn't understand what a girl understood, would be the last indignity.

When the cricket show-off was finished, Joe talked India and ragged Tara, in a big-brotherly way, ignored Christine, as if five and a half simply didn't count. That roused Roy; and by way of tacit rebuke, he bestowed such marked attention on his small sister, that Christine (who adored him, and was feeling miserably shy) sparkled like a dewdrop when the sun flashes out.

She was a tiny creature, exquisitely proportioned; fair, like her father, yet in essence a replica of her mother, with the same wing-like brows and dark limpid eyes. Dimly jealous of Tara, she was the only one of the three who relished the presence of the intruder and wished strange boys oftener came to tea.

Millicent, the nursery-maid, presided. She was tall and smiling and obviously a lady. She watched and listened and said little during the meal.

Once, in the course of it, Lilámani came in and hovered round them, filling Roy's tea-cup, spreading Christine's honey—extra thick. Her Eastern birthright of service, her joy in waiting on those she loved, had survived ten years of English marriage, and would survive ten more. It was as much an essential part of her as the rhythm of her pulses and the blood in her veins.

She was no longer the apple-blossom vision of the morning. She wore her mother-o'-pearl sari with its narrow gold border. Her dress, that was the colour of a dove's wing, shimmered changefully as she moved, and her aquamarine pendant gleamed like drops of sea water on its silver chain.

Roy loved her in the mother-o'-pearl mood best of all; and he saw, with a throb of pride, how the important Boy-from-India seemed too absorbed in watching her even to show off. She did not stay many minutes and she said very little. She was still, by preference, quiet during a meal; and it gave her a secret thrill of pleasure to see the habit of her own race reappearing as an instinct in Roy. So, with merely a word or two, she just smiled at them and gave them things and patted their heads. And when she was gone, Roy felt better. The scales had swung even again. What was a school blazer and twenty runs at cricket, compared with the glory of having a mother like that?

But if tea was not much fun, after tea was worse.

They were told to run and play in the garden; and obediently they ran out, dog and all. But what *could* you play at with a superior being who had made twenty runs not out, in a House Match—whatever that might be? They showed him their ring-doves and their rabbits; but he didn't even pretend to be interested, though Tara did her best, because it was she who had brought this infliction on Roy.

"How about the summer-house?" she suggested, hopefully. For the summer-house locker contained an assortment of old tennis-bats, mallets and balls, that might prove more stimulating than rabbits and doves. Roy offered no objection; so they straggled across a corner of the lawn to a narrower strip behind the tall yew hedge.

The grown-ups were gathered under the twin beeches; and away at the far end of the lawn Roy's mother and Tara's mother were strolling up and down in the sun.

Again Roy noticed how Joe Bradley stared: and as they rounded the corner of the hedge he remarked suddenly: "I say! There's that swagger ayah of yours walking with Lady Despard. She's jolly smart, for an ayah. Did you bring her from India? You never said you'd been there."

Roy started and went hot all over. "Well, I *have*—just on a visit. And she's *not* an ayah. She's my Mummy!"

Joe Bradley opened his mouth as well as his eyes, which made him look plainer than ever.

"Golly! what a tale! White people don't have ayahs for Mothers—not in my India. I s'pose your Pater married her out there?"

"He didn't. And I tell you she's *not* an ayah."

Roy's low voice quivered with anger. It was as if ten thousand little flames had come alight inside him. But you had to try and be polite to visitors; so he added with a virtuous effort: "She's a really and truly Princess—so there!"

But that unspeakable boy, instead of being impressed, laughed in the rudest way.

"Don't excite, you silly kid. I'm not as green as you are. Besides—who cares——?"

It flashed on Roy, through the blur of his bewildered rage, that perhaps the Boy-from-India was jealous. He tried to speak. Something clutched at his throat; but instinct told him he had a pair of hands. . . .

To the utter amazement of Tara, and of the enemy, he silently sprang at the bigger boy; grabbed him unscientifically by the knot of his superior neck-tie and hit out, with more fury than precision, at cheeks and eyes and nose——

For a few exciting seconds he had it all his own way. Then the enemy—recovered from the first shock of surprise—spluttered wrathfully and hit out in return. He had weight in his favour. He tried to bend Roy backwards; and failing began to kick viciously wherever he could get at him. It hurt rather badly and made Roy angrier than ever. In a white heat of rage, he shook and pummelled, regardless of choking sounds and fingers clutching at his hair. . . .

Tara, half excited and half frightened, could only grab Prince's collar, to keep him from rushing into the fray; and when Joe started kicking, it was all she could do not to let him go. But she knew Athol—her dearest brother—would say it wasn't fair play. So she tugged, and Prince tugged; while the boys, fiercely silent, rocked to and fro; and Christine sobbed piteously—"He's hurting Roy—he's *killing* Roy!"

Tara, fully occupied with Prince, could only jerk out: "Don't be a baby, Chris. Roy's all right. He loves it." Which Christine simply didn't believe. There was blood on his tussore shirt. It mightn't be his, but still——

It made even Tara feel rather sick; and when a young gardener appeared on the scene she called out: "Oh, Mudford, do stop them—or something'll happen."

But Mudford—British to the bone—would do nothing of the kind. He saw at once that Roy was getting the better of an opponent nearly twice his weight; and setting down his barrow he shamelessly applauded his young master.

By now, the enemy's nose was bleeding freely and spoiling the brand-new blazer. He gasped and spluttered: "Drop it, you little beast!" But Roy, fired by Mudford's applause, only hit out harder.

"'Pologise—'pologise! Say she isn't!"

His forward jerk on the words took Joe unawares. The edge of the lawn tripped him up and they rolled on the grass, Joe undermost in a close embrace——

And at that critical moment there came strolling round the corner of the hedge a group of grown-ups—Sir Nevil Sinclair with Mrs Bradley, Lady Roscoe, Lady Despard and Roy's godfather, the distinguished novelist, Cuthbert Broome.

Mudford and his barrow departed; and Tara looked appealingly at her mother.

Roy—intent on the prostrate foe—suddenly felt a hand on his shoulder and heard his father's voice say sharply: "Get up, Roy, and explain yourself!"

They got up, both of them—and stood there, looking shy and stupefied and very much the worse for wear:—hair ruffled, faces discoloured, shirts torn open. One of Roy's stockings was slipping down; and, in the midst of his confused sensations, he heard the excited voice of Mrs Bradley urgently demanding to know what her "poor dear boy" could have done to be treated like that.

No one seemed to answer her; and the poor dear boy was too busy comforting his nose to take much interest in the proceedings.

Lady Despard (you could tell at a glance she was Tara's mother) was on her knees comforting Christine; and as Roy's senses cleared, he saw with a throb of relief that his mother was not there. But Aunt Jane was—and Uncle Cuthbert——

He seemed to stand there panting and aching in an endless silence, full of eyes. He did not know that his father was giving him a few seconds to recover himself.

Then: "What do you mean by it, Roy?" he asked; and this time his voice was really stern. It hurt more than the bruises. "Gentlemen don't hammer their guests." This was an unexpected blow. And it wasn't fair. How could he explain before "all those"? His cheeks were burning, his head was aching; and tears, that must not be allowed to fall, were pricking like needles under his lids.

It was Tara who spoke—still clutching Prince, lest he overwhelm Roy and upset his hardly maintained dignity.

"Joe made him angry—he *did*," she thrust in with feminine officiousness; and was checked by her mother's warning finger.

Mrs Bradley—long and thin and beaky—bore down upon her battered son, who edged away sullenly from proffered caresses.

Sir Nevil, not daring to meet the humorous eye of Cuthbert Broome—still contemplated the dishevelled dignity of his own small son—half puzzled, half vexed.

"You've done it now, Roy. Say you're sorry," he prompted; his voice a shade less stern than he intended.

Roy shook his head.

"It's him to say—not me."

"Did he begin it?"

"No."

"Of course he didn't," snapped the injured mother. "He's been properly brought up," which was not exactly polite, but she was beside herself—simply an irate mother-creature, all beak and ruffled feathers. "You deserve to be whipped. You've hurt him badly."

"Oh, dry up, mother," Joe murmured behind his sanguinary handkerchief, edging still further away from maternal fussings and possible catechism.

Nevil Sinclair saw clearly that his son would neither apologise nor explain. At heart he suspected young Bradley, if only on account of his insufferable mother. but the laws of hospitality must be upheld.

"Go to your own room, Roy," he said with creditable severity, "and stay there till I come."

Roy gave him one look—mutely reproachful. Then—to every one's surprise and Tara's delight—he walked straight up to the Enemy.

"I *did* hammer hardest. 'Pologise!"

The older boy mumbled something suspiciously like the fatal word: a suspicion confirmed by Roy's next remark: "I'm sorry your blazer's spoilt. But you made me."

And the elders, watching with amused approbation, had no inkling that the words were spoken not by Roy Sinclair but by Prithvi Raj.

The Enemy, twice humbled, answered nothing; and Roy,—his dignity unimpaired by such trifles as a lump on his cheek, a dishevelled tie and one stocking curled lovingly round his ankle—walked leisurely away, with never a glance in the direction of the "grown-ups," who had no concern whatever with this—the most important event of his life——

Tara—torn between wrath and admiration—watched him go. In her eyes he was a hero, a victim of injustice and the density of grown-ups.

She promptly released Prince, who bounded after his master. She wanted to go too. It was all her fault, bringing that horrid boy to tea. She did hope Roy would explain things properly. But boys were stupid sometimes and she wanted to make sure. While her mother was tactfully suggesting a homeward move, she slipped up to Sir Nevil and insinuated a small hand into his.

"Uncle Nevil, *do* believe," she whispered urgently. "Truly it isn't fair——"

His quick frown warned her to say no more; but the pressure of his hand comforted her a little.

All the same she hated going home. She hated 'that putrid boy'—a forbidden adjective; but what else *could* you call him? She was glad he would be gone the day after to-morrow. She was even more glad his nose was bleeding and his eye bunged up and his important blazer all bloodied. Girl though she was, there ran a fiercer strain in her than in Roy.

As they moved off, she had an inspiration. She was given that way.

"Mummy darling," she said in her small clear voice, "mayn't I stay back a little and play with Chris. She's *so* unhappy. Alice could fetch me—couldn't she? Please."

The innocent request was underlined by an unmistakable glance through her lashes at Joe. She wanted him to hear; and she didn't care if he understood—him and his beaky mother! Clearly her own Mummy understood. She was nibbling her lips, trying not to smile.

"Very well, dear," she said. "I'll send Alice at half-past six. Run along."

Tara gave her hand a grateful little squeeze—and ran. She would have hated the "beaky mother" worse than ever could she have heard her remark to Lady Despard, when they were alone.

"Really, a most obstinate, ungoverned child. His mother, of course—a very pretty creature—but what can you expect? Natives always ruin boys."

Lady Despard—Lilámani Sinclair's earliest champion and friend—could be trusted to deal effectually with a remark of that quality.

As for Tara—once "the creatures" were out of sight they were extinct. All the embryo mother in her was centred on Roy. It was a shame sending him to his room, like a naughty boy, when he was really a champion, a King-Arthur's-Knight. But if only he properly explained, Uncle Nevil would surely understand——

And suddenly there sprang a dilemma. How could Roy make himself repeat to Uncle Nevil the rude remarks of that abominable boy? And if not—how was he going to properly explain——?

## CHAPTER IV.

> "What a great day came and passed;
> Unknown then, but known at last."
>
> —ALICE MEYNELL.

THAT very problem was puzzling Roy as he lay on his bed, with Prince's head against his shoulder, aching a a good deal, exulting at thought of his new-born knighthood, wondering how long he was to be treated like a sinner,—and, through it all, simply longing for his mother. . . .

It was the conscious craving for her sympathy, her applause, that awakened him to his dilemma.

He had championed her with all his might against that lumpy Boy-of-ten,—who kicked in the meanest way; and he couldn't explain why, so she couldn't know ever. The memory of those insulting words hurt him so that he shrank from repeating them to anyone—least of all to her. Yet how could he see her and feel her and not tell her everything? She would surely ask—she would want to know—and then—when he tried to think beyond that point he felt simply lost.

It was an *impasse* none the less tragic because he was only nine. To tell her every little thing was as simple a necessity of life as eating or sleeping; and—till this bewildering moment—as much a matter of course. For Lilámani Sinclair, with her Eastern mother-genius, had forged between herself and her first-born a link woven of the tenderest, most subtle fibres of heart and spirit; a link so vital, yet so unassertive, that it bid fair to stand the strain of absence, the test of time. So close a link with any human heart, while it makes for beauty, makes also for pain and perplexity,—as Roy was just realising to his dismay.

At the sound of footsteps he sat up, suddenly very much aware of his unheroic dishevelment. He tugged at the fallen stocking and made hasty dabs at his hair. But it was only Esther the housemaid with an envelope on a tray. Envelopes, however, were always mysterious and exciting.

His name was scribbled on this one in Tara's hand; and as Esther retreated he opened it, wondering. . . .

It contained a half-sheet of note-paper, and between the folds lay a circle of narrow blue ribbon plaited in three strands. But only two of the strands were ribbon; the third was a tress of her gleaming hair. Roy gazed at it a moment, lost in admiration, still wondering; then he glanced at Tara's letter—not scrawled, but written with laboured neatness and precision.

"DEAR ROY,—It was splendid. You are Prithvi Raj. I am sending you the bangel like Aunt Lila told us. It can't be gold or jewels. But I pulled the ribbon out of my petticote and put in sum of my hair to make it spangly. So now you are Braselet Bound Brother. Don't forget. From TARA."

"I hope you aren't hurting much. Do splain to Uncle Nevil properly and come down soon. I am hear playing with Chris. TARA."

Roy sat looking from the letter to the bangle with a distinctly pleasant kind of mixed-up feeling inside. He was so surprised, so comforted, so elated by this tribute from his High Tower Princess, who was an exacting person in the matter of heroes. Now—besides being a Knight and a champion he was Bracelet-Bound Brother as well.

Only the other day his mother had told them a tale about this old custom of bracelet-sending in Rajputana: —how, on a certain holy day, any woman—married or not married—may send her bracelet token to any man. If he accepts it, and sends in return an embroidered bodice, he becomes from that hour her bracelet brother, vowed to her service, like a Christian Knight in the days of chivalry. The bracelet may be of gold or jewels or even of silk interwoven with spangles—like Tara's impromptu token. The two who are bracelet-bound might possibly never meet face to face. Yet she, who sends, may ask of him who accepts, any service she pleases; and he may not deny it—even though it involve the risk of his life.

The ancient custom, she told them, still holds good, though it has declined in use, like all things chivalrous, in an age deafened by the clamour of industrial strife; an age grown blind to the beauty of service, that, in defiance of "progress," still remains the keynote of an Indian woman's life.

So these privileged children had heard much of it, through the medium of Lilámani's Indian tales; and this particular one had made a deeper impression on Tara than on Roy; perhaps because the budding woman in her relished the power of choice and command it conferred on her own sex. Certainly no thought of possible future commands dawned on Roy. It was her pride in his achievement, so characteristically expressed that flattered his incipient masculine vanity and added a cubit to his stature. He knew now what he meant to be when he grew up. Not a painter, or a soldier or a gardener—but a Bracelet-Bound Brother. . . .

Gingerly, almost shyly, he slipped over his hand the deftly woven trifle of ribbon and gleaming hair. As the first glow of pleasure subsided, there sprang the instinctive thought—"Won't Mummy be pleased!" And straightway he was caught afresh in the toils of his dilemma—How could he possibly explain——?

What was she doing? Why didn't she come——?

There——! His ear caught far-off footsteps—too heavy for hers. He slipped off the Bracelet, folded it in Tara's letter and tucked it away inside his shirt.

Hurriedly—a little nervously—he tied his brown bow and got upon his feet, just as the door opened and his father came in.

"*Well*, Roy!" he said, and for a few seconds he steadily regarded his small son with eyes that tried very hard to be grave and judicial. Scoldings and assertions of authority were not in his line: and the tug at his heart-strings was peculiarly strong in the case of Roy. Fair himself, as the boy was dark, their intrinsic likeness of form and feature was yet so striking that there were moments—as now—when it gave Nevil

Sinclair an eerie sense of looking into his own eyes,—which was awkward, as he had come steeled for chastisement, if needs must, though his every instinct revolted from the mutual indignity. He had only once inflicted it on Roy for open defiance in one of his stormy ebullitions of temper; and, at this moment, he did not seem to see a humble penitent before him.

"What have you got to say for yourself?" he went on, hoping the pause had been impressive; strongly suspecting it had been nothing of the kind. "Gentlemen, as I told you, don't hammer their guests. It was rather a bad hammering, to judge from his handkerchief. And you don't look particularly sorry about it either."

"I'm not—not one littlest bit."

This was disconcerting; but Nevil held his ground.

"Then I suppose I've got to whack you. If boys aren't sorry for their sins, it's the only way."

Roy's eyelids flickered a little.

"You better not," he said with the same impersonal air of conviction. "You see, it wouldn't make me sorry. And you don't hurt badly. Not half as much as Joe did. He was mean. He kicked. I wouldn't have stopped, all the same—if *you* hadn't come."

The note of reproach was more disconcerting than ever.

"Well, if whacking's no use, what am I to do with you? Shut you up here till bedtime—eh?"

Roy considered that dismal proposition, with his eyes on the summer world outside.

"Well—you can if you like. But it wouldn't be fair." A pause. "You don't know what a horrid boy he was, Daddy. *You'd* have hit him harder—even if he *was* a guest."

"I wonder!" Nevil fatally admitted. "Of course it would all depend on the provocation."

"What's 'provication'?"

The instant alertness, over a new word, brought back the smile to Nevil's eyes.

"It means—saying or doing something bad enough to make it right for you to be angry."

"Well, it was bad enough. It was"—a portentous pause—"about Mummy."

"About Mummy?" The sharp change in his father's tone was at once startling and comforting. "Look here,

Roy. No more mysteries. This is my affair as much as yours. Come here."

Pulling a bedside chair near the window, he sat down and drew Roy close to him, taking his shoulders between his hands.

"Now then, old boy, tell me just exactly what happened—as man to man."

The appeal was irresistible. But—how could he——? The very change in his father's manner made the telling at once more difficult and more urgent.

"Daddy—it hurts too much. I don't know how to say it——" he faltered, and the blood tingled in his cheeks.

If Nevil Sinclair was not a stern father, neither was he a very demonstrative one. Even his closest relations were tinged with something of the artist's detachment, and innate respect for the individual even in embryo. But at sight of Roy's distress and delicacy of feeling, his heart melted in him. Without a word, he slipped an arm round the boy's shoulder and drew him closer still.

"That better, eh? You've got to pull it through, somehow," he said gently, so holding him that Roy could, if he chose, nestle against him. He did choose. It might be babyish; but he hated telling: and it was a wee bit easier with his face hidden. So, in broken phrases and in a small voice that quivered with anger revived—he told.

While he was telling, his father said nothing; and when it was over, he still said nothing. He seemed to be looking out of the window, and Roy felt him draw one big breath.

"Have you got to whack me—now, Daddy?" he asked, still in his small voice.

His father's hand closed on his arm. "No. You were right, Roy," he said. "I would have hit harder. Ill-mannered little beast! All the same——"

A pause. He, no less than Roy, found speech difficult. He had fancied himself, by now, inured to this kind of jar—so frequent in the early years of his daringly unconventional marriage. It seemed he was mistaken. He had been vaguely on edge all the afternoon. What young Joe had rudely blurted out, Mrs Bradley's manner had tacitly expressed. He had succeeded in smothering his own sensations, only to be confronted with the effect of it all on Roy—who must somehow be made to understand.

"The fact is, old man," he went on, trying to speak in his normal voice, "young Bradley and a good many of his betters spend years in India without coming to know very much about the real people over there. You'll understand why when you're older. They all have Indians for servants, and they see Indians working in shops and villages, just like plenty of our people do here. But they don't often meet many of the other sort—like Mummy and Grandfather and Uncle Rama—except sometimes in England. And then—they make stupid mistakes—just because they don't know better. But they needn't be rude about it, like Joe; and I'm glad you punched him—hard."

"So'm I. Fearfully glad." He stood upright now, his head erect :—proud of his father's approval, and being treated as "man to man." "But, Daddy—what are we going to do . . . about Mummy? I *do* want her to know . . . it was for her. But I *couldn't* tell—what Joe said. Could you?"

Nevil shook his head.

"Then—what?"

"You leave it to me, Roy. I'll make things clear without repeating Joe's rude remarks. She'd have been up before this; but *I* had to see you first—because of the whacking!" His eye twinkled. "She's longing to get at your bruises——"

"Oh nev' mind my bruises. They're all right now."

"And beautiful to behold!" He lightly touched the lump on Roy's cheek. "I'd let her dab them, though. Women love fussing over us when we're hurt—especially if we've been fighting for them!"

"Yes—they do," Roy agreed gravely; and to his surprise, his father drew him close and kissed his forehead.

His mother did not keep him waiting long. First the quick flutter of her footsteps; then the door gently opened—and she flew to him, her sari blowing out in beautiful curves. Then he was in her arms, gathered into her silken softness and the faint scent of sandalwood; while her lips, light as butterfly wings, caressed the bruise on his cheek.

"Oh, what a bad, wicked Sonling!" she murmured, gathering him close.

He loved her upside-down fashion of praise and endearment; never guessing its Eastern significance—to avert the watchfulness of jealous gods swift to spy out our dearest treasures, that hinder detachment, and snatch them from us. "Such a big rude boy—and you tried to kill him only because he did not understand your queer kind of mother! That you will find often, Roy; because it is not custom. Everywhere it is the same. For some kind of people not to be like custom is much worse than not to be good. And that boy has a mother too much like custom. Not surprising if he didn't understand."

"I made him though—I did," Roy exulted shamelessly, marvelling at his father's cleverness, wondering how much he had told. "I hammered hard. And I'm not sorry a bit. Nor Daddy isn't either."

For answer she gave him a convulsive little squeeze—and felt the crackle of paper under his shirt. "Something hidden there! What is it, Sonling?" she asked with laughing eyes: and suddenly shyness overwhelmed him. For the moment he had forgotten his treasure; and now he was wondering if he could show it—even to her.

"It is Tara—I think it's rather a secret——" he began.

"But I may see?" Then as he still hesitated, she added with grave tenderness: "Only if you are wishing it, son of my heart. To-day—you are a man."

From his father that recognition had been sufficiently uplifting. And now—from her . . . ! The subtle flattery of it and the deeper prompting of his own heart demolished his budding attempt at reserve.

"I am—truly," he said: and she, sitting where his father had sat, unfolded Tara's letter—and the bangle lay revealed.

Roy had not guessed how surprised she would be—and how pleased! She gave a little quick gasp and murmured something he could not catch. Then she looked at him with shining eyes, and her voice had its low serious note that stirred him like music.

" Now—you are Bracelet-Bound, my son. So young ! "

Roy felt a throb of pride. It was clearly a fine thing to be.

" Must I give a ' broidered bodice ' ? "

" I will broider a bodice—the most beautiful ; and you shall give it. Remember, Roy, it is not a little matter. It is for always."

" Even when I'm a grown-up man ? "

" Yes, even then. If she shall ask from you any service, you must not refuse—ever."

Roy wrinkled his forehead. He had forgotten that part of it. Tara might ask anything. You couldn't tell with girls. He had a moment of apprehension.

" But, Mummy, I don't think—Tara didn't mean all that. It's only—our sort of game of play——"

Unerringly she read his thoughts, and shook her head at him with smiling eyes, as when he made naughty faces about Aunt Jane.

" Too sacred thing for only game of play, Roy. By keeping the bracelet, you are bound." Her smile deepened. " You were not afraid of the big rude boy. Yet you are just *so* much afraid—for Tara." She indicated the amount with the rose-pink tip of her smallest finger. " Tara—almost like sister—would never ask anything that could be wrong to do."

At this gentle rebuke he flushed and held his head a shade higher.

" I'm not afraid, Mummy. And I will keep the bracelet —and I *am* bound."

" That is my brave son."

" She said—I am Prithvi Raj."

" She said true." Her hand caressed his hair. " Now you can run down and tell you are forgiven."

" You too, Mummy ? "

" In a little time. Not just now. But see——" Her brows flew up. " I was coming to mend your poor bruises ! "

" I haven't got any bruises."

The engaging touch of swagger delighted her. A man to-day—in very deed. Her gaze dwelt upon him. It was as if she looked through the eyes of her husband into the heart of her son.

Gravely she entered into his mood.

"That is good. Then we will just make you tidy—and one littlest dab for this not-bruise on your cheek."

So much he graciously permitted: then he ran off to receive the ovation awaiting him from Tara and Chris.

# CHAPTER V.

"Thy bosom is endearéd with all hearts,
For there reigns love, and all love's loving parts."
—SHAKSPERE.

"Women are not only deities of the household fire, but the flame of the soul itself."—RABINDRANATH TAGORE.

LEFT to herself, Lilámani moved back to the window with her innate, deliberate grace. There she sat down again, very still, resting her cheek on her hand; drinking in the serenity, the translucent stillness of clear green spaces robed in early evening light, like a bride arrayed for the coming of her lord. The higher tree-tops were haloed with glory. Young leaves of beeches and poplars gleamed like minted gold; and on the lawn, the great twin beeches cast a stealthily encroaching continent of shadow. Among the shrubs, under her window, birds were trilling out their ecstasy of welcome to the sun, in his Hour of Union with Earth—the Divine Mother, of whom every human mother is, in Eastern eyes, a part, a symbol, however imperfect.

Yet, beneath her carven tranquillity, heart and spirit were deeply stirred. For all Nevil's skill in editing the tale of Roy's championship, she had read his hidden thoughts as unerringly as she had divined Mrs Bradley's curiosity and faint hostility beneath the veneer of good manners, not yet imparted to her son.

Helen Despard—wife of a retired Lieut.-Governor—had scores of Anglo-Indian friends; but not all of them shared her enthusiasm for India,—her sympathetic understanding of its peoples. Lilámani had too soon discovered that the ardent declaration, "I love India," was apt to mean merely that the speaker loved riding and dancing and sunshine and vast spaces, with 'the real India' for a dim effective background. And by now, she could almost tell at a glance which were the right and which the wrong kind of Anglo-Indian, so far as she and Nevil were concerned. It was not like Helen to inflict the wrong kind on her; but it had all been Mrs Bradley's doing. She had been tactlessly insistent in her demand to see the beautiful old garden and the famous artist-Baronet, who had so boldly flouted tradition. Helen's lame excuses had been airily dismissed, and the discourtesy of a point-blank refusal was beyond her.

She had frankly explained matters to her beloved Lilámani as they strolled together on the lawn, while Roy was enlightening Joe on the farther side of the yew hedge.

His championship had moved her more profoundly than she dared let him see without revealing all she knew. For the same reason, she could not show Nevil her full appreciation of his tact and delicacy. How useless—trying to hide his thoughts—he ought to know by now: but how beautiful—how endearing!

That she, who had boldly defied all gods and godlings, all claims of caste and family, should have reaped so rich a harvest——! For her—high priestess of the inner life—that was the miracle of miracles: scarcely less so to-day than in that crowning hour when she had placed her first man-child in the arms of her husband—still, at heart, lord of her being. For the tale of her inner life might almost be told in two words—she loved.

Even now—so many years after—she thrilled to remember how, in that one magical moment, without nearness or speech or touch, the floating strands of their destinies had become so miraculously entangled, that neither gods nor godlings, nor household despots of East or West, had power to sever them. From one swift pencil sketch, stolen without leave—he sitting on the path below, she dreaming on the Hotel balcony above—had blossomed the twin flower of their love: the deeper revealing of marriage—its living texture woven of joy and pain; and the wonder of their after-life together—a wonder that, to her ardent, sensitive spirit, still seemed new every morning, like the coming of the sun. A poet in essence, she shared with all true poets that sense of eternal freshness in familiar things that, perhaps, more than any other gift of God, keeps the bloom on every phase and every relation of life. By her temperament of genius, she had quickened in her husband the flickering spark that might else have been smothered under opposing influences. Each, in a quite unusual degree, had fulfilled the life of the other, and so wrought harmony from conflicting elements of race and religion that seemed fated to wreck their brave adventure. To gain all, they had risked all: and events had amazingly justified them.

Within a year of his ill-considered marriage Sir Nevil had astonished all who knew him with the unique Exhibition of the now famous Ramayana pictures, inspired by his wife: a series of arresting canvases, setting forth the story of India's great epic, her confession of faith in the two supreme loyalties—of the Queen to her husband, of the King to his people. His daring venture had proved successful beyond hope. Artistic and critical London had hailed him as a newcomer of promise, amounting to genius: and Lilámani Sinclair, daughter of Rajputs, had only escaped becoming the craze of the moment by her precipitate withdrawal to Antibes, where she had come within an ace of losing all, largely through the malign influence of Jane—her evil genius during those wonderful, difficult, early months of marriage.

Nevil had returned to find himself a man of note; a prophet, even in his own county, where feathers had been ruffled a little by his erratic proceedings. Hence a discreetly changed attitude in the neighbourhood, when Lilámani, barely nineteen, had presented her husband with a son.

But—for all the gracious condescension of the elderly, and the frank curiosity of the young—only a discerning few had made any real headway with this attractive, oddly disconcerting child of another continent; this creature of queer reserves and aloofness and passionate pride of race. The friendliest were baffled by her incomprehensible lack of social instinct, the fruit of India's purdah system. Loyal wives and mothers who 'adored' their children—yet spent most of their day in pursuit of other interests—were nonplussed by her complete absorption in the joys and sanctities of home. Yet, in course of time, her patent simplicity and sincerity had disarmed prejudice. The least perceptive could not choose but see that she was genuinely, intrinsically different, not merely in the matter of iridescent silks and saris, but in the very colour of her soul.

Not that they would have expressed it so. To talk about the soul and its colour savoured of being psychic or morbid—which Heaven forbid! The soul of the right-minded Bramleigh matron was a neutral-tinted, decently veiled phantom, officially recognised morning and evening, also on Sundays, but by no means permitted to interfere with the realities of life.

The soul of Lilámani Sinclair—tremulous, passionate and aspiring—was a living flame, that lighted her thoughts, her prayers, her desires; and burned with clearer intensity because her religion had been stripped of all feastings and forms and ceremonies by a marriage that set her for ever outside caste. The inner Reality—free of earth-born mists and clouds—none could take from her.

God manifest through Nature, the Divine Mother, must surely accept her incense and sacrifice of the spirit, since no other was permitted. Her father had given her that assurance; and to it she clung, as a child in a crowd clings confidingly to the one familiar hand.

She was none the less eager to glean all she could assimilate of the religion to which her husband conformed, but in which, it seemed, he did not ardently believe. Her secret pangs on this score had been eased a little by later knowledge that it was he who shielded her from tacit pressure to make the change of faith expected of her by certain members of his family. Jane—out of regard for his wishes—had refrained from frontal attacks; but more than one flank movement had been executed by means of the Vicar (a second cousin) and of Aunt Julia—a mild elder Sinclair, addicted to foreign missions.

She had not told Nevil of these tentative fishings for her soul, lest they annoy him and he put a final veto on them. Being well versed in their Holy Book, she wanted to try and fathom their strange illogical way of believing. The Christianity of Christ she could accept. It was a faith of the heart and the life. But its crystallised forms and dogmas proved a stumbling-block to this embarrassing slip of a Hindu girl, who calmly reminded the Reverend Jeffrey Sale that the creed of his Church had not really been inspired by Christ, but dictated by Constantine and the Council of Nicea; who wanted to know why, in so great a religion, was there no true worship of woman—no recognising, in the creative principle, the Divine Motherhood of God? Finally, she had scandalised them both by quarrelling with their exclusive belief in one single instance, through endless ages, of the All-embracing, and All-creating revealed in terms of human life. Was not that same idea a part of her own religion—a world-wide doctrine of Indo-Aryan origin? Was every other revealing false, except that one made to an unbelieving race only two thousand years ago? To her—unregenerate but not unbelieving—the message of Krishna seemed to strike a deeper note of promise. "Wherever irreligion prevails and true religion declines, there I manifest myself in a human form to establish righteousness and to destroy evil."

So she questioned and argued, in no spirit of irreverence, but simply with the logic of her race, and the sweet reasonableness that is a vital element of the Hindu faith at its best. But, after that final confession, Aunt Julia, pained and bewildered, had retired from the field. And Lilámani, flung back on the God within, had evolved a private creed of her own;—shedding the husks of Christian dogmas and the grosser superstitions of her own faith, and weaving together the mystical elements that are the life-blood of all religious beliefs.

For the lamps are many, but the flame is one. . . .

Not till the consummation of motherhood had lifted her status—in her own eyes at least—did she venture to speak intimately with Nevil on this vital matter. Though debarred from sharing of sacred ceremonies, she could still aspire to be true *Sahardamini*—'spiritual helpmate.' But to that end he also must co-operate; he must feel the deeper need. . . .

For many weeks after the coming of Roy she had hesitated, before she found courage to adventure farther into the misty region of his faith or unfaith, in things not seen.

"If I am bothering you with troublesome questions —forgive. But, in our Indian way of marriage, it is taught that without sharing spiritual life there cannot arrive true union," she had explained, not without secret tremors lest she fail to evoke full response. And what such failure would mean, for her, she could hardly expect him to understand.

But—by the blessing of Sarasvati, Giver of Wisdom—she had succeeded, beyond hope, in dispelling the shy reluctance of his race to talk of the 'big little things.' Even to-day she could recall the thrill of that moment :—he, kneeling beside the great chair in his studio—their sanctuary ; she holding the warm bundle of new life against her breast.

In one long look his eyes had answered her. "Nothing *short* of 'true union' will satisfy me," he had said with a quiet seriousness more impressive than any lovers' fervour. "God knows if I'm worthy to enter your inner shrine. But unwilling—never. In the 'big little things' you are pre-eminent. I am simply your extra child—mother of my son."

That tribute was her charter of wifehood. It linked love with life ; it set her, once for all, beyond the lurking fear of Jane ; and gave her courage to face the promised visit to India, when Roy was six months old, to present him to his grandfather, Sir Lakshman Singh.

They had stayed nearly a year ; a wonderful year of increasing knowledge, of fuller awakening . . . and yet !

The ache of anticipation had been too poignant. The foolish half-hope that Mataji might relent and sanctify this first grandchild with her blessing, was—in the nature of things Oriental—foredoomed to failure. And not till she found herself back among sights and sounds hauntingly familiar, did she fully awake to the changes wrought in her by marriage with one of another race. For, if she had profoundly affected Nevil's personality, he had no less profoundly influenced her sense of values both in art and life.

She had also to reckon with the insidious process of idealising the absent. Indian to the core, she was deeply imbued with the higher tenets of Hindu philosophy—that lofty spiritual fabric woven of moonlight and mysticism, of logic and dreams. But the new Lilámani, of Nevil's making, could not shut her eyes to debasing forms of worship, to subterranean caverns of gross superstition, and lurking demons of cruelty and despair. While Nevil was imbibing impressions of Indian Art, Lilámani was secretly weighing and probing the Indian spirit that inspired it; sifting the grain from the chaff—a process closely linked with her personal life; because, for India, religion and life are one.

But no shadow had clouded the joy of reunion with her father; for both were adepts in the fine art of loving, the touchstone of every human relation. And in talk with him she could straighten out her tangle of impressions, her secret doubts and fears.

Also there had been Rama, elder brother, studying at college and loving as ever to the sister transformed into English-wife—yet sister still. And there had been fuller revelation of the wonders of India, in their travels northward, even to the Himalayas, abode of Shiva, where Nevil must go to escape the heat and paint more pictures—always more pictures. Travelling did not suit her. She was too innately a creature of shrines and sanctities. And in India—home of her spirit—there seemed no true home for her any more. . . .

Five years later, when Roy was six and Christine two and a half, they had been tempted to repeat their visit, even in the teeth of stern protests from Jane, who regarded the least contact with India as fatal to the children they had been misguided enough to bring into the world. That second time, things had been easier; and there had been the added delight of Roy's eager interest; his increasing devotion to the grandfather, whose pride and joy in him rivalled her own.

"In this little man we have the hope of England and India!" he would say, only half in joke. "With East and West in his soul—the best of each—he will cast out the devils of conflict and suspicion and draw the two into closer understanding of one another."

And, in secret, Lilámani dreamed and prayed that some day . . . possibly . . . who could tell——?

Yet, still there had persisted the sense of a widening

gulf between her and her own people, leaving her doubtful if she ever wanted to see India again. The spiritual link would be there always; for the rest—was she not wife of Nevil, mother of Roy? Ungrateful to grieve if a price must be paid for such supreme good fortune.

For herself she paid it willingly. But—must Roy pay also? And in what fashion? How could she fail to imbue him with the finest ideals of her race? But how if the magnet of India proved too strong——? To hold the scales even was a hard task for human frailty. And the time of her absolute dominion was so swiftly slipping away from her. Always, in the back of her mind, loomed the dread shadow of school; and her Eastern soul could not accept it without a struggle. Only yesterday, Nevil had spoken of it again—no doubt because Jane made trouble—saying too long delay would be unfair for Roy. So it must be not later than September next year. Just only fifteen months! Nevil had told her, laughing, it would not banish him to another planet. But it would plunge him into a world apart—utterly foreign to her. Of its dangers, its ideals, its mysterious influences, she knew herself abysmally ignorant. She must read. She must try and understand. She must believe Nevil knew best—she, who had not enough knowledge and too much love. But she was upheld by no sustaining faith in this English fashion of school, with its decree of too early separation from the supreme influences of mother and father—and home. . . .

Later on, that evening, when she knelt by Roy's bed for good-night talk and prayer, his arms round her neck, his cool cheek against hers, the rebellion she could not altogether stifle surged up in her afresh. But she said not a word.

It was Roy who spoke, as if he had read her heart.

"Mummy, Aunt Jane's been talking to Daddy again about school. Oh, I do *hate* her!" (This in fervent parenthesis.)

She only tightened her hold and felt a small quiver run through him.

"Will it be fearfully soon? Has Daddy told you?"

"Yes, my darling. But not too fearfully soon, because he knows I don't wish that."

"When?"

"Not till next year, in the autumn. September."

"Oh, you good—*good*est Mummy!"

He clutched her in an ecstasy of relief. For him a year's respite was a lifetime. For her it would pass like a watch in the night.

## CHAPTER VI.

"Thou knowest how, alike, to give and take gentleness in due season . . . the noble temper of thy sires shineth forth in thee."—PINDAR.

IT was a clear mild Sunday afternoon of November;—pale sunlight, pale sky, long films of laminated cloud. From the base of orange-tawny cliffs, the sands swept out with the tide, shining like rippled silk, where the sea had uncovered them; and sunlight was spilled in pools and tiny furrows: the sea itself grey-green and very still, with streaks and blotches of purple shadow flung by no visible cloud. The beauty and the mystery of them fascinated Roy, who was irresistibly attracted by the thing he could not understand.

He was sitting alone, near the edge of a wooded cliff; troubles forgotten for the moment; imbibing it all. . . .

His fifteen months of reprieve had flown faster than anyone could have believed. It was over—everything was over. No more lessons with Tara under their beech-tree. No more happy hours in the studio, exploring the mysteries of 'maths' and Homer, of form and colour, with his father, who seemed to know the 'Why' of everything. Worse than all—no more Mummy, to make the whole world beautiful with the colours of her saris and the loveliness and the dearness of her face, and her laugh and her voice.

It was all over. He was at school: not Coombe Friars, decreed by Aunt Jane; but St Rupert's, because the Head was an artist friend of his father, and would take a personal interest in Roy.

But the Head, however kind, was a distant being; and the boys, who could not exactly be called kind, hemmed him in on every side. His shy sensitive spirit shrank fastidiously from the strange faces and bodies that herded round him, at meals, at bedtime, in the schoolroom, on the playground; some curious and friendly; others curious and hostile:—a very nightmare of boys, who would not let him be. And the more they hemmed him in, the more he felt utterly, miserably alone.

As the endless weeks dragged on, there were interesting, even exciting moments—when you hardly felt the ache. But other times—evenings and Sundays—it came back sharper than ever. And in the course of those weeks he had learnt a number of things not included in the school curriculum. He had learnt that it was better to clench your teeth and not cry out when your ears were tweaked or your arm twisted, or an unexpected pin stuck into the soft part of your leg. But, inside him, there burned a fire of rage and hate unsuspected by his tormentors. It was not so much the pain, as the fact that they seemed to enjoy hurting him, that he could neither understand nor forgive.

And by now he felt more than half ashamed of those early letters to his mother, pouring out his misery of loneliness and longing; of frantic threats to run away or jump off the cliff, that had so strangely failed to soften his father's heart. It seemed, he knew all about it. He had been through it himself. But Mummy did not know; so she got upset. And Mummy must not be upset, whatever happened to Roy, who was advised to 'shut his teeth and play the man' and he would feel the happier for it. That hard counsel had done more than hurt and shame him. It had steadied him at the moment when he needed it most. He *had* somehow managed to shut his teeth and play the man; and he *was* the happier for it already.

So his faith in the father who wouldn't have Mummy upset, had increased ten-fold: and the letter he had nearly torn into little bits was treasured, like a talisman, in his letter-case—Tara's parting gift.

It was on the Sunday of the frantic threats that he had wandered off alone and discovered the little wood on the cliff in all its autumn glory. It was a very ordinary wood of mixed trees with a group of tall pines at one end. But for Roy any wood was a place of enchantment; and this one had trees all leaning one way, with an air of crouching and hurrying that made them seem almost alive; and the moment they closed on him he was back in his old familiar world of fancy, where nothing that happened in houses mattered at all. . . .

Strolling on, careless and content, he had reached a gap where the trees fell apart, framing blue deeps and distances of sea and sky. For some reason they looked more blue, more beautiful so framed than seen from the open shore; and there—sitting alone at the edge of all things, he had felt strangely comforted; had resolved to keep his discovery a profound secret; and to come there every Sunday for 'sanctuary'; to think stories, or write poetry—a very private joy.

And this afternoon was the loveliest of all. If only the sheltering leaves would not fall so fast!

He had been sitting a long time, pencil in hand, waiting for words to come; when suddenly there came instead the very sounds he had fled from—the talk and laughter of boys.

They seemed horribly close, right under the jutting cliff; and their laughter and volleys of chaff had the jeering note he knew too well. Presently his ear caught a high-pitched voice of defiance, that broke off and fell to whimpering—a sound that made Roy's heart beat in quick jerks. He could not catch what they were saying, nor see what they were doing. He did not want to see. He hated them all.

Listening—yet dreading to hear—he recognised the voice of Bennet Ma., known—strictly out of earshot—as Scab Major. Is any school, at any period, quite free of the type? It sounded more like a rough than an ill-natured rag; but the whimpering unseen victim seemed to have no kick in him: and Roy could only sit there wondering helplessly what people were made of who found it amusing to hurt and frighten other people, who had done them no harm. . . .

And now the voice of Scab Major rang out distinctly: "After *that* exhibition, he'll jolly well salaam to the lot of us, turn about. If he's never learnt, we'll show him how."

The word salaam enlightened Roy. Yesterday there had been a buzz of curiosity over the belated arrival of a new boy—an Indian—weedy-looking and noticeably dark, with a sullen mouth and shifty eyes. Roy, though keenly interested, had not felt drawn to him; and a new self-protective shrinking had withheld him from proferring advances that might only embroil them both. He had never imagined the boy's colour would tell against him. Was *that* what it meant—making him salaam?

At the bare suspicion, shrinking gave place to rage. Beasts, they were! If only he could take a flying leap on to them, or roll a few stones down and scare them out of their wits. But he could not stir without giving away his secret. And while he hesitated, his eye absently followed a moving speck far off on the shining sand.

It was a boy on a bicycle—hatless, head in air, sitting very erect. There was only one boy at St Rupert's who carried his head that way and sat his bicycle just so. From the first Roy had watched him covertly, with devout admiration; longing to know him, too shy to ask his name. But so far the godlike one, surrounded by friends, had hardly seemed aware of his existence.

Swiftly he came nearer; and with a sudden leap of his pulses, Roy knew he had seen——

Springing off his bicycle, he flung himself into the little group of tormentors, hitting out vigorously right and left. Sheer surprise and the fury of his onslaught gave him the advantage; and the guilty consciences of the less aggressive were his allies. . . .

This was not cruelty, but championship: and Roy, determined to see all, lay flat on his front—danger of discovery forgotten—grabbing the edge of the cliff, that curved inward, exulting in the triumph of the deliverer and the scattering of the foe.

Bennet Major, one of the first to break away, saw and seized the prostrate bicycle. At that Roy lost his head; leaned perilously over and shouted a warning, "Hi! Look out!"

But the Scab was off like the wind: and the rest, startled by a voice from nowhere, hurriedly followed suit.

Roy, raising himself on his hands, gave a convulsive wriggle of joy—that changed midway, into a backward jerk . . . too late!

The crumbling edge was giving way under his hands, under his body. No time for terror. His jerk gave the finishing touch. . . .

Down he went—over and over; his Sunday hat bouncing gaily on before; nothing to clutch anywhere; but by good luck, no stones——

The thought flashed through him, "I'm killed!" And five seconds later he rolled—breathless and sputtering—to the feet of the two remaining boys, who had sprung back just in time to escape the dusty avalanche.

There he lay—shaken and stupefied—his eyes and mouth full of sand; and his pockets and boots and the inside of his shirt. Nothing seemed to be broken. And he wasn't killed!

Some one was flicking the sand from his face; and he opened his eyes to find the deliverer kneeling beside him, amazed and concerned.

"I say, that was a pretty average tumble! What sort of a lark were you up to? Are you hurt?"

"Only bumped a bit," Roy panted, still out of breath. "I spec' it startled you. I'm sorry."

The bareheaded one laughed. "You startled the Scab's minions a jolly sight more. Cleared the course! And a rare good riddance—eh, Chandranath?"

To that friendly appeal the Indian boy vouchsafed a muttered assent. He stood a little apart, looking sullen, irresolute, and thoroughly uncomfortable, the marks of tears still on his face.

"Thanks veree much. I am going now," he blurted out abruptly; and Roy felt quite cross with him. Pity had evaporated. But the other boy's good-humour seemed unassailable.

"If you're not in a frantic hurry, we can go back together."

Chandranath shook his head. "I don't wish—to go back. I would rather—be by myself."

"As you please. Those cads won't bother you again."

"If they do—I will *kill* them."

He made that surprising announcement in a fierce whisper. It was the voice of another race.

And the English boy's answer was equally true to type. "Right you are. Give me fair warning and I'll lend a hand."

Chandranath stared blankly. "But—they are of *your* country," he said; and turning, walked off in the opposite direction.

"A queer fish," Roy's new friend remarked. "Quite out of water here. Awfully stupid sending him to an English school."

"Why?" asked Roy. He was sitting up and dusting himself generally.

"Oh, because——" the boy frowned pensively at the horizon. "That takes some explaining, if you don't know India."

"D'*you* know India?" Roy could not keep the eagerness out of his tone.

"Rather. I was born there. North-West Frontier. My name's Desmond. We all belong there. I was out till seven and a half, and I'll go back like a bird the minute my schooling's over."

He spoke very quietly; but under the quietness Roy guessed there was purpose—there was fire. This boy knew exactly what he meant to do in his grown-up life—that large, vague word crowded with exciting possibilities. He stood there, straight as an arrow, looking out to sea; and straight as an arrow he would make for his target when school and college let go their hold. Something of this Roy dimly apprehended: and his interest was tinged with envy. If they all 'belonged,' were they Indians, he wondered; and decided not, because of Desmond's coppery brown hair. He wanted to understand—to hear more. He almost forgot he was at school.

"We belong too——" he ventured shyly; and Desmond turned with a kindling eye.

"Good egg! What Province?"

"Rajputana."

"Oh—miles away. Which service?"

Roy looked puzzled. "I—don't know You see—it's my mother—that belongs. My grandfather's a Minister in a big Native State out there."

"Oh—I say!"

There was a shadow of change in his tone. His direct look was a little embarrassing. He seemed to be considering Roy in a new light.

"I—I wouldn't have thought it," he said; and

added a shade too quickly: "*We* don't belong—that way. We're all Anglo-Indians—Frontier Force." (Clearly a fine thing to be, thought Roy, mystified, but impressed.) "Is your father in the Political?"

More conundrums! But, warmed by Desmond's friendliness, Roy grew bolder.

"No. He hates politics. He's just—just a gentleman."

Desmond burst out laughing.

"Top hole! He couldn't do better than that. But—if your mother—he must have been in India?"

"Afterwards—they went. I've been too. He found Mother in France. He painted her. He's a rather famous painter."

"What name?"

"Sinclair."

"Oh, I've heard of him.—And your people are always at home. Lucky beggar!" He was silent a moment watching Roy unlace his boot. Then he asked suddenly, in a voice that tried to sound casual: "I say—have you told any of the other boys—about India—and your Mother?"

"No—why? Is there any harm?" Roy was on the defensive at once.

"Well—no. With the right sort, it wouldn't make a scrap of difference. But you can see what some of 'em are like—Bennet Ma. and his crew. Making a dead set at that poor blighter, just because he isn't their colour——"

Roy started. "Was it only because of *that?*" he asked with emphasis.

"'Course it was. Plain as a pike-staff. I suppose they'd bullied him into cheeking them. And they were hacking him on to his knees—forcing him to salaam." Twin sparks sprang alight in his eyes. "That sort of thing—makes me feel like a kettle on the boil. Wish I'd *had* a boiling kettle to empty over Bennet."

"So do I—the mean Scab! And he's pinched your bicycle."

"No fear! You bet we'll find it round the corner. He wouldn't have the spunk to go right off with it. But look here—what I mean is"—hesitant, yet resolute, he harked back to the main point—"if any of that lot came to know—about India and—your mother, well—they're proper skunks, some of them. They might say things that would make *you* feel like a kettle on the boil."

"If they did—I would kill them."

Roy stated the fact with quiet deliberation, and without noticing that he had repeated the very words of the vanished victim.

This time Desmond did not treat it as a joke.

"'Course you would," he agreed gravely. "And that sort of shindy's no good for the school. So I thought—better give you the tip——"

"I—see," Roy said in a low voice, without looking up. He did not see; but he began dimly to guess at a so far unknown and unsuspected state of mind.

Desmond sat silent while he shook the sand out of his boots. Then he remarked in an easier tone: "Quite sure there's no damage?"

Roy, now on his feet, found his left leg uncomfortably stiff—and said so.

"Bad luck! We must walk it off. I'll knead it first, if you like. I've seen them do it on the Border."

His unskilled manipulation hurt a good deal; but Roy, overcome with gratitude, gave no sign.

When it was over they set out for their homeward tramp, and found the bicycle, as Desmond had prophesied. He refused to ride on; and Roy limped beside him, feeling absurdly elated. The godlike one had come to earth indeed! Only the remark about his mother still rankled; but he felt shy of returning to the subject. The change in Desmond's manner had puzzled him. Roy glanced admiringly at his profile—the straight nose, the long mouth that smiled so readily, the resolute chin, a little in the air. A clear case of love at sight, schoolboy love; a passing phase of human efflorescence; yet, in passing, it will sometimes leave a mark for life. Roy, instinctively a hero-worshipper, registered a new ambition—to become Desmond's friend.

Presently, as if aware of his thought, Desmond spoke.

"I say, Sinclair, how old are you? You seem less of a kid than most of the new lot."

"I'm ten and a half," said Roy, wishing it was eleven.

"Bit late for starting. I'm twelve. Going on to Marlborough next year."

Roy felt crushed. In a year he would be gone! Still—there were three more terms: and *he* would go on to Marlborough too. He would insist.

"Does Scab Ma. bother you much?" Desmond asked with a friendly twinkle.

"Now and then—nothing to fuss about."

Roy's nonchalance, though plucky, was not quite convincing.

"Righto! I'll head him off. He isn't keen to knock up against me." A pause. "How about sitting down my way at meals? You don't look awfully gay at your end."

"I'm not. It would be ripping."

"Good. We'll hang together, eh? Because of India; because we both belong—in a different way. And we'll stick up for that miserable little devil Chandranath."

"Yes—we will." (The glory of that 'we.') "All the same,—I don't much like the look of him"

"No more don't I. He's the wrong 'ját.' He won't stay long—you'll see. But still—he shan't be bullied by Scabs, because he's not the same colour outside. You see that sort of thing in India too. My father's fearfully down on it, because it makes more bad blood than anything; I've heard him say that it's just the blighters who buck about the superior race who do all the damage with their inferior manners. Rather neat—eh?"

Roy glowed. "Your father must be a splendid sort. Is he a soldier?"

"Rath*er*! He's a V.C. He got it saving a Jemadar—a Native Officer."

Roy caught his breath.

"I would awfully like to hear how——"

Desmond told him how. . . .

It was a wonderful walk. By the end of it Roy no longer felt a lonely atom in a strange world. He had found something better than his Sanctuary—he had found a friend. .

Looking back, long afterwards, he recognised that Sunday as the turning-point. . . .

Later in the evening he poured it all out to his mother in four closely-written sheets.

But not a word about herself, or Desmond's friendly

warning, which still puzzled him. He worried over it a little before he fell asleep. It was the very first hint—given, in all friendliness—that the mere fact of having an Indian mother might go against you, in some people's eyes. Not the right ones, of course; but still—in the nature of things,—he couldn't make it out. That would come later

At the time its only effect was to deepen his private satisfaction at having hammered Joe Bradley; to quicken his attitude of championship towards his mother and towards India, till ultimately the glow of his fervent devotion fused them both into one dominant idea.

## CHAPTER VII.

"He it is—the innermost one who awakens my being with his deep hidden touches."—TAGORE.

LILÁMANI read and re-read that letter curled among her cushions in the deep window-seat of the studio, a tower room with tall windows looking north, over jagged pine tops, to the open moor

And while she read, Nevil stood at his easel, seizing and recording, the unconscious grace of her pose, the rapt stillness of her face. He was never weary of painting her—never quite satisfied with the result; always within an ace of achieving the one perfect picture that should immortalise a gleam from her inner uncaptured loveliness—the essence of personality that eternally foils the sense, while it sways the spirit. Impossible, of course. One might as well try and catch the fragrance of a rose, the bloom of an April dawn, or any other fragment of the world's unseizable beauty. But there remained the joy of pursuing—and pursuing, not achieving, is the salt of life.

Something in her pose, her absorption—lips just parted, shadow of lashes on her cheek, primrose-pale sari against the green velvet curtain—had fired him, lit a spark of inspiration. . . .

If he made a decent thing of it, Roy should have it for a companion to the Antibes pastel: her two aspects —wife of Nevil; mother of Roy. Later on, the boy would understand. His star stood higher than usual, just then. For Nevil had detested writing that letter of rebuke; had not dared show it to his wife; and Roy had taken it like a man. No more lamentations, so far. Certainly not on this occasion, judging by her rapt look, her complete absorption that gave him the chance of catching her unawares.

For, in truth, she was unaware; lost to everything but the joy of contact with her son. The pang of parting had been dulled to a hidden ache; but always the blank was there, however richly filled with other claims on heart and spirit. A larger schoolroom now: and Nevil, with his new Eastern picture on hand, making constant demands on her—as usual—in the initial stages; till the subject of the moment eclipsed everything, every one—sometimes even herself. Her early twinges of jealousy, during that phase, rarely troubled her now. As wife and mother, she better understood the dual allegiance—the twofold strain of the creative process, whether in spirit or flesh. Now she knew that, when art seemed most exclusively to claim him, his need was greater, not less, for her woman's gift of self-effacing tenderness, of personal physical service. And through deeper love, came clearer insight. She saw Nevil—the artist—as a veritable Yogi, impelled to ceaseless striving for mastery of himself, his atmosphere, his medium: saw her wifely love and service as the life-giving impetus without which he might flag and never reach the heights.

Women of wide social and intellectual activities might raise perplexed eyebrows over her secluded life, still instinct with the 'spirit of purdah.' She found the daily pattern of it woven with threads so richly varied that to cherish a hidden grief seemed base ingratitude. Yet always—at the back of things—lurked her foolish mother-anxieties, her deep unuttered longing. And letters were cold comfort. In the first few weeks she had come to dread opening them. Always the bitter cry of loneliness and longing for home. What was it Nevil had said to make so surprising a change? Craving to know, she feared to ask; and more than suspected that he blessed her for refraining.

And now came this long, exultant letter, written in the first flush of his great discovery——

And as she read on, she became aware of a new sensation. This was another kind of Roy. On the first page he was pouring out his heart in careless unformed phrases. By the end of the second, his tale had hold of him; he was enjoying—perhaps unaware—the exercise of a newly-awakened gift. And, looking up, at last, to share it with Nevil, she caught him in the act of tracing a curve of her sari in mid-air.

With a playful movement—pure Eastern—she drew it half over her face.

"Oh, Nevil—you wicked! I never guessed——"

"That was the beauty of it. I make my salaams to Roy! What's he been up to that it takes four sheets to confess?"

"Not confessing. Telling a tale. It will surprise you."

"Let's have a look."

She gave him the letter; and while he read it, she intently watched his face. "The boy'll write—I shouldn't wonder," was his verdict, handing back her treasure, with an odd half-smile in his eyes.

"And you were hoping—he would paint?" she said, answering his thought.

"Yes, but—scarcely expecting. Sons are a perverse generation. I'm glad he's tumbled on his feet and found a pal."

"Yes. It is good."

"We'll invite young Desmond here and inspect him, eh?"

"Yes—we will."

He was silent a moment, considering her profile—humanly, not artistically. "Jealous, is she? The hundredth part of a fraction?"

"Just so much!" she admitted in her small voice. "But underneath—I am glad. A fine fellow. We will ask him—later."

The projected invitation proved superfluous. Roy's next letter informed them that after Christmas Desmond was coming for ten whole days. He had promised.

He kept his promise. After Christmas he came and saw—and conquered. At first they were all inclined to be secretly critical of the new element that looked as if it had come to stay. For Roy's discreetly repressed admiration was clear as print to those who could read him like an open page. And, on the whole, it was not surprising, as they were gradually persuaded to admit. There was more in Lance Desmond than mere grace and good looks, manliness and a ready humour. In him two remarkable personalities were blended with a peculiarly happy result.

They discovered, incidentally, his wonderful gift of music. "Got it off my mother," was his modest disclaimer. "She and my sister are simply top-hole. We do lots of it together."

His intelligent delight in pictures and books commended him to Nevil; but, at twelve and a half, skating, tramping, and hockey matches held the field. Sometimes—when it was skating—Tara and Chris went with them. But they made it clear, quite unaggressively, that the real point was to go alone.

Day after day, from her window, Lilámani watched them go, across the radiant sweep of snow-covered lawn; and, for the first time, where Roy was concerned, she knew the prick of jealousy,—a foretaste of the day when her love would no longer fill his life. Ashamed of her own weakness, she kept it hid—or fancied she did so; but the little stabbing ache persisted, in spite of shame and stoic resolves.

Tara and Christine also knew the horrid pang; but they knew neither shame not stoic resolves. Roy mustn't suspect, of course; but they told each other, in strictest confidence, that they hated Desmond; firmly believing they spoke the truth. So it was particularly vexatious to find that the moment he favoured them with the most casual attention, they were at his feet.

But that was their own private affair. Whether they resented, or whether they adored, the boys remained entirely unconcerned, entirely absorbed in each other. It was Desmond's opinion of them that mattered supremely to Roy; in particular—Desmond's opinion of his mother. After those first puzzling remarks and silences, Roy had held his peace; had not even shown Desmond her picture. His invitation accepted, he had simply waited, in transcendent faith, for the moment of revelation. And now he had his reward. After a prelude of mutual embarrassment, Lance had succumbed frankly to Lady Sinclair's unexpected charm and her shy irresistible overtures to friendship:—so frankly, that he was able, now, to hint at his earlier perplexity.

He had seen no Indian women, he explained, except in bazaars or in service; so he couldn't quite understand, until his own mother made things clearer to him and recommended him to go and see for himself. Now he had seen—and succumbed: and Roy's very private triumph was unalloyed. Second only to that triumph, the really important outcome of their glorious Ten Days was that, with Desmond's help, Roy fought the battle of going on to Marlborough when he was twelve—and won. . . .

It was horrid leaving them all again; but it did make a wonderful difference knowing there was Desmond at the other end; and together they would champion that doubtfully grateful victim—Chandranath. Their zeal proved superfluous. Chandranath never reappeared at St Rupert's. Perhaps his people had arrived at Desmond's conclusion, that he was not the right "ját" for an English school. In any case, his disappearance was a relief—and Roy promptly forgot all about him.

Years later—many years later—he was to remember.

After St Rupert's—Marlborough:—and just at first he hated it, as he had hated St Rupert's, though in a different fashion. Here it was not so much the longing for home, as a vague yet deepening sense that, in some vital way—not yet fully understood—he was different from his fellows. But once he reached the haven of Desmond's study, the good days began in earnest. He could read and dream along his own lines. He could scribble verse or prose, when he ought to have been preparing quite other things; and the results, good or bad, went straight to his mother.

Needless to say, she found them all radiant with promise; here and there a flicker of the divine spark: and, throughout the years of transition, the locked and treasured book that held them was the sheet-anchor to which she clung, till the new Roy should be forged out of the backslidings and renewals incidental to that time of stress and becoming. What matter their young imperfections, when—for her—it was as if Roy's spirit reached out across the dividing distance and touched her own. In the days when he seemed most withdrawn, that dear illusion was her secret bread.

And all the while, subconsciously, she was drawing nearer to the given moment of religious surrender that would complete the spiritual link with husband and children. As the babies grew older, she saw, with increasing clearness, the increasing difficulty of her position. Frankly, she had tried not to see it. Her free spirit, having reached the Reality that transcends all forms, shrank from returning to the dogmas, the limitations of a definite creed. In her eyes, it seemed a step backward. Belief in a personal God, above and beyond the Universe, was reckoned by her own faith a primitive conception; a stage on the way to that ultima Thule where the soul of man perceives its own inherent divinity, and the knower becomes the Known, as notes become music, as the river becomes the sea. It was this that troubled her logical mind and delayed decision.

But the final deciding factor—though he knew it not—was Roy. By reason of her own share in him, religion would probably mean more to him than to Nevil. For his sake—for the sake of Christine and Tara and the babies, fast sprouting into boys—she felt at last irresistibly constrained to accept, with certain mental reservations, the tenets of her husband's creed; and so qualify herself to share with them all its outward and visible forms, as already she shared its inward and spiritual grace.

The conviction sprang from no mere sentimental impulse. It was the unhurried work of years. So—when there arose the question of Roy's confirmation, and Tara's, at the same Easter-tide, conviction blossomed into decision, as simply and naturally as the bud of a flower opens to the sun. That is the supreme virtue of changes not imposed from without. When the given moment came—the inner resolve was there.

Quite simply she spoke of it to Nevil, one evening over the studio fire. And behold a surprise awaited her. She had rarely seen him more deeply moved. From the time of Roy's coming, he told her, he had cherished the hidden hope.

"Yet too seldom you have spoken of such things—why?" she asked, moved in her turn and amazed.

"Because from the first I made up my mind I would

not have it, except in your own way and in your own time. I knew the essence of it was in you. For the rest—I preferred to wait till you were ready—Sita Devi."

"Nevil—lord of me!" She slipped to her knees beside him. "I *am* ready. But oh, you wicked, how *could* I know that all the time you were caring that much in your secret heart."

He gathered her close and said not a word.

So the great matter was settled, with no outward fuss or formalities. She would be baptized before Roy came home for the Easter holidays and his confirmation.

"But not here—not Mr Sale," she pleaded. "Let us go away quietly to London—we two. Let it be in that great Church, where first the thought was born in my heart that some day . . . this might be."

He could refuse her nothing. Jeffrey might feel aggrieved when he knew. But after all—this was their own affair. Time enough afterwards to let in the world and its thronging notes of exclamation.

Roy was told when he came home. For imparting such intimate news, she craved the response of his living self. And if Nevil's satisfaction struck a deeper note, it was simply that Roy was very young and had always included her Hindu-ness in the natural order of things.

Wonderful days! Preparing the children, with Helen's help; preparing herself, in the quiet of her "House of Gods"—a tiny room above the studio—in much the same spirit as she had prepared for the great consecration of marriage, with vigil and meditation and unobtrusive fasting—noted by Nevil, though he said no word.

Crowning wonder of all, that golden Easter morning of her first Communion with Roy and Tara, with Nevil and Helen:—unfolding of heart and spirit, of leaf and blossom; dual miracle of a world new made. . . .

END OF PHASE I.

# PHASE II.

# THE VISIONARY GLEAM

## CHAPTER I.

"Youth is lifted on Wings of his strong hope and soaring valour; for his thoughts are above riches."—PINDAR.

OXFORD on a clear, still evening of June: silver reaches of Isis and Cher; meadows pied with moon daisies and clover, and the rose madder bloom of ripe grasses; the trill of unseen birds tuning up for evensong; the passing and repassing of boats and canoes and punts, gay with cushions and summer frocks; all bathed in the level radiance that steals over earth like a presence in the last hours of a summer day. . . .

Oxford—shrine of the oldest creeds and the newest fads—given over, for one hilarious week, to the yearly invasion of mothers and sisters and cousins, and girls that were neither; especially girls that were neither. . . .

Two of the punts, clearly containing one party, kept close enough together for the occupants to exchange sallies of wit, or any blissful foolishness in keeping with the blissfully foolish mood of a moonlight picnic up the river in 'Commem.'

Roy Sinclair's party boasted the distinction of including one mother, Lady Despard; and one grandfather, Cuthbert Broome; and Roy himself—a slender, virile figure in flannels, and New College tie—was poling the first punt.

As in boyhood, so now, his bearing and features were Nevil incarnate. But to the shrewd eye of Broome the last seemed subtly overlaid with the spirit of the East—a brooding stillness wrought from the clash of opposing forces within. When he laughed and talked it vanished. When he fell silent, and drifted away from his surroundings, it reappeared.

It was precisely this hidden quality, so finely balanced,

that intrigued the brain of the novelist, as distinct from the heart of the godfather. Which was the real Roy? Which would prove the decisive factor at the critical corners of his destiny? To what heights would it carry him—into what abyss might it plunge him—that gleam from the ancient soul of things? Would India—and his young glorification of India—be, for him, a spark of inspiration or a stone of stumbling?

Broome had not seen much of the boy, intimately, since the New Year; and he did not need spectacles to discern some inner ferment at work. Roy was more talkative and less communicative than usual; and Broome let him talk, reading between the lines. He knew to a nicety the moment when a chance question will kill confidence—or evoke it. He suspected one of those critical corners. He also suspected one of those Indian cousins of his: delightful, both of them; but still . . .

The question remained, which was it—the girl or the boy?

The girl, Arúna—student at Somerville College—was reclining among vast blue and pink cushions in the bows, pensively twirling a Japanese parasol, one arm flung round the shoulders of her companion—a fellow-student; fair and stolid and good-humoured. Broome summed her up mentally: "Tactless but trustworthy. Anglo-Saxon to the last button on her ready-made Shantung coat and the blunted toe of her white suède shoe."

Arúna—in plain English, Dawn—was quite arrestingly otherwise. Not beautiful, like Lilámani, nor quite so fair of skin; but what the face lacked in symmetry was redeemed by lively play of expression, piquante tilt of nose and chin, large eyes, velvet-dark like brown pansies. The modelling of the face—its breadth and roundness and upturned aspect—gave it a pansy-like air. Over her simple summer frock of carnation pink she wore a paler sari flecked with gold; and two ropes of coral beads enhanced the deeper coral of her full lower lip. Not yet eighteen, she was studying "pedagogy" for the benefit of her less adventurous sisters in Jaipur.

Clearly a factor to be reckoned with, this creature of girlish laughter and high purpose; a woman to the tips of her polished finger nails. Yet Broome had by no means decided that it *was* the girl——

After Desmond—Dyán Singh: each, in his turn and type, own brother to Roy's complex soul. Broome—in no insular spirit—preferred the earlier influence. But Desmond had sped like an arrow to the Border, where his eldest brother commanded their father's old regiment; and Dyán Singh—handsome and fiery, young India at its best—reigned in his stead. The two were of the same college. Dyán, twelve months younger, looked the older by a year or more. Face and form bore the Rajput stamp of virility, of a racial pride, verging on arrogance; and the Rajput insignia of breeding—noticeably small hands and feet.

He was poling the second punt with less skill and assurance than Roy. His attention was palpably distracted by a vision of Tara among the cushions in the bows; an arm linked through her mother's, as though defending her against the implication of being older than any one else, or in the least degree out of it because of that trifling detail—tacitly admitted, while hotly denied; which was Tara all over.

Certainly Lady Despard still looked amazingly young; still emanated the vital charm she had transmitted to her child. And Tara at twenty, in soft butter-coloured frock and roses in her hat, was a vision alluring enough to distract any young man from concentration on a punt pole. Vivid, eager and venturesome, singularly free from the bane of self-consciousness; not least among her graces—and rare enough to be notable—was the grace of her chivalrous affection for the older generation. In Tara's eyes, girls who patronised their mothers and tolerated their fathers were anathema. It was a trait certain to impress Roy's Rajput cousin; and Broome wondered whether Helen was alive to the disturbing possibility; whether, for all her genuine love of the East, she would acquiesce. . . .

Only the other day, it seemed, he and she had sat together among the rocks of the dear old Cap, listening to Nevil's amazing news. She it was who had championed his choice of a bride: and Lilámani had justified her championship to the full. But then—Lilámani was one in many thousands; and this affair would be the other way about :—Tara, the apple of their eye ; Tara, with her wild-flower face and her temperament of clear flame——?

How sharply they tugged at his middle-aged heart, these casual and opinionated young things, with their follies and fanaticisms, their Jacob's ladders hitched perilously to the stars ; with their triumphs and failures and disillusions all ahead of them ; airily impervious to proffered help and advice from those who would agonise to serve them if they could. . . .

A jarring bump in the small of his back cut short his flagrantly Victorian musings. Dyán's punt was the offender ; and Dyán himself, clutching the pole that had betrayed him, was almost pitched into the river.

His achievement was greeted by a shout of laughter, and an ironic " Played indeed ! " from Cuthbert Gordon —Broome's grandson. Roy, tumbled from some starry dream of his own, flashed out imperiously : " Look alive, you blithering idiot. ' Who are you a-shoving ' ? "

The Rajput's face darkened ; but before he could retort, Tara had risen and stepped swiftly to his side. Her fingers closed on the pole ; and she smiled straight into his clouded eyes.

" Let *me*, please. I'm sick of lazing and fearfully keen. And I can't allow my Mother to be drownded by anyone *but* me. I'd be obliged to murder the other body, which would be awkward—for us both ! "

" Miss Despard—there is no danger——" he muttered —impervious to humour ; and—as if by chance—one of his hands half covered hers.

" Let go," she commanded, so low that no one else knew she had spoken ; so sternly that Dyán's fingers unclosed as if they had touched fire.

" Now, don't fuss. Go and sit down," she added, in her lighter vein. " You've done your share. And you're jolly grateful to me, really. But too proud to own it ! "

" *Not* too proud to obey you," he muttered.

She saw the words rather than heard them ; and he turned away without daring to meet her eyes.

It all passed in a few seconds, but it left him tingling with repressed rage. He had made a fool of himself in her eyes ; had probably given away his secret to the whole party. After all, what matter ? He could not much longer have kept it hidden. By the touch of hands and his daring words he had practically told her. . . .

As he settled himself, her clear voice rang out: "Wake up, Roy! I'll race you to the backwater."

They raced to the backwater; and Tara won by half a length, amid cheers from the men.

"Well, you see, I *had* to let you," Roy explained, as she confronted him, flushed with triumph. "Seemed a shame to cut you out. Not as if you were a giddy suffragette!"

"*Qui s'excuse—s'accuse!*" she retorted. "Anyway —*I'm* the winner."

"Right you are. The way of girls was ever so. No matter what line you take, it's safe to be the wrong one."

"Hark at the Cynic!" jeered young Cuthbert. "Were you forty on the 9th, or was it forty-five?"

Roy grinned. "Good old Cuthers! Don't exhaust yourself trying to be funny! Fish out the drinks. We've earned them, haven't we—High Tower Princess?" The last, confidentially, for Tara's ear alone.

And Dyán, seeing the smile in her eyes, felt jealousy pierce him like a red-hot wire.

The supper, provided by Roy and Dyán, was no scratch wayside meal, but an ambrosial affair:—salmon mayonnaise, ready mixed; glazed joints of chicken; strawberries and cream; lordly chocolate boxes; sparkling moselle—and syphons for the abstemious.

It was a lively meal: Roy, dropped from the clouds, the film of the East gone from his face, was simply Nevil again; even as young Cuthbert, with his large build and thatch of tawny hair, was a juvenile edition of Broome. And the older man, watching them, bandying chaff with them, renewed his youth for one careless golden hour.

The punts were ranged alongside; and they all eat together, English and Indian. No irksome caste rules on this side of the water; no hint of condescension in the friendly attitude of young Oxford. Nothing to jar the over-sensibility of young India—prone to suspect slight where no thought of it exists; too often, also, treated to exhibitions of ill-bred arrogance that undo in an hour the harmonising work of years.

Dyán sat by Tara, anticipating her lightest need; courage rising by leaps and bounds. Arúna, from her nest of cushions, exchanged lively sallies with Roy. Petted by a college full of friendly English girls, she had very soon lost what little shyness she ever possessed. Now and again, when his eyes challenged hers, she would veil them and watch him surreptitiously; one moment approving his masculine grace; the next, boldly asking herself: "Does he see how I am wearing the favourite sari—and how my coral beads make my lips look red?" And again: "Why do they make foolish talk of a gulf between East and West?"

To that profound question came no answer in words; only in hidden stirrings, that she preferred to ignore. Both brother and sister had persuaded themselves that talk of a gulf was exaggerated by unfriendly spirits. They, at all events, having built their bridge, took its stability for granted. Children of an emotional race, it sufficed to discover that they loved the cool green freshness of England, the careless kindly freedom of her life and ways; the hum of her restless, smoky, all-embracing London; her miles and miles of books and pictures. Above everything they loved Oxford, where all were brothers in spirit—with a proper sense of difference between the brothers of one's own college and the mere outsider:—Oxford, at this particular hour of this particular June evening. And at this actual moment, they loved salmon mayonnaise and crushed strawberries fully as much as any other manifestation of the delectable land.

And down in subconscious depths—untroubled by the play of surface emotions—burned their passionate, unreasoned love of India that any chance breath might rekindle to a flame.

Presently, as the sun drew down to earth, trees and meadows swam in a golden haze. Arrows of gold, stealing through alders and willows, conjured mere leaves into discs of pure green light. Clouds of pollen brightened to dust of gold. In the near haze midges flickered; and, black against the brightness, swallows wheeled and dipped, uttering thin cries in the ecstasy of their evening flight.

On the two punts in the backwater a great peace

descended after the hilarity of their feast. Clouds of cigarette smoke kept midges at bay. In the deepening stillness small sounds asserted themselves—piping of gnats, the trill of happy birds, snatches of disembodied laughter and talk from other parties in other punts, somewhere out of sight. . . .

Only Arúna did not smoke; and Emily Barnard, her fanatic devotee, retired with her to the bank, where they made a lazy pretence of "washing up." But Arúna's eyes *would* stray toward the recumbent figure of Roy, when she fancied Emmie was not looking. And Emmie—who could see very well without looking—wished him at the bottom of the river.

Propped on an elbow, he lay among Arúna's cushions, his senses stirred by the faint carnation scent she used, enlarging on his latest enthusiasm—Rabindranath Tagore, the first of India's poet-saints to challenge the ethics of the withdrawn life. When the mood was on, the veil of reserve swept aside, he could pour out his ardours, his protests, his theories, in an eloquent rush of words. And Arúna—absently wiping spoons and forks—listened entranced. He seemed to be addressing no one in particular; but as often as not his gaze rested on Broome, as though he were indirectly conveying to him thoughts he felt shy of airing when they were alone.

A pause in the flow of his talk left a space of silence into which the encompassing peace and radiance stole like an inflowing tide. None loved better than Roy the ghostly music of silence; but to-night his brain was filled with the music of words—not his own.

"Just listen to this," he said, without preamble. His eyes took on their far-away look; his voice dropped a tone.

"The night is night of mid-May; the breeze is the breeze of the South.

"From my heart comes out and dances the image of my Desire.

"The gleaming vision flits on.

"I try to clasp it firmly, it eludes me and leads me astray.

"I seek what I cannot get; I get what I do not seek."

To that shining fragment of truth and beauty, his

audience paid the fitting tribute of silence; and his gaze—returning to earth—caught, in Tara's eyes, a reflection of his exalted mood. Dyán saw it also; and once more that red-hot wire pierced his heart.

It passed in a second; and Roy was speaking again—not to Tara, but to her mother.

"Is there any poet, East or West, who can *quite* so exquisitely capture the essence of a mood, hold it lightly, like a fluttering bird, and as lightly let it go?"

Lady Despard smiled approval at the simile. "In that one," she said, "he has captured more than a mood—the very essence of life.—Have you met him?"

"Yes, once—after a lecture. We had a talk—I'll never forget. There's wonderful stuff in the new volume. I know most of it by heart."

"Spare us, good Lord," muttered Cuthbert—neither prejudiced nor perverse, but British to the core. "If you start again, I'll retaliate with Job and the Psalms!"

Roy retorted with the stump of an extinct cigarette. It smote the offender between the eyebrows, leaving a caste-mark of warm ash to attest the accuracy of his aim.

"Bull's eye!" Tara scored softly; and Roy, turning on his elbow, appealed to Broome. "Jeffers, please extinguish him!" ("Jeffers" being a corruption of G.F., alias Godfather).

Broome laughed. "I had a hazy notion he was your show candidate for the Indian Civil!"

"He's supposed to be. That's the scandal of it. A mighty lot of interest he's cultivating in the people and the country he aspires to administer."

"High art and sloppy sentiment are not in the bond," Cuthbert retorted, with a wink at Dyán Singh.

That roused Lady Despard. "Insight and sympathy *must* be in the bond, unless England and India are to drift apart altogether. The Indian Civilian should be caught early, like the sailor, and trained on the spot. Exams make character a side issue. And one might almost say there's no *other* issue in the Indian services."

Cuthbert nodded. "Glorious farce, isn't it? They simply cram us like Christmas turkeys. Efficiency's the war-cry, these enlightened days."

"Too *much* efficiency," Dyán struck in, with a kindling

eye. "Already turning our ancient cities into nightmares like Manchester and Birmingham, killing the true sense of beauty, giving us instead the poison of money and luxury worship. And what result? Just now, when the West at last begins to notice our genius of colour and design—even to learn from it—we find it slipping out of our own fingers. Nearly all the homes of the English educated are like caricatures of your villas—the worst kind. Yet there are still many on both sides who wish to make life—not so ugly, to escape a little from gross superstition of *facts*——"

"Hear, hear!" Broome applauded him. "But I'm afraid, my dear boy, the Time Spirit is out to make tradesmen and politicians of us all. Thank God, the soul of a race lives in its books, its philosphy and art."

"Very well then"—Roy was the speaker,—"the obvious remedy lies in getting the souls of both races into closer touch—philosophy, art, and all that—eh, Jeffers? That's what we're after—Dyán and I—on the lines of that society Dad belongs to."

Broome looked thoughtfully from one to the other. "A tall order," said he.

"A vision splendid!" said Lady Despard.

Roy leaned eagerly towards her. "*You* don't sneer at dreams, Aunt Helen."

"Nor do I, my son. Dreamers are our strictly unpaid torch-bearers. They light the path for us; and we murmur 'Poor fools!' with a kind of sneaking self-satisfaction, when they come a cropper."

"'Which I 'ope it won't 'appen to me!'" quoted Roy, cheered by Lady Despard's approval. "Anyway, we're keen to speed up the better understanding move—on the principle that Art unites and politics divide."

"Very pithy—and approximately true! May I be allowed to proffer a sound working maxim for youth on the war-path? 'Freedom and courage in thought—obedience in act.' When I say obedience, I don't mean slavish conformity. When I say freedom, I don't mean licence. Only the bond are free."

"Jeffers, you're a Daniel! I'll pinch that pearl of wisdom! But what about democracy—Cuthers' pet panacea? Isn't it making for *dis*obedience in act—rebellion; and enslavement in thought—every man reared on the same catch-words, minted with the same hall-mark?"

That roused the much-enduring British Lion—in the person of Cuthbert Gordon.

"Confound you, Roy! This is a picnic, not a bally Union debate. You can't argue for nuts; and when you start spouting you're the limit. But two can play at that game!" He flourished a half-empty syphon of lemonade, threatening the handle with a very square thumb.

"Fire away, old bean." Roy opened his mouth by way of invitation. Cuthbert promptly pressed the trigger—and missed his mark.

There was a small shriek from Tara and from the girls on the bank: then the opponents proceeded to deal with one another in earnest. . . .

Dyán soon lost interest when India was not the theme; and, as the elders fell into an undercurrent of talk, his eyes sought Tara's face. Her answering smile spurred him to a bold move; and he leaned towards her, over the edge of the boat. "Miss Despard," he said under his breath, "won't you come for a stroll in the field?—Do."

She shook her head. "I'm too lazy! We've had enough exercise. And there's the walk home."

Her refusal jarred him; but desire overruled pride. "You couldn't call it exercise. Do come."

"Truly—I'm tired," she insisted gently, looking away from him towards her mother.

It was Lady Despard's boast that she could listen to three conversations at once; but even Tara was surprised when she casually put out a hand and patted her knee. "Wise child. Better keep quiet till we start home."

The hand was not removed. Tara covered it with her own, and further maddened the discomfited Dyán by saying, with her very kindest smile: "I'm so sorry. Don't be vexed."

Vexed! The bloodless word was insult piled on injury. All the pride and passion of his race flamed in him. Without answering her smile or her plea, he drew abruptly away from her; stepped out of the punt and went for his stroll alone.

## CHAPTER II.

"Who knows what days I answer for to-day . . . ?
Thoughts yet unripe in me, I bend one way. . . ."
—ALICE MEYNELL.

WHILE Broome and Lady Despard were concerned over indications of a critical corner for Roy, there was none —save perhaps Arúna—to be concerned for the dilemma of Dyán Singh, Rajput—half savage, half chivalrous gentleman; idealist in the grain; lover of England and India; and now—fiercely, consumedly—lover of Tara Despard, with her Indian name and her pearl-white English skin and the benign sunshine of England in her hair.

It is the danger-point for the young Indian overseas, unused to free intercourse with women other than his own; saddled, very often, with a girl-wife in the background—the last by no means a matter of course in these enlightened days. In Dyán Singh's case the safeguard was lacking. His mother being dead, he had held his own against a rigidly conventional grandmother, and insisted on delaying the inevitable till his education was complete. Waxing bolder still, he had demanded the same respite for Arúna; a far more serious affair. For months they had waged a battle of tongues and temper and tears, with Mataji—high-priestess of the Inside—with the family matchmaker and the family *guru*, whom to offend was the unforgiveable sin. Had he not power to call down upon an entire household the curse of the gods?

More than once Arúna had been goaded to the brink of surrender; till her brother grew impatient and spurned her as a weakling. Yet her ordeal had been sharper than his own. For him, mere moral suasion and threats of ostracism. For her, the immemorial methods of the Inside; forbidden by Sir Lakshman, but secretly applied, when flagrant obstinacy demanded drastic measures. So neither Dyán nor his grandfather had suspected that Arúna, for days together, had suffered the torment of Tantalus—food set before her so mercilessly peppered that a morsel would raise blisters on her lips and tongue; water steeped in salt; the touch of the 'fire-stick' applied where her skin was tenderest; not to mention the more subtle torment of jibes and threats and vile insinuations that suffused her with shame and rage. A word to the menfolk, threatened Mataji, and worse would befall. If *men* cared nothing for family honour, the women must vindicate it in their own fashion. For the two were doing their duty, up to their lights. Only the knowledge that Dyán was fighting her battle, as well as his own, had kept the girl unbroken in spirit, even when her body cried out for respite at any price. . . .

All this she had confided to him when, at last, they were safe on the great ship, with miles of turbulent water between them and the ruthless dominion of *dastúr*. That confession—with its unconscious revealing of the Rajput spirit hidden in her laughter-loving heart—had drawn them into closest union and filled Dyán with self-reproach. Small wonder if Oxford seemed to both a paradise of knowledge and of friendly freedom. Small wonder if they believed that, in one bold leap, they had bridged the gulf between East and West.

At Bramleigh Beeches, Lilámani—who knew all without telling—had welcomed them with open arms: and Lady Despard no less. It was here that Dyán met Tara, who had 'no use' for colleges—and, in the course of a few vacation visits, the damage had been done.

At first he had felt startled, even a little dismayed. English education and delayed marriage had involved no dream of a possible English wife. With the Indian Civil in view, he had hoped to meet some girl student of his own race, sufficiently advanced to remain outside purdah and to realise that a modern Indian husband might crave companionship from his wife no less than motherhood, worship, and service.

And now . . . *this——!*

Striding across the field, in the glimmer of a moon just beginning to take colour, he alternately raged at her light rebuff, and applauded her maidenly hesitation. As a Hindu and a man of breeding, his natural instinct had been to approach her parents; but he knew enough of modern youth, by now, to realise that English parents were a side issue in these little affairs. For himself, the primitive lover flamed in him. He wanted to kneel and worship her. In the same breath, he wanted simply to possess her, would she or no. . . .

And in saner moods, uncertainty racked him. What did they amount to, her smiles and flashes of sympathy, her kind, cousinly ways? What did Roy's cousinly kindness amount to, with Arúna? If in India they suffered from too much restriction, it dawned on him that in England trouble might arise from too much freedom. Always, by some cause, there would be suffering. The gods would see to it. But not through loss of her—he mutely implored them. Any way but that!

Everything hung on the walk home. Those two must have finished their sparring match by now. . . .

They had. Roy was on the bank, helping Arúna pack the basket; and Cuthbert in possession of Tara—not for long.

He was called upon to punt back; and at the boat-house, where a taxi removed the elders and the picnic impedimenta, he essayed a futile manœuvre to recapture Tara and saddle Dyán with the solid Emily. Failing, he consoled himself by keeping in touch with Arúna and Roy.

Dyán patently delayed starting, patently lagged behind. Unskilled and desperately in earnest, he could not lead up to his moment. He was laboriously framing the essential words when Tara scattered them with a light remark, rallying him on his snail's pace.

"You *would* go for that stroll; and you strolled so violently——!"

"Because my heart in me was raging—aching, violently!" he blurted out with such unexpected vehemence, that she started and stepped back a pace. "Of course I knew—there must be difficulties—so I have been waiting and hoping . . ." An idiotic catch in his throat brought a sudden hot wave of self-consciousness. He flung out both hands. "Tara——!"

Instinctively, she drew her own out of reach. A ghost of a shiver ran through her. "No—no. I don't . . . I never have . . . If I've misled you, I'm ever so sorry."

"If you are sorry—*give me hope*," his voice, his eyes implored her. "You come so near—then you draw back; like offering a thirsty man a cup of water he must not drink. Give me only a little time—a little chance——"

She shook her head. "Please believe me. I'm *not* the wavering kind. I'm keen to go on being friends—because of Roy. But, truthfully, it's no use hoping for anything more—ever."

Her patent sincerity, the sweet seriousness of her face, carried conviction. And conviction turned his ardour to bitterness.

"Why no use—*ever?*" he flung out, maddened by her emphasis on the word.

"I suppose—because I know my own mind."

"No. Because—*I* am Indian." His voice was changed and harsh. "We are all British subjects—oh yes—when convenient! But the door is opened only—so far. If we make bold to ask for the best, it is slammed in our faces."

"Dyán Singh, if I have hurt you, it was quite unintentional. You know that. But now, *with* intention, you are hurting me." Her dignity and gentleness, the justice of her reproof, smote him silent; and she went on: "You forget, it is the same among your own people. Aunt Lila was cast out—for always. With an English girl that could never be."

Too distraught for argument, he harked back to the personal issue. "With *you* there would be no need. I would live altogether like an Englishman——"

"Oh, *stop!*" she broke out desperately. "Don't start all over again——"

"Look alive, you two slackers," shouted Roy, from the far corner of the road. "I'm responsible for keeping the team together."

"Coming!" called Tara, and turned on Dyán a final glance of appeal. "I'm *sorry* from the bottom of my heart. I can't say more."—And setting the pace, she hurried forward.

For the fraction of a second, he hesitated. An overmastering impulse seized him to walk off in the opposite direction. His eager love for them all had suddenly turned to gall. But pride forbade. He would not for the world have them guess at his rebuff—not even Arúna. . . .

He slept little that night; and it was not Dyán Singh of New College who awoke next morning. It was Dyán Singh, Rajput, Descendant of the Sun. Yet the foolish round of life must go on as if no vital change had come to pass.

That afternoon, he was going with Roy to a select drawing-room meeting. A certain Mr Ramji Lal had been asked to read a paper on the revival of Indian arts and crafts. Dyán had been looking forward to it keenly; but now, sore and miserable as he was—all sense of purpose and direction gone—he felt out of tune with the whole thing.

He would have been thankful to cry off. Roy, however, must not suspect the truth—Roy, who himself might be the stumbling-block. The suspicion stung like a scorpion; though it soothed a little his hurt pride of race.

Embittered and antagonistic, he listened only with half his mind to his own countryman's impassioned appeal for renewal of the true Swadeshi [1] spirit in India; renewal of her own innate artistic culture, her faith in the creative power of thought and ideas. That spirit—said the speaker—has no war-cries, no shoutings in the market-place. It is a way of looking at life. Its true genesis and inspiration is in the home. Like flame, newly-lit, it needs cherishing. Instead, it is in danger of being stamped out by false Swadeshi—an imitation product of the West; noisy and political, crying out for more factories, more councils; caring nothing for true Indian traditions of art and life. It will not buy goods from Birmingham and Manchester; but it will create Birmingham and Manchester in India. In effect, it is

[1] Own country.

the age-old argument whether the greatness of a nation comes from the dominion of men or machinery. . . .

For all this, Dyán had cared intensely twenty-four hours ago. Now it seemed little better than a rhapsody of fine phrases—'sounding brass and tinkling cymbals.'

Could the mere word of a woman so swiftly and violently transform the mind of a man? His innate masculinity resented the idea. It succumbed, nevertheless. He was too deeply hurt in his pride and his passionate heart to think or feel sanely while the wound was still so fresh. He was scarcely stirred even by the allusion to Rajputana in Mr Ramji Lal's peroration.

"I ask you to consider, in conclusion—my dear and honoured English friends—the words of a veteran lover of India, who is also a son of England. It was his conviction—it is also mine—that 'the still living art of India, the still living chivalry of Rajputana, the still living religion of the Hindus, are the only three points on which there is any possibility of regenerating the national life of India—the India of the Hindus . . .'"

Very fine; doubtless very true; but what use—after all—their eternal talk? By blowing volumes of air from their lungs, did they shift the mountains of difficulty one single inch?

More talk followed; tea and attentions that would have flattered him yesterday. To-day it all passed clean over his head. They were ready enough to pamper him, like a lap-dog, these good ladies; forgetting he was a man, with a man's heart and brain, making demand for something more than carefully chosen sugar-plums.

He had never been so thankful to get away from that hospitable house, where he had imagined himself so happy. . . .

They were out in the street again, striding back to New College: Roy—not yet alive to the change in him—full of it all; talking nineteen to the dozen. But Dyán's urgent heart spoke louder than his cousin's voice. And all the while he kept wondering consumedly—*Was* it Roy?

He could not bring himself to ask outright. The answer would madden him either way. And Goodness—or Badness—knew he was miserable enough: hurt, angry, with Fate, with England, even with Tara—

lovely and unattainable! She had spoilt everything; his relation with her, with her people, with Roy. She had quenched his zeal for their joint crusade. All the same, he would hold Roy to the India plan; since there was just a chance—and it would take him away from her. He hated himself for the thought; but jealousy, in the East, is a consuming fire. . . .

Roy's monologue ceased abruptly. "Your innings, old chap, I think?" he said. "You're mum as a fish this afternoon. I noticed it in there—I thought you'd have lots to say to Ramji Lal."

Dyán frowned. He could not for long play at pretences with Roy.

"Those ladies did all the saying. They would not have liked it at all if I had spoken my true thought,"—he paused and added deliberately—"that we are all cracking our skulls against stone walls."

"My dear chap——!" Roy stared in frank bewilderment. "What's gone wrong? Your liver touched up? Too much salmon mayonnaise and cream?"

His light tone goaded Dyán to exasperation. "Quite likely," he retorted, a sneer lurking in his tone. "Plenty of mayonnaise and cream, for all parties. But when we make bold to ask for more satisfying things, we find 'No Indians need apply.'"

"But—my good Dyán——!"

"Well—it's true. Suppose I wish to promote that closer union we all chatter about by marrying an English girl—what then?"

Up went Roy's eyebrows. "Are *you* after an English wife?"

"I am submitting a case—that might easily occur." He spoke with a touch of irritation; and fearing self-betrayal, swerved from the main issue. "Would *you* marry an Indian girl?"

"I believe so. If I was keen. I'm not at all sure, though, if it's sound — in principle — mixing such opposite strains. And in your case — hypothetical, I suppose——?"

Dyán's grunt confessed nothing and denied nothing.

"Well—from what one hears, an English wife, out there, might make a bit of complication, if you get the 'Civil.'"

Dyán started. "I shan't go up for it. I've changed my mind."

"Good Lord! And you've been sweating all this time."

Dyán's smile was tinged with bitterness.

"Well—one lives and learns. I can make good use of my knowledge without turning myself into an imitation Englishman. An Indian wife might make equal difficulty. So—with all my zeal—I am between two grindstones. My father joined the Civil. He was keen. He did well. But—no promotion; and little friendliness, except from very few. I believe he was never happy. I believe—it killed him. I was cherishing a hope that, now, things might be better. But I am beginning to see—I may be wrong. Safer to see it in time——"

Roy looked genuinely distressed. "Poor old Dyán. Perhaps you're right. I don't know much about British India. But it does seem hard lines—and bad policy—to choke off men like you."

"Yes. They might consider *that* more, if they heard some of our fire-eaters. One was at me last week. He gave the British ten years to survive. Said their lot could raise a revolution to-morrow if they had money—a trifle of five millions! He was swearing the Indian princes are not loyal, in spite of talk and subscriptions; that the Army will join whichever side gives best pay. We who *are* loyal need *some* encouragement—some recognition. We are only human——!"

"Rather. But *you* won't go back on our little show, old chap. Just when I'm dead keen—laying my plans for India——"

He took hold of Dyán's upper arm and gave it a friendly shake.

"No, I'll stick to that. But are you sure you can work it—with your people? If *you* back out, I swear, by the sin of the sack of Chitor, I'll join the beastly crowd who are learning to make bombs in Berlin."

At that—the most solemn oath that can pass the lips of a Rajput—Roy looked startled. Then he laughed.

"'Commem' seems to have disagreed with you all round! But I won't be intimidated. Likewise—I won't back out. I intend opening diplomatic conversations with Jeffers to-night. Recherché dinner for two in my room. All his little weaknesses! He'd be a strong ally. Wish me luck."

Dyán wished him luck in a rather perfunctory tone, considering his vehemence of a moment earlier. All the fire seemed suddenly to have gone out of him.

They had just entered the college gate; and a few yards ahead, they caught sight of Lady Despard and Tara—the girl's hand linked through her mother's arm.

"Oh, I clean forgot," remarked Roy. "I said they could look in."

## CHAPTER III.

"It is the spirit of the quest which helps. I am the slave of this spirit of the quest."—KABIR.

ROY'S recherché little dinner proved an unqualified success. With sole and chicken sauté, with trifle and savoury, he mutely pleaded his cause; feeling vaguely guilty, the while, of belittling his childhood's idol, whom he increasingly admired and loved. But this India business was tremendously important, and the dear old boy would never suspect——

Roy watched him savouring the chicken and peas; discussing the decay of falling in love, its reasons and remedies; and thought, for the hundredth time, what a splendid old boy he was; so big and breezy, nothing bookish or newspapery about him. Quite a masterpiece of modelling, on Nature's part; the breadth and bulk of him; the massive head, with its thatch of tawny-grey hair that retreated up the sides of his forehead, making corners; the nose, rugged and full of character; the beard and the sea-blue eyes that gave him the sailor aspect Roy had so loved in nursery days. Now he appraised it consciously, with the artist's eye. A vigorous bust of his godfather was his acknowledged masterpiece, so far, in the modelling line, which he preferred to brush or pencil. But first and foremost, literature claimed him: poetry, essays, and the despised novel—truest and most plastic medium for interpreting man to man and race to race: the most entirely obvious medium, thought Roy, for promoting the cause he had at heart.

Though his brain was overflowing with the one subject, he was reserving it diplomatically for the more intimate atmosphere of port wine, coffee and cigars.

Meantime they always had plenty to talk about, these two. Broome held the unorthodox view that he probably had quite as much to learn from the young as they from him; and at the moment, the question whether Roy should take up literature in earnest was very much to the fore.

Once or twice during a pause, he caught the shrewd blue eye watching him from under shaggy brows; but each kept his own counsel till the scout had removed all superfluities. Then Broome chose a cigar, sniffed it, and beheaded it.

"My particular weakness!" he remarked pensively, while Roy filled his glass. "What an attentive godson it is! And after this intriguing prelude—what of the main plot? India?"

Under a glance as direct as the question Roy reddened furiously. The 'dear old boy' had done more than suspect; he had seen through the whole show—the indignity of all others that youth can least abide.

At sight of his crestfallen countenance, Broome laughed outright. "Bear up, old man! Don't grudge me a fraction of the wits I live by. Weren't you trying to give me an inkling yesterday?"

Roy nodded, mollified a little. But his self-confidence wilted under the false start. "How about arm-chairs?" he remarked tentatively, very much engaged with a cigarette.

They removed their coffee-cups, and sipped once or twice in silence. "I'm waiting," said Broome, encouragement in his tone.

But Roy still hesitated. "You see—" he temporised, "I'm so fearfully keen, I feel shy of gassing about it. Might seem to you mere soppy sentiment."

Broome's sailor eyes twinkled. "You pay me the compliment, my son, of treating me as if I were a fellow-undergrad! It's only the 'teens and the twenties of this very new century that are so mortally afraid of sentiment—the main factor in human happiness. If you had *not* a strong sentiment for India, you would be unworthy of your mother. You want to go out there—is that the rub?"

"Yes. With Dyán."

"In what capacity?"

"A lover and a learner. Also—by way of—a budding author. I was hoping you might back me up with a few commissions for my preliminary stuff."

"You selected your godfather with unerring foresight! And preliminaries over—a book, or books, would be the end in view?"

"Yes—and other things. Whatever one can do—in a small way—to inspire a friendlier feeling all round; a clearer conviction that the destinies of England and India are humanly bound up together. I'm sure those cursed politics are responsible for most of the friction. It's art and literature, the emotional and spiritual forces that draw men together, isn't it, Jeffers? *You* know that——"

He leaned forward, warming to his subject; the false start forgotten; shyness dispelled. . . .

And, once started, none was more skilful than Broome in luring him on to fuller, unconscious self-revealing. He knew very well that, on this topic, and on many others, Roy could enlarge more freely to him than to his father. Youth is made that way. In his opinion, it was all to the good that Roy should aspire to use his double heritage, for the legitimate and noble purpose of interpreting—as far as might be—East to West, and West to East: not least, because he would probably learn a good deal more than he was qualified to teach. It was in the process of qualifying himself, by closer acquaintance with India, that the lurking danger reared its head. But some outlet there must be for the Eastern spirit in him; and his early efforts pointed clearly to literary expression, if Broome knew anything of the creative gift. Himself a devotee, he agreed with Lafcadio Hearne that 'a man may do quite as great a service to his country by writing a book as by winning a battle'; and just so much of these thoughts as seemed fit he imparted to Roy, who—in response to the last—glowed visibly.

"Priceless old Jeffers! I knew I could reckon on you to back me up—and buck me up! Of course one will be hugely encouraged by the bleating of the practical crowd—Aunt Jane and Co. '*Why* waste your time writing silly novels?' And if you try to explain that novels *have* a real function, they merely think *you*'ve got a swelled head."

"Never mind, Roy. 'The quest is a noble one and the hope great.' And we scribblers have our glorious compensations. As for Aunt Jane——" He looked very straight at her nephew—and winked deliberately.

"Oh, of course—she's *the* unlimited limit," Roy agreed without shame. "I suppose if Dad plays up, she'll give him hell?"

"Good measure, pressed down.—By the way—have you spoken to *him* yet of all this——?"

"No. Mother probably guesses. But you're the first. I made sure *you*'d understand——"

"You feel doubtful—about Father?"

"M-yes. I don't quite know why."

Broome was silent a moment. "After all—it's natural. Put yourself in his place, Roy.—He sees India taking a stronger hold of you each year. He knows you've a deal of your mother and grandfather in your make-up. He may very well be afraid of the magnet proving too strong at close quarters. And I suspect he's jealous—for England. He'd like to see your soul centred on Bramleigh Beeches: and I more than suspect they'd both prefer to keep you nearer home."

Roy looked distressed. "Hard lines. I hadn't got to that yet. But it wouldn't be for always. And—there's George and Jerry sprouting up."

"I gather that George and Jerry are not precisely—Roy——"

"Jeffers—you old sinner! I can't flatter myself——!"

"Don't be blatantly British, Roy! You can flatter yourself—you know as well as I do!"

"I know it's undiplomatic to contradict my elders!" countered Roy, lunging after pipe and pouch.

"Especially convenient godfathers, with press connections?"

Roy fronted him squarely, laughter lurking in his eyes. "Are you *going* to be convenient—that's the rub! *Will* you give Dad a notion I may turn out something decent when I've scraped up some crumbs of knowledge——?"

Broome leaned forward and laid a large reassuring hand on his knee. "Trust me to pull it off, old man—provided Mother approves. We couldn't press it against *her* wish—either of us."

"No—we couldn't." There was a new gravity in Roy's tone. "As I said, she probably knows all about it. That's her way. She understandeth one's thoughts long before." The last in a lower tone—his eyes dwelling on her portrait above the mantelpiece: the one in the studio window-seat.

And Broome thought: "With all his brains, the man's hardly astir in him yet; and the boy's still in love with her. This notion may be an unconscious outlet. A healthy one—if Nevil can be got to see it that way."

After a perceptible pause, he said quietly: "Remember, Roy, just because she's unique, she can't be taken as representative. She naturally stands for India in your eyes. But no country can produce beings of her quality by the score——"

"I suppose not." Roy reluctantly shifted his gaze. "But she does represent what's best in the Indian spirit: the spirit that people over here might take more pains to understand."

"And you are peculiarly well fitted to assist them, I admit—if Father's willing to bear the cost of your trip. It's a compact between us. The snare of your A1 dinner shall not have been laid in vain!"

They sat on together for more than an hour. Then Broome departed, leaving Roy to dream—in a blue mist of tobacco smoke—the opal-tinted ego-centric dreams of one-and-twenty.

And to-night one dream eclipsed them all.

For years the germ of it had lived in him like a seed in darkness—growing with him as he grew. All incidents and impressions that struck deep had served to vitalise it: that early championship of his mother; her tales of Rajputana; his friendship with Desmond and Dyán; and, not least, his father's Ramayána pictures in the long gallery at home, that had seized his imagination in very early days, when their appeal was simply to his innate sense of colour, and the reiterate wonder and beauty of his mother's face in those moving scenes from the story of Sita—India's crown of womanhood. . . .

Then there was the vivid memory of a room in his

grandfather's house; the stately old man, with his deep voice, speaking words that he only came to understand years after; and the look in his mother's eyes, as she clapped her hands without sound, in the young fashion he loved. . . .

And Chandranath—another glimpse of India; the ugly side . . . And stories from Tod's 'Rajasthan'—that grim and stirring panorama of romance and chivalry, of cruelty and cunning; orgies of slaughter and miracles of high-hearted devotion. . . .

Barbaric; utterly foreign to life, as he had lived it, those tales of ancient India most strangely awakened in him a vague, thrilling sense of familiarity . . . He *knew* . . .! Most clearly he knew the spirit that fired them all, when Akbar's legions broke, wave on wave, against the mighty rock-fortress of Chitor—far-famed capital of Mewar, thrice sacked by Islam and deserted by her royal house; so that only the ghost of her glory remains—a protest, a challenge, an inspiration. . . .

Sometimes he dreamed it all, with amazing vividness. And in the dreams there was always the feeling that he knew . . . It was a very queer, very exciting sensation. He had spoken of it to no one but his mother and Tara; except once at Marlborough, when he had been moved to try whether Lance would understand.

Priceless old Desmond! It had been killing to watch his face—interested, sceptical, faintly alarmed, when he discovered that it was not an elaborate attempt to pull his leg. By way of reassuring him, Roy had confessed it was a family failing. When things went wrong his mother nearly always knew: and sometimes she came to him, in dreams that were not exactly dreams. What harm?

Desmond, puzzled and sceptical, was not prepared to hazard an opinion. If Roy was made that way, of course he couldn't help it. And Roy, half indignant, had declared he wouldn't for worlds be made any other way. . . .

To-night, by some freak of memory, it all came back to him through the dream-inducing haze of tobacco smoke. And there, on his writing-table, stood a full-length photograph of Lance in Punjab cavalry uniform. Soldiering on the Indian Border, fulfilling himself in his own splendid fashion, he was clearly in his element; attached to his father's old regiment, with Paul for second-in-command; proud of his strapping Sikhs and Pathans; watched over, revered and implicitly obeyed by the sons of men who had served with his father—men for whom the mere name Desmond was a talisman. For that is India's way.

And here was he, Roy, still at his old trick of scribbling poems and dreaming dreams. For a fleeting moment, Desmond was out of the picture; but when time was ripe he would be in it again. The link between them was indestructible—elemental. Poet and Warrior; the eternal complements. In the Rig Veda[1] both are one; both *Agni Kula*—'born of fire'; no fulness of life for the one without the other.

The years dominated by Desmond had been supreme. They had left school together, when Roy was seventeen; and, at the time, their parting had seemed like the end of everything. Yet, very soon after, he had found himself in the thick of fresh delights—a wander-year in Italy, Greece, the Mediterranean, with the parents and Christine——

And now, here he was, nearing the end of the Oxford interlude—dominated by Dyán and India; and, not least, by Oxford herself, who counts her lovers by the million; holds them for the space of three or four years and sets her impress for life on their minds and hearts. For all his dreamings and scribblings, he had played hard and worked hard. In the course of reading for Greats, he had imbibed large draughts of the classics; had browsed widely on later literature, East and West; won the Newcastle, and filled a vellum-bound volume—his mother's gift—with verse and sketches in prose, some of which had appeared in the more exclusive weeklies. He had also picked up Hindustani from Dyán, and looked forward to tackling Sanskrit. In the Schools, he had taken a First in Mods; and, with reasonable luck, hoped for a First in the Finals. Once again, parting would be a wrench, but India glowed like a planet on the horizon; and he fully intended to make that interlude the pick of them all. . . .

[1] Ancient Hindu Scriptures.

What novels he would write! Not modern impressionist stuff; not mean streets and the photographic touch. No—his adventuring soul, with its tinge of Eastern mysticism, craved colour and warmth and light;—not the mere trappings of romance, but the essence of it that imparts a deeper sense of the significance and mystery of life; that probes to the mainsprings of personality, the veiled yet vital world of spiritual adventure . . . Pain and conflict; powers of evil, of doubt and indecision:—no evading these. But in any imaginative work he essayed, beauty must be the prevailing element—if only as a star in darkness. And nowadays Beauty had become almost suspect. Cleverness, cynicism, sex and sensation—all had their votaries and their vogue. Mere Beauty, like Cinderella, was left sitting among the ashes of the past; and Roy—prince or no—was her devout lover.

To the son of Nevil and Lilámani, her clear call could never seem either a puritanical snare of the flesh or a delusion of the senses; but rather, a grace of the spirit, the joy of things seen detached from self-interest: the visible proof that love, not power, is the last word of Creation. Happily for him, its outward form and inward essence had been his daily bread ever since he had first consciously looked upon his mother's face, consciously delighted in his father's pictures. They lived it, those two: and the life lived transcends argument.

At this uplifted moment—whatever might come later—he blessed them for his double heritage; for the perfect accord between them that inspired his hope of ultimate harmony between England and India, in spite of barriers and complexities and fomenters of discord; a harmony that could never arrive by veiled condescension out of servile imitation. Intimacy with Dyán and his mother had made that quite clear. Each must honestly will to understand the other; each holding fast the essence of individuality, while respecting in the other precisely those baffling qualities that strengthen their union and make it vital to the welfare of both. Instinctively he pictured them as man and woman; and on general lines the analogy seemed to hold good. He had yet to discover that analogies are often deceptive things; peculiarly so, in this case, since India is many, not one. Yet there lurked a germ of truth in his seedling idea: and he was at the age when ideas and tremendous impulses stir in the blood like sap in spring-time; an age to be a reformer, a fanatic or a sensualist.

Too often, alas, before the years bring power of adjustment, the live spark of enthusiasm is extinct. . . .

To-night it burned in Roy with a steady flame. If only he could enthuse his father——!

He supposed he would go in any case: but he lacked the rebel instinct of modern youth. He wanted to share, to impart his hidden treasure; not to argue the bloom off it. And his father seemed tacitly to discourage rhapsodies over Indian literature and art. You couldn't say he was not keen: only the least little bit unresponsive to outbursts of keenness in his son; so that Roy never felt quite at ease on the subject. If only he could walk into the room now, while Roy's brain was seething with it all, high on the upward curve of a wave. . . .

# CHAPTER IV.

"You could humble at your feet the proudest heads in the world.
But it is your loved ones . . . whom you choose to worship.
Therefore I worship you."

—RABINDRANATH TAGORE.

ROY, after due consideration, decided that he would speak first to his father—the one doubtful element in the home circle. But habit and the obsession of the moment proved too strong, when his mother came to 'tuck him up,' as she had never failed to do since nursery days.

Seated on the edge of his bed, in the shaded light, she looked like some rare, pale moth in her moon-coloured sari flecked and bordered with gold; amber earrings and a rope of amber beads—his own gift; first fruits of poetic earnings. The years between had ripened and embellished her; rounded a little the oval of her cheek; lent an added dignity to her grace of bearing and enriched her wisdom of the heart.

It was as he supposed. She had understood his thoughts long before. He flung out his hand—a fine, nervous hand—and laid it on her knee.

"You're a miracle. I believe you know all about it."

"I believe—I do," she answered, letting her own hand rest on his; moving her fingers, now and then, in the ghost of a caress:—an endearing way she had. "You are wishing—to go out there?"

"Yes. I simply must. *You* understand?"

She inclined her head and, for a moment, veiled her eyes. "I am proud. But you cannot understand how difficult . . . for us . . . letting you go. And Dad . . ."

She paused.

"You think he'll hate it—want to keep me here?"

"My darling—'hate' is too strong. He cares very much for all that makes friendship between England and India. But—is it wonder if he cares more for his own son? You will speak to him soon?"

"To-morrow. Unless—a word or two, first, from you——"

"No, not that!" She smiled at his old boyish faith in her. "Better to keep me outside. You see—I *am* India. So I am already too much in it that way."

"You are in it up to the hilt!" he declared with sudden fervour: and—his tongue unloosed—he poured out to her a measure of his pent-up feeling; how they had inspired him—she and his father; how he naturally hoped they would back him up; and a good deal more that was for her private ear alone. . . .

Her immense capacity for listening, her eloquent silence and gentle flashes of raillery, her occasional caress—all were balm to him in his electrical mood. Were ever two beings quite so perfectly in tune——? Could he possibly leave her? Could he face the final wrench?

When at last she stooped to kiss him, the faint clear whiff of sandalwood waked a hundred memories; and he held her close a long time, her cheek against his hair.

"Bad boy! Let me go," she pleaded; and, with phenomenal obedience, he unclasped his hands.

"See if you *can* go now!"

It was his old childish game. The moment she stirred, his hands were locked again.

"Son of my heart—I must!"

"One more kiss then—for luck!"

So she kissed him, for luck, and left him to his midnight browsings. . . .

Next morning she sat among her cushions in the studio, ostensibly reading a long letter from her father. Actually, her mind was intent on Nevil, who stood at his easel absorbed in fragmentary studies for a new picture—flying draperies; a man's face cleverly foreshortened.

Though nearing fifty, he looked more like five-and-thirty; his face singularly free of lines; his fair hair scarcely showing the intrusion of grey. To her he seemed perennially young; and dearer than ever—if that could be—as the years mellowed and deepened the love on which they had boldly staked everything that counted most for them both. Yet, for all her skill in divination, she could not tell precisely how he would take the things Roy had to say; nor whether Roy himself would say them in just the right way. With Nevil, so much depended on that.

Till this morning, she had scarcely realised how unobtrusively she had been, as it were, their connecting link in all difficult or delicate matters, where their natures were not quite in tune. But now, Roy being a man, they must come to terms in their own fashion. . . .

At the first far-off sound of his step on the stairs, she rose and came over to the easel, and stood there a few moments—fascinated always by the swift sure strokes.

"Good—eh?" he asked, smiling into her serious eyes.

She nodded. "Quite evident—you are in the mood!" Her fingers lightly caressed the back of his hand. "I will come back later. *Such* a tray of vases waiting for me in the drawing-room!"

As Roy entered, she passed him and they exchanged a smile. Her eyes, mutely blessing him, besought him not to let his eager tongue run away with itself. Then she went out, leaving them together—the two who were her world.

Down in the drawing-room, roses and sweet-peas, cut by Christine—her fairy daughter—lay ready to hand. Between them they filled the lofty room with fragrance and harmonies of delicate colour. Then Christine flew to her beloved piano; and Lilámani wandered away to her no less beloved rose-garden. Body and mind were restless. She could settle to nothing till she knew what had passed between Nevil and Roy. His boyish confidences and adorations of the night before had filled her cup to overflowing. She felt glad and proud that her first-born should have set his heart on the high project of trying to promote deeper sympathy between his father's great country and her own people, in this time of dangerous antagonism and unrest.

But beneath her pride and gladness, stirred a fear lest the scales she had tried to hold even, should be inclining to tilt the wrong way. For duty to his father's house was paramount. Too strong a leaning towards India —no matter for what high purpose—would still be a tilt the wrong way. She had seen the same fear lurking in Nevil's heart also; and now, unerringly, she divined the cause of that hidden trouble which baffled Roy. Nevil feared that—if Roy went to India—history might repeat itself. She admitted the danger was real; and she knew his fear implied no reflection on herself or her country. Best of all, she knew that—because of his chivalrous loyalty that had never failed her—he would not speak of it, even to his son.

Clearly then, if Roy insisted on going to India, and if a word of warning must be spoken to ease Nevil's mind, only one person in the world could speak it—herself. For all her sensitive shrinking she could not, at this critical turning-point, stand outside. She was "in it"—as Roy dramatically assured her—up to the hilt. . . .

Time passed—and he did not come. Troubled, she wandered back towards the house; caught sight of him, lonely and abstracted, pacing the lawn: saw him stop near the great twin beeches—that embowered a hammock, chairs and rugs—and disappear inside. Then she knew her moment had come. . . .

She found him prone in the hammock: not even smoking: staring up into the cool green dome, fretted with graceful convolutions of trunk and branches. One lightly-clenched hand hung over the edge. Attitude and abstraction alike suggested a listless dejection that sharply caught at her heart.

He started at sight of her. "Blessed little Mummy—no hiding from *you!*"

He flung out his left hand. She took it and laid it against her cheek: a form of caress all her own.

"Were you wishing to hide? I was waiting among the roses, to show you the new sweet-peas."

"And I never came. Proper beast I am! And sprawling here——" He swung his long legs over the side and stood up, tall and straight—taller than Nevil—smiling down at her. "I wasn't exactly hiding. I was shirking—a little bit. But now you've found me, you won't escape!"

Pressing down the edge of the hammock, he half lifted her into it and settled her among the cushions, deftly tucking in her silks and muslins.

"Comfy?" he asked, surveying her, with Nevil's own smile in his eyes.

"Comfy," she sighed, wishing discreet warnings at the bottom of the sea. Just to be foolish with him—the bliss of it! To chime in with his moods, his enthusiasms, his nonsense—she asked nothing better of life, when he came home. "Very clever, Sonling. But no,"—she lifted a finger—"that won't do. You are twenty-one. Too big for the small name now. So far away up there!"

"If I shot up as high as a lamp-post, my heart would still be down there—at your feet."

He said it lightly—that was the Englishman. But he said it—that was the Rajput. And she knew not which she loved the best. Strange to love two such opposites with equal fervour.

She blew him a kiss from her finger-tips. "Very well. We will not be unkind to the small name and throw him on the rubbish-heap. But now sit, please—Sonling. You have been talking—you and Dad? Not any decision? Is he not wishing you should—work for India?"

"Mummy, I don't know." He secured a chair and sat down facing her. "He insists that I'm officially free to kick over the traces, that he's not the kind of father who 'thunders veto from the family hearthrug!'"

Lilámani smiled very tenderly at that so characteristic touch; but she said nothing. And Roy went on: "All the same, I gathered that he's distinctly not keen on my going out there. So—what the devil am I to do? He rubbed it in that I'm full young, and no hurry—but I feel there's something else at the back of his mind."

He paused—and she could hesitate no longer.

"Yes, Roy—there is something else——"

"Then *why* can't he speak out?"

"Not to be so impatient," she rebuked him gently. "It is because he so beautifully remains—my lover, he cannot put in words—any thought that might give——" She flung out an appealing hand. "Oh, Roy—can you not guess the trouble? He is afraid—for your marriage——"

"My marriage!" It was clear he did not yet grasp

the truth. "Really, Mummy, that's a trifle previous. I'm not even thinking of marriage."

"No, Stupid One! But out there you might come to think of it! No man can tell when Kama, godling of the arrows, will throw magic dust in his eyes. You might meet other cousins—like Arúna, and there would come trouble, because"—she faced him steadily and he saw the veiled blush creep into her cheeks—"that kind of marriage—for you—must not be."

Now he understood; and, for all her high resolve, she thrilled at the swift flash of anger in his eyes.

"Who says—it must not be?" he demanded with a touch of heat. "Aunt Jane—confound her! When I do marry, it will be to please myself—not *her!*"

"Oh, hush, Roy—and listen! You run away too fast. It is not Aunt Jane—it is *I* who am saying must not, because I know—the difficult thought in Dad's heart. And I know it is right——"

"Why is it right?" He was up in arms again. Obstinate—but how lovable!—"Why mayn't I have the same luck as he had—if it comes my way? I've never met a girl or woman that could hold a candle to you for all-round loveliness. And it's the East that gives you—inside and out—a quality, a bloom—unseizable—like moonlight——"

"But, my darling! You make me blush!" She drew her sari across her face, hiding, under a veil of lightness, her joy at his outspoken praise.

"Well, you made me say it. And I'm not sentimentalising. I'm telling a home truth!"

His vehemence was guarantee of that. Very gently he drew back the sari and looked deep into her eyes.

"Why should we only tell the ugly ones, like Aunt Jane? Anyway, I've told you my truest one now—and I'm not ashamed of it."

"No need. It is a jewel I will treasure in my heart." She dropped the veil of lightness, giving him sincerity for sincerity as he deserved. "But—Ancient one, have you seen so many girls and women in your long life——?"

"I've seen a pretty good mixture of all sorts—Oxford, London, and round here," he insisted unabashed. "And I've had my wits about me. Of course they're most of them jolly and straight. Good fellows in fact; talking our slang; playing our games. No harm, of course. But it kills the charm of contrast—the supreme charm. They understand *that* in India better than we do here."

The truth of that last Lilámani could not deny. Too clearly she saw in the violent upheaval of Western womanhood the hidden germs of tragedy, for women themselves, for the race.

"You are right, Roy," she said, smiling into his serious face. "From our—from Hindu point of view, greatest richness of life come from greatest possible difference between men and women. And most of all it is so in Rajputana. But over here . . ." She sighed, a small shivering sigh. The puzzle and pain of it went too deep with her. "All this screaming and snatching and scratching for wrong kind of things hurts my heart; because—I am woman and they are women—desecrating that in us which is a symbol of God. Nature made women for ministering to Life and Love. Are they not believing, or not caring, that by struggling to imitate man (while saying with their lips how they despise him!) they are losing their own secret, beautiful differences, so important for happiness—for the race. But marriage in the West seems more for convenience of lovers than for the race——"

"Yet your son, though he *is* of the West—must not consider his own inclination or convenience——"

"My son," she interposed, gently inflexible, "because he is *also* of the East, must consider this matter of the race; must try and think it with his father's mind."

"All the same—making such a point of it seems like an insult—to you——"

"No, Roy. *Not* to say that——" The flash in her eyes, that was almost anger, startled and impressed him more than any spoken word. "No thought that ever came in your father's mind could be—like insult to me. Oh, my dear, have you not sense to know that for an old English family like his, with roots down deep in English soil and history, it is not good that mixture of race should come twice over in two generations. To you—our kind of marriage appears a simple affair. You see only how close we are now, in love and understanding. You cannot imagine all the difficulties that went before.

We know them—and we are proud, because they became like dust under our feet. Only to you—Dilkusha, I could tell . . . a little, if you wish—for helping you to understand."

"Please tell," he said, and his hand closed on hers.

So, leaning back among her cushions—speaking very simply in the low voice that was music to his ears—she told. . . .

The telling—fragmentary, yet vivid—lasted less than half an hour. But in that half-hour Roy gleaned a jewel of memory that the years would not dim. The very words would remain. . . .

For Lilámani—wandering backward in fancy through the Garden of Remembrance—revealed more than she realised of the man she loved and of her own passionate spirit, compact of fire and dew, the sublimated essence of the Eastern woman at her best.

Yet in spite of that revealing—or rather because of it—rebellion stirred afresh. And, as if divining his thoughts, she impulsively raised her hand. "Now, Roy, you must promise. Only so, I can speak to Dad and rest his mind."

Seizing her hand, he kissed it fervently.

"Darling—after all that, a mere promise would be a fatuous superfluity. If you say 'No Indian wife,' that's enough for me. I suppose I must rest content with the high privilege of possessing an Indian mother."

Her radiant surprise was a beautiful thing to see. Leaning forward, she took his head in her hands and kissed him between his eyebrows where the caste-mark should be.

"Must it be October—so soon?" she asked.

He told her of Dyán, and she sighed. "Poor Dyán! I wonder? It is so difficult—even with the best kind—this mixing of English education and Indian life. I hope it will make no harm for those two——"

Then they started, almost like lovers; for the drooping branches rustled and Tara stood before them—a very vision of June; in her straight frock of Delphinium blue; one shell-pink rose in her hat and its counterpart in her waist-belt. Canvas shoes and tennis-racquet betrayed her fell design on Roy.

"Am I despritly superfluous?" she queried, smiling from one to the other.

"Quite too despritly," Roy assured her with emphasis.

She wrinkled her nose at him, so far as its delicate aquiline would permit. "Speak for yourself, spoilt boy!"

But she favoured him with her left hand, which he retained, while she stooped over the hammock and kissed Lilámani on both cheeks. Then she stood up and gently disengaged her hand.

"Christine's to blame. She guessed you were here. I came over in hopes of tennis. It's just perfect. Not too hot."

"Still more perfect in here, lazing with Mummy," said graceless Roy.

"I disown you, I am ashamed!" Lilámani rebuked him only half in jest. "No more lazing now. I have done with you. Only you have to get me out of this."

They got her out, between them; fussed over her and laughed at her; and then went off together for Roy's racquet.

She stood in the silvery sunlight watching them till they disappeared round the corner of the house. Not surprising that Nevil said—"No hurry!" If he would only wait . . ! He was still too young, too much in love with India—with herself. Yet, had he already begun inditing sonnets, even to the most acceptable eyebrow, her perverse heart would doubtless have known the prick of jealousy—as in Desmond's day.

Instead she suddenly knew the first insidious prick of middle age; felt dazed, for a mere moment, by the careless radiance of their youth; to them an unconsidered thing: but to those who feel it relentlessly slipping through their fingers . . .

Her small fine hands clenched in unconscious response to her thought. She was nearing forty. In her own land she would be reckoned almost an old woman. But some magic in the air and way of life in this cool green England seemed to keep age at bay: and there remained within a flame-like youth of the spirit—not so easy, even for the Arch-Thief to steal away. . . .

# CHAPTER V.

"The bow saith to the arrow, 'Thy freedom is mine.'"
—RABINDRANATH TAGORE.

AND while Lilámani reasoned with the son—whose two-fold nature they had themselves bestowed and inspired—Nevil was pacing his shrine of all the harmonies, heart and brain disturbed, as they had not been for years.

Out of the troubled waters of family friction and delicate adjustments, this adventurous pair had slid into a haven of peace and mutual understanding. And now behold, fresh portent of trouble arising from the dual strain in Roy—the focal point of their life and love.

Turning in his stride, his eye encountered a head and shoulders portrait of his father, Sir George Sinclair: an honest, bluff, unimaginative face: yet suddenly, arrestingly, it commanded his attention. Checking his walk, he stood regarding it: and his heart went out to the kindly old man in a quite unusual wave of sympathetic understanding. He saw himself—the "damned unsatisfactory son," Bohemian and dilettante, frankly at odds with the Sinclair tradition—now standing, more or less, in that father's shoes; his heart centred on the old place and on the boy for whom he held it in trust; and the irony of it twisted his lips into a rueful smile. By his own over-concentration on Roy, and his secret dread of the Indian obsession, he could gauge what his own father must have suffered in an aggravated form, blind as he was to any point of view save his own. And there was Roy—like himself in the twenties, but how much more purposeful!—drawn irresistibly by the lure of the horizon; a lure bristling with dangers the more insidious because they sprang from the blood in his veins.

Yet a word of warning, spoken at the wrong moment, in the wrong tone, might be disastrously misunderstood; and the distracting sense of being purely responsible for his own trouble, stung him to renewed irritation. All capacity for work had been dispelled by that vexatiously engaging son of his, with his heart in India and his head among the stars. . . .

Weary of pacing, he took out his pipe and sat down in the window-seat to fill it. He was interrupted by the sound of an unmistakable footstep; and the response of his whole being justified to admiration Lilámani's assurance that his hidden trouble implied no lightest reflection on herself. Lilámani and irritation simply could not co-exist within him; and he was on his feet when she opened the door.

She did not come forward at once. Pushing it shut with both hands, she stood so—a hovering question in her eyes. It recalled, with a tender pang, the earlier days of worshipful aloofness, when only by special invitation wou'd she intimately approach her lord.

That she might guess his thought he held out his arms. "Come along—English wife!"

It had been their private password. But her small teeth imprisoned her lip.

"No—King of me—Indian wife: making too much trouble again!"

"Lilámani! How dare you! Come here."

His attempt at sternness took effect. In one swift rush—sari blown backward—she came: and he, smitten with self-reproach, folded her close; while she clung to him in mute passionate response.

"Beloved," she whispered. "Not to worry any more in your secret heart. I told—he understands."

"Roy——? My darling! But *what*——?" His incoherence was a shameless admission of relief. "You couldn't—you haven't told him——?"

"Nevil, I have told him all. I saw lately this trouble in your thoughts: and to-day it came in my mind that only I could speak—could give command that—one kind of marriage must *not* be."

He drew her closer, and she suppressed a small sigh.

"Wasn't the boy angry?"

"Only at first—on account of me. He is—so very darling, so worshipping—his foolish little Mother."

"A weakness he shares with his father," Nevil assured her: and in that whispered confession she had her reward. For after twenty-three years of marriage, the note of loverly extravagance is as rare as the note of the cuckoo in July.

"Sit, little woman." He drew her down to the window-seat, keeping an arm round her. "The relief it is to feel I can talk it all over with you freely. Where the dickens would we be, Roy and I, without our interpreter? And she does it all unbeknownst; like a Brownie. I *have* been worrying lately. The boy's clean gone on his blessed idea. No reasoning with him; and the modern father doesn't venture to command! It's as much as his place is worth! Yet *we* see the hidden dangers clearer than he can. Wouldn't it be wiser to apply the curb discreetly before he slips off into an atmosphere where all the influences will tug one way?"

It was the sane masculine wisdom of the West. But hers—that was feminine and of the East—went deeper.

"Perhaps it is mother-weakness," she said, leaning against him and looking away at a purple cloud that hung low over the moor. "But it seems to me, by putting on the curb, you keep only his body from those influences. They would tug all the stronger in his soul. Not healthy and alive with joy of action, but cramped up and aching, like your legs when there is no room to stretch them. Then there would come impatience, turning his heart more to India, more away from you. Father had that kind of thwarting when young—so I know. Dearest one, am I too foolish?"

"You are my Wisest of Wise.—Is there more?"

"Yes. It is this. Perhaps, through being young and eager, he will make mistakes; wander too far. But even if he should wander to farthest end, all influence will *not* tug one way. He will carry in his heart the star of you and the star of me. These will shine brighter if he knows how we longed—for ourselves—to keep him here; yet, for himself, we let him go. I have remembered always one line of poetry you showed me at Como. 'To take by leaving, To hold by letting go.' That is true truth for many things. But for parents truest of all."

High counsel indeed! Good to hear; hard to act upon. Nevil Sinclair—knowing they would act upon it—let out an involuntary sigh and tightened his hold of the gentle, adoring woman, whose spirit towered so far above his own.

"Lilámani—you've won," he said, after a perceptible pause. "You deserve to win—and Roy will bless you. It's the high privilege of Mothers, I suppose, to conjure the moon out of heaven for their sons."

"Sometimes, by doing so, they nearly break their hearts," she answered very low.

He stooped and kissed her. "Keep yours intact—for me. I shall need it." Her fingers closed convulsively on his—"England will seem sort of empty—without Roy. Is he dead keen on going this autumn?"

"Yes—I am afraid. A little because of young impatience. A little because he is troubled over Dyán; and he has much influence. There are so many now in India dragged two ways."

Nevil sighed again. "Bless the boy! It's an undeniable risk. And what the family will say to our Midsummer madness, God knows! Jane can be trusted to make the deuce of a row. And we can't even smooth matters by telling her of our private precaution——"

"No—not one little *word.*"

Lilámani sat upright, a gleam of primitive hate in her eyes.

Nevil smiled, in spite of secret dismay. "You implacable little sinner! Can't you ever forgive her like a Christian?"

"No—not ever." The tense quiet of her tone carried conviction. "Not only far-off things, I can never forget—nearly killing me and—and Roy. But because she is always stabbing at me with sharp words and ugly thoughts. She cannot ever forgive that I am here—that I make you happy, which she could not believe. She is angry to be put in the wrong by mere Hindu wife——" She paused in her vehement rush of speech: saw the look in Nevil's face that recalled an earlier day; and anger vanished like a light blown out. "King of me—I am sorry. Only—it is true. And *she* is Christian born.

But I—down in my deepest places I am still—Rajputni. Just the same as after twenty-three years of English wife, I am still in my heart—like the 'Queen who stood erect!'"

On the word she rose and confronted him, smiling into his troubled eyes; grace of girlhood and dignity of womanhood adorably mingled in her pose.

"Who was she?" Nevil asked, willingly lured from thoughts of Jane.

"Careless one! Have you forgotten the story of my Wonder-Woman—how a King, loving his Queen with all his soul, bowed himself in ecstasy, and 'took the dust off her feet' in presence of other wives who, from jealousy, cried: 'Shameless one, lift up the hands of the King to your head.' But the Queen stood erect, smiling gladly. 'Not so: for both feet and head are my Lord's. Can I have aught that is mine?'"

The swiftness of transition, the laughing tenderness of her eyes so moved him—and so potent in her was the magical essence of womanhood—that he, Sir Nevil Sinclair, Baronet, of Bramleigh Beeches, came near to taking the dust off her feet in very deed.

## CHAPTER VI.

"Qui n'accepte pas le regret, n'accepte pas la vie."

NEVIL'S fears were justified to the full. Lady Roscoe was one of those exasperating people of whom one can predict, almost to a word, a look, what their attitude will be on any given occasion. So Nevil, who shirked a "scene"—above all when conducted by Jane—put off telling her the unwelcome news as long as he dared, without running the dire risk of its reaching her "round the corner."

Meantime he was fortified and cheered by a letter from Cuthbert Broome—a shrewd, practical letter amounting to a sober confession of faith in Roy the embryo writer, as in Roy the budding man.

"I don't minimise the risk," he concluded, with his accustomed frankness (no relation to the engaging candour that dances a war-dance on other people's toes), "but, on broad lines, I hereby record my conviction that the son of you two and the grandson of Sir Lakshman Singh can be trusted to go far—to keep his head as well as his feet, even in slippery places. He is eager for knowledge, for work along his own lines. If you dam up this strong current, it may find other outlets, possibly less desirable. I came on a jewel the other day. As it's distinctly applicable, I pass it on.

"'The sole wisdom for man or boy who is haunted with the hovering of unseen wings, with the scent of unseen roses, and the subtle enticement of melodies unheard, is *work*. If he follow any of these, they vanish. If he work, they will come unsought . . .'

"Well, when Roy goes out, I undertake to provide him with work that will keep his brain alert and his pen busy. That's my proposed contribution to his start in life; and—though *I* say it!—not to be despised. Tell him I'll bear down upon the Beeches the first available week-end, and talk both your heads off!—Yours ever, C. B."

"After *that*," was Nevil's heroic conclusion, "Jane can say what she damn well pleases."

He broke the news to her forthwith—by post; the usual expedient of those who shirk "scenes." He furthermore took the precaution to add that the matter was finally settled.

She replied next morning—by wire. "Cannot understand. Coming down at once."

And, in record time, on the wings of her new travelling car—she came.

As head of the Sinclair clan—in years and worldly wisdom at least—she could do no less. From her point of view, it was Nevil's clear duty to discourage the Indian strain in the boy, as far as that sentimental, headstrong wife of his would permit. But Nevil's sense of duty needed constant galvanising, lest it die of inanition. It was her sacred mission in life to galvanise it, especially in the matter of Roy; and no one should ever say *she* shirked a disagreeable obligation. It may safely be added that no one ever did!

Nevil—who would have given a good deal to be elsewhere—awaited her in the library: and at the first shock of their encountering glances, he stiffened all through. He was apt to be restive under advice, and rebellious under dictation; facts none knew better than Jane, who throve on advice and dictation—given, not received! She still affected the neat hard coat and skirt and the neat hard summer hat that had so distressed the awakening beauty-sense of nine-year-old Roy: only, in place of the fierce wing there uprose in majesty a severely wired bow. Jane was so unvarying, outside and in; a worse failing, almost, in the eyes of this hopelessly artistic household, than her talent for pouncing, or advising or making up other people's minds.

But to-day, as she glanced round the familiar room, her sigh—half anger, half bitterness of heart—was genuine. She did care intensely, in her own way, for the brother whom she hectored without mercy. And he too cared—in his own way—more than he chose to reveal. But their love was a dumb thing, rooted in ancestral mysteries. Their surface clash of temperament was more loquacious.

"I suppose we're fairly safe from interruption?" she asked, with ominous emphasis; and Nevil gravely indicated the largest leather chair.

"I believe the others are out," he said, half sitting on the edge of the writing-table and proceeding to light a cigarette. "But, upon my soul, I don't know *why* you put yourself out to come down all this way when I told you plainly everything was fixed up."

"You thought I'd swallow that—and keep my mouth shut?" she retorted, bristling visibly. "*I'm* no fool, Nevil, if *you* are. I *told* you how it would be, when you went out in '99. You wouldn't listen then. Perhaps you'll at least have the sense to listen *now?*"

Nevil shrugged. "As you've come all this way for the satisfaction of airing your views—I've not much choice in the matter."

And the latitude, thus casually given, she took in full measure. For twenty minutes, by the clock, she aired her views in a stream of vigorous colloquial English, lapsing into ready-made phrases of melodrama, common to the normally inexpressive, in moments of excitement. . . .

To the familiar tuning-up process, Nevil listened unmoved. But his anger rose with her rising eloquence: —the unwilling anger of a cool man, more formidable than mere temper.

Such fine distinctions, however, were unknown to Jane. If you were in a temper, you were in a temper. That was flat. And she rather wanted to rouse Nevil's. Heated opposition would stiffen her own. . . .

"India of all countries in the world!" she culminated —a desperate note invading her wrath. "The one place where he should *not* be allowed to sow his wild oats—if the modern anæmic young man has enough red blood in his veins—for that sort of thing. And it's your obvious duty to be quite frank with him on the subject. If you had an ounce of common-sense in your make-up, you'd see it for yourself. But I always say the clever people are the biggest fools. And Roy's in the same boat—being your son. No ballast. All in the clouds. *That's* the fruits of Lil's fancy education. And you can't say I didn't warn you. What he needs is discipline—a tight hand. Why not one of the Services? If he gets bitten with India—at his age, it's quite on the cards that he may go turning Hindu—or even repeat *your* folly——"

She paused, simply for lack of breath—and became suddenly alive to the set stillness of her brother's face.

"*My* folly—as you are pleased to call it," he said with concentrated scorn, "has incidentally made our name famous, and cleared the old place of mortgage. For that reason alone, you might have the grace to refrain from insulting my wife."

She flung up her head, like a horse at a touch of the curb.

"Oh, if it's an insult to speak the simple truth, I'm *quite* out of it. I never could call spades agricultural instruments: and I can't start new habits at my time of life. I don't deny you've made a good thing out of your pictures. But no one in their senses *could* call your marriage an act of wisdom."

Nevil winced visibly. "I married for the only defensible reason," he said, in a low controlled voice. "And events have more than justified me."

"Possibly—so far as *you*'re concerned. But you can't get over the fact that—even if Roy marries the best blood of England—his son may revert to type. Dr Simons tells me——"

"*Will* you hold your tongue!" Nevil blazed out, in a white fury. "I'll thank you *not* to discuss my affairs—or Roy's—with your damned Doctor. And the subject's barred between us—as you're very well aware."

She blenched at the force and fire of his unexpected onslaught, never dreaming how deeply her thrust had gone home.

"Goodness knows it's as painful for me as it is for you——"

"I didn't say it was painful. I said it was barred."

"Well, you goad me into it, with your unspeakable folly; too much under Lil's thumb to check Roy, even for his own good. For heaven's sake, Nevil, put your foot down firmly, for once, and reverse your crazy decision."

He gave her a long, direct look. "Sorry to disappoint, after all the trouble you've taken," he said in a level tone, "but I've already told you the matter's settled. My foot is down on that as firmly as even *you* could wish."

"You *mean* it?" she gasped, too incredulous for wrath.

"I mean it."

"Yet you see the danger?"

"I see the danger."

The fact that he would not condescend to lie to her eased a little her bitter sense of defeat.

She rose awkwardly—all of a piece.

"Then I have no more to say. I wash my hands of you all. Until you come to your senses, I don't cross this threshold again."

In spite of the threadbare phrases, genuine pain vibrated in her tone.

"Don't rant, old thing. You know you'll never keep it up," Nevil urged more gently than he had spoken yet.

But anger still dominated pain.

"When *I* say a thing, I mean it," she retorted stiffly, "as you will find to your cost." Without troubling to answer, he lunged for the door handle; but she waved him aside. "All humbug—playing at politeness—when you've spurned my advice."

"As you please." He stood back for her to pass. "Sorry it's upset you so. But we'll see you here again—when you've got over it."

"The *boy* would have got over it in no time," she flung back at him from the threshold. "Mark my words, disaster will come of it. Then perhaps you'll admit I was right."

He felt no call to argue that point. She was gone . . . And she had carefully refrained from slamming the door. Somehow that trifling act of restraint impressed him with a sense of finality oddly lacking in her dramatic asseveration.

He stood a few moments staring at the polished oak panels. Then he turned back and sat down in the chair she had occupied; and all the inner tension of the last hour went suddenly, completely to pieces. . . .

It was the penalty of his artist nature, this sharp nervous reaction from strain; and with it came crowding back all the insidious doubts and anxieties that even Lilámani's wisdom had not entirely charmed away. He felt torn at the moment between anger with Roy for causing all this pother; and anger with Jane, who, for all her lack of tenderness and tact, was right—up to a point. It was just Family Herald heroics about "not crossing the threshold." At least—rather to his surprise—he found himself half hoping it was. Roy and Lilámani could frankly detest her—and there an end. Nevil—in spite of unforgiveable interludes—was liable to be tripped up by the fact that, after all, she was his sister; and her aggression was proof that, in her own queer fashion, she loved him. Half the trouble was that the love of each for the other took precisely the form that other could least appreciate or understand: no uncommon dilemma in family life. At all events, he had achieved his declaration of independence. And he had not failed to evoke the "deuce of a row."

With a sigh of smothered exasperation, he leaned forward and hid his face in his hands. . . .

The door opened softly. He started and looked up. It was Roy—in flannels and blazer, his dark hair slightly ruffled: considered dispassionately (and Nevil believed he so considered him) a singularly individual and attractive figure of youth.

At the look in his father's face, he hesitated, wrinkling his brows in a way that recalled his mother.

"Anything wrong, Daddums? I'm fearfully sorry. I came for a book. Is it"—still further hesitation—"Aunt Jane?"

"Why? Have you seen her?" Nevil asked sharply.

"Yes. Was it a meteoric visitation? As I came up the path, she was getting into her car.—And she cut me dead!" He seemed more amused than impressed. Then the truth dawned on him. "Dad—*have* you been telling her? *Is* she 'as frantic as a skit'?"

Their favourite Hardy quotation moved Nevil to a smile. "She's angry—naturally—because she wasn't consulted," he said (a happy idea). "And—well, she doesn't understand."

"'Course she doesn't. Can she ever?" retorted impertinent youth. "She lacks the supreme faculty —imagination." Which was disrespectful, but unanswerable.

Nevil had long ago recognised the futility of rebuke in the matter of "Aunt Jane"; and it was a relief to find the boy took it that way. So he smiled, merely —or fancied he did. But Roy was quick-sighted; and his first impression had dismayed him.

No hesitation now. He came forward and laid a hand on his father's shoulder. "Dads, don't get worrying over me—out there," he said with shy tenderness that was balm after the lacerating scene Nevil had just passed through. "That'll be all right. Mother explained—beautifully."

But louder than Roy's comfortable assurance sounded within him the parting threat of Jane: "Disaster will come of it. *Then* perhaps you'll admit I was right." It shook the foundations of courage. He simply could not stand up to the conjunction of disaster—and Roy. With an effort he freed himself of the insidious thing, —and just then, to his immense surprise, Roy stooped and kissed the top of his head.

"Confound Aunt Jane! She's been bludgeoning you. And you *are* worrying. You mustn't—I tell you. Bad for your work. Look here"— a portentous pause. "Shall I chuck it—for the present, anyhow?"

The parental attitude of the modern child has its touching aspect. Nevil looked up to see if Roy were chaffing; and there smote him the queer illusion (rarer now, but not extinct) of looking into his own eyes.

Roy had spoken on impulse—a noble impulse. But he patently meant what he said, this boy stigmatised by Jane as "all in the clouds," and needing a "tight hand." Here was one of those "whimsical and perilous moments of daily life" that pass in a breath; light as thistledown, heavy with complex issues. To Nevil it seemed as if the gods, with ironical gesture, handed him the wish of his heart, saying: "It is yours —if you are fool enough to take it." Stress of thought so warred in him that he came to himself with a fear of having hurt the boy by ungracious silence.

The pause, in fact, had been so brief that Roy had

only just become aware that his cherished dream was actually trembling in the balance—when Nevil stood up and faced him, flatly defying Jane and Olympian irony.

"My dear old boy, you shall *not* chuck it," he said with smiling decision. "I've never believed in the older generation being a drag on the wheel. And now it's my turn, I must play up. What's life worth without a spice of risk? I took my own—a big one—family or no——"

He broke off—and Roy filled the gap. "You mean—marrying Mother?"

"Yes—just that," he admitted frankly. "The greatest bit of luck in my life. She shared the risk—a bigger one for her. And I'm damned if we'll cheat you of yours. There's a hidden key somewhere that most of us have to find. Yours may be in India—who knows?"

He spoke rapidly, as if anxious to convince himself no less than the boy. And he had his reward.

"Dad—you're simply stunning—you two," Roy said quietly, but with clear conviction.

At that moment the purring of the gong vibrated through the house, and he slipped a hand through his father's arm. "That reminds me—I'm *starving* hungry! If they're still out, let's be bold, and propitiate the teapot on our own!"

Lady Roscoe was, after all, a benefactor in her own despite. Her meteoric visitation had drawn these two closer together than they had been since schoolroom days.

# CHAPTER VII.

"Ce que nous quittons c'est une partie de nous même. Il faut mourir à une vie, pour entrer dans une autre."—ANATOLE FRANCE.

AFTER all, human perversity decreed it should be Roy himself who shrank most acutely from the wrench of parting, when it loomed near enough to bring him down from Pisgah heights to the dust of the actual.

Dyán was overjoyed, of course, and untroubled by qualms. Towards the end of July, he and Arúna came for a brief visit. His excuses for its brevity struck Roy as a trifle 'thin'; but Dyán kept his secret and paid Tara Despard the compliment of taking her answer as final.

It was during his visit that Roy suffered the first incipient qualms; the first sharp contact with practical details:—date of sailing, details of outfit, the need for engaging a passage betimes. As regards his destination, matters were simplified by the fact that the new Resident of Jaipur, Colonel Vincent Leigh, C.S.I., D.S.O., very considerately happened to be the husband of Desmond's delightful sister Thea. The schoolboy link between Lance and Roy had created a lasting friendship between their respective families; and it was General Sir Theo Desmond—now retired—who had invited Roy, in the name of his 'Twin,' to start with an unlimited visit to the Leighs; the sort of casual elastic visit that no one would dream of proposing outside India,—unless it were Ireland, of an earlier, happier day. The prospect was a secret consolation to Roy. It was also a secret jar to find he needed every ounce of consolation available.

Very carefully he hid his ignominious frame of mind —even from his mother; though she probably suspected it and would not fail to understand. What, precisely, would life be worth without that dear, daily intimacy —life uncoloured by the rainbow-tinted charm of her gentle, passionate, humorous, delicately-poised personality? Relations of such rare quality exact their own pitiless price; and the woman influence would always be, for Roy—as for most men of genuine gifts and high purpose—his danger point or salvation. The dim and distant prospect of parting was thinkable—though perturbing. But all this talk of steamers and outfits startlingly illumined the fact that in October he was actually going—to the other end of the earth.

With Dyán's departure, realisation pounced upon his heart and brain. Vaguely, and quite unjustly, he felt as if his cousin were in some way to blame; and for the moment, he was not sorry to be rid of him. Partings over, he went off for a lone prowl—hatless, as usual—to quiet his jangling sensations and tell that inner, irresolute Roy not to be a treble-distilled fool. . . .

Nothing like the open moor to clear away cobwebs. The sweeps of heady colour and blue distances could be trusted to revive the winged impulse that lured him irresistibly away from the tangible and assured. Is there no hidden link—he wondered—between the wander-instinct of the home-loving Scot and the vast spaces of moor and sky that lie about him in his infancy . . . ?

But first he must traverse the enchanted green gloom of his beech-wood, memory-haunted at every turn. Under his favourite tree, a wooden cross, carved by Tara and himself, marked the grave of Prince, dead these three years of sheer old age. And at sight of it there sprang to memory that unforgotten day of May,—the fight with Joe; Tara's bracelet, still treasured in his letter-case, even as Tara treasured the "broidered bodice," in a lavender-scented sachet, set apart from mere blouses and scarves. . . .

And again that troublesome voice within urged —"What an utter fool you are—running away from them all."

To him had fallen the privilege of knowing family life at its best—the finest and happiest on earth; and he could not escape the price exacted, when the call comes to act and decide and suffer alone. Associations that grow up with us are more or less taken for granted while their roots lie deep in the heart. Only when the threat of parting disturbs the delicate fibres, their depth and tenacity are revealed. And so it was with Roy. Hurrying through his wood of knightly adventures he felt besieged, in spirit, by the many loves that had hitherto simply been a part of his life; yet to-day pressed urgently, individually, upon his consciousness, his heart . . .

And over against them was the counter-pull of deep ancestral stirrings; large vague forces of the outer world; the sense of ferment everywhere; of storm-clouds on the greater horizon, big with dramas that might rock the spheres. . . .

All these challenging forces seemed to dwarf his juvenile agitations; even to arraign his own beautiful surroundings as almost too peaceful, too perfect. Life could not be altogether made up of goodness and sweetness and poetry and philosophy. Somewhere—remote, unseen, implacable—there must lurk strong things, big things, perhaps inimical things, waiting to pounce on him, to be tackled and overcome. Anyhow there could be no question, after all his vapourings, of playing the fool and backing out——

He was on the ridge now; clear space all about him, heather underfoot; his stride keeping pace with the march of his thoughts. Risks . . .? Of course there were risks. He recognised that more frankly now; and the talk with his mother had revealed a big one that had not so much as occurred to him. For Broome was right. Concentration on her had, in a sense, delayed his emotional development; had kept him—for all his artistry and his First in Greats—very much a boy at heart. Certainly, Arúna's grace and gaiety had struck him more consciously during this last visit. No denying, the Eastern element had its perilous fascination. And the Eastern element was barred. As for Tara—sister and friend and High Tower Princess in one—she was as much a part of home as his mother and Christine. He had simply not seen her yet as a budding woman. He had, in fact, been too deeply absorbed in Oxford and writing and his dream, and the general deliciousness of life, to challenge the future definitely, except in the matter of going to India, somewhen, somehow . . .

Lost in the swirl of his thoughts and the exhilaration of light and colour, he forgot all about teatime. . . .

It was after five when, at last, he swung round the yew hedge on to the long lawn; and there, at the far end, was Tara, evidently sent out to find him. She was wearing her delphinium frock and the big blue hat with its single La France rose. She walked pensively, her head bowed; and, in that moment, by some trick of sense or spirit, he saw her vividly, as she was. He saw the grace of her young slenderness, the wild-flower colouring, the delicate aquiline of her nose that revealed breeding and character; the mouth that even in repose seemed to quiver with sensibility. And he thought: "Good Lord! How lovely she is!"

Of course he had known it always—at the back of his mind. The odd thing was, he had never thought it, in so many words, before. And from the thought sprang an inspiration. If only *she* could come out with them—for a time, at least. So imbued was he with a sense of their brother and sister relation, that the idea seemed as natural as if it had concerned Christine. He had certainly been aware, the last year or so, of a gossamer veil dropped between them. He attributed this to mere grown-up-ness; but it made him feel appreciably shy at thought of broaching his brilliant idea.

She raised her head at that point; saw him, and waved a commanding hand. Impelled by eagerness, he condescended to hurry.

"Casual demon—what *have* you been up to?" she greeted him with mock severity.

"Prowling on the ridge. It was gorgeous up there," he answered, noticing in detail the curve of her eyelid and thick dark lashes.

"Well, tea's half cold and most of it eaten; and Aunt Lila seemed wondering a little. So I offered to go and unearth you."

"How could you tell?"

A dimple dipped in one cheek. "I couldn't! I was going to the wood, on chance. Come along."

"No hurry. If tea's half cold, it can wait a bit longer." He drew a breath, nerving himself; then: "Tara—I've got a proposal to make."

"Roy!" Her lips quivered, just perceptibly, and were still.

"Well, it's this. Wouldn't it be splendid if *you* came along out—with us three?"

"Roy!" It was a changed intonation. "That's *not* a subject for a practical joke."

"But I'm in earnest. High Tower Princess, wouldn't you love to come?"

"Of course I would." Was it his fancy, or did the blood stir ever so little in her cheeks? "But it's utterly, crazily impossible. The sort of thing only *you* would suggest. So please let be—and come along in."

"Not till you promise. I'm dead set on this. And I'm going to have it out with you."

"Well, you won't have *me* out with you—if you talk till midnight."

"Why not?"

Her smile had its delicious tremulous quality. "Were you twenty-one last birthday—or twelve? If you think you'll be lonely, ask for Christine. She's your sister—I'm not!"

The emphasis and faint inflection of the last words had their intended effect. Roy's face fell. "O-oh, I see. But you've always been my sort of sister. Thea would understand. And nowadays girls do all sorts of things."

"Yes—they do!" Tara agreed demurely. "They scratch faces and burn down beautiful harmless houses. But they don't happen to belong to mother. Roy—it's what I said—crazily—utterly—— If it wasn't, d'you suppose I'd say No?"

Then Roy knew he was beaten. Also he knew she was right and that he had been an impulsive fool—depressing convictions both. For a moment he stood nonplussed while Tara fingered a long chain he had given her, and absently studied a daisy-plant that had dared to invade the oldest, loveliest lawn in that part of the country.

But Roy was little used to being thwarted—by home elements, at least: and when an idea seized him he could be pertinacious, even to the point of folly. He was determined Tara should come with him. And Tara wanted to come. Add her permanent dearness and her newly-found loveliness, and there sprang from the conjunction a second inspiration, even bolder than the first.

"Tara—dear," he ventured, in a changed tone that halted between tenderness and appeal. "I'm going to say—something tremendous."

She deserted the daisy and faced him, blue eyes wide; her tell-tale lower lip drawn in.

"Would it be—quite so 'crazily—utterly'—if . . . well, if we were engaged?"

The tremendous word was out; and the effect on her was unmistakable. Colour stirred visibly in her face. She straightened herself with an air that seemed physically to increase the distance between them.

"Really, Roy—have you *quite* lost your senses to-day?"

He looked—and felt—crestfallen. "But, Tara," he urged, "it's such a supreme idea. Wouldn't you—think of it, ever? We'd fit like a pair of gloves. Mummy would love it—extravagantly. And we've been kind of —caring all these years. At least"—sudden doubt assailed him—"I suppose you *do* care still—a little bit?"

"Silly boy! Of course I—care . . . a lot."

That was more like the Tara he knew. "Very well. *Why* accuse me of incipient lunacy? I care, too. Always have done. Think how topping it would be, you and I together, exploring all the wonderland of our Game and Mummy's tales—Udaipur, Amber, Chitor, perhaps the shrine of the real Tara——"

Still demurely distant, she thought "how topping it would be"; and the thought kept her silent so long that he grew impatient.

"High Tower Princess—do give over. Your grown-up airs are awfully sweet—but not to the point. You are coming? It'll spoil everything now, if you don't."

She shook her head with a small wise smile that seemed to push him away from her, gently yet inexorably;

to make him feel little more than a schoolboy confronted by a woman; very young in her new shyness and dignity, but still—a woman.

"No, Roy—I'm not coming. It's—dear of you to want me. But I can't—for lots of reasons. So please understand, once for all. And don't fuss."

"But you said—you cared," Roy murmured blankly.

"Of course I do. Only—there's caring—and caring . . . since you make me say it. You must know that by now. Anyway, I know we simply can't get married just because we're very fond of each other and it would please 'Mummy' and be convenient for India."

Roy sighed portentously. He found himself feeling younger and younger with every smiling, reasonable word she uttered. It was all so unlike his eager, fiery Tara that perplexity tempered a little his genuine dismay.

"I s'pose you're right," he grudgingly admitted. "But I'm fearfully disappointed."

"You are now. You won't be afterwards. It's not marrying time for you—yet. You've lots of big things to do first. Go out to India and do them. Then—when the time really comes, you'll understand—and you'll be grateful to *me*—for understanding now. There, what a lecture! But the point is—we can't: and I won't be badgered about it. *I'm* going back to tea; and if you don't come, I'll have to tell Aunt Lila—why?"

He sighed. "I'll probably tell her myself to-night. Would you mind?"

"N-no, she'll understand."

"Bet she won't."

"She will. You're not the only person the darling understands, though you *are* her spoilt boy."

She swung round on that impetuous little speech, more like her normal self; and her going was so swift that Roy had some ado to keep pace with her. He had still more ado to unravel his own tangle of thought and emotion. A few clear points emerged from a chaos of sensations, like mountain peaks out of a mist. He knew she was all of a sudden distractingly lovely; that her charm and obstinacy combined had thoroughly churned him up; that all the same, she was right about his unreadiness for marrying now; that he hoped she didn't utterly despise him; that he hated the idea of leaving her more than ever. . . .

Her pace, perhaps intentionally, made talk difficult; and he still had a lot to say.

"Tara—why *are* you sprinting like this?" he broke out, reproachfully. "Are you angry with me?"

She vouchsafed him a small smile.

"Not yet. But I soon will be, if you don't take care. And I'm dangerous in a temper!"

"Don't I know that? I once had a scratch that didn't heal for a month. But do walk slower. You're not chucking me—for good—eh?"

She slowed down a little, perforce; needing her breath for this new and hopelessly intractable Roy.

"Really, I've never known you ask so many foolish questions in one hour before. You must have drunk some potion up on the moor! Have you forgotten you're my Bracelet-bound Brother?"

"But that doesn't bar—the other thing. It's not one of the Prayer-book affinities! I say, Tara—you might promise to think it over. If you can't do that much, I won't believe you care a bean about me, for all you say——"

Her blue eyes flashed at that—genuine fire; and she stood still again, confronting him.

"Roy—be *quiet!* You make me furious. I want to slap you. First you suggest a perfectly crazy plan; then you worry me into a temper by behaving like a spoilt boy, who won't take 'No' for an answer."

Roy straightened himself sharply. "I'm not spoilt—and I'm not a boy. I'm a man."

"Well then, try and *behave* like one."

The moment her impulsive retort was spoken, she saw how sharply she had hurt him, and, with a swift softening of her expressive face, she flung out a hand. He held it hard. And suddenly she leaned nearer; her lips tremulous; her eyes melting into a half smile.

"Roy—darling," she murmured, barely above her breath. "You are really—a little bit of all three. That's part of your deliciousness and troublesomeness. And it's not your fault—the spoiling. We've all helped. I've been as bad as the others. But this time—please believe—I simply, utterly can't—even for you."

Words went from him. He could only cling to her hand.

But with a deft movement she freed herself—and fled round the corner of the house; leaving him in a state of confusion worse confounded, to seek his mother and the outraged teapot—alone.

He found her, companioned by the ruins of tea, in the depths of her great arm-chair; eyes and fingers intent on a square of elaborate embroidery; thoughts astray with her unpunctual son.

Bramleigh Beeches drawing-room—as recreated by Sir Nevil Sinclair for his Indian bride—was a setting worthy of its mistress: lofty and spacious, light filled by three tall French windows, long gold curtains shot through with bronze; gold and cream colour the prevailing tone; ivory, brass, and bronze the prevailing incidentals, mainly Indian; and flowers in profusion—roses, lilies, sweet-peas. Yet, in the midst of it all, the spirit of Lilámani Sinclair was restless, lacking the son, of whom, too soon, both she and her home would be bereft——

At the sound of his step she looked up.

"Wicked one! What came to you?"

Impossible to hide from her the disarray of his emotions. So he spoke the simple truth.

"Tara came to me——! I'd been prowling on the moor, and forgetting the time. I met her on the lawn——"

"Yes—where is she?—And you——?"

He caught the note of apprehension. Next moment he was kneeling by her chair, confessing all.

"Mummy, I've just asked her—to marry me. And she simply . . . won't hear of it. I thought it would be so lovely, going out together—that it would please you so——"

The smile in her eyes recalled Tara's own. "Did you say it that way—to her, my darling?"

"No—not exactly. Naturally I did mention you—and India. She admits she's fond of me. Yet she got quite angry. I can't make her out."

A faintly aggrieved note in his voice, implied expectation of sympathy. To his inexpressible surprise she said pensively, as if to herself: "Such a wise Tara!"

"Well, *I* don't see where the wisdom comes in," he muttered a trifle disconcerted.

"Not yet, son of my heart. Some day perhaps when your eyes are not too dazzled from the many-coloured sparkle of youth—of yourself—you will see—many surprises. You are not yet ready for a wife, Roy. Your heart is reaching out to far-away things. That—*she* has been woman enough to guess."

"Perhaps, I'm not so sure. She seemed—not a bit like herself, part of the time." He looked pensively at a slim vase overflowing with sprays of blush rambler, that, for some reason, evoked a tantalising vision of the girl who had so suddenly blossomed into a woman; and his shy, lurking thought found utterance: "I've been wondering, Mummy, is it . . . can she be—in love with somebody else? Do you think she is?"

Lilámani shook her head at him. "That is a man's question! Hard to tell. At this kind of age, when girls have so much character—like my Tara—they have a natural instinct for hiding the thoughts of their hearts." She dropped her needlework now and lightly took his head between her hands, looking deep into his eyes. "Do you think *you* are yet—in love with her, Roy? Honest answer."

The touch of her hands stirred him all through. The question in her eyes probed deep.

"Honest answer, Mummy—I'm blest if I know," he said slowly. "I don't think I've ever been so near it before; beyond thrills at dances . . . and all that. She somehow churned me up just now and made me want her tremendously. But I truly hadn't thought of it—that way, before. And—I did feel it might ease you and Dad about . . . the other thing, if I went out fixed up."

She drew his head to her and kissed him, then let her hands fall in her lap. "Wonderful Sonling! Indeed it *would* ease me and please me—if coming from the true motive. Only remember, so long as you are thinking first of me, you can be sure That Other has not yet arrived."

"But I shall always think first of you," he declared, catching at her hands. "There's no one like you. There never will be."

"No—not like, but different—in dearness and nearness. Love is one big impulse, but many forms. Like white light made from many colours. No rival for me, That Other; but daughter-in-law—best gift a son can bring to his father's house. Just now there is room inside you only for one big thing—India."

"And you——"

"But I am India."

"Sublimated essence of it, according to Jeffers."

"Jeffers says many foolish things!" But she did not disguise her pleasure.

"I've noticed occasional flashes of wisdom!—But, I say, Motherling, what price tea?"

"Tea?" She feigned exaggerated surprise. "I thought you were much too far in the clouds!"

"On the contrary. I'm simply famished!"

And forthwith he fell upon a plate of sugar cakes; while she rang for the fresh teapot, so often in requisition for 'Mr Roy.'

## CHAPTER VIII.

> "Comfort, content, delight, the ages' slow-bought gain,
> They shrivelled in a night. Only ourselves remain
> To face the naked days in silent fortitude.
> Through perils and dismays renewed and re-renewed."
>
> —KIPLING.

NEVIL was up in town on business; not returning till next day. The papers were seething with rumours; but the majority of everyday people, immersed in their all-important affairs, continued cheerfully to hope against hope. Sir Nevil Sinclair was not of these; but he kept his worst qualms to himself. Neither his wife nor his son were keen newspaper readers; which, in his opinion, was just as well.

Certainly it did not occur to Lilámani that any trouble in Europe could invade the sanctities of her home, or affect the shining destiny of Roy. That he was destined to shine, her mother's heart knew beyond all doubt. And round that knowledge, like an aura, glimmered a dream-like hope that perhaps his shining might some day, in some way, strengthen the bond between Nevil's people and her own. For the problem of India's changing relation to England lay intimately near her heart. Her poetic brain saw England always as "husband of India"; while misguided or malicious meddlers—who would "make the Mother a widow"—were fancifully incorporated in the person of Jane. And, in this matter of India, Roy had triumphed over Jane:—surely good omens, for bigger things:—for at heart she was still susceptible to omens; more so than she cared to admit. Crazy mother-arrogance, Nevil would say. But she seemed to feel the spirit of his grandfather at work in Roy; and well she knew that the old man's wisdom would guide and temper his young zeal. Beyond that, no human eyes could see; only the too-human heart of a mother could dream and hope. . . .

Long ago her father had told that nations had always been renewed by individuals; that India—aristocratic to the deeps of her Brahmin-ridden soul—would never acknowledge the crowd's unstable sway. For her it must always be the *man*—ruler, soldier, or saint.

Not that she had breathed a word of her 'arrogance' to Nevil, or even to Roy. Nor had she shown to either a certain letter from a distinguished Indian woman; pure Indian by birth; also by birth a Christian; her sympathy with East and West as evenly poised as Lilámani's own. The letter lived in a slim blue bag, lovingly embroidered. Lilámani—foolish and fanciful—wore it like a talisman, next her heart; and at night slipped it under her pillow with her gold watch and wisp of scented lawn.

To-night, being alone, and her mind very full of Roy, she drew it out and re-read it for the hundredth time; lingering, as always, on its arresting finale.

"I have seen much and grieved more over the problem of the Eurasian, as multiplied in our beloved country—the fruit, most often, of promiscuous unions between low-caste types on both sides, with sense of stigma added to drag them lower still. But where the crossing is of highest caste—as with you and your 'Nevil'—I can see no stigma; perhaps even spiritual gain to your children. For I love both countries with my whole heart. And to my love God has given the vision that India may some day be saved by the son of just such a union as your own. He will have the strength of his handicap; the soul of the East; the forceful mind and character of the West. He will bring to the task of uniting them such twofold love and understanding that the world must needs take infection. What if the ultimate meaning of British occupation of India be just this—that the successor of Buddha should be a man born of high-caste, high-minded British and Indian parents; a fusion of the finest that East and West can give. That vision may inspire you in your first flush of happy motherhood. So I feel impelled to pass it on . . ."

Such a vision—whether fantasy or prophecy—could

not fail to stir Lilámani Sinclair's Eastern heart to its depths. But she shrank from sceptical comment; and sceptical Nevil would surely be. As for Roy, intuition warned her it was too heady an idea to implant in his ardent brain. So she treasured it secretly, and read it at intervals, and prayed that, some day, it might be fulfilled—if not through her, then through some other Lilámani, who should find courage to link her life with England. Above all, she prayed he who should achieve India's renewal might spring from Rajasthán. . . .

In the midst of her thinking and praying, she fell sound asleep—to dream of Roy tossed out of reach on the waves of some large vague upheaval. The 'how' and 'why' of it all eluded her. Only the vivid impression remained. . . .

And before the week was out, an upheaval, actual and terrible, burst upon a startled, unheeding world; a world lulled into a false sense of security; and too strenuously engaged in rushing headlong round a centrifugal point called 'progress,' to concern itself with a mythical peril across the North Sea.

But at the first clear note of danger, devotees of pleasure and progress and the franchise were transformed, as by magic, into a crowd of bewildered, curious and resentful human beings, who had suddenly lost their bearings; who snatched at newspapers; confided in perfect strangers; protested that a European War was unspeakable, unthinkable, and all the while could speak and think of nothing else. . . .

It was the nightmare terror of earthquake, when the solid ground underfoot turns traitor. And it shook even the stoutest nerves in the opening weeks of the Great War, destined to shatter their dear and familiar world for months, years, decades perhaps. . . .

But underlying all the froth and fume of the earlier restlessness, of the later fear and futility, the strong, kindly, imperturbable heart of the land still beat, sanely—if inconspicuously—in the home life of her cottages and her great country houses. Twentieth-century England could not be called degenerate while she counted among her hidden treasures homes of such charm and culture and mutual confidence as those that produced the Grenfells, the Charltons, a Lord Elcho, an Edward Tennant and a Charles Sorley—to pick a few names at random from that galaxy of 'golden boys' who ungrudgingly gave their lives—for what?

The answer to that staggering question is not yet. But the splendour of their gift remains: a splendour no after-failure can tarnish or dim. . . .

To the inmates of Bramleigh Beeches—Nevil excepted—the crash came with startling abruptness; dwarfing all personal problems, heart-searchings and high decisions. Even Lady Roscoe forgot Family Herald heroics, and 'crossed the threshold' without comment from Nevil or herself. The weightiest matters became suddenly trivial beside the tremendous questions that hovered in every mind and on every tongue: 'Can We hold Them?' 'Can They invade Us?' 'Can it be true—this whispered horror, that rumoured disaster?' And the test question—most tremendous of all, for the mere unit—'Where do *I* come in?'

Nevil came in automatically through years of casual connection with the Artists' Rifles. He was a Colonel by now; and would join up as a matter of course—to his wife's secret amazement and far from secret pride. Without an ounce of the soldier in him, he acted on instinct like most Englishmen; not troubling to analyse motives; simply in the spirit of *Noblesse oblige;* or, in the more casual modern equivalent—'one just does.'

Roy—poet and dreamer—became electrically alive to his double heritage of the soldier spirit. From age to age the primeval link between poet and warrior is reaffirmed in time of war: and the Rajput in him recognised only one way of fighting worthy the name—the triune conjunction of man and horse and sword. Disillusion, strange and terrible, awaited him on that score: and as for India—what need of his young activities, when the whole Empire was being welded into one resistant mass by the triple hammer-strokes of a common danger, a common enemy, a common aim?

It was perhaps this sense of a clear call in an age of intellectual ferment, of sex problems and political friction, that sent so many unlikely types of manhood straight as arrows to that universal target—the Front. The War offered a high and practical outlet for their dumb idealism; to their realism, it offered the 'terrific verities of fatigue, suffering, bodily danger—beloved life and staggering death.'

For Roy, Cavalry was a matter of course. In the saddle, even Jane could find no fault with him; little guessing that, in his genius for horsemanship, he was Rajput to the marrow. His compact, nervous make, strong thigh and light hand, marked him as the inevitable centaur; and he had already gained a measure of distinction in the cavalry arm of the Officers' Training Corps. But a great wish to keep in touch with his father led him to fall in with Sir Nevil's suggestion that he should start in the Artists' Rifles and apply for a transfer later on—when one could see more clearly how this terrific business was likely to develop. George and Jerry—aged fifteen and sixteen and a half—raged at their own futile juvenility—which, in happier circumstances, nothing would have induced them to admit. Jerry—a gay and reckless being—had fell designs on the Flying Corps, the very first moment he could 'wangle it.' George—the truest Sinclair of them all—sagely voted for the Navy, because it took you young. But no one heeded them very much. They were all too absorbed in newspapers and their own immediate plans.

And Lilámani, also, found her niche, when the King's stirring proclamation announced the coming of Indian troops. There was to be a camp on the estate. Later on, there would be convalescents. Meantime, there was wholesale need of 'comforts' to occupy her and Helen and Christine.

Tara's soaring ambition would carry her farther afield. Her spirit of flame—that rose instinctively to tragic issues and heroic demands—could be at peace nowhere but in the splendid, terrible, unorganised thick of it all. Without making any ado, she proposed to get there in the shortest possible time; and, in the shortest possible time, by sheer concentration and hard work, she achieved her desire. Before Roy left England, before her best-loved brother—a man of brilliant promise—had finished learning to fly, she was driving her car in Belgium, besieged in Antwerp, doing and enduring terrible things. . . .

After Tara, Nevil—for the Artists' Rifles were early

in the field. After Nevil, Roy—his exchange effected—very slim and soldierly in cavalry uniform; his grey-blue eyes, with the lurking gleam in them, more than ever noticeable in his sunburnt face.

The last day, the last hour were at once sad and glad beyond belief; so that Lilámani's coward heart was thankful for urgent trifles that helped to divert attention from the waiting shadow. Even to-day, as always, dress and sari were instinctively chosen to express her mood:—the mother-of-pearl mood; iridescence of glad and sad: glad to give; yet aching to keep. Daughter of Rajputs though she was, she had her moment of very human shrinking when the sharp actuality of parting was upon them; when he held her so close and long that she felt as if the tightened cord round her heart must snap—and there an end. . . .

But, by some miracle, some power not her own, courage held; though, when he released her, she was half blinded with tears.

Her last words—entirely like herself though they were—surprised him.

"Son of my heart—live for ever," she whispered, laying light hands on his breast. "And when you go into the battle, always keep strongly in your mind that They must *not* win, because no sacred or beautiful thing would be left clean from their touch. And when you go into the battle always remember—Chitor."

"It is *you* I shall always remember—looking like this," he answered under his breath. But he never forgot her injunctions; and through years of fighting, he obeyed them to the letter. . . .

That was in April, after Neuve Chapelle, when even optimists admitted that the War might last a year.

At Christmas time he came home on short leave—a changed Roy; his skin browner; his sensitive lips more closely set under the shadow line of his moustache; the fibre of body and spirit hardened, without loss of fineness or flexibility. Livelier on the surface, he was graver, more reticent, underneath—even with her. By the look in his eyes she knew he had seen things that could never be put into words. Some of them she too had seen, through his mind; so close was the spiritual link between them. In that respect at least, he was beautifully, unaffectedly the same. . . .

Nevil was home too, for that wonderful Christmas; and Tara, changed also, in her own vivid way; frank and friendly with Roy; though the grown-up veil between them was seldom lifted now. For the War held them both in its unrelaxing grip; satisfied, in terrible and tremendous fashion, the hidden desire—not uncommon in young things, though concealed like a vice—to suffer for others. Everything else, for the time being, seemed a side issue. Personal affairs could wait. . . .

When it came to letting Nevil and Roy go again, after their brief, beautiful interlude together, Lilámani discovered how those fifteen months of ceaseless anxiety and ceaseless service had shaken her nerve. Gladness of giving could now scarce hold its own against dread of losing; till she felt as if her heart must break under the strain. It did not break, however. It endured—as the hearts of a million mothers and wives have endured in all ages—to breaking-point . . . and beyond. The immensity of the whole world's anguish at once crushed and upheld her, making her individual pain seem almost a little thing——

They left her. And the War went on—disastrously, gloriously, stubbornly, inconclusively; would go on, it seemed, to the end of Time. One came to feel as if life free from the shadow of War had never been. As if it would never be again——

END OF PHASE II.

# PHASE III.

# PISGAH HEIGHTS

# CHAPTER I.

"No receipt openeth the heart, but a true friend."—FRANCIS BACON.

As early as 1819 there had been a Desmond in India; a soldier-administrator of mark, in his day. During the Sikh Wars there had been a Desmond in the Punjab; and at the time of the Great Mutiny there was a Punjab Cavalry Desmond at Kohat; a notable fighter, with a flowing beard and an easy-going uniform that would not commend itself to the modern military eye. In the year of the second Afghan War, there was yet another Desmond at Kohat; one that earned the cross 'For Valour,' married the daughter of Sir John Meredith, and rose to high distinction. Later still, in the year of grace 1918, his two sons were stationed there, in the self-same Punjab Cavalry Regiment. There was also by now, a certain bungalow in Kohat known as 'Desmond's bungalow,' occupied at present by Colonel Paul Desmond, now in Command.

That is no uncommon story in India. She has laid her spell on certain families; and they have followed one another through the generations, as homing birds follow in line across the sunset sky. And their name becomes a legend that passes from father to son; because India does not forget. There is perhaps nothing quite like it in the tale of any other land. It makes for continuity; for a fine tradition of service and devotion; a tradition that will not be broken till agitators and theorists make an end of Britain in India. But that day is not yet; and the best elements of both races still believe it will never be.

Certainly neither Paul nor Lance Desmond, riding home together from kit inspection, on a morning of early September, entertained the dimmest idea of a break with the family tradition. Lance, at seven-and-twenty—spare and soldierly, alive to the finger-tips—was his father in replica, even to the V.C. after his name, which he had 'snaffled out of the War,' together with a Croix de Guerre and a brevet-Majority. Though Cavalry had been at a discount in France, Mesopotamia and Palestine had given the Regiment its chance—with fever and dysentery and all the plagues of Egypt thrown in to keep things going.

It was in the process of filling up his woeful gaps that Colonel Desmond had applied for Roy Sinclair, and so fulfilled the desire of his brother's heart: also, incidentally, Roy's craving to serve with Indian Cavalry. To that end, his knowledge of the language, his horsemanship, his daring and resource in scout work, had stood him in good stead. Paul—who scarcely knew him at the time—very soon discovered that he had secured an asset for the Regiment—the great Fetish, that claimed his paramount allegiance, and began to look like claiming it for life.

"He's just John over again," Lady Desmond would say, referring to a brother who had served the great Fetish from subaltern to Colonel and left his name on a cross in Kohat cemetery.

Certainly, in form and feature, Paul was very much a Meredith:—the coppery tone of his hair, the straight nose and steadfast grey-blue eyes, the height and breadth and suggestion of power in reserve. It was one of the most serious problems of his life to keep his big frame under weight for polo, without impairing his immense capacity for work. Apart from this important detail, he was singularly unaware of his striking personal appearance, except when others chaffed him about his look of Lord Kitchener, and were usually snubbed for their pains; though, at heart, he was inordinately proud of the fact. He had only one quarrel with the hero of his boyhood:—the decree that officially extinguished the Frontier Force; though the spirit of it survives, and will survive, for decades to come. Like his brother, he had 'snaffled' a few decorations out of the War: but to be in Command of the Regiment, with Lance in charge of his pet squadron, was better than all.

The strong bond of affection between these two—first

and last of a family of six—was enhanced by their very unlikeness. Lance had the élan of a torrent; Paul the stillness and depth of a mountain lake. Lance was a rapier; Paul a claymore—slow to smite, formidable when roused. Both were natural leaders of men; both, it need hardly be added, 'Piffers'[1] in the grain. They had only returned in March from active service, with the Regiment very much the worse for wear; heartily sorry to be out of the biggest show on record; yet heartily glad to be back in India, a sadly changing India though it was.

Two urgent questions were troubling the mind of Lance as they rode at a foot's pace up the slope leading to the Blue Bungalow. Would the board of doctors, at that moment 'sitting' on Roy, give him another chance? Would the impending reliefs condemn them to a 'down-country' station? For they had only been posted to Kohat till these came out.

To one of those questions Colonel Desmond already knew the answer.

"I had a line from the General this morning," he remarked, after studying his brother's profile and shrewdly gauging his thoughts.

True enough—his start betrayed him. "The General? —Reliefs?"

"Yes." A pause. "We're for—Lahore Cantonments."

"Damn!"

"I've made that inspired remark already. You needn't flatter yourself it's original!"

"I'm not in the mood to flatter myself or any one else. I'm in a towering rage. And if dear old Roy is to be turned down into the bargain——!" Words failed him. He had his father's genius for making friends; and among them all Roy Sinclair reigned supreme.

"I'm afraid he will be if I know anything of medical boards."

"Why the *devil*——?" Lance flashed out. "It's not as if A1 officers were tumbling over each other in the service. If Roy was a Tommy they'd jolly soon think of something better than leave and futile tonics."

[1] Punjab Irregular Frontier Force.

Colonel Desmond smiled at the characteristic outburst.

"Certainly their tinkering isn't up to much. But I'm afraid there's more wrong with Roy than mere doctoring can touch. Still—he doesn't seem keen on going Home."

Lance shook his head. "Naturally—poor old chap. Feels he can't face things, yet. It's not only the delights of Mespot that have knocked him off his centre. It's losing—that jewel of a mother." His eyes darkened with feeling. "You can't wonder. If anything was to happen——" He broke off abruptly.

Paul Desmond set his teeth and was silent. In the deep of his heart, the Regiment had one rival—and Lady Desmond knew it. . . .

They found the bungalow empty. No sign of Roy.

"Getting round 'em," suggested Paul optimistically, and passed on into his dufter.

Lance lit a cigar, flung himself into a verandah chair and picked up the 'Civil and Military.' He had just scanned the war telegrams when Roy came up at a round trot.

Lance sat forward and discarded the paper. An exchange of glances sufficed. Roy's determination to 'bluff the board' had failed.

He looked sallow in spite of sunburn; tired and disheartened; no lurking smile in his eyes. He fondled the velvet nose of his beloved Suráj—a graceful creature, half Arab, half Waler; and absently acknowledged the frantic jubilations of his Irish terrier puppy, christened by Lance the Holy Terror—Terry for short. Then he mounted the steps, subsided into the other chair and dropped his cap and whip on the ground.

"Damn the doctors," said Lance, questions being superfluous.

That so characteristic form of sympathy moved Roy to a rueful smile. "Obstinate devils. I bluffed 'em all I knew. Overdid it, perhaps. Anyway they weren't impressed. They've dispensed with my valuable services. Anæmia, mild neurasthenia, cardiac symptoms —and a few other pusillanimous ailments. Wonder they didn't throw in housemaid's knee! Oh, confound 'em all!" He converted a sigh into a prolonged yawn.

"Let's make merry over a peg, Lance. Doctors are exhausting to argue with. And Cuthers always said I couldn't argue for nuts! Now then—how about pegs?"

"A bit demoralising—at midday," Lance murmured without conviction.

"Well, I *am* demoralised; dead—damned—done for. I'm about to be honoured with a blooming medical certificate to that effect. As a soldier, I'm extinct—from this time forth for evermore. You see before you the wraith of a Might-Have-Been. After *that* gold-medal exhibition of inanity, kindly produce said pegs!"

Lance Desmond listened with a grave smile, and a sharp contraction of heart, to the absurdities of this first-best friend, who for three years had shared with him the high and horrible and ludicrous vicissitudes of war. He knew only too well that trick of talking at random to drown some inner stress. With every word of nonsense he uttered, Roy was implicitly confessing how acutely he felt the blow; and to parade his own bitter disappointment seemed an egotistical superfluity. So he merely remarked with due gravity: "I admit you've made out an overwhelming case for 'said pegs'!" And he shouted his orders accordingly.

They filled their tumblers in silence, avoiding each other's eyes. Every moment emphasised increasingly all that the detested verdict implied. No more polo together. No more sharing of books and jokes and enthusiasms and violent antipathies, to which both were prone. No more 'shoots' in the Hills beyond Kashmir.

From the first of these they had lately returned—sick leave, in Roy's case; and the programme was to be repeated next April, if they could 'wangle' first leave. Each knew the other was thinking of these things. But they seemed entirely occupied in quenching their thirst, and their disappointment, in deep draughts of sizzling ice-cool whisky-and-soda. Moreover—ignominious, but true—when the tumblers were emptied, things did begin to look a shade less blue. It became more possible to discuss plans. And Desmond was feeling distinctly anxious on that score.

"You won't be shunted instanter," he remarked; and Roy smiled at the relief in his tone.

"Next month, I suppose. We must make the most of these few weeks, old man."

"And then—what? . . . Home?"

Roy did not answer at once. He was lying back again, staring out at the respectable imitation of a lawn, at rose beds, carpeted with over-blown mignonette, and a lone untidy tamarisk that flung a spiky shadow on the grass. And the eye of his mind was picturing the loveliest lawn of his acquaintance, with its noble twin beeches and a hammock slung between—an empty casket; the jewel gone. It was picturing the drawing-room; the restful simplicity of its cream and gold: but no dear and lovely figure, in gold-flecked sari, lost in the great arm-chair. Her window-seat in the studio—empty. No one in a 'mother-o'-pearl mood' to come and tuck him up and exchange confidences, the last thing. His father, also invalided out; his left coat sleeve half empty, where the forearm had been removed.

"N—no," he said at last, still staring at the unblinking sunshine. "Not Home. Not yet—anyway."

Then, having confessed, he turned and looked straight into the eyes of his friend—the hazel-grey eyes he had so admired, as a small boy, because of the way they darkened with anger or strong feeling. And he admired them still. "A coward—am I? It's not a flattering conclusion. But I suppose it's the cold truth."

"It hasn't struck *me* that way." Desmond frankly returned his look.

"That's a mercy. But—if one's name happened to be Lance Desmond, one would go—anyhow."

"I doubt it. The place must be simply alive—with memories. We Anglo-Indians, jogged from pillar to post, know precious little about homes like yours. A man—can't judge——"

"You're a generous soul, Lance!" Roy broke out with sudden warmth. "Anyway—coward or no—I simply *can't* face—the ordeal, yet awhile. I believe my father will understand. After all—here I am in India, as planned, before the Great Interruption. So—given the chance, I might as well take it. The dear old place is mostly empty, these days—with Tiny married and Dad's Air Force job pinning him to Town. *So*—as I remarked before——!"

"You'll hang on out here for the present? Thank God for that much."

Desmond's pious gratitude was so fervent that they both burst out laughing; and their laughter cleared the air of ghosts.

"Jaipur it is, I suppose, as planned. Thea will be overjoyed. Whether Jaipur's precisely a health resort——?"

"I'm not after health resorts. I'm after knowledge—and a few other things. Not Jaipur first, anyway. The moment I get the official order of the boot—I'm for Chitor."

"Chitor?" Faint incredulity lurked in Desmond's tone.

"Yes—the casket that enshrines the soul of a race; buried in the wilds of Rajasthan. Ever heard tell of it, you arrant Punjabi? Or does nothing exist for *you* south of Delhi?"

"Just a thing or two—not to mention Thea!"

"Of course—I beg her pardon! *She* would appreciate Chitor."

"Rather. They went there—and Udaipur, last year. She's death on getting Vincent transferred. And the Burra Sahibs are as wax in her hands. If they happen to be musical, and she applies the fiddle, they haven't an earthly——!"

Roy's eyes took on their far-away look.

"It'll be truly uplifting to see her—and hear her fiddle once more, if she's game for an indefinite dose of my society. Anyway, there's my grandfather——"

"Quite superfluous," Desmond interposed a shade too promptly. "If I know Thea, she'll hang on to you for the cold weather; and ensure you a *pied à terre* if you want to prowl round Rajputana and give the bee in your bonnet an airing! You'll be in clover. The Residency's a sort of palace. Not precisely Thea's ideal of bliss. She's a Piffer at heart; and her social talents don't get much scope down there. Only half a dozen whites; and old Vinx buried fathoms deep in ethnology, writing a book. But, being Thea, she has pitched herself head foremost, into it all. Got very keen on Indian women. She's mixed up in some sort of a romance now. A girl who's been educated at home.

It seems an unfailing prescription for trouble. I rather fancy she's a cousin of yours."

Roy started. "What—Arúna?"

"She didn't mention the name. Only ructions—and Thea to the rescue!"

"Poor Arúna!—She stayed in England a goodish time, because of the War—and Dyán. I've not heard of Dyán for an age; and I don't believe they have either. He was knocked out in 1915. Lost his left arm. Said he was going to study art in Calcutta. —I wonder——?" Desmond—who had chiefly been talking to divert the current of his thoughts—noted, with satisfaction, how his simple tactics had taken effect.

"We'll write to-morrow—eh?" said he. "Better still—happy thought!—I'll bear down on Jaipur myself, for Christmas leave. Rare fine pig-sticking in those parts."

The happy thought proved a masterstroke. In the discussion of plans and projects Roy became almost his radiant self again: forgot, for one merciful hour, that he was dead, damned, and done for—the wraith of a 'Might-Have-Been.'

## CHAPTER II.

"Oh, not more subtly silence strays
  Amongst the winds, between the voices . . .
Than thou art present in my days.

My silence, life returns to thee
  In all the pauses of her breath.
And thou, wake ever, wake for me!

—ALICE MEYNELL.

SOME five weeks later, Roy sat alone—very completely and desolately alone—in a whitewashed, unhomely room that everywhere bore the stamp of dák bungalow; from the wobbly teapoy [1] at his elbow to the board of printed rules that adorned the empty mantelpiece. The only cheering thing in the room was the log fire that made companionable noises and danced shadow-dances on the dingy white walls. But the optimism of the fire was discounted by the pessimism of the lamp that seemed specially constructed to produce a minimum of light with a maximum of smell—and rank kerosene at that.

Dák bungalows had seemed good fun in the days of his leave, when he and Lance made merry over their well-worn failings. But it was quite another affair to smoke the pipe of compulsory solitude, on the outskirts of Chitor, hundreds of miles away from Kohat and the Regiment; to feel oneself the only living being in a succession of empty rooms—for the servants were housed in their own little colony apart. Solitude, in the right mood and the right place, was bread and wine to his soul; but acute loneliness of the dák bungalow order was not in the bond. For four years he had felt

[1] Tripod table.

himself part of a huge incarnate purpose; intimately part of his regiment—a closely-knit brotherhood of action. Now, the mere fact of being an unattached human fragment oddly intensified his feeling of isolation. With all his individuality, he was no egoist; and very much a lover of his kind. Imbued with the spirit of the quest, yet averse by temperament to ploughing the lonely furrow.

It had been his own choice—if you could call it so, —starting this way, instead of in the friendly atmosphere of the Jaipur Residency. But was there really such a thing as choice? The fact was, he had simply obeyed an irresistible impulse,—and to-morrow he would be glad of it. To-night, after that interminable journey, his head ached atrociously. He felt limp as a wet dish-clout; his nerves all out of gear . . . Perhaps those confounded doctors were not such fools as they seemed. He cursed himself for a spineless ineffectual—messing about with nerves when he had been lucky enough to come through four years of war with his full complement of limbs and faculties unimpaired. Two slight wounds, a passing collapse, from utter fatigue and misery, soon after his mother's death; a spell of chronic dysentery, during which he had somehow managed to keep more or less fit for duty:—that was his record of physical damage, in a War that had broken its tens of thousands for life.

But there are wounds of the mind; and the healing of them is a slow, complex affair. Roy, with his fastidious sense of beauty, his almost morbid shrinking from inflicted pain, had suffered acutely, where more robust natures scarcely suffered at all. Yet it was the robust that went to pieces—which was one of the many surprises of a War that shattered convictions wholesale, and challenged modern man to the fiercest trial of faith at a moment when Science had almost stripped him bare of belief in anything outside himself.

Roy, happily for him, had not been stripped of belief; and his receptive mind had been ceaselessly occupied registering impressions, to be flung off, later, in prose and verse, that *She* might share them to the full. A slim volume—published, at her wish, in 1916—had attracted no small attention in the critical world. At the time, he had deprecated premature rushings into print; but afterwards it was a blessed thing to remember the joy he had given her that last Christmas—the very last. . . .

On the battlefield, if there had been nerve-shattering moments, these had their counterpart in moments when the spirit of his Rajput ancestors lived again in him, when he knew neither shrinking nor horror nor pity: and in moments of pure pleasure, during some quiet interlude, when larks rained music out of the blue; when he found himself alone with the eerie wonder of dawn over the scarred and riven fields of death; or when he discovered his Oriental genius for scout work that had rapidly earned him distinction and sated his love of adventure to the full.

And always, unfailingly he had obeyed his mother's parting injunction. As a British officer, he had fought for the Empire. As Roy Sinclair—son of Lilámani—he had fought for the sanctities of Home and Beauty—intrinsic beauty of mind and body and soul—against hideousness and licence and the unclean spirit that could defile the altar sanctuaries of God.

And always, when he went into battle, he remembered Chitor. Mentally, he put on the saffron robe, insignia of 'no surrender.' To be taken prisoner was the one fate he could not bring himself to contemplate: yet that very fate had befallen him and Lance, in Mesopotamia—the sequel of a daring and successful raid.

Returning, in the teeth of unexpected difficulties, they had found themselves ambushed, with their handful of men—outnumbered, no loophole for escape.

For three months, that seemed more like years, they had lost all sense of personal liberty—the oxygen of the soul. They had endured misery, semi-starvation, and occasionally other things, such as a man cannot bring himself to speak about or consciously recall: not least, the awful sense of being powerless—and hated. From the beginning, they had kept their minds occupied with ingenious plans for escape, that, at times, seemed like base desertion of their men, whom they could neither help nor save. But when—as by a miracle—the coveted chance came, no power on earth could have stayed them. . . .

It had been a breathless affair, demanding all they possessed of bodily fleetness and suppleness, of cool, yet reckless, courage. And it had been crowned with success; the good news wired home to mothers who waited and prayed. But Roy's nerves had suffered more severely than Desmond's. A sharp attack of fever had completed his prostration. And it was then, in the moment of his passing weakness, that Fate turned and smote him with the sharpest weapon in her armoury. . . .

He had not even heard his mother was ill. He had just received her ecstatic response to his wire—and that very night she came to him, vividly, as he hovered on the confines of sleep.

There she stood by his bed, in her mother-o'-pearl gown and sari; clear in every detail; lips just parted; a hovering smile in her eyes. And round about her a shimmering radiance, as of moonbeams, heightened her loveliness, yet seemed to set her apart; so that he could neither touch her nor utter a word of welcome. He could only gaze and gaze, while his heart beat in long slow hammer-strokes, with a double throb between.

With a gesture of mute yearning her hands went out to him. She stooped low and lower. A faint breeze seemed to flit across his forehead as if her lips, lightly brushing it, had breathed a blessing.

Then, darkness fell abruptly—and a deep sleep. . . .

He woke late next morning: woke to a startling, terrible certainty that his vision had been no dream; that her very self had come to him—that she was gone. . . .

When the bitter truth reached him, he learnt, without surprise, that on the night of his vision, her spirit passed. . . .

It was a sharp attack of pneumonia that gave her the *coup de grâce*. But, in effect, the War had killed her, as it killed many another hyper-sensitive woman, who could not become inured to horror on horror, tragedy on tragedy, whose heart ached for the sorrows of others as if they were her own. And her personal share had sufficiently taxed her endurance, without added pangs for others, unseen and unknown. George—her baby—had gone down in the Queen Mary. Jerry, too early sent out to France, had crashed behind the German lines; and after months of uncertainty they had heard he was alive, wounded—in German hands. Tara, faithful to the Women's Hospital in Serbia, had been constantly in danger, living and moving among unimaginable horrors. Nevil, threatened with septic poisoning, had only been saved at the cost of his left forearm. Not till he was invalided out, near the close of 1916, had he realised—too late—that she was killing herself by inches, with work that alone could leaven anxiety—up to a point.

But it was the shock of Roy's imprisonment and the agony of suspense that finally stretched her nerve to breaking-point; so that the sudden onslaught of pneumonia had slain her in the space of a week. And Roy, knowing her too well, had guessed the truth, in spite of his father's gallant attempt to shield him from it.

His first letter from that bereft father had been little short of a revelation to the son, who had ventured to suppose he knew him: a rash supposition where any human being is concerned. There had been more than one such revelation in the scores of letters that at once uplifted and overwhelmed him, and increased tenfold his pride in being her son. But outshining all, and utterly unexpected, was a letter from herself, written in those last days, when the others still hoped against hope, but she knew——

It had come, with his father's, in a small, gold-embroidered bag—scent and colour and exquisite needlework all eloquent of her: and with it came the other, her talisman since he was born. Reaching him while brain and body still reeled under the bewildering sense of loss, it had soothed his agony of pain and rebellion like the touch of her fingers on his forehead; had taken the sting from death and robbed the grave of victory. . . .

To-night, in his loneliness, he drew the slim bag out of an inner pocket, and re-read with his eyes the words that were imprinted on his memory.

"Roy, son of my heart,—This is good-bye—but not altogether good-bye. Between you and me that word can never be spoken. So I am writing this, in my foolish weakness, to beg of you—by the love between us, too deep for words—not to let heart and courage be *quite* broken because of this big sorrow. You were brave in battle, my Prithvi Raj. Be still more brave for me. Remember I am Lilámani—Jewel of Delight. *That* I have tried to be in my life, for every one of you. That I wish to be always. So I ask you, my darling, not to make me a Jewel of Sorrow because I have passed into the Next Door House too soon. Though not seen, I will never for long be far from you. That is my faith; and you must share it; helping your dear father, because for him the way of belief is hard.

"Never forget those beautiful words of Fouquet in which you made dedication of your poems to me: 'How blessed is the son to whom it is allowed to gladden his mother's heart with the blossom and fruit of his life!' And you will still gladden it, Dilkusha.[1] I will still share your work, though in different fashion than we hoped. Only keep your manhood pure and the windows of your spirit clear, so the Light can shine through. Then you will know if I speak truth, and you will not feel altogether alone.

"Oh, Roy, I could write and write till the pen drops. My heart is too full, but my hand is too feeble for more. Only this, when your time comes for marriage, I pray you will be to your wife all that your splendid father has been for me—king and lover and companion of body and spirit. Draw nearer than ever, you two, because of your so beautiful love for me—unseen now, but with you always. God bless you. I can write no more.

"Your devoted

MOTHER."

The last lines wavered and ran together. In spite of her injunction, tears *would* come. Chill and unheeded, they slipped down his cheeks, while he folded his treasure, and put it away with the other, that went to his head, a little, as she had foreseen; though in the event, it had been overshadowed by her own, than which she could have left him no dearer legacy. In life she had been an angel of God. In death, she was still his angel of

[1] Joy of my Heart.

comfort and healing. She had bidden him share her belief; and he never *had* felt altogether alone. Sustained by that inner conviction, he had somehow adapted himself to the strangeness of a life empty of her physical presence. The human being, in a world of pain, like the insect in a world of danger, lives mainly by that same ceaseless, unconscious miracle of adaptation. Dearly though he craved a sight of his father and Christine, he had not asked for leave home. There were bad moments when he wondered if he could ever bring himself to face the ordeal. He sincerely hoped they understood. Their letters left an impression that it was so. Jeffers obviously did.

And Tara——? Her belated letter, from the wilds of Serbia, had revealed, in every line, that she understood only too well. For Tara, not long before, had passed through her own ordeal—the death, in a brilliant air fight, of her second brother Atholl, her devotee and hero from nursery days. So when Roy's turn came, her fulness of sympathy and understanding were outstretched like wings to shield him, if might be, from the worst, as she had known it.

For that once, she flung aside the veil of grown-up reserves and wrote straight from her eager passionate heart to the Bracelet-bound Brother, unseen for years, yet linked with her by an imperishable memory; and now linked closer still by a mutual grief.

The comfort to Roy of that spontaneous, Tara-like outpouring had been greater than she knew—than he could ever let her know. For the old intimacy had never been quite re-established between them since the day of his tactless juvenile proposal—for so he saw it now. They had only met that once, when he was home for Christmas. On the second occasion, they had missed. Throughout the War they had corresponded fitfully; but her letters, though affectionate and sisterly, lacked an unseizable something that affected the tone of his response. He had been rash enough, once, to presume on their special relation. But he was no longer a boy; and he had his pride.

He wondered sometimes how it would be if they met again. Would he fall in love with her? She was supreme. No one like her. But he knew now—as she had instinctively known then—that his conviction on that score did not amount to being in love. Conviction must be lit and warmed with the fire of passion. And you couldn't very well fall in love across six thousand miles of sea. Certainly none of the girls he had danced with and ridden with since his arrival in India had affected him that way. And for him marriage was an important consideration. Some day he supposed it would confront him as an urgent personal issue. But there was a tremendous lot to be done first; and girls were kittle cattle.

Unsuspected by him, the intimate relation with his mother—while it quickened his need for woman's enveloping tenderness and sympathy—held his heart in leash by setting up a standard, to which the modern girl rarely aspired, much less attained.

And now she was gone, in some strange, enthralling way, she held him still. At rare intervals, she came again to him in dreams; or when he hovered on the verge of sleep. Dreams, or visions—they persisted as clearly in memory as any waking act; and unfailingly left a vivid after-sense of having been in touch with her very self. More and more conviction deepened in him that she still had joy in 'the blossom and fruit of his life'; that even in death she was nearer to him than many living mothers to their sons.

A strange experience: strangest of all, perhaps, the simplicity with which he came to accept it as part of the natural order of things. The intuitive brain is rarely analytical. Moreover, he had seen; he had felt; he knew. It is the invincible argument of the mystic. Against belief born of vivid, reiterate experience, the loquacity of logic, the formulæ of pure intellect break like waves upon a rock—and with as little result. The intensity and persistence of Roy's experience simply left no room for insidious whispers of doubt; nor could he have tolerated such scepticism in others, natural though it might be, if one had not seen, nor felt, nor known.

So he neither wrote nor spoke of it to any one. He could scarce have kept it from Tara, the sister-child who had shared all his thoughts and dreams; but the grown-up Tara had become too remote in every sense for a confidence so intimate, so sacred. To his father he would fain have confided everything, remembering her last command; but Sir Nevil's later letters—though unfailingly sympathetic—were not calculated to evoke filial outpourings. For the time being, he seemed to have shut himself in with his grief. Perhaps he, of all others, had been least able to understand Roy's failure to press for short leave home. He had said very little on the subject. And Roy—with the instinct of sensitive natures to take their tone from others—had also said little: too little, perhaps. Least said may be soonest mended; but there are times when it may widen a rift to a gulf.

In the end, he had felt impelled at least to mention his dream experiences, and let it rest with his father whether he said any more.

And by return mail came a brief but poignant answer: "Thank you, my dearest Boy, for telling me what you did. It is a relief to know you have some sort of comfort—if only in dreams. You are fortunate to be so made. After all, for purposes of comfort and guidance, one's capacity to believe in such communion is the measure of its reality. As for me, I am still utterly, desolately alone. Perhaps some day she will reach me in spite of my little faith. People who resort to mediums and the automatic writing craze are beyond me: though the temptation I understand. You may remember a sentence of Maeterlinck—'We have to grope timidly and make sure of every footstep, as we cross the threshold. And even when the threshold is crossed, where shall certainty be found——? One cannot speak of these things—the solitude is too great.' That is my own feeling about it—at present."

The last had given Roy an impression that his solitude, however desolating, was a sort of sanctuary, not to be shared as yet, even with his son. And, in the face of such loneliness, it seemed almost cruel to enlarge on his own clear sense of intimate communion with her who had been unfailingly their Jewel of Delight.

So, by degrees—in the long months of separation from them all—his ethereal link with her had come to feel closer and more real than his link with those others, still in the flesh, yet strangely remote from his inner life.

To-night—after reading both letters—that sense of nearness seemed stronger than ever. Could it be that the magnetism of India was in the nature of an intimation from her that for the present his work lay here? By the hidden forces that mould men's lives, he had been drawn to the land of heart's desire; and at home, neither his family nor his country seemed to have any particular need of him. Whether or no India had need of him, he assuredly had need of her. And it was the very strength of that feeling which had given him pause.

But now, at last, he knew beyond cavil that, for all his mind—or was it his conscience?—might haver and split straws, he had been drawn to Rajputana, as irresistibly as if that vast desert region were the moon and he a wavelet on the tidal shore.

With a great sigh he rose, yawned cavernously and shivered. Better get to bed and to sleep:—a bed that didn't clank and jolt and batter your brains to a pulp. Things would look amazingly different in the morning.

## CHAPTER III.

"Darkness and solitude shine for me:
For life's fair outward part, are rife
The silver noises: let them be.
It is the very soul of life
Listens for thee, listens for thee."
—ALICE MEYNELL.

THE depressingly bare, whitewashed bedroom owned a French bedstead, with brass rails;—a welcome 'find' in a dák bungalow, especially after three very broken nights in an Indian train. Tired to the point of stupefaction, Roy promised himself he would sleep the clock round; eat a three-decker Anglo-Indian breakfast, and thereafter be his own man again. In that faith he laid his head on the least lumpy portion of the pillow—and in less than five minutes found himself quite intolerably wide awake.

Though the bedstead neither repudiated him, nor took liberties with his person, ghostly clankings and vibrations still jarred his nerves and played devil's tunes in his brain. Though he kept his eyelids severely closed, sleep—the coveted anodyne—seemed to hover on the misty edge of things, always just out of reach. His body was over-tired, his brain abnormally alert. Each change of position, that was to be positively the last, lost its virtue in the space of three minutes, till the sheet—that was too narrow for the mattress—became ruckled into hills and valleys and made things worse than ever. Having started like this, he knew himself capable of keeping it up gaily till the small hours; and to-night, of all nights——!

Even through his closed eyelids, he was still aware that his verandah doorway framed a wide panel of moonlight—the almost incredible moonlight of India.

He had flung it open as usual and rolled up the chick. A bedroom hermetically sealed made him feel suffocated, imprisoned; so he must, perforce, put up with the moon; and when the world was drowned in her radiance, sleep seemed almost a sin. But to-night, moon or no, he craved sleep as an opium-eater craves his magic pellets,—because he wanted to dream. It was many weeks since he last had sight of his mother. But surely she must be near him in his loneliness; aware, in some mysterious fashion, of the deep longing with which he longed for sight or sense of her, to assure him that—in spite of qualms and indecisions—he had chosen aright. Conviction grew that directly the veil of sleep fell he would see her. It magnified his insomnia from mere discomfort to a baffling inimical presence withholding him from her:—till utter weariness blotted out everything; and even as he hovered on the verge of sleep, she was there. . . .

She was lying in her hammock under the beeches, in her apple-blossom sari, sunlight flickering through the leaves. And he saw his own figure moving towards her, without the least surprise, that he could see and hear himself as another being, while still remaining inside himself.

He heard his own voice say, low and fervently, "Beloved little Mother—I am here. Always in the battle I remembered Chitor. Now—turned out of the battle—I have come to Chitor."

Then he was on his knees beside her; and her fingers, light as thistledown, strayed over his hair, in the ghost of a caress that so unfailingly stilled his excitable spirit. Without actual words, by some miracle of interpenetration, she seemed to know all that was in his heart—the perplexities and indecisions; the magnetism of Home and the dread of it; the difficulty of making things clear to his father. And the magic of her touch charmed away all inner confusions, all headache and heartache. But when he rose impulsively, and would have taken her in his arms—she was gone; everything was gone; . . . the hammock, the beeches, the sunbeams. . . .

He was standing alone on a moonlit plain, blotched and streaked with shadows of dák-jungle and date-palm; and rising out of it abruptly—as he had seen it last night—loomed the black bulk of Chitor; the sacred, solitary ghost of a city, linked with his happiest days of childhood and his mother's heroic tales. The great rock was scarped and bastioned, every line of it. The walls, ruined in parts, showed ghostly shades of ruins beyond; and soaring high above all, Khumba Rána's nine-storied Tower of Victory lifted a giant finger to the unheeding heavens. Watching it, fascinated, trying in vain to make out details, he was startlingly beset by the strangest among many strange sensations that had visited his imaginative brain: nothing less than a revival of the long-ago dream-feeling, the strange sense of familiarity—he knew! Beyond all cavil, he knew every line of that looming shadow, every curve of the hills. He knew the exact position of the old bridge over the Gamberi river. From the spot where he stood, he could find his way unerringly to the Padal Pol—the fortified entrance to the road of Seven Gates;—the road that had witnessed, three times in three hundred years, that heroic alternative to surrender, the terrible rite of Johur:—the final down-rush of every male defender, wearing the saffron robe and coronet of him who embraces death as a bride; the awful slaughter at the lowest gate, where they fell, every man of them, before the victors entered in. . . .

The horror and savage exaltation of it all stirred, so sensibly, in his veins that he caught himself dimly wondering—was it he, Roy Sinclair, who stood there remembering these things—or another . . . ?

And before that crazy question could resolve itself—behold he was lying wide awake again in his ruckled bed, on the lumpy pillow, staring at the wide patch of moonlight framed by his open door.

Not morning *yet*, confound it all! But the tiredness and loneliness were clean gone. It was always so when she came to him thus. Tacitly, he knew it, and she knew it, for a visitation. There was no delusion of having got her back again; only the comforting assurance that she was near him still. There was also, on this occasion, a consuming curiosity and impatience not to be denied.

Switching on his electric torch, he consulted his watch. Nearly half-past four—why not . . . ? It was no distance to the lower gate, and only a mile of zigzag road up to the city.

Thought and action were almost simultaneous. He was out of bed, standing in the doorway. The moon's unclouded brilliance seemed to flood his brain; to clear it of cobwebs and dispel all desire of sleep. For he loved the veiled spirit of night as most men love the unveiled face of morning; and in no way, perhaps, was he more clearly of the East. In a land where the sun slays his thousands, the moon comes triumphantly to her own: and Roy decided, there and then, that in the glamour of her light he would take his first look at Chitor. Whether or no it really was his first look, he might possibly find out when he got there.

His train-basket provided him with a hurried cup of tea, biscuits and a providential hard-boiled egg. He had no qualms about rousing Bishun Singh to saddle Suráj, or disturbing the soldiery quartered at the gates. His grandfather had written of him to the Maharana of Udaipur—a cousin in the third degree: and he had leave to go in and out, during his stay, at what hour he pleased. He would remain on the rock till dawn; and from the ninth storey of Khumba Rána's Tower he would see the sun rise over Chitor. . . .

Half an hour later, he was in the saddle trotting along the empty road; Terry, a scurrying shadow in his wake; Bishun Singh left to finish his night's rest. Right before him loomed the magnet that had dragged him out of bed at this unearthly hour—the great rock-fortress, three miles long, less than a mile broad, aptly likened to a battleship ploughing through the disturbed sea of bush-grown hills at its base.

Riding quickly through new Chitor—a dirty little town, fast asleep—he reached the fortified gateway: was challenged by sleepy soldiery; gave his name and passed on—into another world; a world that grew increasingly familiar with every hundred yards of ascent.

At one point he halted abreast of two rough monuments, graves of the valiant pair who had fought and died, like Rajputs, in that last terrible onslaught when the hosts of Akbar entered in, over the bodies of eight thousand saffron-robed warriors, and made Chitor a place of desolation for ever. One—a mere boy of sixteen—was the only son of his house. Beside him, lance in hand, fought his widowed mother and girl wife; and in death they were not divided. The other, Jaimul of Bednore, was a far-away ancestor of his own mother. How often she had told him the tale—adding proudly that, while Rajasthan endured, the names of those two would shine clear in the firmament of time, as stars in the firmament of space.

Through gateway after gateway—under the lee of a twenty-foot wall, pierced for musketry,—he passed, a silent shadow. And gradually there stole over him afresh the confused wonder of his dream,—was it he himself who rode—or was it—that other, returning to the sacred city after long absence? For the moment he could hardly tell. But—what matter? The astonishing thrill of recognition was all. . . .

Round about the seventh gateway clustered the semblance of a village; shrouded, slumbering forms strewn around in the open;—ghosts all. The only instant realities were himself and Surâj and Chitor, and the silence of the sleeping earth, watched over by unsleeping stars. Within, and about him, hovered a stirring consciousness of ancient, unchanging India; utterly impervious to mere birds of passage from the West; veiled, elusive, yet almost hideously real. So real, just then, to Roy, that—for a few amazing moments—he was unaware that he rode through a city forsaken by man. Ghosts of houses and temples slid by on either side of him, as he spurred Surâj to a canter and made unerringly for the main palace. There was news for the Rana—news of Akbar's army—that did not brook delay. . . .

Not till Surâj stopped dead—there where the Palace had once stood in its glory—did he come to himself, as abruptly as when he waked in the French bedstead an hour ago.

Gone was the populous city through which he had ridden in fancy; gone the confusion of himself with that other self—how many centuries old? But the familiar look of the palace was no dream; nor the fact that he had instinctively made his way there at full speed. Bastioned and sharply domed, it stood before him in clear outline; but within sides it was hollow as a skull;

a place of ghosts. Suddenly there came over him the old childish dread of dark, that he had never quite outgrown. But dread or no, explore it he must. . . .

As his foot touched earth, a low hiss warned him he was trespassing, and clutching Terry's collar, he stood rigid, while the whip-like shadow of death writhed across a strip of moonlight—and disappeared. There was life,—of a sort, in Chitor. So Roy trod warily as he passed from room to room; dread of dark forgotten in the weird fascination of foreknowledge verified without fail.

Through riven walls and roofs, moonlight streamed: its spectral brightness intensifying every patch or streak of shadow. And there, where Kings and Princes had held audience—watched by their womenfolk through fretted screens—was neither roof nor walls; only a group of marble pillars, as it were assembled in ghostly conference. The stark silence and emptiness—not of yesterday, but of centuries—smote him with a personal pang. From end to end of the rock it brooded; a haunting presence,—tutelary goddess of Chitor. There is an emptiness of the open desert, of an untrodden snowfield that lifts the soul and sets it face to face with God; but the emptiness of a city forsaken is that of a body with the spark of life extinct:—'the silver cord loosed, the golden bowl broken, and the pitcher broken at the fountain . . .'

Terry's sharp bark, a squawk and a scuffle of wings, made him start violently and jarred him all through. It seemed almost profane—as if one were in a cathedral. Calling the marauder to heel, he mounted and rode on toward the Tower of Victory. For the moon was dipping westward; and he must see that vast view bathed in moonlight. Then the dawn. . . .

Once more deserting Suráj he confronted Khumba's Tower; scatheless as the builder's hand left it four centuries ago. Massive and arrogant, it loomed above him; scarcely a foot of stone uncarven, so far as he could see—exploring the four-square base of it with the aid of the moon and his torch. Figures, in high relief, everywhere—animal, human and divine; a riot of impossible forms, impossibly intertwined; ghoulish in any aspect, and in moonlight hideously so:—bewildering, repellent, frankly obscene. But even while his cultured eye rejected it all, some infinitesimal fragment of himself knew there was symbolic meaning in that orgy of sculpture, could one but find the key.

Up and up, round and round the inner spiral staircase he climbed, in a creepsome darkness, invaded by moonbeams, hardly less creepsome, admitted through window-like openings set in every face of every storey. With each inrush of light, each flash of his torch, in deepest darkness, those thronging figures, weirdly distorted, sprang at him afresh, sending ignominious trickles down his spine. Walls, window slabs, door beams—the vast building was encrusted with them from base to summit; a nightmare of prancing, writhing, gesticulating unrest; only one still face repeated at intervals—the Great God holding the wheel of Law. . . .

Never had Roy more keenly appreciated the company of Terry, who, in spite of a Celtic pedigree, was not enjoying this prolonged practical joke.

It was relief unspeakable to emerge at last, into full light and clean sweet morning air. For the ninth storey, under the dome, was arcaded on all four sides and refreshingly innocent of decoration. Not a posturing figure to be seen. Nothing but restful slabs of polished stone. There was meaning in this also—could one catch the trend of the builder's thought.

On a slab near an arcaded opening Roy sat gratefully down; while Terry, bored to extinction with the whole affair, curled himself up in a shadowed corner and went fast asleep. "Unfriendly little beast," thought Roy; and promptly forgot his existence.

For below him, in the silvery moonlight of morning, lay Chitor; her shattered arches and battlements, her temples and palaces dwarfed to mere footstools for the gods. And beyond, and again beyond, lay the naked strength and desolation of northern Rajputana—white with poppy-fields, velvet-dark with scrub, jagged with outcrops of volcanic rock; the gaunt warrior country, battered by centuries of struggle and slaughter; making calamity a whetstone for courage; saying, in effect, to friend and enemy, 'Take me or leave me. You cannot change me.'

The Border had fascinated Roy. The Himalayas had

subjugated him. But this strong unlovely region of rock and sand, of horses and swords, of chivalry and cruelty and daring, irresistibly laid siege to his heart; gave him the authentic sense of being one with it all.

On a day, in that summer of blessed memory, his mother had almost promised him that, once again she would revisit India if only for the joy of making a pilgrimage with him to Chitor. And here he sat on the summit of Khumba Rána's Tower—alone. That was the way of life. . . .

Gradually there stole over him a great weariness of body and spirit; pure reaction from the uplift of his strange adventure. His lids drooped heavily. In another moment he would have fallen sound asleep; but he saved himself, just in time. When he craved the thing, it eluded him; now, undesired, it assailed him. But it would never do. He might sleep for hours. And at the back of his mind lurked a clear conviction that he was waiting for more than the dawn. . . .

To shake off drowsiness he rose, stretched himself, paced to and fro several times—and did not sit down again. Folding his arms, he leaned his shoulders against the stone embrasure; and stood so, a long while, absorbing—with every faculty of flesh and spirit—the stillness, the mystery, the pearl-grey light and bottomless gulfs of shadow; his mind emptied of articulate thought . . . his soul poised motionless, as it were a bird on outspread wings. . . .

Was it fantasy, this gradual intensifying of his uplifted mood, this breathless stir in the region of his heart, till some vital part of him seemed gradually withdrawn—up into the vastness and the silence . . .?

And suddenly, in every nerve, he knew—he was not alone. In the seeming emptiness of the place, something, some one hovered near him. Amazed, yet exultant, he held his breath; and an answering leap of the heart set him tingling from head to foot.

It was more than a vague 'sense of presence.' Fused in the central happiness that flooded him—as the moonlight flooded the desert—was an almost startling awareness; not the mere emotional effect of music or a poem; but sure knowledge that she was there with him in that upper room; her disembodied tenderness yearning towards him across a barrier of empty space that neither she nor he could traverse, for all their nearness, for all their longing. . . .

If Lance himself had come audibly up those endless stairs and stood beside him, he could not have felt more certain of his presence than he felt, at this moment, of her companionship, her unspoken assurance that he *had* chosen aright. He felt himself, if possible, the less real of the two.

For that brief space, his world seemed empty of everything, every one, but they two—so irrevocably sundered, so mysteriously united.

Could he only have sight of her to complete the marvel of it! But although he kept his eyes on the spot whence the 'feel of her' seemed to come, not the shadow of a shade could he see; only—was it fancy?—a hint of brighter radiance than mere moonbeams—there, near the opposite archway?

He dared not move a finger lest he break the spell. Yet he could not restrain altogether the emotion that surged in him, that filled his ears with a soft roar as of breaking waves.

"God bless you, little Mother!" he murmured, barely above his breath—and waited; expecting he knew not what.

A ghost of a breeze passed close to him;—truly a ghost, for the night was dead still. Almost he could have sworn that if he put out a hand he would have touched her. But reverence withheld him, rather than fear.

And the next moment, the place was empty. He was alone. . . .

He felt the emptiness as unmistakably as he had felt her presence. But the pang of her going was shot through with elation that at last his waking brain had knowledge of her—a knowledge that no man could wrest from him, even if she never so came again. He had done her bidding. He had kept his manhood pure and the windows of his soul clear—and, behold, the Light *had* shone through. . . .

Impossible to tell how long he stood there. In those few moments of intensified life, time was not. The ordinary sense of his surroundings faded. The inner sense of reality quickened in like measure; the reality of her presence, all the more felt, because it was unseen. . . .

When he came clearly to himself again, the moon had vanished. Eastward, the sky was full of primrose light. It deepened and blazed; till, all in a moment, the sun leaped from the scabbard of the hills, keen and radiant as a drawn sword.

A full minute Roy stood there, eyes and brain blinded with brilliance. Then he knelt down and covered his face; and so remained, a long while, his whole being uplifted in a wordless ecstasy of thanksgiving.

# CHAPTER IV.

> "The snow upon my life-bloom sits
> And sheds a dreary blight;—
> Thy spirit o'er my spirit flits,
> And crimson comes for white."
>
> —ANON.

ON an unclouded afternoon of October, Roy sat alone with Thea Leigh in a shady corner of the Residency garden, smoking and talking, feeling blissfully at ease in body, and very much at home in spirit. After the wrench of parting with Desmond, it was balm to be welcomed by the sister who shared his high courage and enthusiasm for life, and who was smiling at Roy now with the same hazel-grey eyes that both had gotten from their father. But Thea's hair—her crown of glory—belonged exclusively to herself. The colour of it reminded him, with a pang, of autumn beech leaves, in his own woods. It enhanced the vivid quality of her beauty, and added appreciably to his pleasure in watching her while she talked.

Roy had arrived that morning, in the mist-laden chill of dawn; had enjoyed a long talk with Colonel Leigh; had made the acquaintance of Vernon and Phyllis, aged six and four; also of Flossie Eden, a kind of adopted daughter, aged twenty; and, tiffin being over, had announced his intention of riding out to re-discover the rose-red wonderland of his childish dreams—the peacocks and elephants and crocodiles and temple bells. Thea, however, had counselled patience, threatening him with dire disillusion, if he went seeking his wonderland at that glaringly unpoetic time of day.

"An early cup of tea, and a ride afterwards," she prescribed, in her best autocratic manner. "Only sunset, or the first glimmer of dawn, can throw a spell over the municipal virtues and artistic backslidings of Jaipur! I speak with feeling; because *I* rushed forth untimely; and, in the full glare of afternoon sunshine, your rose-red city looked like nothing on earth but a fearful and wonderful collection of pink and white birthday cakes, set out for a giants' tea-party! It seemed almost a pity the giants had never come and eaten them up. Vinx said I was ribald. As a matter of fact, he was simply jealous of my brilliant metaphor! Look at him now—bored to death with me, because I'm telling the truth!"

Colonel Leigh—a tall pensive-looking man, who talked little and listened assiduously—met her challenge with the indulgent smile of a husband who can be at once amused and critical and devoted: an excellent conjunction in marriage.

"If you can stay Roy's impatience with your metaphors, I'll begin to have some respect for them!" said he.

And she was staying Roy's impatience now, with cigarettes and coffee and the tale of Arúna—'England-returned.' She had revealed little by letter; an uncharacteristic touch of caution derived from her husband, who questioned the wisdom of her bold incursion into the complexities and jarring elements of a semi-modern Hindu household. But Thea Leigh, daughter of Honor Desmond, was strongly imbued with the responsibility of the ruling race. She stoutly refused to preserve, in Jaipur, the correct official detachment of Anglo-India. More: she possessed a racial wisdom of the heart, not to be gainsaid; as who should know better than her husband, since it had saved him from himself. And now, having secured Roy for half an hour, she confided to him, unreservedly, all she could gather of the tragic tangle she was unravelling in her own effective fashion.

"Arúna's the dearest thing," she told him—as well he knew. "And I'm truly fond of her. But sometimes I feel helpless. They're so hard to come at—these gentle, inscrutable Hindu women. Talk of English reserve! However, I'm getting quite nimble at guessing and inferring; and I gather that your splendid old grandfather is rather pathetically helpless with that hive of hidden womenfolk and gurus. Also that the old lady—Mátaji—is a bit of a tartar. Of course, having lost caste, makes the poor child's home position almost impossible. Yet she flatly refuses to go through their horrid rites of restitution. And Miss Hammond—our lady doctor at the hospital—backs her up."

"Well played, Miss Hammond!" quoth Roy; and remembering Arúna's cheerful letters (no word of complications), all his sympathy went out to her. Might not he—related, yet free of grandmotherly tyranny—somehow be able to help? Too cruel that from her happy time in England there should spring such tragic issues. And she was not a creature made for tragedy, but for laughter and love and 'man's delight.' Yet, in the Hindu nature of things, this very matter of marriage was the crux of her troubles.

To the Power behind the curtain it spelt disgrace, that the eldest grand-daughter—at the ripe age of twenty-two—should be neither wife nor mother. It would need a very advanced suitor to overlook that damning item. Doubtless a large dowry would be demanded by way of compensation; and, before all, caste must be restored. While Arúna remained obdurate, nothing could be definitely arranged; and her grandfather had not the heart to enforce his wife's insistent demands. But if the Indian woman's horizon be limited, her shrewdness and intuitive knowledge are often amazing; and this formidable old lady—skilled in the art of imposing her will on others—knew herself a match for her husband's evasions and Arúna's flat rebellion.

She reckoned, however, without the daughter of Sir Theo Desmond, who, at this point, took action—sudden and disconcerting.

"You see the child came regularly to my purdah parties," she explained to Roy, who was impatient no longer, only absorbed. "Sometimes I had her alone for reading and music; and it was heart-breaking to see her wilting away before my eyes. So, at last, in desperation, I broke loose—as Vinx politely puts it—and asked searching questions, regardless of etiquette. After all, the poor lamb has no mother. And I never disobey an impulse of the heart. I believe I was only in the *nick* of time. It seemed the old tartar and her widowed sister-in-law were in touch with a possible husband. So they had given the screw a fresh turn, assisted by the family *guru*. He had just honoured them with a special visit, expecting to find the lost sheep regenerate and eager for his blessing. Shocked at the tale of her obstinacy, he announced that, unless he heard otherwise within a week, he would put a nameless curse upon her; in which case her honourable grandmother would not allow the poor child to eat or sleep under her honourable roof."

Roy's hand closed sharply on the arm of his chair. "Confound the fellow! It's chiefly the mental effect they rely on. They're no fools; and even men like Grandfather—who can't possibly believe such rot—seem powerless to stand up against them. Does *he* know all this?"

"It's hard to tell. They're so guarded—even the most enlightened—in alluding to domestic matters. Without a shade of discourtesy, they simply keep one outside. Poor Arúna was terrified at having told me. Broke down utterly. But no idea of giving in. It's astonishing the grit one comes upon under their surface gentleness. She said she would starve or drown rather. *I* said she should do nothing of the kind; that I would speak to Sir Lakshman myself—oh, very diplomatically, of course! Afterwards, all in a rush, came my inspiration. Some sort of secretarial work for me would sound fairly plausible. (Did you know—I'm making a name, in a small way, over my zeal for Indian women?) On the strength of that, one could suggest a couple of rooms in the Residency; and she could still keep on at the hospital with Miss Hammond, giving me certain afternoons. It struck me as flawless—*till* I imparted it to Vinx and saw him tweak his left eyebrow. Of course he was convinced it 'wouldn't do'; Sir Lakshman . . . my position . . . and so on. I said I proposed to make it do—and the eyebrow twitched worse than ever. So I mildly reminded him that *he* had not held Arúna sobbing in his arms, and he didn't happen to be a mother! Which was unanswerable.—And, my dear Roy, I had a hectic week of it, manipulating Sir Lakshman and Arúna *and* the honourable grandmother—strictly unseen! I'm sure she's anti-English. I've got at all the other high-borns ; but I can't get at her. However—with a bold front and a tactful tongue, I carried the day. So I hope the holy man will transfer his potent curse to me. Naturally, the moment I'd fixed things up, came Lance's letter about you. But I couldn't back out. And I suppose it's all right ? "

"Well, of course." Roy was troubled with no doubts on that score. "What a family you are ! I was hoping to pick up threads with Arúna."

"You shall. But you must be discreet. Jaipur isn't exactly Oxford. Brother and cousin are almost the same word with them ; but still——"

"Is she at the hospital now ? " Roy cut in irrelevantly. Her insistence on discretion—with Arúna, of all people—struck him as needless fussing and unlike Thea. And by now he was feeling more impatient to see Arúna than to see Jaipur.

"No. But she seemed shy of appearing at tiffin. So I said if she came out here afterwards, she would find you and me alone. She's looked happier and less fragile lately. Even Vinx admits the event has justified me. But of course it's simply an emergency plan—a transition——"

"To *what ?* " Roy challenged her with surprising emphasis.

"That's my puzzle of puzzles. Perhaps you can help me solve it. Sometimes I wonder if she knows herself, what she wants out of life . . . But perhaps I haven't the key to her waverings . . ."

At that moment, a slight unmistakable figure stepped from the shadow of the verandah down the shallow steps flanked with pots of begonia ; moving with the effortless grace that Roy's heart knew too well. Dress and sari were carnation pink. Her golden shoes glittered at every step : and she pensively twirled a square Japanese parasol—almond blossoms and butterflies scattered abroad on silk of the frailest blue.

"*Is* their instinct for that sort of thing unconscious, I wonder ? " murmured Thea. "You shall have half an hour with her, to pick up threads. Help me if you can, Roy. But—*be discreet !* "

Roy scarcely heard her. He had gone suddenly very still—his gaze riveted on Arúna. The Indian dress, the carriage of her veiled head, the leisured grace, so sharply smote him that tears pricked his eyelids; and, for one intoxicating moment he was wafted, in spirit, across the chasm of the War to that dear dream-world of youth, when all distances were blue and all the near prospect bright with the dew of the morning. Only under a mask-like stillness could he hide that startling uprush of emotion; and had Broome been watching him, he would have seen the subtle film of the East steal over his face.

Thea saw only his sudden abstraction and the whitened knuckles of his left hand. She also realised, with a faint prick of anxiety, that he had simply not heard her remark. Was it possible—could Roy be at the back of Arúna's waverings? Would his coming mean fresh complications? Too distracting to be responsible for anything of that kind. . . .

Without a word, he had risen—and went quickly forward to meet her. Thea saw how, on his approach, all her studied composure fell away; and both, when they joined her, looked so happy, yet so plainly discomposed, that Thea felt ridiculously at a loss for just the right word with which to effect a casual retreat. Responsibility for Sir Lakshman's grand-daughter was no light matter: at least she had done well in warning Roy. These emerging Indian girls . . . !

It was a positive relief to see the prosaic figure of Floss Eden, in brief tennis skirts and shady hat, hurrying across the lawn, with her boyish stride; racquet swinging, her round face flushed with exercise.

"I say, Aunt Thea—you're wanted *jut put*," [1] she announced briskly. "Verney's in one of his moods—and Mr Neill will soon be in one of his tempers, if he isn't forcibly removed. Instead of helping with the balls, he's been parading up and down the verandah; two tin pails, tied on to him with string, clattering behind—making a beast of a row. Shouting wasn't any earthly. So I rushed in and grabbed him. 'Verney—drop it! What *are* you doing?' I said sternly; and he looked up at me like a sainted cherub. 'Flop, don't hinder me. I'm walkin' froo the valley of the shadow, an' goodness

[1] Instantly.

an' mercy are following me *all* the days of my life.' That's the fruits of teaching the Bible to innocents!"

Thea's laugh ended in a sigh. "I warned Miss Mills. But the creature *is* getting out of hand. I suppose it means he ought to go home. Mr Neill," she explained to Roy, "is Vinx's shorthand secretary: volcanic, but indispensable to the Great Work! So I must fly off and obliterate my superfluous son."

Her eyes tried to impart the warning he had not heard. Useless. His attention was centred on Arúna.

"Wonderful—isn't she?" the girl murmured, looking after her. Then swiftly, half-shyly, she glanced up at him. "Still more wonderful that, at last, you have come, that I am here too—only through her. She—told you?"

"Yes. A little. I want to hear more."

"Presently. I would rather push away sad things—now you are here. If there was only Dyán too—like Oxford days. And—oh, Roy, I was bad never writing . . . about her. I did try. But so difficult . . . And—you knew——?"

"Yes—I knew," he said in a repressed voice. On that subject he could not trust himself just yet. Every curve and fold of her sari, and the half-seen coils of her dark hair, every movement, every quaint turn of phrase, set his nerves vibrating with an ecstasy that was pain. For the moment, he wanted simply to be aware of her; to hug the dear illusion that the years between were a dream. And illusion was heightened by the trivial fact that her appearance was identical in every detail. Was it chance? Or had she treasured them all this time? Only she herself looked older. Though her face kept its pansy aspect, her cheek-bones were a shade too prominent; no veiled glow of health under her dusky skin. But her smile could still atone for all shortcomings.

"Let's sit down," he added after a strained silence. "And tell me—what's come to Dyán?"

She shook her head. "Oh—if we could *know*. Not much use, after all, trying to push away sadness!" She sank into her chair and looked up at him. "The more you push it away, the more it comes flowing in from everywhere. Everything so broken and confused from this terrible War. At the beginning how they said all would be made new; East and West firmly united. But here, at home, while the best were fighting, the worst were too busy with ugly whispers and untrue talk. Even holy men, behind the purdah . . ."

"As bad as that, is it?" asked Roy, distracted from his own sensations by the subject that lay nearest his heart. "And you think Dyán's in with that crew?"

"Yes, we are afraid . . . A pity he came back from France too soon, because half his left arm must be cut off. Then—you heard—he went to Calcutta?"

"Yes, I wrote at the time. He didn't answer. I haven't heard since."

She nodded. Sudden tears filled her eyes. "Always now . . . no answer. Like trying to speak with some one dead. So Grandfather fears he was not only studying art. You know how he is too quick to catch fire. And too easily, he might believe those men who spin words like spider's webs. Also he was very sore losing his arm, by some small stupid chance; and there was bitterness for that trouble . . . of Tara . . ."

Roy started. "Lord—was it *Tara?*" Instantly there flashed a vision of the walled lane leading to New College; Dyán's embittered mood and bewildering change of front . . . Looking back now, the thing seemed glaringly obvious; but, through the opalescent mist of his own dreams, he had seen Dyán in one relation only. Just as well perhaps. Even at this distance, the idea amazed and angered him. Tara! The arrogance of it . . .!

"You didn't know—never thought? . . . Poor Dyán!" One finger-tip furtively intercepted a tear that was stealing down the side of her nose.

"I am *too* silly just now," she apologised meekly. "To me, he only spoke of it long after, when coming wounded from France. Then I saw how the bitterness was still there, changing the noble thoughts of his heart. That is the trouble with Dyán. First—nothing good enough for England. But too fierce love may bring too fierce hate—if they poison his mind with cunning words dressed up in high talk of religion——"

"How long since you heard? Have you any address?" Roy dared not encourage her melting mood.

"Six months now." She stoically blinked back her tears. "Not any word. Not any address, since he left Calcutta. Last week, I wrote, addressing to the office of a paper there, because once he said that editor gave him work. I told him all the pain in my heart. If that letter finds him—some answer *must* come."

"Well, if it does, I promise you this much;—I'll unearth him—somehow, wherever he is——"

"Oh, Roy! I hoped—I knew——!" She clasped her hands to hide their tremor, and the look in her eyes came perilously near adoration.

Roy had spoken with the cool assurance of his father's race, and without a glimmering idea how his rash promise was going to be fulfilled. "I'll do my level utmost, anyhow," he added more soberly. "But there's you—your home complications——"

She turned her hands outward with the expressive gesture of her race. "That foolish sadness we *can* push away. What matter for anything—now? I rest—I breathe—I am here——!" Her smile shone out, sudden and brilliant. "Almost like England—this big green garden and children and sound of playing tennis. Let us be young again. Let us, for a small time, not remember that all outside is Jaipur and the desert—dusty and hot and cruel; and dark places full of secret and terrible things. Here we are safe. Here it is almost England!"

Her gallant appeal so moved him, and the lighter vein so charmingly became her, that Roy humoured her mood willingly enough. . . .

When his tea arrived, she played hostess with an alluring mixture of shyness and happy importance, capping his lively sallies with the quick wit of old days. And when Suráj was announced—"Oh, please—may I see him?" she begged eagerly as a child.

Suráj graciously permitted his velvet nose to be stroked by alien fingers, light as rose petals. Then Roy sprang into the saddle; and Arúna stood watching him as he went—*sais* and dog trotting to heel—a graceful lonely figure, shadowed by her semi-transparent parasol.

At a bend in the drive, where a sentry sprang to attention, he turned for a parting salute. Her answering gesture might or might not have been intended for him. She at least knew all about the need for being discreet. For, on leaving the tea-table, they had passed from the dream of 'almost England' into the dusty actuality of Jaipur.

# CHAPTER V.

"Broadly speaking, there are two blocks of people—East and West; people who interfere and people who don't interfere; . . . East is a fatalist, West is an idealist, of a clumsy sort."—STACY AUMONIER.

A MILE, or less, of tree-bordered road sloped gently from the Residency gate-posts to the walled City of Victory, backed by craggy, red-grey spurs of the Aravalli range, hidden almost in feathery heads of banyan, acacia, and neem—a dusty, well-ordered oasis, holding its own against the stealthy oncoming of the desert.

North and east ran the screen of low hills with their creeping lines of masonry; but from south and west the softly encroaching thing crept up to the city walls, in through the gates, powdering every twig and leaf and lattice with the fine white dust of death. Shadeless and colourless, to the limit of vision, it rose and fell in long billowing waves; as if some wizard, in the morning of the world, had smitten a living ocean to lifeless sand, where nothing flourished but the camel thorn and the *ak* plant and gaunt cactus bushes—their limbs petrified in weird gesticulation.

But on the road itself was a sufficiency of life and colour—parrokeets flashing from tree to tree, like emeralds made visible and vocable; village women swathed in red and yellow veils; prancing Rajput cavaliers, straight from the Middle Ages; ox-carts and camels—unlimited camels, with flapping lip and scornful eye; a sluggish stream of life, rising out of the landscape and flowing, from dawn to dusk, through the seven Gates of Jaipur. And there, on the low spurs, beyond the walls, he sighted the famous Tiger Fort, and the marble tomb of Jai Sing—he that built the rose-red City; challenging the desert, as Canute the sea; saying, in terms of stone and mortar, 'Here shall thy proud waves be stayed!' Nearing the fortified gateway, Roy noted how every inch of flat surface was silkily powdered, every opening silted with sand. Would it rest with desert or city, he wondered, the ultimate victory of the last word . . . ?

Close against the ramparts, sand and dust were blown into a deep drift; or was it a deserted pile of rags——? Suddenly, with a sick sensation, he saw the rags heave and stir. Arms emerged—if you could call them arms—belonging to pinched, shadowy faces. And from that human dust-heap came a quavering wail, "Maharáj! Maharáj!"

"What *is* it, Bishun Singh?" he asked sharply of the *sais*, trotting at his stirrup.

"Only the famine, Hazúr. Not a big trouble this year, they say. But from the villages these come crawling to the city, believing the Maharáj has plenty, and will give."

"Does he give?"

Bishun Singh's gesture seemed to deprecate undue curiosity. "The Maharáj is great, but the people are like flies. If their Karma is good, they find a few handfuls; if evil—they die."

Roy said no more. That simple statement was conclusive as a dropped stone. But, on reaching the gateway, he scattered a handful of loose coins.

Instantly a cry went up: "He gives money for food! *Jai déa Maharáj!*"[1] Not merely arms, but entire skeletons emerged, seething, scrambling, with hands wasted to mere claws. A few of the boldest caught at Roy's stirrup; whereat Bishun Singh brushed them off, as if they were flies indeed.

Unresisting, they tottered and fell one against another, like ninepins: and Roy, hating the man, turned sharply away. But rebuke was futile. One could *do* nothing. It was that which galled him. One could only pass on; mentally brushing them aside—like Bishun Singh.

Spectres vanished, however, once he and Suráj were absorbed into the human kaleidoscope of the vast main

[1] Victory to thee, Maharáj!

street, paved with wide strips of hewn stone; one half of it sun-flooded; one half in shadow. The colour and movement; the vista of pink-washed houses speckled with white florets; the gay muslins, the small turbans and inimitable swagger of the Rajput—Sun-descended, re-awakened in him those gleams of ancestral memory that had so vividly beset him at Chitor. Sights and sounds and smells—the pungent mingling of spices and dust and animals—assailed his senses with a vague yet poignant familiarity: fruit and corn-shops with their pyramids of yellow and red and ochre, and the fat brown bunnia in the midst; shops bright with brass-work and Jaipur enamel; lattice windows, low-browed arches, glimpses into shadowed courts; flitting figures of veiled women; humbler women, unveiled, winnowing grain, or crowned with baskets of sacred cow-dung, stepping like queens. . . .

And the animals——! Extinct, almost, in modern machine-ridden cities, here they visibly and audibly prevailed. For Asia lives intimately—if not always mercifully—with her animals; and Roy's catholic affection embraced them all. Horses first—a long way first. But bullocks had their charm: the graceful trotting zebus, horns painted red and green. And the ponderous swaying of elephants—sensitive creatures, nervous of their own bulk, resplendently caparisoned. And there—a flash of the jungle, among casual goats, fowls, and pariahs—went the royal cheetahs, led on slips; walking delicately, between scarlet peons, looking for all the world like amiable maiden ladies with blue-hooded caps tied under their chins. In the wake of their magnificence two distended donkeys, on parodies of legs, staggered under loads more distended still, plump dhobies perched callously on the cruppers. Above all, Roy's eye delighted in the jewelled sheen of peacocks, rivalling in sanctity the real lords of Jaipur —Shiva's sacred bulls. Some milk-white and onyx-eyed, some black and insolent, they sauntered among the open shop fronts, levying toll and obstructing traffic —assured, arrogant, immune. . . .

And, at stated intervals, like wrong notes in a succession of harmonies, there sprang wrought-iron gas-lamps fitted with electric bulbs!

So riding, he came to the heart of the city—a vast open space, where the shops seemed brighter, the crowds gayer; and, by contrast, the human rag and bone heaps, beggars and cripples, more terrible to behold.

Here the first ray of actual recognition flashed through the haze of familiar sensations. For here architectural exuberance culminated in the vast bewildering façade of the Hall of the Winds and the Palace flaunting its royal standard—five colours blazoned on cloth of gold. But it was not these that held Roy's gaze. It was the group of Brahmin temples, elaborately carven, rose-red from plinth to summit, rising through flights of crows and iridescent pigeons; their monolithic forms clean cut against the dusty haze; their shallow steps flanked with marble elephants, splashed with orange-yellow robes of holy men and groups of brightly-veiled women.

At sight of them Roy instinctively drew rein;—and there, in the midst of the shifting, drifting crowd, he sat motionless, letting the vision sink deep into his mind, while Terry investigated a promising smell, and Bishun Singh, wholly incurious, gossiped with a potter, from whose wheel emerged an endless succession of *chirághs* —primitive clay lamps, with a lip for the cotton wick. His neighbour, with equal zest, was creating very ill-shapen clay animals, birds and fishes.

"Look, Hazúr—for the Dewáli," Bishun Singh thrust upon Roy's attention the one matter of real moment, just then, to all right-minded Hindus. "Only two more weeks. So they are making lamps, without number, for houses and shops and the palace of the Maharája. Very big tamasha, Hazúr."

He enlarged volubly on the coming festival, to this Sahib, who took such unusual interest in the ways of India; while Roy sat silent, watching, remembering. . . .

Nearly nineteen years ago he had seen the Dewáli —Feast of Lights; had been driven, sitting on his mother's knee, through a fairy city outlined in tremulous points of flame, down to the shore of the Man Sagar Lake, where the lights quavered and ran together and the dead ruins came alive with them. All night they had seemed to flicker in his fanciful brain; and next morning—unable to think or talk of anything else—he had been moved to dictate his very first attempt at a poem. . . .

Suddenly, sharply, there rose above the chatter of the crowd and the tireless clamour of crows, a scream of mingled rage and anguish that tore at his nerves and sent a chill down his spine.

Swinging round in the saddle, he saw a spectral figure of a woman—detached from a group of spectres, huddled ironically against bulging sacks of grain. One shrivelled arm was lifted in denunciation; the other pressed a shapeless bundle to her empty breasts. Obviously little more than a girl—yet with no trace of youth in her ravaged face—she stood erect, every bone visible, before the stall of a bangle-seller, fat and well liking, exuding rolls of flesh above his *dhoti*,[1] and enjoying his savoury chupattis hot and hot; entirely impervious to unseemly ravings; entirely occupied in pursuing trickles of *ghi* [2] with his agile tongue that none might be lost.

"That shameless one was begging a morsel of food," the toymaker explained conversationally. "Doubtless her stomach is empty. *Wah! Wah!* But she has no pice. And a man's food is his own . . ."

As he spoke a milk-white bull ambled by, plundering at will; his privileged nose adventuring near and nearer to the savoury smell. Promptly, with reverential eagerness, the man proffered half a fresh chupatti to the sacred intruder.

At that the starving girl-mother lunged forward with the yell of a hunted beast; lunged right across the path of a dapper young man in an English suit, green turban, and patent-leather shoes.

"Peace, she-devil! Make way," he cried; and catching her wrist—that looked as if it would snap at a touch—he flung her aside so roughly that she staggered and fell, the child beneath her emitting a feeble wail. . . .

Since the days of his imprisonment, cruelty witnessed had a startling effect on Roy. Between the moment when he sprang from the saddle, in a blaze of fury, to the moment when he stood confronting the suave, Anglicised Indian—riding-crop in one hand, the other

[1] Loin-cloth. [2] Melted butter.

supporting the girl and her babe—his mind was a blank. The thing was done almost before the impulse reached his brain. He wondered if he had struck the fellow, whom he was now arraigning furiously in fluent Hindustani, and whose sullen, shifty face was reminding him of some one—somewhere. . . .

"Have you *no* respect for suffering—or for women other than your own?" he demanded, scorn undisguised in his look and tone.

The man's answering shrug was frankly contemptuous. "All you English are mad," he said in the vernacular. "If she die not to-day, she will die to-morrow. And already there are too many to feed——"

"She will not die to-day or to-morrow," Roy retorted with Olympian assurance. "Courage, little mother,"—he addressed the girl—"you shall have food, you and the sonling."

As she raised herself, clutching at his arm, he became uncomfortably aware that her rags of clothing were probably verminous; that his chivalrous pity was tinged with repulsion. But pity prevailed. Supporting her to a neighbouring stall, he bought fruit, which she devoured like a wild thing. He begged a little milk in a lotah and gave her money for more. Half dazed, she dropped the money, emptied the small jar almost at a gulp, and flung herself at his feet, pressing her forehead on his dusty boot; covering him with confusion. Imperatively he bade her get up. No result. So he stooped to enforce his command. . . .

She had fainted.

"Help, mother—quick!" he appealed to an elder woman who hovered near the stall, and responded, instinctively, to the note of command.

As she stooped over the girl he said in low rapid tones: "Listen! It is an order. Give warm food to her and the child. Take her to the Burra Sahib's compound. There she will be cared for. I will give word."

He slipped two rupees into her hand, adding: "Two more—when all is done according to order."

"*Hai! Hai!* The Sahib is a Son of Princes," murmured the favoured one, reflecting shrewdly that eight annas would suffice to feed those poor empty creatures;

and gathering up her light burden she bore it away —to Roy's unfeigned relief.

Would Thea scold him—or uphold him, he wondered, —having committed himself. The whole thing had been so swift, so unreal, that he seemed half a world away from the green Residency garden, with its atmosphere of twentieth-century England, scrupulously, yet unconsciously, preserved in a setting of sixteenth-century India. And Roy had a strain of both in his composition.

Across the road Bishun Singh—tolerant of his Sahib's vagaries—was still chatting with the potter; a blare of discord in a minor key announced an approaching procession; and there, in talk with the bangle-seller, stood the cause of these strange doings; keeping a curious eye on the mad Englishman, but otherwise frankly unconcerned. Again there dawned on Roy the conviction that he had seen that face before. It was not in India. It was linked with the same sensations, in a milder form. It would come in a moment. . . .

It came.

Behind the slight, foppish figure, the eye of his mind saw suddenly—not the sunlight and colour of Jaipur, but a stretch of grey-green sea, tawny cliffs, and sandy shore . . . St Rupert's! Of course, unmistakable: the sullen mouth, the shifty eyes. . . .

Instantly he went forward and said in English: "I say—excuse me—but is your name Chandranath?"

The man started and stiffened. "That is no matter to you."

"Perhaps not. Only . . . you're very like a boy who was one term at St Rupert's School with me."

"Well, I *was* at St Rupert's. A beastly hole——" He, too, spoke English, and scanned Roy's face with narrowed eyes. "Sinclair—is it? You tumbled down the cliff on to me—and that Desmond fellow——?"

"Yes, I did. Lucky for you," Roy answered, stiffening in his turn. But because of old days—because this unpromising specimen of manhood had incidentally brought him and Desmond together, he held out his hand. "'Fraid I lost my temper," he said casually, for form's sake. "But you put my blood up."

Chandranath's fingers lay limply in his grasp.

"Still so sensitive——? Then better to clear out of India. I only pushed that crazy girl aside. Englishmen knock and kick our people without slightest compunction. Perhaps you are a tourist—or new to this country?"

Words and manner set Roy's nerves on edge; but he had been imprudent enough for one day. "I've spent seven months on the Frontier in a cavalry Regiment," he said; "but I only came to Jaipur yesterday."

"Well, take my advice, Mr Sinclair, and leave these people alone. They don't want Englishmen making pretence of sentimental fuss over them. They like much better to be pushed—or even starved—by their own *ját*. You may not believe it. But I belong to them. So I know."

Roy, who also 'belonged' in a measure, very nearly said so—but again prudence prevailed. "I'm rash enough to disagree with you," he said placably. "The question of non-interference, of letting ill alone—because one's afraid or can't be bothered—isn't merely a race question; it's a root question of human character. Some men can't pass by on the other side. Right or wrong, it simply isn't arguable. It's a matter of the individual conscience—the heart——"

"Conscience and heart—if not drastically disciplined by the logically reasoning brain, propagate the majority of troubles that afflict mankind," quoth Chandranath in the manner of one familiar with platform oratory. "Are you stopping in Jaipur?"

"Yes. At the Residency. Mrs Leigh is Desmond's sister. Did you know?"

"That is curious. I did not know. Too much heart and conscience there also. Mrs Leigh is thrusting her fingers into complicated issues of which she is lamentably ignorant."

Roy, taken aback, nearly gave himself away—but not quite. "I gather she acted with Sir Lakshman Singh's approval," was all he said.

Chandranath shrugged. "Sir Lakshman is an able but deluded man. His dreams of social reform are obsolete. We of the new school adhere patriotically to social and religious ordinances of the Mother. All we agitate for is political independence." He unfurled the polysyllables, like a flag; sublimely unaware of having stated a contradiction in terms. "But your Sir Lakshman is of the old-fashioned school—English-mad."

"And your particular friends—are sane, eh?"

The apostle of Hindu revival pensively twirled an English button of his creditably-cut English coat.

"Yes. We are sane—thanks to more liberalising influences. Coloured dust cannot be thrown in our eyes by bureaucratic conjuring tricks, or imperialistic talk about prestige. To-day it is India's turn for prestige. 'Arya for the Aryans' is the slogan of the rising generation." He paused, blinked, and added with an ingratiating chuckle: "You will go running away with an impression that I am metamorphosed into red-hot revolutionary. No, thank you! I am intrinsically a man of peace!" With a flourish he jerked out a showy gold watch. "Ah—getting late! Very agreeable exchanging amenities with old schoolfellows. But I have an appointment in the Palace Gardens, at the time they feed the muggers. *That* is a sight you should see, Mr Sinclair—when the beasts are hungry and have not lately snapped up a washerwoman or an erring wife!"

"I'd rather be excused this evening, thanks," Roy answered, with a touch of brusqueness. "I confess it wouldn't appeal to my sense of humour—seeing crocodiles gorge, while women and children starve."

"That is what they call in a book I once read 'little ironies of life.' Good fortune, at least, for the muggers! Better start to sharpen your sense of humour, my friend. It is incomparable asset against the slings and arrows of outrageous contingencies." This time his chuckle had an undernote of malice; and Roy, considering him thoughtfully—from green turban to patent-leather shoes—felt an acute desire to take him by the scruff of his English coat and dust the Jaipur market-place with the remnant of him.

Aloud he said coolly: "Thanks for the prescription. Are you stopping here long?"

"Oh, I am meteoric visitant. Never very long anywhere. I come and go."

"Business—eh?"

"Yes—many kinds of business—for the Mother." He flashed a direct look at Roy; the first since their encounter; fluttered a foppish hand—the little finger lifted to display a square uncut emerald—and went his way. . . .

Roy, left standing alone in the leisurely crowd of men and animals—at once so alien and so familiar—returned to Bishun Singh and Suráj in a vaguely troubled frame of mind.

"Which way to the house of Sir Lakshman Singh?" he asked the maker of chirághs, his foot in the stirrup.

Enlightened, he set off at a trot, down another vast street, all hazy in the level light that conjured the dusty air to gold. But contact with human anguish, naked and unashamed—as he had not seen it since the war—and that sudden queer encounter with Chandranath, had rubbed the bloom off delicate films of memory and artistic impressions. These were the drop-scene, merely: negligible, when Life took the stage. He had an exciting sense of having stepped straight into a crisis. Things were going to happen in Jaipur.

# CHAPTER VI.

"God has a few of us, whom He whispers in the ear;
The rest may reason and welcome. . . ."

—BROWNING.

"Living still, and the more beautiful for our longing."

THE house of Sir Lakshman Singh, C.S.I.—like many others in advancing India—was a house divided against itself. And the cleavage cut deep. The furnishing of the two rooms, in which he mainly lived, was not more sharply sundered from that of the Inside, than was the atmosphere of his large and vigorous mind from the twilight of ignorance and superstition that shrouded the mind and soul of his wife. More than fifty years ago —when young India ardently admired the West and all its works—he had dreamed of educating his spirited girl-bride, so that the way of companionship might gladden the way of marriage.

But too soon the spirited girl had hardened into the narrow, tyrannical woman; her conception of the wifely state limited to the traditional duties of motherhood and household service. Happily for Sir Lakshman, his unusual gifts had gained him wide recognition and high service in the State. He had schooled himself, long since, to forget his early dreams: and if marriage had failed, fatherhood had made royal amends. Above all, in Lilámani, daughter of flesh and spirit, he had found —had in a measure created—the intimate companionship he craved; a woman skilled in the fine art of loving —finest and least studied of all the arts that enrich and beautify human life. But the gods, it seemed, were jealous of a relation too nearly perfect for mortal man. So Rama, eldest son, and Lilámani, beloved daughter, had been taken, while the estranged wife was left. Remained the grandchildren, in whom centred all his hope and pride. So far as the dividing miles and years would permit, he had managed to keep in close touch with Roy. But the fact remained that England had first claim on Lilámani's children; and Rama's were tossed on the troubled waters of transition.

As for India herself—sacred Mother-land—her distraught soul seemed more and more at the mercy of the voluble, the half-baked, the disruptive, at home and abroad.

Himself, steeped in the threefold culture of his country—Vedantic, Islamic, and European—he came very near the prevailing ideal of composite Indian nationality. Yet was he not deceived. In seventy years of life, he had seen intellectual India pass through many phases, from ardent admiration of the West and all its works, to no less ardent denunciation. And in these days he saw too clearly how those same intellectuals—with catchwords, meaningless to nine-tenths of her people—were breaking down, stone by stone, their mighty safeguard of British administration. Useless to protest. Having ears, they heard not. Having eyes, they saw not. The spirit of destruction seemed abroad in all the earth. After Germany—Russia. Would it be India next? He knew her peoples well enough to fear. He also knew them well enough to hope. But of late, increasingly, fear had prevailed. His shrewd eye discerned, in every direction, fresh portents of disaster—a weakened executive, divided counsels, and violence that is the offspring of both. His own Maharája, he thanked God, was of the old school, loyal and conservative; his face set like a flint against the sedition-monger in print or person. And as concessions multiplied and extremists waxed bolder, so the need for vigilance waxed in proportion. . . .

But to-day his mind had room for one thought only—the advent of Roy; legacy of her, his vanished Jewel of Delight.

A message from the Residency had told of the boy's arrival, of his hope to announce himself in person that evening; and now, on a low divan, the old man sat awaiting him with a more profound emotion at his heart than the mere impatience of youth. But the impassive face under the flesh-pink turban betrayed no sign of disturbance within. The strongly-marked nose and eyebones might have been carved in old ivory. The snowy beard, parted in the middle, was swept up over his ears; and the eyes were veiled. An open book lay on his knee. But he was not reading. He was listening for the sound of hoofs, the sound of a voice. . . .

The two had not met for five years: and in those years the boy had proved the warrior blood in his veins; had passed through the searching test of a bitter loss. Together, they could speak of her—gone from them; yet alive in their hearts for evermore. Seen or unseen, she was the link that kept them all united, the pivot on which their lives still turned. There had been none with whom he could talk of her since she went. . . .

Over his writing-table hung the original Antibes portrait—life-size; Nevil's payment for the high privilege of painting her; a privilege how reluctantly accorded none but himself had ever known. And behold his reward: her ever-visible presence—the girl-child who had been altogether his own.

Hoofs at last—and the remembered voice; deeper, more commanding; the embroidered curtain pushed aside. Then—Roy himself, broader, browner; his father's smile in his eyes; and, permeating all, the spirit of his mother, clearly discernible to the man who had given it life.

He was on his feet now, an imposing figure, in loose white raiment and purple choga. In India, he wisely discarded English dress, deeming it as unsuitable to the country as English political machinery. Silent, he held out his arms and folded Roy in a close embrace: then —still silent—stood away and considered him afresh. Their mutual emotion affected them sensibly, like the presence of a third person, making them shy of each other, shy of themselves.

It was Sir Lakshman who spoke first. "Roy, son of my Heart's Delight, I have waited many years for this day. It was the hidden wish of her heart. And her spirit, though withdrawn, still works in our lives. It is only so with those who love greatly, without base mixture of jealousy or greed. They pass on—yet they remain; untouched by death, like the lotus, that blooms in the water, but opens beyond its reach."

Words and tone so stirred Roy that sudden tears filled his eyes. And through the mist of his grief, dawned a vision of his mother's face. Blurred and tremulous, it hovered before him with a startling illusion of life: then—he knew. . . .

Without a word, he went over to the picture and stood before it, drowned fathoms deep. . . .

A slight movement behind roused him; and with an effort he turned away. "I've not seen a big one since—since my last time at home," he said simply. "I've only two small ones out here."

The carven face was not impassive now. "After all, Dilkusha,[1] what matter pictures when you have—herself?"

Roy started. "It's true. I *have*—herself. How could you know?"

Five minutes later, he was sitting beside his grandfather on the deep divan, telling him all.

Before setting out, he would not have believed it possible. But instinctively he knew himself in touch with a quality of love that matched his own; and the mere telling revived the marvel, the thrill of that strange and beautiful experience at Chitor. . . .

Sir Lakshman had neither moved nor spoken throughout. Now their eyes met in a look of deep understanding.

"I am very proud you told me, Roy. It is not easy."

"No. I've not told any one else. I couldn't. But just now—something seemed to draw it all out of me. I suppose—something in you——"

"Or perhaps—herself? It almost seemed—she was here with us, while you talked."

"Perhaps—she is here still."

Their voices were lowered, as in the presence of sacred things. Never, till now, had Roy so keenly felt his individual link with this wonderful old man, whose blood ran in his veins.

"Grandfather," he asked after a pause, "I suppose it doesn't often happen—that sort of thing? I suppose

[1] Joy of my heart.

most common-sense people would dismiss it all as—sheer delusion?"

The young simplicity of the question lit a smile in Sir Lakshman's eyes.

"Quite possible. All that is most beautiful in life, most real to saints and lovers, must seem delusion to those whose hearts and spirits are merely vassals to the body and the brain. But those who say of the soul, 'It is not,' have still to *prove* it is not to those who have felt and known. Also I grant—the other way about. But they speak in different languages. Kabir says, 'I disclose my soul in what is hidden.' And again, 'The bird is beyond seeking, yet it is most clearly visible.' For us, that is living truth. For those others, a mere tangle of words."

"I see." Roy's gaze was riveted on the picture above the writing-table. "You can't explain colours to the colour-blind. And I suppose experiences like mine only come to those for whom words like that are—living truth?"

"Yes—like yours. But there are other kinds; not always true. Because, in this so sacred matter, clever people, without scruple, have made capital out of the heart's natural longing; and the dividing line is dim where falsehood ends and truth begins. So it has all come into suspicion and contempt. Accept what is freely given, Roy. Do not be tempted to try and snatch more."

"No—no. I wouldn't if I could." A pause. "*You* believe it is true . . . what I feel? That she is often —very near me?"

Sir Lakshman gravely inclined his head. "As I believe in Brahma, Lord of all."

And for both the silence that fell seemed pulsating with her unseen presence. . . .

When they spoke again it was of mundane things. Roy vividly described his sensations, riding through the City; the culminating incident, and his recognition of the offender.

"The queerest thing, running into the beggar again like that! He looks as sulky and shifty as ever. That's how I knew."

"Sulky and shifty—and wearing English clothes?"

Sir Lakshman's brows contracted sharply. "What name did you say?"

"Chandranath, we called him."

"And you don't know his whereabouts?"

"No, I'm sorry. I didn't suppose his whereabouts mattered a damn to any one."

The stern old Rajput smiled. It did his heart good to hear the familiar slang phrases again. "Whether it matters a damn—as you say—depends on whether he is the undesirable I have in mind. Quite young; but much influence, and a bad record. Mixed up with German agents, before the War, and the Ghadr party in California; arrested for seditious activity and deported: but of course, on appeal, allowed to return. Always the same tale. Always the same result. Worse mischief done. And India—the true India—must be grateful for these mercies! Sometimes I think the irony is too sharp between the true gifts given, unnoticed, by Englishmen working sincerely for the good of our people, and the false gifts proclaimed from the house-tops, filling loyal Indians with bewilderment and fear. I have had letters from scores of these, because I am known to believe that loyal allegiance to British government gives India the best chance for peaceful progress she is likely to have for many generations. And from every one comes the same cry, begging to be saved from this crazy nightmare of Home Rule, not understood and not desired except by those who invented it. But what appeal is possible to those who stop their ears? And all the time, by stealthy and open means, the poison of race-hatred is being poured into India's veins——"

"But, Grandfather—what about the War—and pulling together—and all that?"

Sir Lakshman's smile struck Roy as one of the saddest he had ever seen. "Four years ago, my dear Boy, we all had many radiant illusions. But this War has dragged on too long. It is too far away. For our Princes and warlike races it has had some reality. For the rest it means mostly news in the papers and rumours in bazaars, high prices, and trouble about food. No better soil for sowing evil seeds. And friends of Germany are still working in India—remember that!

While the loyal were fighting, these were talking, plotting, hindering: and now they are waving, like a flag, the services of others, to gain their own ends, from which the loyal pray to be delivered! Could irony be more complete? Indian Princes can keep some check on these gentlemen. But it is not always easy. If this Chandranath should be the same man—he is here, no doubt, for Dewáli. At sacred feasts they do most of their devil's work. Did you speak of connection with me?"

"No. But he seemed to know about Arúna: said you were English mad."

Sir Lakshman frowned. "English mad! That is their jargon. Too narrow to understand how I can deeply love both countries, while remaining as jealous for all true rights of my Motherland as any hot-head who swallows their fairy-tale of a Golden Age, and England as Raksha—destroying demon! By help of such inventions, they have deluded many fine young men, like my poor Dyán, who should be already married and working to fill my place. Such was my hope in sending him to Oxford. And now—see the result . . ."

On that topic he could not yet trust himself; and Roy, leaning forward impulsively, laid a hand on his knee.

"Grandfather, I have promised Arúna—and I promise you—that somehow, I *will* get hold of him; and bring him back to his senses."

Sir Lakshman covered the hand with his own. "True son of Lilámani! But I fear he may have joined some secret society; and India is a large haystack in which to seek one human needle!"

"But Arúna has written again. She is convinced he will answer."

Sir Lakshman sighed. "Poor Arúna! I am not sure if I was altogether wise letting her go to the Residency. But I am deeply grateful to Mrs Leigh. India needs many more such English women. By making friends with high-born Indian women, it is hardly too much to say they might, together, mend more than half the blunders made by men on both sides."

Thus, skilfully, he steered clear of Arúna's problem that was linked with matters too intimately painful for discussion with a grandson, however dear.

So absorbed was Roy in the delight of reunion, that not till he rose to go did he take in the details of the lofty room. Everywhere Indian workmanship was in evidence. The pictures were old Rajput paintings; fine examples of Vaishnava art—pure Hindu, in its mingling of restraint and exuberance, of tenderness and fury; its hallowing of all life and idealising of all love. Only the writing-table and swivel-chair were frankly of the West, and certain shelves full of English books and reviews.

"I *like* your room," Roy announced after leisurely inspection. "But I don't seem to remember——"

"You would be a miracle if you did! The room *you* saw had plush curtains, gilt mirrors and gilt furniture; in fact, the correct 'English-fashion' guest-room of the educated Indian gentleman. But of late years I have seen how greatly we were mistaken, making imitation England to honour our English friends. Some frankly told me how they were disappointed to find in our houses only caricatures of middle-class England or France. Such rooms are silent barriers to friendship: proclaiming that East may go to the West but West cannot come to the East."

"In a way that's true, isn't it?"

"Yes—in a way. This room, of course, is not like my inner apartments. It is like myself, however; cultivated—but still Indian. It is my way of preaching true Swadeshi:—Be your own self, even with English guests. But so far I have few followers. Some are too foolishly fond of their mirrors and chandeliers and gramophones. Some will not believe such trifles can affect friendliness. Yet—strange, but true—too much Anglicising of India instead of drawing us nearer, seems rather to widen the gulf."

Roy nodded. "I've heard that. Yet most of us are so keen to be friends. Queer, perverse things—human beings, aren't they?"

"And for that reason, more interesting than all the wonders of Earth!" Setting both hands on Roy's shoulders he looked deeply into his eyes. "Come and see me often, Dilkusha. It lifts my tired heart to have this very human being so near me again."

Ten minutes later, Roy was riding homeward through

a changed city; streets and hills and sky wrapped in the mystery of encroaching dusk.

South and west the sky flamed, like the heart of a fire opal, through a veil fine as gauze—dust no longer; but the aura of Jaipur. Seen afar, through the coloured gloom, familiar shapes took on strange outlines; moved and swayed, mysteriously detached, in a sea of shadows, scattered, here and there, by flames of little dinner fires along the pavements. The brilliant shifting crowd of two hours ago seemed to have sunk into the earth. For there is no night life in the streets of Jaipur. Travellers had passed on and out. Merchants had stowed away their muslins and embroideries, their vessels of brass and copper and priceless enamels. Only the starving lay in huddled heaps as before—ominously still; while above them vultures and eagles circled, expectant, ink-black against the immense radiance beyond. Grey, deepening to black, were flat roofs, cornices, minarets and massed foliage, and the flitting shadows, with lifted tails, that careered along the house-tops; or perched on some jutting angle, skinny elbows crooked, absorbed in the pursuit of fleas. For sunset is the monkey's hour, and the eerie jibbering of these imps of darkness struck a bizarre note in the hush that shrouded the city.

Roy knew, now, why Thea had stayed his impatience; and he blessed her sympathetic understanding. But just then—steeped in India at her most magical hour—it was hard to believe in the Residency household; in English dinner-tables and English detachment from the mediæval medley of splendour and squalor, of courage and cruelty and dumb endurance, of arts and crafts and all the paraphernalia of enlightened knowledge that was Jaipur. It seemed more like a week than a few hours since he had turned in the saddle to salute Arúna and ridden out into another world:—her world, which was also in a measure his own. . . .

On and on he rode, at a foot's pace, followed by his twin shadows; past the temples of Maha Deo, still rosy where they faced the west, still rumbling and throbbing with muffled music; past wayside shrines, mere alcoves for grotesque images—Shiva, Lord of Death, or Ganesh the Elephant God—each with his scented garlands and his flickering chirágh; past shadowy groups round the dinner fires, cooking their evening meal: on and out through the double fortified gateways into the deserted road, his whole being drenched in the silence and the deepening dusk.

Here, outside the city, emptiness loomed almost like a presence. Only the trees were alive; each with its colony of peacocks and parrots and birds of prey noisily settling to rest. The peacocks' unearthly cry, and the far, ghostly laugh of jackals—authentic voice of India at sundown—sent a chill down Roy's spine. For he, who had scarcely known fear on the battlefield, was ignominiously at the mercy of imagination and the eerie spirit of the hour.

At a flick of the reins, Suráj broke into a smart canter, willingly enough. What were sunsets or local devils to him compared with stables and gram?

And as they sped on, as trees on either side slid by like stealthy ghosts, the sunset splendour died, only to rise again in a volcanic afterglow, on which trunks and twigs and battlemented hills were printed in daguerreotype; and desert voices were drowned in the clamour of cicadas, grinding their knives in foolish ecstasy; and, at last, he swerved between the friendly gate-posts of the Residency—the richer for a spiritual adventure that could neither be imparted, nor repeated, nor forgotten while he lived.

## CHAPTER VII.

"The deepest thing in our nature is this dumb region of the heart, where we dwell alone with our willingnesses and unwillingnesses, our faiths and our fears."—WILLIAM JAMES.

NOT least among the joys of Arúna's return to the freer life of the Residency was her very own verandah balcony. Here, secure from intrusion, she could devote the first and last hours of her day to meditation or prayer. Oxford studies had confused a little, but not killed, the faith of her fathers. The real trouble was that too often, nowadays, that exigent heart of hers would intrude upon her sacred devotions, transforming them into day-dreams, haloed with a hope the more frankly formulated because she was of the East.

For Thea had guessed aright. Roy was the key to her waverings, her refusals, her eager acceptance of the emergency plan :—welcome in itself; still more welcome because it permitted her simply to await his coming.

They had been very wonderful, those five years in England; in spite of anxieties and disappointed hopes. But when Dyán departed and Mesopotamia engulfed Roy, India had won the day.

How unforgettable that exalted moment of decision, one drenched and dismal winter evening; the sudden craving for sights and sounds and smells of her own land. How slow the swiftest steamer to the speed of her racing thoughts! How bitter, beyond belief, the first faint chill of disappointment; the pang of realising —how reluctantly—that, within herself, she belonged whole-heartedly to neither world.

She had returned qualified for medical work, by experience in a College hospital at Oxford; yet hampered by innate shrinking from the sick and maimed, who had been too much with her in those years of war. Not less innate was the urge of her whole being to fulfil her womanhood through marriage rather than through work. And in the light of that discovery, she saw her dilemma plain. Either she must hope to marry an Englishman and break with India, like Aunt Lilámani; or accept, at the hands of the matchmaker, an enlightened bridegroom, unseen, unknown, whose family would overlook—at a price—her advanced age and English adventures.

Against the last, all that England and Oxford had given her rose up in revolt . . . But the discarded, subconscious Arúna was centuries older than the half-fledged being who hovered on the rim of the nest, distrustful of her untried wings and the pathless sky. That Arúna had, for ally, the spirit of the ages; more formidable, if less assertive, than the transient spirit of the age. And the fledgling Arúna knew perfectly well that the Englishman of her alternative was, confessedly—Roy. His mother being Indian, she innocently supposed there would be no trouble of prejudice; no stupid talk of the gulf that she and Dyán had set out to bridge. The fact that Dyán had failed only made her the more anxious to succeed. . . .

Soon after arriving, she had taken up hospital work in the women's ward, because Miss Hammond was kind; and her educated self had need of occupation. Her other self—deeply loving her grandfather—had urged her to try and live at home,—so far as her unregenerate state would permit.

As out-of-caste, she had been exempt from kitchen work; debarred from touching any food except the portion set aside for her meals, that were eaten apart in Sir Lakshman's room—her haven of refuge. In the Inside, she was at the mercy of women's tongues and the petty tyranny of Mátaji; antagonistic as ever; sharpened and narrowed with age, even as her grandfather had mellowed and grown beautiful, with the unearthly beauty of the old, whose spirit shines visibly through the attenuated veil of flesh. Arúna, watching him, with clearer understanding, marvelled how he had preserved his serenity of soul through a lifetime of Mátaji's dominion.

And the other women—relations in various degrees

—took their tone from her, if only for the sake of peace:—the widowed sister-in-law, suavely satirical; a great-aunt, whose tongue clacked like a rice-husker; two cousins, correctly betrothed to unseen bridegrooms, entitled to look askance at the abandoned one, who was neither wife nor mother; and two children of a poor relation—embryo women, who echoed the jeers of their elders at her English friends, her obstinacy in the matter of caste and the inevitable husband. *Hai! hai!* At her age, what did she fear? Had the English bewitched her with lies? Thus Peru, aged nine, jocosely proceeding to enlighten her; egged on by giggles and high-pitched laughter from the prospective brides. For in the zenana reticence is not, even before children. Arúna herself had heard such talk; but for years her early knowledge had lain dormant; while fastidiousness had been engendered by English studies and contact with English youth. Useless to answer. It simply meant tears or losing her temper; in which case, Mátaji would retaliate by doctoring her food with red pepper to sweeten her tongue.

Meanwhile, sharpened pressure in the matter of caste rites and rumours of an actually maturing husband, had brought her very near the end of her tether. Again Thea was right. Her brave impulse of the heart had only been just in time. And hard upon that unbelievable good fortune followed the news that Roy was coming.

Tremulously at first, then with quickening confidence, her happy nature rose like a sea-bird out of troubled waters, on the wings of a secret hope. . . .

And now he was here, under this friendly roof that sheltered her from the tender mercies of her own kind. There were almost daily meetings, however brief, and the after-glow of them when past; all the well-remembered tricks of speech and manner; and the twinkle of fun in his eyes. Lapped in an ecstasy of content, hope scarcely stirred a wing. Enough that he was there——

Great was her joy when Mrs Leigh—after scolding him in the kindest way over the girl mother and two more starving children, picked up afterwards—had given her leave to take special charge of them and lodged them with the dhobi's wife. This also brought her nearer to Roy. And what could she ask more?

But with the approach of the Dewáli, thoughts of the future came flocking like birds at sundown. Because, on Dewáli night, all tried their luck in some fashion; and Mai Lakshmi's answer failed not. The men tossed coin or dice. The maidens, at sunset, when the little wind of evening stirred the waters, carried each her chirágh—lamp of her life—and set it afloat on tank or stream, praying Mai Lakshmi to guide it safe across. If the prayer was heard, omens were favourable. If the lamp should sink, or be shattered, omens were evil. And the centuries-old Arúna—still at the mercy of dastur—had secretly bought her little chirágh; secretly resolved to try her fate on the night of nights. If the answer were unfavourable—and courage failed her—there was always one way of escape. The water that put out her lamp would as carelessly put out the flame of her life—in a little moment—without pain. . . .

A small shiver convulsed her—kneeling there in her balcony; her bare arms resting on the balustrade. The new Arúna shrank from thought of death. She craved the fulness of life and love—kisses and rapture and the clinging arms of little children. . . .

For, as she knelt in the moonlight, nominally she was invoking Mai Lakshmi; actually she was dreaming of Roy; chiding herself for the foolishness that had kept her from appearing at dinner; hoping he might wonder, and perhaps think of her a little—wishing her there. And all the while, perhaps he was simply not noticing—not caring one little bit——!

Stung by the thought, she clenched her hands and lifted her bowed head. Then she started—and caught her breath——

Could it be he, down there among the shadows—wandering, dreaming, thinking of her, or making poems? She knew most of his slim volume by heart.

More likely, he was framing bold plans to find Dyán—now the answer to her letter had come. It was a strange unsatisfying answer; full of affection, but too full of windy phrases that she was shrewd enough to recognise as mere echoes from those others, who had ensnared him in a web of words.

"Fear not for me, sister of my heart," he wrote. "Rejoice because I am dedicated to service of the Mother, that she may be released from political bondage and shine again in her ancient glory—no longer exploited by foreigners, who imagine that with bricks and stones they can lock up Veda—eternal truth! The gods have spoken. It is time. Kali rises in the East, with her necklet of skulls—Giants of evil she has slain. It is she who speaks through the voice of the patriot: 'Do not wall up your vision, like frogs in a well . . . Rise above the Penal Code to the rarefied atmosphere of the Gita and consider the actions of heroic men.'

"You ask if I still love Roy? Why not? He is of our own blood and a very fine fellow. But I don't write now because he would not understand my fervour of soul. So don't you take all his opinions for gospel; like my grandfather's, they are well meant, but obsolete. If only you had courage, Arúna-ji, to accept the enlightened husband, who might not keep you in strict purdah, then we could work together for liberation of the Mother. Sing *Bande Mátaram*,[1] forty thousand brothers! That is our battle-cry. And one of those is your own fond brother—Dyán Singh."

Arúna had read and re-read that bewildering effusion till tears fell and blotted the words. Could this be the same Dyán who had known and loved England even as she did? His eloquence somehow failed to carry conviction. To her, the soul of new India seemed like a book, full of contradictions, written in many strange languages, hard to read. But behind that tangle of words beat the heart of Dyán—the brother who was her all.

Still no address was given. But Roy had declared the Delhi postmark sufficient clue. Directly Dewáli was over, he would go. And, by every right impulse, she ought to be more glad than sad. But the heart, like the tongue, can no man tame. And sometimes his eagerness to go hurt her a little. Was he thinking of Delhi down there—or of her——?

The shadow had turned and was moving towards her. There was a white splash of shirt-front, the glow of a cigarette.

[1] Hail, Mother.

Suddenly his pace quickened. He had seen her. Next moment he was standing under her balcony. His low-pitched voice came distinctly to her ears.

"Good evening—Juliet! Quit your dreaming. Come and be sociable down here."

Delicious tremors ran through her. Much too bold, going down in the dark. But how to resist?

"I think—better not," she faltered, incipient surrender in her tone. "You see—not coming down to dinner . . . Mrs Leigh . . ."

"Bother Mrs Leigh. I've got a ripping inspiration about Delhi—— Hurry up. I'll be by the steps."

Then he *had* been thinking of Delhi. But he wanted her now; and the note of command extinguished hesitation. Slipping on a cloak, she reached the verandah without meeting a soul. He put out a hand. Purely on impulse she gave him her left one; and he conducted her down the steps with mock ceremony, as if leading her out to tread a measure to unheard strains of the viola and spinet.

Happiness ran like wine in her veins: and catching his mood she swept him a curtsey, English fashion.

"Fit for the Queen's Drawing-room!" he applauded; and she smiled up at him under her straight lashes. "Why didn't you appear at dinner? Is it a whim—hiding your light under a bushel? Or do you get headaches and heartaches working in the ward, and feel out of tune with our frivol?"

The solicitude in his tone was worth many headaches and heartaches to hear again. But with him she could not pretend.

"No—not that!" she said, treading the grass beside him, as if it were a moonlit cloud. "Only sometimes . . . I am foolish—not inclined for so many faces; and all the lights and the talk."

He nodded. "I know the feeling. The same strain in us, I suppose. But, look here, about Dyán. It suddenly struck me I'd have ten times better chance if I went as an Indian. I can talk the language to admiration. What d'you think?"

She caught her breath. A vision of him so transformed seemed to bring him surprisingly nearer. "How exciting! How bold!"

"Yes—but not impossible. And no end of a lark. If I could lodge with some one who knew, I believe I could pull it through. Grandfather might arrange that. It would give me a chance to get in among Dyán's set and hear things. Don't breathe a word to any one. I must talk it all over with Grandfather."

"Oh! I would love to see you turned into a Rajput," she breathed.

"You *shall* see me. I'll come and make my salaams and ask your blessing on my venture."

"And I will make *prasad* for your journey!" Her unveiled eyes met his frankly now. "A portion for Dyán too. It may speak to his heart clearer than words."

"*Prasad?* What's that?"

"Food prepared and consecrated by touch of mother or sister or—or nearest woman relation. And by absence of those others . . . it is . . . my privilege——"

"*My* privilege. I would not forgo it for a kingdom," Roy interposed, such patent sincerity in the reverend quiet of his tone that she was speechless. . . .

For less than half an hour they strolled on that moon-enchanted lawn. Nothing was said by either that the rest might not have heard. Yet it was a transfigured Arúna who approached the verandah, where Thea stood awaiting them; having come out to look for Roy and found the clue to his prolonged meditations.

"What have you been plotting, you two?" she asked lightly when they reached her. To Roy her eyes said: "D'you call *this* being discreet?" To Arúna her lips said: "Graceless one! I thought you were *purdah nashin* this evening!"

"So she was," Roy answered for her. "I'm the culprit. I insisted. Some details about my Delhi trip, I wanted to talk over."

Thea wrinkled her forehead. "Roy—you mustn't. It's a crazy plan——"

"Pardon me—an inspired plan!" He drew himself up half an inch the better to look down on her. "Nothing on earth can put me off it—except Grandfather. And I know he'll back me up."

"In that case, I won't waste valuable verbal ammunition on you! Come along in—— We're going to have music."

But as Roy moved forward, Arúna drew back. "Please—I would rather go to bed now. And—please, forgive, little Mother," she murmured caressingly. For this great-hearted English woman seemed mother indeed to her now.

For answer, Thea took her by the shoulders and kissed her on both cheeks. "Not guilty this time, *piári.*[1] But don't do it again!"

Roy's hand closed hard on hers, but he said not a word. And she was glad.

Alone again on her balcony, gladness rioted through all her being. Yet—nothing had really happened. Nothing had been said. Only—everything felt different inside. Of such are life's supreme moments. They come without flourish of trumpets; touch the heart or the lips with fire, and pass on. . . .

While undressing, an impulse seized her to break her chirágh and treasure the pieces—in memory of to-night. Why trouble Mai Lakshmi with a question already half answered? But, lost in happy thoughts—inwoven with delicate threads of sound from Thea's violin—she forgot all about it, till the warmth of her cheek nestled against the cool pillow. Too lazy and comfortable to stir, she told her foolish heart that to-morrow morning would do quite as well.

But the light of morning dimmed, a little, her mood of exalted assurance. Habit and superstition prevailed over that so arrogant impulse, and the mystic chirágh of destiny was saved—for another fate.

[1] Darling.

# CHAPTER VIII.

> "The forces that fashion, the hands that mould,
> Are the winds fire-laden, the sky, the rain :—
> . . . . . . . .
> They are gods no more, but their spells remain."
> —SIR ALFRED LYALL.

DEWÁLI night at last; and all Jaipur astir in the streets at sundown awaiting the given moment that never quite loses its quality of miracle. . . .

For weeks every potter's wheel had been whirling, double tides, turning out clay chirághs by the thousand, that none might fail of honouring Mai Lakshmi—a compound of Minerva and Ceres,—worshipped in the living gold of fire and the dead gold of minted coin.

And all day long there ebbed and flowed through the temple doors a rainbow-coloured stream of worshippers: while the dust-laden air vibrated with jangle of metal bells, wail of conches and raucous clamour of crows. Within doors, the rattle of dice rivalled the jangle of bells. Young or old, none failed to consult those mysterious arbiters on this auspicious day. Houses, shops, and balconies had been swept and plastered with fresh cow dung, in honour of Vishnu's bride; and gayest among festal shop-fronts was the dazzling array of toys. For the Feast of Lights is also a feast of toys in bewildering variety; in sugar, in paper, in burnt clay; tinselled, or gorgeously painted with colours such as never were on ox or elephant, fish or bird.

What matter? To the uncritical Eastern eye, colour is all.

And, as the day wore on, colour, and yet more colour, was spilled abroad in the wide main streets that are an arresting feature of Jaipur. Men, women, and children, in gala turbans and gala draperies, laughing and talking at full pitch of their lungs; gala elephants sheathed in cloth of gold, their trunks and foreheads patterned in divers colours; scarlet outriders clearing a pathway through the maze of turbans that bobbed to and fro like a bed of parrot-tulips in a wind. Crimson, agate, and apricot, copper and flame colour, greens and yellows; every conceivable harmony and discord; nothing to rival it anywhere, Sir Lakshman told Roy; save perhaps in Gwalior or Mandalay.

Roy had spent most of the morning in the city, lunching with his grandfather and imbibing large draughts of colour from an airy minaret on the roof top. Then home to the Residency for tea, only to insist on carrying them all back in the car—Thea, Arúna, Flossie, and the children, who must have their share of strange sweets and toys, if only 'for luck,' the watchword of Dewáli.

As for Arúna—to-day everything in the world seemed to hang on the frail thread of those two words. And what of to-night . . . ?

All had been arranged in conjunction with Roy. His insistence on the cousinly privilege of protecting her had arisen from a private confession that she shrank from joining the orthodox group of maidens who would go forth at sundown, to try their fate. She was other than they were; out of purdah; out of caste; a being apart. And for most of them it was little more than a 'game of play.' For her—but that she kept to herself—this symbolical act of faith, this childish appeal for a sign, was a matter of life and death. So—to her chosen angle of the tank, she would go alone; and there—unwatched, save by Dewáli lights of earth and heaven—she would confide her lamp to the waters and the breeze that rippled them in the first hour of darkness.

But Roy would not hear of her wandering alone in a Dewáli crowd. In Dyán's absence, he claimed the right to accompany her, to be somewhere within hail. Having shed the Eastern protection of purdah, she must accept the Western protection of escort. And straightway there sprang an inspiration: he would wear his Indian dress, ready and waiting in every detail, at Sir Lakshman's house. From there, he could set out unnoticed on the Delhi adventure—which his grandfather happily approved, with what profound heart-searchings and heart-stirrings Roy did not even dimly guess.

At sundown the Residency party would drive through the city and finish up at the gardens, before going on to dine at the Palace. That would be Arúna's moment for slipping away. Roy—having slipped away in advance—would rejoin her at a given spot. And then——?

The rest was a tremulous blur of hopes and fears and the thrill of his presence, conjured into one of her own people. . . .

Sundown at last; and the drive, in her exalted mood, was an ecstasy no possible after-pain or disappointment could dim. As the flaming tint of sunset faded and shafts of amethyst struck upward into the blue, buildings grew shadowy; immense vistas seemed to melt into the landscape, shrouded in a veil of desert dust.

Then—the first flickering points of fire—primrose-pale, in the half light; deepening to orange, as night rolled up out of the East, and the little blown flames seemed to flit along of their own volition, so skilled and swift were the invisible hands at work.

From roof to roof, from balcony to balcony they ran: till vanished Jaipur emerged from her shroud, a city transfigured: cupolas, arches, balconies, and temples, palace of the Maharája and lofty Hall of the Winds—every detail faultlessly traced on darkness, in delicate, tremulous lines of fire. Only here and there illusion was shattered by garish globes of electric light, dimming the mellow radiance of thousands on thousands of modest chirághs.

Arúna had seen many Dewáli nights in her time; but never at a moment so charged with conflicting emotions. Silent, absorbed, she sat by Thea in the barouche; Roy and Vernon opposite; Phyllis on her mother's knee; the others in the car on ahead—including a tourist of note—outriders before and behind, clearing a pathway through the press. Vernon, jigging on his feet, was lost in wonder. Roy, like Arúna, said little. Only Thea kept up a low ripple of talk with her babe. . . .

By now, not only the city was alight, but the enclosing hills, where bonfires laughed in flame. Jewelled coronets twinkled on bastions of the Tiger Fort. Threads of fire traced every curve and line of Jai Singh's tomb. And on either side of the carriage, the crowd swayed and hummed; laughing, jesting, boasting; intoxicated with the spirit of festival, that found an echo in Arúna's heart and rioted in her veins. To-night she felt merged in India, Eastern to the core; capable, almost, of wondering—could she put it away from her, even at the bidding of Roy——?

On they drove, away from crowded pavements, towards the Mán Sagar Lake, where ruined temples and palaces dreamed and gleamed, knee deep in the darkling water; where jackals prowled and cranes nested and muggers dozed unheeding. At a point of vantage above the Lake, they halted and sat there awhile in darkness—a group of silent shadows. Words did not meet the case. Even Vernon ceased his jigging and baby Phyllis uttered no sound: for she had fallen asleep.

Arúna, resting an elbow on the side of the carriage, sat lost in a dream. . . .

Suddenly, electrically, she was aware of contact with Roy's coat-sleeve. He had leaned forward to catch a particular effect, and was probably not aware of his trespassing arm; for he did not shift it till he had gazed his fill. Then with a long sigh, he leaned back again. But Arúna's dream was shattered by sensations too startingly real to be ignored. . . .

Once, driving back, as they passed under an electric globe, she caught his eyes on her face, and they exchanged a smile. Did he know——? Did he ever feel—like that?

Near Sir Lakshman's house they stopped again and Roy leaned towards her.

"I'll be quick as lightning—don't stir till I come," he said—and vanished.

Some fifteen minutes later, she stood alone in the jewelled darkness, awaiting him; her own flickering jewel held between her hands. She had brought it with her, complete; matches and a tiny bottle of oil, stowed in a cardboard box. Mrs Leigh—angel of goodness—had lit the wick with her own hand—'for luck.' How Roy had made her so completely their ally, she had no idea. But who could resist him,—after all? Waiting alone, her courage ebbed a little; but he came quick as lightning, arrayed in a choga of some dark material and the larger turban of the North;—so changed, she scarcely knew him till he saluted and, with a gesture, bade her go forward.

Through the dark archway, under a block of zenana buildings they passed: and there lay before them the great tank patterned with quivering threads of light. Her chosen corner was an unfrequented spot. A little farther on, shadowy figures moved and talked.

"You see," she explained under her breath, as though they were conspirators, "if the wind is kind, it will cut across there making the mystical triangle; symbol of perfect knowledge—new birth. I am only afraid it is getting a little too strong. And if anything should hinder it from crossing, then—there is no answer. Suspense—all the time. But—we will hope. Now, please, I must be alone. In the shadow of this building, few will notice me. Afterwards, I will call softly. But don't—go too far."

"Trust me. And—see here, Arúna, don't make too much of it—either way. Mai Lakshmi's not Queen of all the Immortals——"

"Oh, hush! She is bride of Vishnu!"

Roy's smile was half amused, half tender. "Well! I hope she plays up—royally."

And with a formal salute, he left her.

Alone, crouching near the water's edge, she held out her cockle-shell with its blown wisp of light.

"Oh Lamp of my life, flame of my heart," she addressed it, just above her breath, "sail safely through the wavelets and answer truly what fate awaits me now? Will Mai Lakshmi grant the blessing I crave?"

With a gentle push, she set it afloat; then, kneeling close against the building, deep in shadow, she covered her face and prayed, childish incoherent prayers, for some solution of her difficult problem that would be best, alike, for her and Roy.

But curiosity was claimant. She must see . . . She must know. . . .

Springing up, she stood near the coping, one hand on a low abutment, all her conscious being centred on the adventuring flame that swayed and curtsied at the caprice of the wind. The effect of her concentration was almost hypnotic: as if her soul, deserting her still body, flickered away there on the water; as if every threat of wind or wavelet struck at her very life. . . .

Footsteps passed, and voices; but the sounds scarcely reached her brain. The wind freshened sharply; and the impact of two ripples almost capsized her chirágh. It dipped—it vanished. . . .

With a low sound of dismay she craned forward; lost her balance, and would have fallen headlong . . . but that masculine fingers closed on her arm and pulled her backward—just in time.

"Roy!" she breathed, without turning her eyes from the water—for the precious flame had reappeared. "Look, there it is—safe . . .!"

"But what of *you*, little sister, had not I stayed to watch the fate of your Dewáli lamp?"

The words were spoken in the vernacular—and not in the voice of Roy. Startled, she drew back and faced a man of less than middle height, bare-headed, wearing the orange-pink draperies of an ascetic. In the half dark she could just discern the colour and the necklace of carved beads that hung almost to his waist.

"I am most grateful, *guru-ji*,"[1] she murmured demurely, also in the vernacular; and stood so—shaken a little by her fright: unreasonably disappointed that it was not Roy; relieved, that the providential intruder chanced to be a holy man. "Will you not speed my brave little lamp with your blessing?"

His smile arrested and puzzled her; and his face, more clearly seen, lacked the unmistakable stamp of the ascetic.

"You are not less brave yourself, sister," he said, "venturing thus boldly and alone . . ."

The implication annoyed her; but anxious not to be misjudged, she answered truthfully: "I am not as those others, *guru-ji*. I am—England-returned; still out of purdah . . . out of caste."

He levelled his eyes at her with awakened interest; then: "Frankness for frankness is fair exchange, sister.

[1] Holy man.

I am no *guru;* but like yourself, England-returned; caste restored, however. Dedicated to service of the Mother——"

It was her turn to start and scrutinise him—discreetly. "Yet you make pretence of holiness——?"

"In the interests of the Mother," he interposed, answering the note of reproach, "I need to mix freely among her sons—and daughters. These clothes are passports to all, and, wearing them in her service is no dishonour. But for my harmless disguise, I might not have ventured near enough to save you from making a feast for the muggers—just for this superstition of Dewáli—not cured by all the wisdom of Oxford.—Was it Oxford?"

"Yes."

"Is it possible——?" He drew nearer. His eyes dwelt on her frankly, almost boldly. "Am I addressing the accomplished daughter of Ram Singh Bahádur——?"

At that she pulled her sari forward, turning away from him. His look and tone repelled her, frightened her; yet she could not call for Roy, who was playing his part too scrupulously well.

"Go——! Leave me!" she commanded desperately, louder than she had spoken yet. "I am not ungrateful. But—making *pujah* [1]—I wish to be alone——"

His chuckling laugh sent a shiver through her.

"Why these airs of the zenana with one enlightened —like yourself . . .?"

He broke off and retreated abruptly. For a shadowy figure had sauntered into view.

Arúna sprang towards it—zenana airs forgotten. "Oh, Roy——!"

"Did you call, Arúna?" he asked. "Thought I heard you. This fellow bothering you——? I'll settle him——" Turning, he said politely: "My cousin is here, under my escort, to make *pujah*, *guru-ji.* She wishes to be alone."

"Your cousin, except for my timely intrusion, would by this time be permanently secure from interruption—in the belly of a *mugger*," [2] retorted the supposed ascetic —in English.

[1] Prayer. [2] Crocodile.

Roy started and stared. The voice was unmistakable.
"Chandranath! Masquerading as a saint? *You* are no *guru*."

"And *you* are no Rajput. You also appear to be masquerading—as a lover, perhaps? Quite useless trying to fool me, Sinclair, with play-acting—about cousins. In my capacity of *guru* I feel compelled to warn this accomplished young lady that her fine cavalier is only a sham Rajput of British extraction . . ."

"*Sham*—curse you! I'm a genuine Seesodia—on one side——" The instant he had spoken, he saw his folly.

"Oho—half-caste only!"

An oath and a threatening forward move, impelled the speaker to an undignified step backward. Roy cooled a little at that. The fellow was beneath contempt.

"I am of highest caste, English and Indian. I admit no slur in the conjunction; and I take no insults from any man . . ." He made another forward move, purely for the pleasure of seeing Chandranath jerk backward. "If my cousin was in danger, we are grateful to you. But I told you, she wishes to be alone. So I must ask you to move on elsewhere."

"Oh, as to that . . . I have no violent predilection for your society."

And, as he sauntered off, with an elaborate air of pleasing no one but himself, Roy kept pace alongside—"For all the world," he thought, "like Terry edging off an intruder. Too polite to go for him; but quite prepared if need be!"

When they had turned the corner of the building, Chandranath fired a parting shot. "I infer you came here fancying you can marry her, because diluted blood of Seesodias runs in your veins. But here in India, you will find forces too powerful militating against it."

But Roy was not to be goaded again into letting slip his self-control. "The men of my stock, British and Rajput, are not in the habit of discussing their women-folk with strangers," said he—and flattered himself he had very neatly secured the last word.

As for Arúna—left alone—she leaned again on the low abutment, but the hypnotic spell was broken: only acute anxiety remained. For the lamp of her life had made scant progress; and now she was aware of a disturbance in the water, little ominous whirlpools not caused by wind. Presently there emerged a long shadow, like a black expanse of rock :—unmistakably a mugger. And in that moment she felt exquisitely grateful to the hand that had seized her in the nick of time. The next—she wrung her own together with a low, shivering cry.

For as the brute rose into fuller view, her chirágh rose with it—and so remained; stranded high and dry somewhere near the horny shoulder; tilted sideways, she judged from the slope of the flame; the oil, its life-blood, trickling away. And as the mugger moved leisurely on, in the wrong direction, breaking up the gold network of reflections, she had her answer—or no answer. The lamp was neither wrecked nor shattered; but it would never, now, reach the farther shore. Mai Lakshmi's face was turned away in simple indifference, from the plea of a mere waverer between two worlds, who ventured to set her lamp on the waters, not so much in faith as in a mute gesture of despair. . . .

She came very near despair, as she crouched sobbing there in the shadow—not entirely for the fate of her lamp, but in simple reaction from the mingled excitements and emotions of the evening. . . .

It was only a few minutes—though it seemed an age—before she felt Roy's hand on her shoulder and heard his voice, troubled and tender beneath its surface note of command.

"Arúna—what the—get up. Don't cry like that—you mustn't . . ."

She obeyed instinctively; and stood there, like a chidden child, battling with her sobs.

"Where's the thing? What's happened?" he asked, seeming to disregard her effort at control.

"There—over there. Look . . . the mugger!"

"Mugger?" He sighted it. "Well, I'm—the thieving brute!" Humour lurked in his voice—more tonic than sympathy; yet in a sense, more upsetting. Her tragedy had its vein of the ludicrous; and at his hint of it, tears trembled into laughter; laughter into tears. The impact unsteadied her afresh; and she covered her face again shaken with sobs.

"Arúna—my *dear*—you mustn't, I tell you . . ." More tenderness now than command.

She held her breath—pain shot through with sudden ecstasy. For in speaking he had laid an arm round her shoulder; just supporting her with a firm gentle grasp that sent tingling shocks along all her sensitised nerves.

"Listen, Arúna—and don't cry," he said, low and urgently. "No answer always leaves room for hope. And you shall have your Dyán, I promise you. I won't come back without him. I can't say fairer than that. So now——" his hand closed on her shoulder. "Give over—breaking your poor heart!"

Comforted a little, she uncovered her face. "I will try. Only to-night—I would rather—not the Palace dinner, the fireworks. I would rather go home with Miss Mills and the children . . ."

"And cry your eyes out all alone. And spoil the whole evening—for us both. No, you don't. Remember—you are Rajputni: not to be hag-ridden by a mere chirágh and a thieving mugger. No more tears and terrors. Look me in the face—and promise."

As usual, he was irresistible. What matter Mai Lakshmi's indifference—since he cared so much? "Faithfully—I promise, Roy," she said; and, for proof of courage, looked straight into his eyes—that seemed mysteriously to hold and draw her into depths beyond depths.

For one incredible moment, his face moved a little nearer to hers—paused, as if irresolute, and withdrew.

So brief was the instant, so slight the movement, that she almost doubted her senses. But her inmost being knew—and ached, without shyness or shame, for the kiss withheld. . . .

"You've the grit—I knew it," Roy said at last, in the level voice that had puzzled her earlier in the evening: and his hand slid from her shoulder. "Come now—we've been too long. Thea will be wondering . . ."

He turned; and she moved beside him, walking in a dream.

"Did you say much, before I came?" he asked, after a pause, "to that fellow—Chandranath?"

"I spoke a little—thinking him a *guru*——" She paused. The name woke a chord of memory. "Chandranath," she repeated, "that is the name they said——"

"*Who?*" Roy asked sharply, coming out of his own dream.

"Mátaji and the widowed Aunt——"

"What do they know of him?"

"How can I tell? I think it was—through our *guru*, he made offer of marriage—for me; wishing for an educated wife. I was wondering—could it be the same——?"

"Well, look here," he rounded on her, suddenly imperious. "If it is—you can tell them I *won't* have it. Grandfather would be furious. He ought to know—and Dyán. Your menfolk don't seem to get a look in."

"Not much—with marrying arrangements. That is for women and priests. But—for now, I am safe, with Mrs Leigh——"

"And you'll stay safe—as far as he's concerned. You see, I know the fellow. He's the man I slanged in the City that day. Besides—at school——"

He unfolded the tale of St Rupert's; and she listened, amazed.

"So don't worry over that," he commanded, in his kind elder-brotherly tone. "As for your poor little chirágh, for goodness' sake don't let it get on your nerves."

She sighed—knowing it would; yet longing to be worthy of him. It seemed he understood, for his hand closed lightly on her arm.

"That won't do at all! If you feel quavery inside, try holding your head an inch higher. Gesture's half the battle of life."

"Is it? I never thought——" she murmured, puzzled, but impressed. And after that, things somehow seemed easier than she had thought possible over there, by the tank.

Secure, under Thea's wing, she drove to the Palace, where they were royally entertained by an unseen host, who could not join them at table without imperilling his soul. Later on, he appeared—grey-bearded, courtly and extensively jewelled—supported by Sir Lakshman, the prince, and a few privileged notables; whereupon they all migrated to the Palace roof for the grand display of fireworks—fitting climax to the Feast of Lights.

Throughout the evening Roy was seldom absent from Arúna's side. They said little, but his presence wrapped her round with a sense of companionship more intimate than she had yet felt even in their happiest times together. While rocket after rocket soared and curved and blossomed in mid-heaven, her gaze reverted persistently to the outline of a man's head and shoulders silhouetted against the sky. . . .

Still later on, when he bade her good-night in the Residency drawing-room, she moved away carrying her head like a crowned queen. It certainly made her feel a few degrees braver than when she had crouched in the shadows praying vain prayers—shedding vain tears. . . .

If only one could keep it up——!

# CHAPTER IX.

"Thou dost beset the path to every shrine;

. . . . . .

And if I turn from but one sin, I turn
Unto a smile of thine."

—Alice Meynell.

For Roy himself, no less than Arúna, the passing of those golden October weeks had been an experience as beautiful as it was unique. The very beauty and bewilderment of it had blinded him, at first, to the underlying danger for himself and her. Bewilderment sprang from an eerie sense—vivid to the verge of illusion—that his mother was with him again in the person of Arúna:—a fancy enhanced by the fact that his entire knowledge of Indian womanhood—the turns of thought and phrase, the charm, at once sensuous and spiritual—was linked indissolubly with her. And the perilous charm had penetrated insidiously deeper than he knew. By the time he realised what was happening, the spell was upon him; his will held captive in silken meshes he had not the heart to snap.

As often as not, in that early stage, he craved sight and sound of her simply because she wore a sari and carried her head and moved her hands just so; because her mere presence stirred him with a thrill that blended exquisite pleasure, exquisite pain. There were times he would contrive to be alone in the room with her; not talking; not even looking at her—because her face disturbed the illusion; simply letting the feel of her presence ease that inner ache—subdued, not stilled—for the mother who had remained more vitally one with him than nine mothers in ten are able, or willing, to remain with their grown-up sons.

Thea Leigh, watching unobtrusively, had caught a glimpse of the strange dual influence at work in him. She had occasionally seen him with his mother; and had gleaned some idea of their unique relation; partly from Lance, partly from her intimate link with her own Theo, half a world away; nearly eighteen now, and eager to join up before all was over. So her troubled scrutiny was tempered with a measure of understanding. Roy had always attracted her. And now, unmothered —the wound not yet healed—she metaphorically gathered him to her heart; would have done so physically without hesitation; but that Vincent had his dear and foolish qualms about her promiscuous capacity for affection. But Arúna was her ewe lamb of the moment; and not even Roy must be allowed to make things harder for her than they were already. . . .

So, after scouting the Delhi idea as preposterous, she suddenly perceived there might be virtue in it—for Arúna. Possibly it would glorify him in her eyes: but it would remove the fatal charm of his presence; give her a chance to pull up before things had gone too far. Whereat, being Thea, she spun round unashamedly, to Roy's secret amusement and relief. All the Desmond in her rose to the adventure of it. A risk, of course; but there must be no question of failure: and success would justify all. She was entirely at his service; discussed details by the hour; put him 'on to Vinx' for coaching in the general situation—underground sedition; reformers, true and false; telling arguments for the reclaiming of Dyán Singh.

To crown all—between genuine relief and genuine affection—she impulsively kissed him on departure under Vincent's very eyes.

"Just only to give you my blessing!" she explained, laughing and blushing like a girl at her own audacity. "Words are the stupidest clumsy things. I'm sure life would be happier and less complicated if we only had the sense to kiss more and talk less——!"

This—in the presence of Arúna and her husband and her six-year-old son!

Roy, deeply moved and a little overcome, nodded assent, while Vincent took her by the arms and gently removed her from further temptation.

"Where *you'd* be, Madam, if talking was rationed——!"

"I'd take it out in kissing—*Sir!*" she retorted unabashed; while Arúna glanced a little wistfully at Roy, who was fondling Terry and talking nonsense to Vernon. For the boy adored him and was on the brink of tears.

But if he seemed unheeding, he was by no means unaware. He was fighting his own battle in his own way; incidentally, he hoped, helping the girl to fight hers. For he had shaken himself almost free of his delicious yet disturbing illusion, only to be confronted by a more profoundly disturbing reality. Loyal to his promise, tacitly given, he had simply not connected her with the idea of marriage. The queer thrill of her presence was for him quite another affair. Not until that night of wandering in the moonlight had it struck him, with a faint shock, that she might be mistaking his friendliness for—something more. That contact with her had come at a critical moment for himself, was a detail he failed to realise. Beyond the sudden bewildering sensations that prompted his headlong proposal to Tara, he had not felt seriously perturbed by girl or woman; and, in the past four years, life had been filled to overflowing with other things——

That he should love Arúna, deeply and dearly, seemed as simple and natural, as loving Tara. But to fall in love was a risk he had no right to run, either for himself or her. Yet the risk had been run before he awoke to the fact. And the events and emotions of Dewáli night had drawn them irresistibly, dangerously close together. For the racial ferment had been strong in him, as in her. And the darkness, the subtle influence of his Indian dress—her tears—her danger! How could any man, frankly loving her, not be carried a little out of himself? That overmastering impulse to kiss her had startlingly revealed the true forces at work.

After all that, what could he do, but sharply apply the curb and remove himself—for a time—in the devout hope that 'things' had not gone too far? He had not the assurance to suppose she was already in love with him; but patently the possibility was there.

So—like Thea—he had come to see the Delhi inspiration in a new and surprising light. Setting forth in search of Dyán, he was, in effect, running away from himself—and Arúna, no less. If not actually in love, he very soon would be—did he dare to let himself go.

And why not—why *not?* The old unreasoning rebellion stirred in him afresh. His mother being gone, temptation tugged the harder. Home, without the Indian element, was almost unthinkable. If only he could take back Arúna! But for him there could be no 'if.' He had tacitly given his word—to *her*. And in any case there was his father—the Sinclair heritage—— So all his fine dreams of helping Arúna amounted to this—that it was he who might be driven, in the end, to hurt her more than any of them. Life that looked such a straight-ahead business for most people, seemed to bristle with pitfalls and obstacles for him; all on account of the double heritage that was at once his pride, his inspiration, and his stone of stumbling.

Endless wakeful hours of the night journey were peopled with thoughts and visions of Arúna—her pansy face and velvet-soft eyes, now flashing delicate raillery, now lifted in troubled appeal. A rainbow creature—that was the charm of her. Not beautiful—he thanked his stars; since his weakness for beauty amounted to a snare, but attractive—perilously so. For, in her case, the very element that drew him was the barrier that held them apart. The irony of it!

Was she lying awake too, poor child—missing him a little? Would she marry an Indian—ever? Would she turn her back on India—even for him? Unanswerable questions hemmed her in. Could she even answer them herself? Too well he understood how the scales of her nature hung balanced between conflicting influences. As he was, racially, so was she, spiritually, a divided being; yet, in spite of waverings, Rajputni at the core, with all that word implies to those who know. If she lacked his mother's high sustained courage, her flashes of spirit shone out the brighter for her lapses into womanly weakness—as in that poignant moment by the tank, which had so nearly upset his own equilibrium. Vividly recalling that moment, it hurt him to realise that weeks might pass before he could see her again. No denying he wanted her; felt lost without her. The coveted Delhi adventure seemed suddenly a very lonely affair; not even a clear inner sense of his mother's presence to bear him company. No dreams lately; no faint mystical intimation of her nearness, since the wonderful hour with his grandfather. Only in the form of that strange and lovely illusion had she seemed vitally near him since he left Chitor.

Graceless ingratitude—that 'only.' For now, looking back, he clearly saw how the beauty and bewilderment of that early phase—so mysteriously blending Arúna with herself—had held his emotions in check, lifted them, purified them; had saved him, for all he knew, from surrender to an overwhelming passion that might conceivably have swept everything before it. Pure fantasy—perhaps. But he felt no inclination to argue out the unarguable. He preferred simply unquestioningly to believe that, under God, he owed his salvation to her. And after all—take it spiritually or psychologically—that was in effect the truth. . . .

Towards morning, utter weariness lulled him into a troubled sleep—not for long. He awoke, chilled and heavy-eyed, to find the unheeded loveliness of a lemon-yellow dawn stealing over the blank immensity of earth and sky.

In a moment he was up, stretching cramped limbs, thanking goodness for a carriage to himself, leaning out and drinking huge draughts of crisp clean air, fragrant with the ghost of a whiff of wood smoke—the inimitable air of a Punjab autumn morning.

# CHAPTER X.

"The tongue is a little member, and boasteth great things . . .
The tongue can no man tame; it is an unruly evil, full of deadly poison."—St James iii. 5-8.

Roy spent ten days in Delhi—lodging with one Krishna Lal, a jewel merchant of high standing, well known to Sir Lakshman—and never a word or a sight of Dyán Singh. The need for constant precautions hampered him not a little; but if the needle he sought was in this particular haystack, he would find it yet.

Meanwhile, at every turn he was imbibing first impressions, a sufficiently enthralling occupation—in Delhi, of all places on earth: Delhi, mistress of many victors; very woman, in that she yields to conquer; and after centuries of romance and tragedy, remains, in essence, unconquered still. The old saying, 'Who holds Delhi, holds India,' has its dark counterpart in the unwritten belief that no alien ruler, enthroned at Delhi, shall endure. Hence the dismay of many loyal Indians when the British Government deserted Calcutta for the Queen of the North. And here, already, were her endless, secretive byways rivalling Calcutta suburbs as hornet-nests of sedition and intrigue.

Roy was to grow painfully familiar with these before his search ended. But the city's pandemonium of composite noises and composite smells was offset by the splendid remnants of Imperial Delhi:—the Pearl Mosque, a dream in marble, dazzling against the blue: inlaid columns of the Dewan-i-Khas—every leaf wrought in jade or malachite, every petal a precious stone; swelling domes and rose-pink minarets of the Jumna Musjid rising superbly from a network of narrow streets and shabby toppling houses. For, in India, the sordid and stately rub shoulders with sublime disregard for effect. In the cool aloofness of tombs and temples, or among crumbling fragments of them on the plain, or away beyond the battered Kashmir Gate—ground sacred to heroic memories—he could wander at will for hours, isolated in body and spirit, yet strangely content. . . .

And there was yet a third Delhi, hard by these two; yet curiously aloof: official, Anglo-Indian Delhi, of bungalows and clubs and painfully new Government buildings. Little scope here for imaginative excursions, but much scope for thought in the queer sensation, that beset him, of seeing his father's people, as it were, through his mother's eyes.

New as he was to Anglo-Indian life, these glimpses from the outskirts were sufficiently illuminating. Once he was present in the crowd at a big Gymkhana; and more than once he strolled through the Club gardens where social Delhi pursued tennis-balls and shuttle-cocks—gravely, as if life hung on the issue; or gaily, with gusts of laughter and chaff, often noisier than need be. And he saw them all, now, from a new angle of vision. Discreetly aloof, he observed, in passing, the complete free-and-easiness of the modern maiden with her modern cavalier; personalities flying; likewise legs and arms; a banter-wrangle interlude over a tennis-racquet; flight and pursuit of the offending maiden, punctuated with shrieks, culminating in collapse and undignified surrender: while a pair of club peons—also discreetly aloof—exchanged remarks whose import would have enraged the unsuspecting pair. Roy knew very well they never gave the matter a thought. They were simply 'rotting' in the approved style of to-day. But, seen from the Eastern standpoint, the trivial incident troubled him. It recalled a chance remark of his grandfather's: "With only a little more decorum and seriousness in their way of life out here, they could do far more to promote good understanding socially between us all, than by making premature 'reforms' or tilting at barriers arising from opposite kinds of civilisation."

Here was matter for the novel—or novels—to be born of his errantry:—the 'fruit of his life' that *she* had so longed to hold in her hands. Were she only at

Home now, what letters-without-end he would be pouring out to her! What letters he could have poured out to Arúna—did conscience permit.

He allowed himself two, in the course of ten days; and the spirit moved him, after long abstention, to indulge in a rambling screed to Tara telling of his quest; revealing more than he quite realised of the inner stress he was trying to ignore. The quest, he emphasised, was a private affair, confided to her only, because he knew she would understand. It hurt more than he cared to admit to feel how completely his father would *not* understand his present turmoil of heart and brain. . . .

Isolated thus, with his hidden thwarted emotion, there resulted a literary blossoming, the most spontaneous and satisfying since his slow struggle up from the depths. Alone at night, and in the clear keen dawns, he wrote and wrote and wrote, as a thirsty man drinks after a desert march:—poems chiefly; sketches and impressions; his dearest theme the troubled spirit of India,—or was it the spirit of Arúna?—poised between crescent light and deepening shadow, looking for sane clear guidance—and finding none. A prose sketch, in this vein, stood out from the rest; a fragment of his soul, too intimately self-revealing for the general gaze: no uncommon dilemma for an artist, precisely when his work is most intrinsically true. Had he followed the natural urge of his heart, he would have sent it to Arúna. As it was, he decided to treasure it a little longer for himself alone.

Meantime Dyán—half forgotten—suddenly emerged. It was at a meeting—exclusively religious and philosophical; but the police had wind of it; and a friendly inspector mentioned it to Krishna Lal. The chief speaker would be a Swami of impeccable sanctity. "But if you have a sensitive palate, you will doubtless detect a spice of political powder under the jam of religion!" quoth Krishna Lal, who was a man of humour and no friend of sedition.

"Thanks for the hint," said Roy—and groaned in spirit. Meetings, at best, were the abomination of desolation; and his soul was sick of the Indian variety. For the 'silent East' is never happier than when it is talking at immense length; denouncing, inaugurating, promoting; and a prolonged dose of it stirred in Roy a positive craving for men who shot remarks at each other in 'straight-flung words and true.' But no stone must be left unturned. So he went;—guided by the friendly policeman, who knew him for a Sahib bent on some personal quest.

Their search ended in a windowless inner room; packed to suffocation; heavy with attar of rose, kerosene, and human bodies; and Roy as usual clung to a doorway that offered occasional respite.

The Swami was already in full flow:—a wraith of a man in a salmon-coloured garment; his eyes, deep in their sockets, gleaming like black diamonds. And he was holding his audience spellbound:—Hindus of every calling; students in abundance; a sprinkling of Sikhs and Dogras from the lines. Some form of hypnotism,—was it? Perhaps. Even Roy could not listen unmoved, when the spirit shook the frail creature like a gust of wind and the hollow chest-notes vibrated with appeal or command. Such men—and India is full of them—are spiritual dynamos. Who can calculate their effect on an emotional race? And they no longer confine their influence to things spiritual. They, too, have caught the modern disease of politics for the million. And the supreme appeal is to youth—plastic and impressionable, aflame with fervours of the blood that can be conjured, by heady words, into fervours infinitely more dangerous to themselves and their country.

In an atmosphere dense with spilled kerosene, with over-breathed air and over-charged emotion, that appeal rang out like a trumpet blast.

"It is to youth the divine message has come in all ages; the call to martyrdom and dedication. 'Suffer little children to come unto me,' said the inspired Founder of Christianity. So also I say in this time of revival, suffer the young to fling themselves into the arms of the Mother. My sons, she cries, go back to the Vedas. You will find all wisdom there. Reject this alien gift—however finely gilded—of a civilisation inferior to your own. Hindu Rishis were old in wisdom when these were still unclothed savages coloured with blue paint. Shall the sacred Motherland be inoculated with Western poison? It is for the young to decide—to act. Nerve your arms with valour. Bring offerings acceptable, to the shrine of Kali Mai. Does she demand a sheep? A buffalo? A cocoanut? Ask yourselves. The answer is written in your hearts——"

His emaciated arms shot up and outward in a gesture the more impressive because it was maintained. For a prolonged moment the holy one seemed to hover above his audience—as it were an eagle poised on outspread wings. . . .

Roy came to himself with a start. His friend the policeman had plucked his sleeve; and they retreated a step or two through the open door.

"The Sahib heard?" queried Mán Singh in cautious undertone.

"There's hearing—and hearing," said Roy, aware of some cryptic message given and understood. "I take it *they* all know what he's driving at."

"True talk. They know. But *he* has not said. Therefore he goes in safety when he should be picking oakum in the jail khana. They are cunning as serpents these holy ones."

"They have the gift of tongues," said Roy. "May one ask what is Mai Kali's special taste in sacrifices?"

The Sikh gave him an odd look. "The blood of white goats—meaning Sahibs, Hazúr."—Roy's 'click' was Oriental to a nicety.—"'A white goat for Kali' is an old Bengali catchword. Hark how their tongues wag. But there is still another—much esteemed by the student-*lòg;* one who can skilfully flavour a *pillau* [1] of learned talk, as the Swami can flavour a pillau of religion. Where he comes, there will be trouble afterwards, and arrests. But no Siri Chandranath. He is off making trouble elsewhere."

"Chandranath—*here?*" Roy's heart gave a jerk, half excitement, half apprehension.

"Your Honour has heard the man?"

"No. I'm glad of the chance."

As they entered, the second speaker stepped on to the platform. . . .

True talk, indeed! There stood the boy who had

[1] An Indian dish.

whimpered under Scab Major's bullying, in the dark coat and turban of the educated Indian; his back half turned, in confidential talk with a friend, who had set a carafe and tumbler ready to hand. The light of a wall lamp shone full on the young man's face—clean-cut, handsome, unmistakable. . . .

*Dyán!* Dyán—and Chandranath! It was the conjunction that confounded Roy and tinged elation with dismay. He could hardly contain himself till Dyán joined the audience; standing a little apart; not taking a seat. Something in his face reminded Roy of the strained fervour in his letter to Arúna. Carefully careless, he edged his way through the outer fringe of the audience, and volunteered a remark or two in Hindustani.

"A full meeting, brother. Your friend speaks well?"

Dyán turned with a start. "Where are *you* from, that you have not heard him?" He scrutinised Roy's appearance. "A hill man——?"

Roy edged nearer and spoke in English under his breath. "Dyán—look at me. Don't make a scene. I am Roy—from Jaipur."

In spite of the warning, Dyán drew back sharply. "*What* are you here for—spying?"

"No. Hoping to find you. Because—I care; and Arúna cares——"

"Better to care less and understand more," Dyán muttered brusquely. "No time for talk now. Listen. You may learn a few things Oxford could not teach."

The implied sneer enraged Roy; but listen he must, perforce: and in the space of half an hour he learnt a good deal about Chandranath and the mentality of his type.

To the outer ear, he was propounding the popular modern doctrine of 'Yoga by action.' To the inner ear he was extolling passion and rebellion in terms of a creed that enjoins detachment from both; inciting to political murder, under sanction of the divine dictum, 'Who kills the body kills naught . . . Thy concern is with action alone, never with results.' And his heady flights of rhetoric, like those of the Swami, were frankly aimed at the scores of half-fledged youths who hung upon his utterance.

"What are the first words of the young child? What

are the first words in your own hearts?" he cried, indicating that organ with a dramatic forefinger. "*I want!* It is the passionate cry of youth. By indomitably uttering it, he can dislodge mountains into the sea. And in India to-day there exist mountains necessary to be hurled into the sea!" His significant pause was not lost on his hearers—or on Roy. "'Many-branched and endless are the thoughts of the irresolute.' But to him who cries ardently, '*I want,*' there is no impediment, except paucity of courage to snatch the seductive object. Deaf to the anæmic whisper of compunction, remembering that sin taints only the weak, he will be translated to that dizzy eminence, where right and wrong, truth and untruth, become as pigmies, hardly discerned by the naked eye. There dwells Káli—the shameless and pitiless; and believing our country that deity incarnate, *her* needs must be our gods. 'Her image make we in temple after temple—Bande Mátaram?'" The invocation was flung back to him in a ragged shout. Here and there a student leapt to his feet brandishing a clenched fist. "Compose your laudable intoxication, brothers. I do not say, 'Be violent.' There is a necromancy of the spirit more potent than weapons of the flesh:—the delusion of irresistible suggestion that will conquer even truth itself . . ."

Abstraction piled on abstraction; perversion on perversion; and that deluded crowd plainly swallowing it all as gospel truth——! To Roy the whole exhibition was purely disgustful; as if the man had emptied a dust-bin under his aristocratic nose. Once or twice he glanced covertly at Dyán, standing beside him; at the strained intentness of his face, the nervous clenched hand. Was this the same Dyán who had ridden and argued and read 'Greats' with him only four years ago—this hypnotised being who seemed to have forgotten his existence——?

Thank God! At last it was over! But while applause hummed and fluttered, there sprang on to the platform, unannounced, a wiry keen-faced man, with the parted beard of a Sikh.

"Brothers—I demand a hearing!" he cried aloud; "I who was formerly hater of the British, preaching all manner of violence—I have been three years detained in Germany; and I come back now, with my eyes open, to say all over India—cease your fool's talk about self-government and tossing mountains into the sea! Cease making yourselves drunk with words and waving your Vedic flags and stand by the British—your true friends——"

At that, cries and counter-cries drowned his voice. Books were hurled; no other weapon being handy; and Roy noted, with amused contempt, that Chandranath hastily disappeared from view.

The Sikh laughed in the face of their opposition. Dexterously catching a book, he hurled it back; and once more made his strong voice heard above the clamour. "Fools—and sheep! You may stop your ears now. In the end I will make you hear——"

Shouted down again, he vanished through a side exit; and, in the turmoil that followed, Roy's hand closed securely on Dyán's arm. Throughout the stormy interlude, he had stood rigidly still: a pained, puzzled frown contracting his brows. Yet it was plain he would have slipped away without a word, but for Roy's detaining grasp.

"You don't go running off—now I've found you," said he good-humouredly. "I've things to say. Come along to my place and hear them."

Dyán jerked his imprisoned arm. "Very sorry. I have—important duties."

"To-morrow night then? I'm lodging with Krishna Lal. And—look here, *don't* mention me to your friend the philosopher! I know more about him than you might suppose. If you still care a damn for me—and the others, do what I ask—and keep your mouth shut——"

Dyán's frown was hostile; but his voice was low and troubled. "For God's sake leave me alone, Roy. Of course—I care. But that kind of caring is carnal weakness. We, who are dedicated, must rise above such weakness, above pity and slave-morality, giving all to the Mother——"

"Dyán—have you forgotten—*my* mother?" Roy pressed his advantage in the same low tone.

"No. Impossible. She was *Dévi*—Goddess; loveliest and kindest——"

"Well, in her name, I ask you—come to-morrow evening and have a talk."

Dyán was silent; then, for the first time, he looked Roy straight in the eyes. "In her name—I will come. Now let me go."

Roy let him go. He had achieved little enough. But for a start it was not so bad.

## CHAPTER XI.

"When we have fallen through storey after storey of our vanity and aspiration, it is then that we begin to measure the stature of our friends."—R. L. S.

NEXT evening Dyán arrived. He stayed for an hour, and did most of the talking. But his unnatural volubility suggested disturbance deep down.

Only once Roy had a glimpse of the true Dyán, when he presented Arúna's '*prasád*,' consecrated by her touch. In silence Dyán set it on the table; and reverently touched, with his finger-tips, first the small parcel, then his own forehead.

"Arúna—sister," he said on an under breath. But he would not be drawn into talking of her, of his grandfather, or of home affairs: and his abrupt departure left Roy with a maddening sense of frustration.

He lay awake half the night; and reached certain conclusions that atoned for a violent headache next morning. First and best—Dyán was not a genuine convert. All this ferment and froth did not spell reasoned conviction. He was simply ensnared; his finer nature warped by the 'delusion of irresistible suggestion,' deadlier than any weapon of War. His fanatical loyalty savoured of obsession. So much the better. An obsession could be pricked like an air-ball with the right weapon at the right moment. That, as Roy saw it, was his task:—in effect, a ghostly duel between himself and Chandranath for the soul of Dyán Singh; and the fate of Arúna virtually hung on the issue.

Should he succeed, Chandranath would doubtless guess at his share in Dyán's defection; and few men care about courting the enmity of the unscrupulous. That is the secret power behind the forces of anarchy, above all in India, where social and spiritual boycott can virtually slay a man without shedding of blood. For himself, Roy decided the game was worth the candle. The question remained—how far that natural shrinking might affect Dyán? And again—how much did he know of Chandranath's designs on Arúna?

Roy decided to spring the truth on him next time—and note the effect. Dyán had said he would come again one evening; and—sooner than Roy expected—he came. Again he was abnormally voluble, as if holding his cousin at arm's length by italicising his own fanatical fervour, till Roy's impatience subsided into weariness and he palpably stifled a yawn.

Dyán, detecting him, stopped dead, with a pained, puzzled look that went to Roy's heart. For he loved the real Dyán, even while he was bored to extinction with the semi-religious verbiage that poured from him like water from a jug.

"Awfully sorry," he apologised frankly. "But I've been over-dosed with that sort of stuff lately; and I'm damned if I can swallow it like you do. Yet I'm dead keen for India to have the best, all round, that she's capable of digesting—yet. So's Grandfather. You *can't* deny it."

Dyán frowned irritably. "Grandfather's prejudiced and old-fashioned."

"He's longer-sighted than most of your voluble friends. He doesn't rhapsodise. He *knows*.—But I'm not old-fashioned. Nor is Arúna."

"No, poor child; only England-infatuated. She is unwise not taking this chance of an educated husband——"

"And *such* a husband!" Roy struck in so sharply that Dyán stared open-mouthed.

"How the devil can *you* know?"

"And how the devil can you *not* know," countered Roy, "when it's your precious paragon—Chandranath."

He scored his point clean and true. "Chandranath!" Dyán echoed blankly, staring into the fire.

Roy said nothing; simply let the fact sink in. Then, having dealt the blow, he proffered a crumb of consolation. "Perhaps he prefers to say nothing till he's pulled it off. But I warn you, if he persists, I shall put every feasible spoke in his wheel."

Dyán faced him squarely. "You seem very intimate with our affairs. Who told you this?"

"Arúna—herself."

"You are also very intimate—with her."

"As she has lost her brother, her natural protector, I do what I can—to make up."

Dyán winced and stole a look at him. "Why not make up for still greater lack—and marry her yourself?"

It was he who hit the mark this time. Roy's blood tingled; but voice and eyes were under control.

"I've only been there a few weeks. The question has not arisen."

"Your true meaning is—it *could not arise.* They were glad enough for her service in England; but whatever her service, or her loving, she must not marry an Englishman, even with the blood of India in his veins. That is our reward—both——"

It was the fierce bitter Dyán of that long ago afternoon in New College Lane. But Roy was too angry on his own account to heed. He rose abruptly.

"I'll trouble you not to talk like that."

Dyán rose also, confronting him. "I *must* say what is in mind—or go. Better accept the fact—it is useless to meet."

"I refuse to accept the fact."

"But—there it is. I only make you angry. And you imply evil of the man—I admire."

He so plainly boggled over the words that Roy struck without hesitation.

"Dyán, tell me straight—*do* you admire him? Would you have Arúna marry him?"

"N—no. Impossible. There is—another kind of wife," he blurted out, averting his eyes; but before Roy could speak, he had pulled himself together. "However—I mustn't stay talking. Good-night."

Roy's anger—fierce but transient, always—had faded. "There are some ties you can't break, Dyán, even with your Bande Mátaram. Come again soon."

Impossible to resist the friendly tone. "But," he asked, "how long are you hanging about Delhi like this?"

"As long as I choose."

"But—why?"

"To see something of you, old chap. It seems the only way—unless I can persuade you to chuck all this poisonous vapouring, and come back to Jaipur with me. Arúna's waiting—breaking her heart—longing to see you . . ."

He knew he was rushing his fences; but the mood was on; the chance too good to lose.

Dyán's eyes lightened a moment. Then he shook his head. "I am too much involved."

"You *will* come, though, in the end," Roy said quietly. "I can wait. Sunday, is it? And we'll bar politics—as we did in the good days. Don't you want to hear of them all at Home?"

"Sometimes—yes. But perhaps—better not. You are a fine fellow, Roy—even to quarrel with. Good-night." They shook hands warmly.

On the threshold, Dyán turned, hesitated; then—in a hurried murmur—asked: "*Where* is she—what's she doing now . . . Tara?"

He was obviously unaware of having used her name: and Roy, though startled, gave no sign.

"She's still in Serbia. She's been simply splendid. Head over ears in it all from the start."—He paused—"Shall I tell her—when I write . . . about you?"

Dyán shrugged his shoulders. "Waste of ink and paper. It would not interest her."

"It would. I know Tara. What you are doing now would hurt her—keenly."

"Tcha!" The sharp sound expressed sheer unbelief. It also expressed pain. "Good-night," he added, for the third time; and went out—leaving Roy electrified; a-tingle with the hope of success at last.

Tara was not forgotten; though Dyán had been trying to pretend she was—even to himself. Ten chances to one, she was still at the core everything; even his present incongruous activities. . . .

Roy paced the room; his imagination alight; his own recoil from the conjunction, overborne by immediate concern for Dyán. Unable to forget her—who could?—he had thrust the pain of remembering into the dark background of his mind; and there it remained—a hard knot of soreness and bitterness—as Arúna had said. And all that bottled-up bitterness had been vented against England—an unconscious symbol of Tara, desired yet withheld ; while the intensity of his thwarted passion sought and found an outlet in fervent adoration of his country visualised as woman.

Right or wrong—that was how Roy saw it. And the argument seemed psychologically sound. Cruel to be kind, he must touch the point of pain ; draw the hidden thing into the open ; and so reawaken the old Dyán, who could arraign the new one far more effectually than could Roy himself or another. Seized with his idea, he indulged in a more hopeful letter to Arúna ; and had scarcely patience to wait for Sunday.

In leisurely course it arrived—that last Sunday of the Great War. The Chandni Chowk was a-bubble with strange and stirring rumours ; but the day waned and the evening waned—and no Dyán appeared.

On Monday morning—still no word : but news, so tremendous, flashed half across the world, that Dyán and his mysterious defection flickered like a match at midday.

The War was over—virtually over. From the Vosges to the sea, not the crack of a rifle nor the moan of a shell ; only an abrupt, dramatic silence—the end ! Belief in the utter cessation of all that wonderful and terrible activity, penetrated slowly. And as it penetrated Roy realised, with something like dismay, that the right and natural sense of elation simply was not. He actually felt depressed. Shrink as he might from the jar of conflict, the sure instinct of a soldier race warned him that hell holds no fury and earth no danger like a ruthless enemy not decisively smitten. The psychology of it was beyond him—shrouded in mystery.

Not till long afterwards did he know how many, in England and France, had shared his bewildered feeling ; how British soldiers in Belgium had cried like children, had raged almost to the point of mutiny. But one thing he knew—steeped as he was in the sub-strata of Eastern thought and feeling. India would never understand. Visible, spectacular victory, alone could impress the East : and such an impression might have counteracted many mistakes that had gone before. . . .

Tuesday brought no Dyán; only a scrawled note: "Sorry—too much business. Can't come just now." *If* one could take that at its face value——! But it might mean anything. Had Chandranath found out—and had Dyán not the moral courage to go his own way?

He knew by now where his cousin lodged; but had never been there. It was in one of the oldest parts of the city; alive with political intrigue. If Roy's nationality were suspected, 'things' might happen, and it was clearly unfair on his father to run needless risks. But this was different. 'Things' might be happening to Dyán.

So, after nearly a week of maddening suspense, he resolved—with all due caution—to take his chance.

A silvery twilight was ebbing from the sky when he plunged into a maze of narrow streets and by-lanes where the stream of Eastern life flows along immemorial channels scarcely stirred by surface eddies of 'advance.'

Threading his way through the crowd, he found the street and the landmark he sought: a doorway, adorned with a faded wreath of marigolds, indication of some holy presence within; and just beyond it, a low-browed arch, almost a tunnel. It passed under balconied houses toppling perilously forward; and as Roy entered it, a figure darkened the other end. He could only distinguish the long dark coat and turbaned head: but there flashed instant conviction—Chandranath!

Alert, rather than alarmed, he hurried forward, hugging the opposite wall. At the darkest point they crossed. Roy felt the other pause, scrutinise him—and pass on. The relief of it! And the ignominy of suddenly feeling the old childish terror, when you had turned your back on a dark room. It was all he could do not to break into a run. . . .

In the open court, set round with tottering houses, a sacred neem tree made a vast patch of shadow. Near it, a rickety staircase led up to Dyán's roof room. Roy, mounting cautiously, knocked at the highest door.

"Are you there? It's Roy," he called softly.

A pause:—then the door flew open and Dyán stood

before him, in loose white garments; no turban; a farouche look in his eyes.

"My God—*Roy!* Crazy of you! I never thought——"

"Well, I got sick of waiting. I suppose I can come in?" Roy's impatience was the measure of his relief.

Dyán moved back a pace, and, as Roy stepped on to the roof, he carefully closed the door.

"Think—if you had come three minutes earlier! He only left me just now—Chandranath."

"And passed me in the archway," added Roy with his touch of bravado. "I've as much right to be in Delhi—and to vary my costume—as your mysteriously potent friend. It's a free country."

"It is fast becoming—not so free." Dyán lowered his voice, as if afraid he might be overheard. "And you don't consider the trouble it might make—for me."

"How about the trouble you've been making for me? What's wrong?"

Dyán passed a nervous hand across his eyes and forehead. "Come in. It's getting cold out here," he said, in a repressed voice. Roy followed him across the roof top, with its low parapet and vault of darkening sky, up three steps, into an arcaded room, where a log fire burned in the open hearth. Shabby, unrelated bits of furniture gave the place a comfortless air. On a corner table strewn with leaflets and pamphlets ("Poisoned arrows, up to date!" thought Roy), a typewriter reared its hooded head. The sight struck a shaft of pain through him. Arúna's Dyán—son of kings and warriors—turning his one skilful hand to such base uses!

"What's wrong?" he repeated with emphasis. "I want a straight answer, Dyán. I've risked something to get it."

Dyán sat down near a small table, and took his head between his hands. "There is—so much wrong," he said, looking steadily up at Roy. "I am feeling—like a man who wakes too suddenly after much sleep-walking."

"Since when?" asked Roy, keeping himself in hand. "What's jerked you awake? D'you know?"

"There have been many jerks. Seeing you; Arúna's offering; this news of the War; and something . . . you mentioned last time."

"What was that . . . Tara?" Roy lunged straight to the middle of the wound.

Dyán started. "But—how——? I never said . . ." he stammered, visibly shaken.

"It didn't need saying. Arúna told me—the fact; and my own wits told me the rest. You're not honestly keen—are you?—to shorten the arm of the British Raj and plunge India into chaos?"

"No—no." A very different Dyán, this, to the one who had poured out stock phrases like water only a week ago.

"Isn't bitterness—about Tara, at the back of it? Face that straight. And—if it's true, say so without false shame."

Dyán was silent a long while, staring into the fire. "Very strange. I had no idea," he said at last. The words came slowly, as if he were thinking aloud. "I was angry—miserable; hating you all; even—very nearly—*her*. Then came the War; and I thought—now our countries will become like one. I will win her by some brave action—she who is the spirit of courage. From France, after all that praise of Indians in the papers, I wrote again. No use. After that, I hoped by some brave action, I might be killed. Instead, through stupid carelessness, I am only maimed—as you see. I was foolishly angry when Indian troops were sent away from France: and my heart became hard like a nut."—He had emerged from his dream now and was frankly addressing Roy—"I knew, if I went home, they would insist I should marry. Quite natural. But for me—not thinkable. Yet I *must* go back to India. And there, in Bombay, I heard Chandranath speak. He was just back from deportation; and to me his words were like leaping flames. All the fire of my passion—choked up in me—could flow freely in service of the Mother. I became intoxicated with the creed of my new comrades: there is neither truth nor untruth, right nor wrong; there is only the Mother. I was filled with the joy of dedication and unquestioning surrender. It gave me visions like opium dreams. Both kinds of opium I have taken freely,—while walking in my sleep. I was ready for taking life; any desperate deed. Instead—Tcha! I have to take money, like a common dacoit, because police must be bribed, soldiers tempted, meetings multiplied . . ."

"It takes more than the blood of white goats to oil the wheels of your chariot," said Roy, very quiet, but rather grim. "And he's not the man to do his own dirty work—eh?"

"No. He is only very clever to dress it up in fine arguments. All money is the Mother's. Only they are thieves who selfishly hide it in banks and safes. Those who release it for her use are deliverers . . ." he broke off with a harsh laugh. "In spite of education, we Indians are too easily played upon, Roy. If you had not spoken—of her, I might have swallowed—even that. Thieving—bah! Killing is man's work. There is sanction in the Gita——"

"Sanction be damned!" Roy cut in sharply. "You might as well say Shakespeare sanctioned theft because he wrote, 'Who steals my purse steals trash!' The only sanction worth anything is inside you. And you didn't seem to find it there. But let's get at the point. Did you refuse?"

"No. Only—for the first time, I demurred; and because the need is urgent, he became very violent—in language. It was almost a quarrel."

"Clear proof you scored! Did you mention—Arúna?"

Dyán shook his head. "If *I* become violent, it is not only language——"

"No. You're a *man*. And now you're awake again, I can tell you things — but I can't stay all night."

"No. He is coming back. Only gone to Cantonments—on business."

"What sort of business?"

Dyán chewed his lip and looked uncomfortable.

"Never mind, old chap. I can see a church by daylight! He's getting at the troops. Spreading lies about the Armistice. And after that——?"

"He is returning—about midnight, hoping to find me in a more reasonable mind——"

"And by Jove we won't disappoint him!" cried Roy, who had seen his God-given chance. Springing up he gripped Dyán by the shoulder. "Your reasonable mind will take the form of scooting back with me, *jut put;*[1] and we can slip out of Delhi by the night mail. Time's precious. So hurry up."

But Dyán did not stir. He sat there looking so plainly staggered that Roy burst out laughing.

"You're not half awake yet. You've messed about so long with men who merely 'agitate' and 'inaugurate,' that you've forgotten the kind who act first and talk afterwards. I give you ten minutes to scribble a tender farewell. Then—we make tracks. It's all I came here for—if you want to know. And I take it you're willing?"

Dyán sighed. "I am willing enough. But—there are many complications. You do not know. They are organising big trouble over the Rowlatt Bill—and other things. I have not much secret information, or my life would probably not be worth a pin. But it is all one complicated network, and there are too easy ways in India for social and spiritual boycott——"

He enlarged a little; quoted cases that filled Roy with surprise and indignation, but no way shook his resolve.

"We needn't go straight to Jaipur. Quite good fun to knock round a bit. Throw him off the scent, till he's got over the shock. We can wire our news; Arúna will be too happy to fret over a little delay. And you won't be ostracised among your own people. They want you. They want your help. Grandfather does. The best *I* could do was to run you to earth—open your eyes——"

"And by Indra you've *done* it, Roy."

"You'll come then?"

"Yes, I'll come—and damn the consequences!"

The Dyán of Oxford days was visibly emerging now: a veritable awakening; the strained look gone from his face.

It was Roy's 'good minute': and in the breathless rush that followed, he swept Dyán along with him—unresisting, exalted, amazed——

The farewell letter was written; and Dyán's few belongings stowed into a basket-box. Then they hurried down, through the dark courtyard into the darker

[1] At once.

tunnel; and Roy felt unashamedly glad not to be alone. His feet would hurry, in spite of him; and that kept him a few paces ahead.

Passing a dark alcove, he swerved instinctively—and hoped to goodness Dyán had not seen.

Just before reaching the next one he tripped over something—taut string or wire stretched across the passage. It should have sent him headlong had he been less agile. As it was, he stumbled, cursed and kept his feet.

"'Ware man-trap!" he called back to Dyán, under his breath.

Next instant, from the alcove, a shot rang out: and it was Dyán who cursed; for the bullet had grazed his arm.

They both ran now; and made no bones about it. Roy's sensations reminded him vividly of the night he and Lance fled from the Turks.

"We seem to have butted in and spoilt somebody's little game!" he remarked, as they turned into a wider street and slackened speed. "How's your arm?"

"Nothing. A mere scratch." Dyán's tone was graver. "But that's most unusual. I can't make it out——"

"You're well quit of it all, anyhow," said Roy, and slipped a hand through his arm.

Not till they were settling down for a few hours' sleep in the night mail, did it dawn on Roy that the little game might possibly have been connected with himself. Chandranath had seen him in that dress before. He had just come very near quarrelling with Dyán. If he suspected Roy's identity, he would suspect his influence. . . .

He frankly spoke his thought to Dyán; and found it had occurred to him already. "Not himself, of course," he added. "The gentleman is not partial to firearms! But suspecting—he might have arranged; hoping to catch you coming back—the swine! Naturally after this, he will go further than suspecting!"

"He can go to the devil—and welcome; now I've collared *you!*" said Roy;—and slept soundly upon that satisfying achievement, through all the rattle and clatter of the express.

## CHAPTER XII.

"God uses us to help each other so."
—Browning.

It was distinctly one of Roy's great moments when, at last, they four stood together in Sir Lakshman's room: the old man, outwardly impassive—as became a Rajput—profoundly moved in the deep places of his heart: Arúna, in Oxford gown and sari, radiant one moment; the next—in spite of stoic resolves—crying softly in Dyán's arms. And Roy understood only too well. The moment he held her hand and met her eyes—he knew. It was not only joy at Dyán's return that evoked the veiled blush, the laugh that trembled into tears. Conceit or no conceit, his intuition was not to be deceived.

And the conviction did not pass. It was confirmed by every day, every hour he spent in her company. On the rare occasions, when they were alone together, the very thing that must be religiously stifled and hid, emanated from her like fragrance from a flower; sharply reawakening his own temptation to respond—were it only to ease her pain. And there was more in it than that—or very soon would be, if he hesitated much longer to clinch matters by telling her the truth; though every nerve shrank from the ordeal—for himself and her. Running away from oneself was plainly a futile experiment. To have so failed with her, disheartened him badly and dwarfed his proud achievement to an insignificant thing.

To the rest, unaware, his triumph seemed complete, his risky adventure justified beyond cavil. They all admitted as much;—even Vincent, who abjured superlatives and had privately taken failure for granted. Roy, in a fit of modesty, ascribed it all to 'luck.' By the merest chance he had caught Dyán, on his own confession, just as the first flickers of doubt were invading his hypnotised soul; just when it began to dawn on him that alien hands were pulling the strings. He had already begun to feel trapped; unwilling to go forward; unable to go back; and the fact that no inner secrets were confided to him, had galled his Rajput vanity and pride. In the event, he was thankful enough for the supposed slight; since it made him feel appreciably safer from the zeal of his discarded friends.

Much of this he had confided to Roy, in fragments and jerks, on the night of their amazing exit from Delhi; already sufficiently himself again to puzzle frankly over that perverted Dyán; to marvel—with a simplicity far removed from mere foolishness—"how one man can make a magic in other men's minds so that he shall appear to them an eagle when he is only a crow."

"That particular form of magic," Roy told him, "has made half the history of the world. We all like to flatter ourselves we're safe from it—till we get bitten! You've been no more of a fool than the others, Dyán—if that's any consolation."

The offending word rankled a little. The truth of it rankled more. "By Indra, I am no fool now. Perhaps he has discovered that already. I fancy my letter will administer a shock. I wonder what he will do?"

"He won't 'do.' You can bank on that. He may fling vitriol over you on paper. But you won't have the pleasure of his company at Jaipur. He left his card on us before the Dewáli. And there's been trouble since; leaflets circulating mysteriously; an exploded attempt to start a seditious 'rag.' So they're on the *qui vive*. He'll count that one up against me: but I'll manage to survive."

And Dyán, in the privacy of his heart, had felt distinctly relieved. Not that he lacked the courage of his race; but, having seen the man for years, as it were, through a magnifying lens, he could not, all in a moment, see him for the thing he was:—dangerous as a snake, yet swift as a snake to wriggle out of harm's way.

He had not been backward, however, in awakening his grandfather to purdah manœuvres. Strictly in private—he told his cousin—there had been ungoverned storms of temper, ungoverned abuse of Roy, who was suspected by 'the Inside' of knowing too much and having undue influence with the old man. 'The Inside,' he gathered, had from early days been jealous of the favourite daughter and all her belongings. Naturally, in Dyán's opinion, his sister ought to marry; and the sooner the better. Perhaps he had been unwise, after all, insisting on postponement. By now she would have been settled in her lawful niche instead of making trouble with this craze for hospital nursing and keeping outside caste. Not surprising if she shrank from living at home, after all she had been through. Better for them both, perhaps, to break frankly with orthodox Hinduism and join the Brahma Samáj.

As Roy knew precisely how much—or rather, how little—Arúna liked working in the wards, he suffered a pang at the pathos of her innocent guile. And if Dyán had his own suspicions, he kept them to himself. He also kept to himself the vitriolic outpouring which he had duly found awaiting him at Jaipur. It contained too many lurid allusions to 'that conceited, imperialistic half-caste cousin of yours'; and Roy might resent the implied stigma as much as Dyán resented it for him. So he tore up the effusion, intended for the eye of Roy, merely remarking that it had enraged him. It was beneath contempt.

Roy would like to have seen it, all the same; for he knew himself quicker than Dyán at reading between the lines. The beggar would not hit back straight. But given the chance, he might try it on some other way—witness the pistol-shot in the arcade; a side light—or a side flash—on the pleasant sort of devil he was!

Back in the Jaipur Residency, in the garden that was 'almost England,' back in his good familiar tweed coat and breeches, the whole Delhi interlude seemed strangely theatrical and unreal; more like a vivid dream than an experience in the flesh.

But there was Dyán to prove it no dream; and the perilous charm of Arúna, that must be resisted to the best of his power. . . .

All this stir and ferment within; yet not a surface

ripple disturbed the flow of those uneventful weeks between the return of Roy and the coming of Lance Desmond for Christmas leave.

It is thus that drama most often happens in life —a light under a bushel; set in the midst, yet unseen. Vincent, delving in ethnological depths, saw little or nothing outside his manuscript and maps. Floss Eden —engrossed in her own drawing-room comedy with Captain Martin—saw less than nothing, except that 'Mr Sinclair's other native cousin' came too often to the house. For she turned up her assertive nose at 'native gentlemen'; and confided to Martin her private opinion that Aunt Thea went too far in that line. She bothered too much about other people all round—which was true.

She had bothered a good deal more about Floss Eden, in early days, than that young lady at all realised. And now—in the intervals of organising Christmas presents and Christmas guests—she was bothering a good deal over Roy, whose absence had obviously failed to clear the air.

Not that he was silent or aloof. But his gift of speech overlaid a reticence deeper than that of the merely silent man; the kind she had lived with and understood. Once you got past their defences, you were unmistakably inside:—Vinx, for instance. But with Roy she was aware of reserves within reserves, which made him the more interesting, but also the more distracting, when one felt entitled to know the lie of the land. For, Arúna apart, wasn't he becoming too deeply immersed in his Indian relations—losing touch, perhaps, with those at home? Did it—or did it not matter—that, day after day, he was strolling with Arúna, riding with Dyán, pig-sticking and buck-hunting with the royal cheetahs and the royal heir to the throne; or plunging neck deep in plans and possibilities, always in connection with those two? His mail letters were few and not bulky, as she knew from handling the contents of the Residency mail-bag. And he very rarely spoke of them all: less than ever of late. To her ardent nature it seemed inexplicable. Perhaps it was just part of his peculiar 'inwardness.' She would have liked to feel sure, however. . . .

Vinx would say it was none of her business. But

Lance would be a help. She was counting on him to readjust the scales. Thank goodness for Lance—giving up the Lahore 'week' and the Polo Tournament to spend Christmas with her and Roy in the wilds of Rajputana. Just to have him about the place again—his music, his big laugh, his radiant certainty that, in any and every circumstance, it was a splendid thing to be alive—would banish worries and lift her spirits sky-high. After the still, deep waters of her beloved Vinx—whose strain of remoteness had not been quite dispelled by marriage—and the starlit mysteries of Arúna and the intriguing complexities of Roy, a breath of Lance would be tonic as a breeze from the Hills. He was so clear and sure; not in flashes and spurts, but continuously, like sunshine; because the clearness and sureness had his whole personality behind them. And he could be counted on to deal faithfully with Roy; perhaps lure him back to the Punjab. It would be sad losing him; but in the distracting circumstances, a clean cut seemed the only solution. She would just put in a word to that effect: a weakness she had rarely been known to resist, however complete her faith in the man of the moment.

She simply dared not think of Arúna, who trusted her. It seemed like betrayal—no less. And yet . . .?

# CHAPTER XIII.

> "One made out of the better part of earth,
> A man born as at sunrise."
>
> —SWINBURNE.

IT was all over—the strenuous joy of planning and preparing. Christmas itself was over. From the adjacent borders of British India, five lonely ones had been gathered in. There was Mr Mayne, Commissioner of Delhi, Vincent's old friend of Kohat days, unmarried and alone in camp with a stray Settlement Officer, whose wife and children were at Home. There was Mr Bourne—in the Canals—large-boned and cadaverous, with a sardonic gleam in his eye. Rumour said there had once been a wife and a friend; now there remained only work and the whisky bottle; and he was overdoing both. To him Thea devoted herself and her fiddle with particular zest. The other two lonelies—a Mr and Mrs Nair—were medical missionaries, fighting the influenza scourge in the Delhi area; drastically disinfected—because of the babies; more than thankful for a brief respite from their daily diet of tragedy, and from labours Hercules' self would not have disdained. For all that, they had needed a good deal of pressing. They had 'no clothes.' They were very shy. But Thea had insisted; so they came—clothed chiefly in shyness and gratitude, which made them shyer than ever.

Roy, still new to Anglo-India, was amazed at the way these haphazard humans were thawed into a passing intimacy by the sunshine of Thea's personality. For himself, it was the nearest approach to the real thing that he had known since that dear and dreamlike Christmas of 1916. It warmed his heart, and renewed the well-spring of careless happiness that had gone from him utterly since the blow fell; gone, so he believed, for ever.

Something of this she divined—and was glad. Yet her exigent heart was not altogether at ease. His reaction to Lance, though unmistakable, fell short of her confident expectation. He was still squandering far too much time on the other two. Sometimes she felt almost angry with him: jealous—for Lance. She knew how deeply he cared underneath; because she too was a Desmond. And Desmonds could not care by halves.

This morning, for instance, the wretch was out riding with Dyán; and there was Lance, alone in the drawing-room strumming the accompaniments of things they would play to-night: just a wandering succession of chords in a minor key; but he had his father's gift of touch, that no training can impart, and the same trick of playing pensively to himself, almost as if he were thinking aloud. It was five years since she had seen her father; and those pensive chords brought sudden tears to her eyes.

What did Lance mean by it—mooning about the piano like that? Had he fallen in love? That was one of the few questions she did not dare ask him. But here was her chance to 'put in a word' about Roy.

So she strolled into the drawing-room and leaned over the grand piano. His smile acknowledged her presence, and his pensive chords went wandering softly away into the bass.

"Idiot—what *are* you doing?" she asked briskly, because the music was creeping down her spine. "Talking to yourself?"

"More or less."

"Well — give over. I'm here. And it's a bad habit."

He shook his head, and went wandering on. "In this form I find it soothing and companionable."

"Well, you oughtn't to be needing either at Christmas time under *my* roof, with Roy here and all—if he'd only behave. Sometimes I want to shake him——"

"Why—what's the matter with Roy?"—That innocent query checked her rush of protest in mid career. Had he not even noticed? Men were the queerest, dearest things!—"He looks awfully fit. Better all round. He's pulling up. *You* never saw him—you don't realise——"

"But, my dear boy, do *you* realise that he's getting rather badly bitten with all this—Indian problems and Indian cousins——"

Lance nodded. "I've been afraid of that. But one can't say much."

"*I* can't. I was counting on you as the God-given antidote. And there he is, still fooling round with Dyán, when *you*'ve come all this way . . . It makes me wild. It isn't *fair*——"

Her genuine distress moved Lance to cease strumming and bestow a friendly pat on her hand. "Don't be giving yourself headaches and heartaches over Roy and me, darlint. We're going strong, thanks very much! It would take an earthquake to throw us out of step. If he chose to chuck his boots at me, I wouldn't trouble—except to return the trees if they were handy! Strikes me women don't yet begin to understand the noble art of friendship——"

"*Which* is a libel—but let that pass! Besides—hasn't it struck you? Arúna——"

"My God!" His hands dropped with a crash on the keyboard. Then, in a low swift rush: "Thea, you don't *mean* it—you're pulling my leg."

"Bible-oath I'm not. It's too safely tucked under the piano!"

"My God!" he repeated softly, ignoring her incurable frivolity. "Has he *said* anything?"

"No. But it's plain they're both smitten more or less."

"Smitten be damned."

"Lance! I won't have Arúna insulted. Let me tell you she's charming and cultivated; much better company than Floss. And I love her like a daughter——"

"Would you have her marry *Roy?*" he flung out wrathfully.

"Of course not. But still——"

"*Me*—perhaps?" he queried with such fine scorn that she burst out laughing.

"You priceless gem! You are *the* unadulterated Anglo-Indian!"

"Well—what *else* would I be? What else are you, by the same token?"

"Not adulterated," she denied stoutly. "Perhaps a wee bit less 'prejudiced.' The awful result, I suppose, of failing to keep myself scrupulously detached from my surroundings. Besides, you couldn't be married twenty years to that Vinx and not widen out a bit. Of course I'm quite aware that widening out has its insidious dangers and limitation its heroic virtues—Hush! Don't fly into a rage. *You*'re not limited, old boy. You loved —Lady Sinclair."

"I adored her," Lance said very low; and his fingers strayed over the keys again. "*But*—she was an accomplished fact. And—she was one in many thousands. She's gone now, though. And there's poor Sir Nevil——"

He rose abruptly and strode over to the fireplace. "Tell you what, Thea. If the bee in Roy's bonnet is buzzing to *that* tune, some one's got to stop it——"

"That's my point!" She swung round confronting him. "Why not whisk him back to the Punjab? It does seem the only way——"

Lance nodded again. "Now you talk sense. Mind, I don't believe he'll come. Roy's a tougher customer than he looks to the naked eye. But I'll have a shot at it to-night. If needs must, I'll tell him why. I can swallow half a regiment of his Dyáns; but not—the other thing. I hope you find us intact in the morning!"

She flew to him and kissed him with fervour; and she was still in his arms, when Roy strolled casually into the room.

There were only three outsiders that night: the State Engineer and two British officers in the Maharajah's employ. But they sat down sixteen to dinner; and, very shortly after, came three others in the persons of Dyán and Sir Lakshman Singh, with his distinguished friend Mahomed Inayat Khan, from Hyderabad. Nothing Thea enjoyed better than getting a mixed batch of men together and hearing them talk—especially shop; for then she knew their hearts were in it. They were happy.

And to-night, her chance assortment was amazingly varied, even for India:—Army, 'Political,' Civil;

P.W.D. and Native States; New India, in the person of Dyán; and not least, the 'medical mish' pair; an element rich in mute inglorious heroism, as the villagers and 'depressed classes' of India know. She took keen delight in the racial interplay of thought and argument, with Roy, as it were, for bridge-builder between. How he would relish the idea! He seemed very much in the vein this evening, especially since his grandfather arrived. He was clearly making an impression on Mr Mayne and Inayat Khan; and a needle-prick of remorse touched her heart. For Arúna, annexed by Captain Martin's subaltern, was watching him too, when she fancied no one was looking; and Lance, attentively silent, was probably laying deep plans for his capture. A wicked shame—but still . . .!

As a matter of fact, Lance, too, was troubled with faint compunction. He had never seen Roy in this kind of company, nor in this particular vein. And, reluctantly, he admitted that it did seem rather a waste of his mentally reviving vigour hauling him back to the common round of tennis and dances and polo—yes, even sacred polo—when he was so dead keen on this infernal agitation business, and seemed to know such a deuce of a lot about it all.

Lance himself knew far too little; and was anxious to hear more, for the intimate, practical reason that he was not quite happy about his Sikh troop. The Pathan lot were all right. But the Sikhs—his pride and joy—were being 'got at' by those devils in the City. And, if these men could be believed, 'things' were going to be very much worse; not only 'down country,' but also in the Punjab, India's sure shield against the invader. To a Desmond, the mere suggestion of the Punjab turning traitor was as if one impugned the courage of his father or the honour of his mother; so curiously personal is India's hold upon the hearts of Englishmen who come under her spell.

So Lance listened intently, if a little anxiously, to all that Thea's 'mixed biscuits' had to say on that absorbing subject. For to-night shop held the field: if that could be called shop, which vitally concerned the fate of England and India, and of British dominion in the East.

Agitation against the sane measures embodied in the Rowlatt Bills was already astir, like bubbles round a pot before it boils. And Inayat Khan had come straight from Bombay, where the National Congress had rejected with scorn the latest palliative from Home; had demanded the release of all revolutionaries, and wholesale repeal of laws against sedition. Here was shop sufficiently ominous to overshadow all other topics: and there was no *gêne*, no constraint. The Englishmen could talk freely in the presence of cultured Indians who stood for Jaipur and Hyderabad, since both States were loyal to the core.

Dyán, like Lance, spoke little and pondered much on the talk of these men, whose straight speech and thoughts were refreshing as their own sea breezes after the fumes of rhetoric, the fog of false values that had bemused his brain these three years. Strange how all the ugliness and pain of hate had shrivelled away; how he could even shake hands, untroubled, with that 'imperialistic bureaucrat' the Commissioner of Delhi, whom he might have been told off, any day, to 'remove from this mortal coil.' Strange to sit there, over against him, while he puffed his cigar and talked, without fear, of increasing antagonism, increasing danger to himself and his kind.

"There's no sense in disguising the unpalatable truth that New India hates us," said he in his gruff, deliberate voice. "Present company excepted, I hope!"

He gravely inclined his head towards Dyán, who responded mutely with a flutter at his heart. Impossible! The man could not suspect——?

And the man, looking him frankly in the eyes, added: "The spirit of the Mutiny's not extinct—and we know it, those of us that count."

Dyán simply sat dumfounded. It was Sir Lakshman who said, in his guarded tone: "Nevertheless, sir, the bulk of our people are loyal and peaceable. Only I fear there are some in England who do not count that fact to their credit."

"If they ever become anything else, it won't be to *our* credit," put in Roy. "If we can't stand up to bluster and sedition with that moral force at our backs, we shall deserve to go under."

"Well spoken, Roy," said his grandfather still more

quietly. "Let us hope it is not yet too late. Sadi says, 'The fountain-head of a spring can be blocked with a stick; but in full flood, it cannot be crossed, even on an elephant.'"

They exchanged a glance that stirred Roy's pulses and gave him confidence to go on: "I don't believe it *is* too late. But what bothers me is this—are we treating our moral force as it deserves? Are we giving them loyalty in return for theirs—the sort they can understand? With a dumb executive and voluble 'patriots,' persuading or intimidating, the poor beggars haven't a dog's chance, unless we openly stand by them; openly smite our enemies—and theirs."

He boldly addressed himself to Mayne, the sole symbol of authority present; and the Commissioner listened, with a gleam of amused approval in his eye.

"You're young, Mr Sinclair—which doesn't mean you're wrong! Most of us, in our limited fashion, are trying to do what we can on those lines. But, after spending half a lifetime in this climate, doing our utmost to give the peasant—*and* the devil—his due, we're apt to grow cynical——"

"Not to mention suicidal!" grunted the slave of work and whisky. "We Canal coolies—hardly visible to the naked eye—are adding something like an Egypt a year to the Empire. But, bless you, England takes no notice. Only let some underbred planter or raw subaltern bundle an Indian out of his carriage, or a drunken Tommy kick his servant in the spleen, and the whole British Constitution comes down about our ears!"

"Very true, sir—very true!" Inayat Khan leaned forward. His teeth gleamed in the dark of his beard. His large firm-featured face abounded in good sense and good humour. "How shall a man see justly if he holds the telescope wrong way round, as too many do over there. It also remains true, however, that the manners of certain Anglo-Indians create a lot of bad feeling. Your so-called reforms do not interest the masses or touch their imagination. But the boot of the low-class European touches their backs and their pride and hardens their hearts. That is only human nature. In the East a few gold grains of courtesy touch the heart more than a *khillat*[1] of political hotch-potch. I myself—though it is getting dangerous to say so!—am frankly opposed to this uncontrolled passion for reform. When all have done their duty in this great struggle, why such undignified clamour for rewards, which are now being flung back in the giver's teeth. It has become a vicious circle. It was British policy in the first place—not so?—that stirred up this superficial ferment; and now it grows alarming, it is doctored with larger doses of the same medicine. We Indians who know how little the bulk of India has really changed, could laugh at the tamasha of Western fancy-dress, in small matters; but time for laughing has gone by. Time has come for saying firmly—all rights and aspirations will be granted, stopping *short* of actual government—otherwise——!"

He flung up his hands, looked round at the listening faces, and realised how completely he had let himself go. "Forgive me, Colonel. I fear I am talking too much," he said in a changed tone.

"Indeed no," Colonel Leigh assured him warmly. "In these difficult days, loyal and courageous friends like yourself are worth their weight in gold mohurs!"

Visibly flattered, the Moslem surveyed his own bulky person with a twinkle of amusement. "If value should go by weight, Inayat Khan would be worth a king's ransom! But I assure you, Colonel, your country has many hundreds of friends like myself all over India, if only she would seek them out and give them encouragement—as Mr Sinclair said—instead of wasting it on volubles, who will never cease making trouble till India is in a blaze."

As the man's patent sincerity had warmed the hearts of his hearers, so the pointed truth of that last pricked them sharply and probed deep. For they knew themselves powerless; mere atoms of the whirling dust-cloud, raised, in passing, by the chariot-wheels of Progress—or perdition?

The younger men rose briskly, as if to shake off some physical discomfort. Dyán—very much aware of Arúna and the subaltern—approached them with a friendly

[1] Dress of honour.

remark. Roy and Lance said, "Play up, Thea! Your innings," almost in a breath—and crooked little fingers.

Thea needed no second bidding. While the men talked, an insidious depression had stolen over her spirit—and brooded there, light and formless as a river mist. Half an hour with her fiddle, and Lance at his best, completely charmed it away. But the creepiness of it had been very real: and the memory remained.

When all the others had dispersed, she lingered over the fire with Roy, while Lance, at the piano, with diplomatic intent, drifted into his friend's favourite Nocturne—the Twelfth; that inimitable rendering of a mood, hushed yet exalted, soaring yet brooding, 'the sky and the nest as well.' The two near the fire knew every bar by heart, but as the liquid notes stole out into the room, their fitful talk stopped dead.

Lance was playing superbly, giving every note its true value; the cadence rising and falling like waves of a still sea; softer and softer; till the last note faded away, ghostlike—a sigh rather than a sound.

Roy remained motionless, one elbow on the mantelpiece. Thea's lashes were wet with the tears of rarefied emotion—tears that neither prick nor burn. The silence itself seemed part of the music; a silence it were desecration to break. Without a word to Roy, she crossed the room; kissed Lance good-night; clung a moment to his hands that had woven the spell, smiling her thanks, her praise; and slipped away, leaving the two together.

Roy subsided into a chair. Lance came over to the fire and stood there warming his hands.

It was a minute or two before Roy looked up and nodded his acknowledgments.

"You're a magician, old chap. You play that thing a damn sight too well."

He did not add that his friend's music had called up a vision of the Home drawing-room, clear in every detail; Lance at the piano—his last week-end from Sandhurst—playing the 'thing' by request; himself lounging on the hearthrug, his head against his mother's knee; the very feel of her silk skirt against his cheek, of her fingers on his hair . . . Nor did he add that the vision had spurred his reluctant spirit to a resolve.

The more practical soul of Lance Desmond had already dropped back to earth, as a lark drops after pouring out its heart in the blue. In spite of concern for Roy, he was thinking again of his Sikhs.

"I suppose one can take it," he remarked thoughtfully, "that Vinx and Mayne and that good old Moslem johnny know what they're talking about?"

Roy smiled—having jumped at the connection. "I'm afraid," he said, "one can."

"You think big trouble is coming—organised trouble?"

"I do. That is, unless some 'strong silent man' has the pluck to put his foot down in time, and chance the consequences to himself. Thank God, we've another John Lawrence in the Punjab."

"And it's the Punjab that matters——"

"Especially a certain P.C. Regiment—eh?"

Lance was in arms at once:—that meant he had touched the spot. "No flies on the Regiment. Trust Paul. It's only—— I get bothered about a Sikh here and there."

"Quite so. The blighters have taken particular pains with the Sikhs. Realising that they'll need some fighting stuff. And Lahore's a bad place. I expect they sneak off to meetings in the City."

"Devil a doubt of it. Mind you, I trust them implicitly. But, outside their own line, they're credulous as children—*you* know."

"Rather. In Delhi, I had a fair sample of it."

Another pause. It suddenly occurred to Lance that his precious Sikhs were not supposed to be the topic of the evening. "You're quite fit again, Roy. And those blooming fools chucked you like a cast horse——" he broke out in a spurt of vexation. "I wish to God you were back with your old Squadron."

And Roy said from his heart, "I wish to God I was."

"Paul misses you, though he never says much. The new lot from home are good chaps. Full of brains and theories. But no knowledge. Can't get at the men. You could still help unofficially in all sorts of ways.—Why not come along back with me? Haven't you been pottering round here long enough?"

Roy shook his head. "Thanks all the same, for the invite. Of course I'd love it. But—I've things to do.

There's a novel taking shape—and other oddments. I've done precious little writing here. Too much entangled with human destinies. I *must* bury myself somewhere and get a move on. April it is. I won't fail you."

Lance kicked an unoffending log. "Confound your old novel!"—A portentous silence. "See here, Roy, I don't want to badger you. But—well—if I'm to go back in moderate peace of mind, I want—certain guarantees."

Roy lifted his eyes. Lance frankly encountered them; and there ensued one of those intimate pauses in which the unspeakable is said.

Roy looked away. "Arúna?" He let fall the word barely above his breath.

"Just that."

"You're frightened—both of you? Oh yes—I've seen——" He fell silent, staring into the fire. When he spoke again, it was in the same low, detached tone. "You two needn't worry. The guarantee you're after was given . . . in July 1914 . . . under the beeches . . . at Home. *She* foresaw—understood. But she couldn't foresee . . . the harder tug—now she's gone. The . . . association . . . and all that."

"Is it—only that?"

"It's mostly that."

To Lance Desmond, very much a man, it seemed the queerest state of things; and he knew only a fragment of the truth.

"Look here, Roy," he urged again. "Wouldn't the Punjab really be best? Aren't you plunging a bit too deep——? Does your father realise? Thea feels——"

"Yes. Thea feels, bless her! But there's a thing or two she doesn't *know!*" He lifted his head and spoke in an easier voice. "One queer thing—it may interest you. Those few weeks of living as an Indian among Indians—amazingly intensified all the other side of me. I never felt keener on the Sinclair heritage and all it stands for. I never felt keener on you two than all this time while I've been concentrating every faculty on—the other two. Sounds odd. But it's a fact."

"Good. And does—your cousin know . . . about the guarantee?"

"N—no. That's still to come."

"*When*——?"

Roy frankly returned his friend's challenging gaze. "Damn you!" he said softly. Then, in a graver tone: "You're right. I've been shirking it. Seemed a shame to spoil Christmas. Remains—the New Year. I fixed it up—while you were playing that thing, to be exact."

"Did I—contribute?"

"You did—if that gives you any satisfaction!" He rose, stretched himself and yawned ostentatiously. "My God, I wish it was over."

Desmond said nothing. If Roy loved him more for one quality than another, it was for his admirable gift of silence.

# CHAPTER XIV.

"Yet shall I bear in my heart this honour of the burden of pain—this gift of thine."—RABINDRANATH TAGORE.

IT was the last day of the year; the last moon of the year, almost at her zenith. Of all the Christmas guests Lance alone remained; and Thea had promised him before leaving, a moonlight vision of Amber, the Sleeping Beauty of Rajasthán. The event had been delayed till now, partly because they waited on the moon; partly because they did not want it to be a promiscuous affair.

To Thea's lively imagination—and to Roy's no less—Amber was more than a mere city of ghosts and marble halls. It was a symbol of Rajput womanhood—strong and beautiful, withdrawn from the clamour of the market-place, given over to her dreams and her gods. For though kings have deserted Amber, the gods remain. There is still life in her temples and the blood of sacrifice on her altar stones. Therefore she must not be approached in the spirit of the tourist. And, emphatically, she must not be approached in a motor-car; at least so far as Thea's guests were concerned. Of course one knew she *was* approached by irreverent cars; also by tourists—unspeakable ones, who made contemptible jokes about 'a slump in house property.' But for these vandalisms Thea Leigh was not responsible.

Her young ones, including Captain Martin, would ride; but, because of Arúna, she and Vincent must submit to the barouche. So transparent was the girl's pleasure at being included, that Thea's heart failed her—knowing what she knew.

Roy and Lance had ridden on ahead; out through the fortified gates into the open desert, strewn with tumbled fragments of the glory that was Rajasthán. There, where courtiers had intrigued and flattered, crows held conference. On the crumbling arch of a doorway, that opened into emptiness, a vulture brooded, heavy with feeding on those who had died for lack of food. Knee-deep in the Mán Sagar Lake, grey cranes sought their meat from God; every tint and curve of them repeated in the quiet water. And there, beside a ruined shrine, two dead cactus bushes, with their stiff distorted limbs, made Roy think suddenly of two dead Germans he had come upon once—killed so swiftly that they still retained, in death, the ghastly semblance of life. Why the devil couldn't a man be rid of them? Dead Germans were not 'in the bond.' . . .

"Buck up, Lance," he said abruptly; for Desmond, who saw no ghosts, was keenly interested. "Let's quit this place of skulls and empty eye-sockets. Amber's dead; but not utterly decayed."

He knew. He had ridden out alone one morning, in the light of paling stars, to watch the dawn steal down through the valley and greet the sleeping city that would never wake again—half hoping to recapture the miracle of Chitor. But Amber did not enshrine the soul of his mother's race. And the dawn had proved merely a dawn. Moonlight, with its eerie enchantment, would be even more beautiful and fitting; but the pleasure of anticipation was shadowed by his resolve.

He had spoken of it only to Thea; asking her, when tea was over, to give him a chance:—and now he was heartily wishing he had chosen any other place and time than this. . . .

The brisk canter to the foothills was a relief. Thence the road climbed, between low, reddish-grey spurs, to the narrow pass, barred by a formidable gate, that swung open at command, with a screech of rusty hinges, as if in querulous protest against intrusion.

Another gateway,—and yet another: then they were through the triple wall that guards the dead city from the invader who will never come, while both races honour the pact that alone saved desperate, stubborn Rajputana from extinction.

Up on the heights, it was still day; but in the valley it was almost evening. And there—among deepening shadows and tumbled fragments of hills—lay Amber: her palace and temples and broken houses crowding round their sacred Lake, like Queens and their handmaids round the shield of a dead King.

Descending at a foot's pace, the chill of emptiness and of oncoming twilight seemed to close like icy fingers on Roy's heart; though the death of Amber was as nothing to the death of Chitor—the warrior-queen, ravished and violently slain by Akbar's legions. Amber had, as it were, died peacefully in her sleep. But there remained the all-pervading silence and emptiness:—her sorrowful houses, cleft from roof to roadway; no longer homes of men, but of the rock-pigeon, the peacock, and the wild boar; stones of her crumbling arches thrust apart by roots of acacia and neem; her streets choked with cactus and brushwood; her beauty—disfigured but not erased—reflected in the unchanging mirror of the Lake.

If Roy and Lance had talked little before, they talked less now. From the Lake-side they rode up, by stone pathways, to the Palace of stone and marble, set upon a jutting rock and commanding the whole valley. There, in the quadrangle, they left the horses with their grooms, who were skilled in cutting corners and had trotted most of the way.

Close to the gate stood a temple of fretted marble—neither ruined nor deserted; for within were the priests of Kali, and the faint, sickly smell of blood. Daybreak after daybreak, for centuries, the severed head of a goat had been set before her, the warm blood offered in a bronze bowl. . . .

"Pah! Beastly!" muttered Lance. "I'd sooner have no religion at all."

Roy smiled at him, sidelong—and said nothing. It *was* beastly: but it matched the rest. It was in keeping with the dusky rooms, all damp-incrusted, the narrow passages and screens of marble tracery; the cloistered hanging garden, beyond the women's rooms, their baths chiselled out of naked rock. And the beastliness was off-set by the beauty of inlay and carving and colour; by the splendour of bronze gates and marble pillars, and slabs of carven granite that served as balustrade to the terraced roof, where daylight still lingered and azure-necked peacocks strutted, serenely immune.

Seated on a carven slab, they looked downward into the heart of desolation; upward, at creeping battlements and a little temple of Shiva printed sharply on the light-filled sky.

"Can't you *feel* the ghosts of them all round you?" whispered Roy.

"No, thank God, I can't," said practical Lance, taking out a cigarette. But a rustle of falling stones made him start—the merest fraction. "Perhaps smoke'll keep 'em off—like mosquitoes!" he added hopefully.

But Roy paid no heed. He was looking down into the hollow shell of that which had been Amber. Not a human sound anywhere; nor any stir of life, but the soft ceaseless kuru-kooing doves, that nested and mated in those dusky inner rooms, where Queens had mated with Kings.

"'Thou hast made of a city an heap, of a defencèd city a ruin . . . Their houses shall be full of doleful creatures; and owls shall dwell there, and satyrs shall dance there,'" he quoted softly; adding after a pause, "Mother had a great weakness for old Isaiah. She used to say he and the minor prophets knew all about Rajasthân. The owls of Amber are blue pigeons. But I hope she's spared the satyrs."

"Globe-trotters!" suggested Lance.

"Or 'Piffers' devoid of reverence!" retorted Roy. "Hullo! Here come the others."

Footsteps and voices in the quadrangle waked hollow echoes as when a stone drops into a well. Presently they sounded on the stairs near by: Flossie's rather boisterous laugh; Martin chaffing her in his husky tones.

"Great sport! Let's rent it off H. H. and gather 'em all in from the highways and hedges for a masked fancy ball!"

Roy stood up and squared his shoulders. "Satyrs dancing, with a vengeance!" said he; but the gleam of Arúna's sari smote him silent. A band seemed to tighten round his heart. . . .

Before tea was over, peacocks and pigeons had gone

to roost among the trees that shadowed the Lake; and the light behind the hills had passed swiftly from gold to flame-colour, from flame-colour to rose. For the sun, that had already departed in effect, was now setting in fact.

"Hush—it's coming," murmured Thea:—and it came.

Hollow thuds, quickening to a vibrant roar, swelled up from the temple in the courtyard below. The Brahmins were beating the great tom-tom before Kali's Shrine.

It was the signal. It startlingly waked the dead city to discordant life. Groanings and howlings and clashings, as of Tophet, were echoed and re-echoed from every temple, every shrine; an orgy of demoniac sounds; blurred in transit through the empty rooms beneath; pierced at intervals by the undulating wail of ram's horns; the two reiterate notes wandering, like lost souls, through a confused blare of cymbals and bagpipes and all kinds of music.

Flossie, with a bewitching grimace at Martin, clapped both hands over her ears. Roy—standing by the balustrade with Arúna—was aware of an answering echo somewhere in subconscious depths, as the discords rose and fell above the throbbing undernote of the drum. It was as if the claimant voices of the East cried out to the blood in his veins: 'You are of us—do what you will; go where you will.' And all the while his eyes never left Arúna's half-averted face.

Sudden and clear from the heights came a ringing peal of bells, as it were the voices of angels answering the wail of devils in torment. It was from the little Shrine of Shiva close against the ramparts, etched in outline, above the dark of the hills.

Arúna turned and looked up at him. "Too beautiful!" she whispered.

He nodded, and flung out an arm. "Look there!"

Low and immense—pale in the pallor of the eastern sky—the moon hung poised above massed shadows, like a wraith escaped from the city of death. Moment by moment, she drew light from the vanished sun. Moment by moment, under their watching eyes, she conjured the formless dark into a new heaven, a new earth. . . .

"Would you be afraid—to stroll round a little . . . with me?" he asked.

"Afraid? I would love it—if Thea will allow." This time she did not look up.

Vincent and Thea were sitting a little farther along the balustrade; Lance beside them, imbibing tales of Rajasthán. Flossie and her Captain had already disappeared.

"*I'm* going to be frankly a Goth and flash my electric torch into holes and corners," Lance announced as the other two came up. "I bar being intimidated by ghosts."

"We're not going to be intimidated either," said Roy, addressing himself to Thea. "And I guarantee not to let Arúna be spirited away."

Vincent shot a look at his wife. "Don't wander too far," said he.

"And don't hang about too long," she added. "It'll be cold going home."

Though he was standing close to her, she could say no more. But, under cover of the dusk, her hand found his and closed on it hard.

The characteristic impulse heartened him amazingly, as he followed Arúna down the ghostly stairway, through marble cloisters into the hanging garden, misted with moonlight, fragrant with orange trees.

And now there was more than Thea's hand-clasp to uphold him. Gradually there dawned on him a faint yet sure intimation of his mother's presence, of her tenderly approving love—dim to his brain, yet as sensible to his spirit as light and warmth to his body.

It did not last many moments; but—as in all contact with her—the clear after-certainty remained. . . .

Exactly what he intended to say he did not know even now. To speak the cruel truth, yet by some means to soften the edge of it, seemed almost impossible. But nerved by this vivid, exalted sense of her nearness, the right moment, the right words could be trusted to come of themselves. . . .

And Arúna, walking beside him in a hushed expectancy, was remembering that other night, so strangely far away, when they had walked alone under the same moon, and assurance of his love had so possessed her, that she had very nearly broken her little chirágh. And to-night—how different! Her very love for him, though the same, was not quite the same. It seemed to depend not at all on nearness or response. Starved of both, it had grown not less, but more.

From a primitive passion it had become a rarefied emotional atmosphere in which she lived and moved. And this garden of eerie lights and shadows was saturated with it; thronged, to her fancy, with ghosts of dead passions and intrigues, of dead Queens, in whom the twin flames of love and courage could be quenched only by flames of the funeral pyre. Their blood ran in her veins—and in his too. *That* closeness of belonging none could snatch from her. About the other, she was growing wofully uncertain, as day followed day, and still no word. Was there trouble after all? Would he speak to-night . . .?

They had reached a dark doorway, and he was trying the handle. It opened inwards.

"I'm keen to go a little way up the hillside," he said, forcing himself to break a silence that was growing oppressive. "To get a sight of the Palace with the moon full on it. We'll be cautious—not go too far."

"I am ready to go anywhere," she answered; and the fervour of that simple statement told him she was not thinking of hillsides any more than he was—at the back of his mind.

Silence was unkinder than speech; and as they passed out into the open, he scanned the near prospect for a convenient spot. Not far above them a fragment of ruined wall, overhung by trees, ended in a broken arch; its lingering keystone threatened by a bird-borne acacia. A fallen slab of stone, half under it, offered a not too distant seat. Slab and arch were in full light; the space beyond, engulfed in shadow.

Far up the hillside a jackal laughed. Across the valley another answered it. A monkey swung from a branch on to the slab, and sat there engaged in his toilet—a very imp of darkness.

"Not be-creeped—are you?" Roy asked.

"Just the littlest bit! Nice kind of creeps. I feel quite safe—with you."

The path was rough in parts. Once she stumbled and

his hand closed lightly on her arm under the cloak. She felt safe with him—and he must turn and smite her——!

At their approach, the monkey fled with a gibbering squeak: and Roy loosened his hold. Between them and the lake loomed the noble bulk of the palace; roof-terraces and façades bathed in silver, splashed with indigo shadow; but for them—mere man and woman—its imperishable strength and beauty had suddenly become a very little thing. They scarcely noticed it even.

"There—sit," Roy said softly, and she obeyed.

Her smile mutely invited him; but he could not trust himself—yet. He might have known the moonlight would go to his head.

"Arúna—my dear——" he plunged without preamble. "I took you away from them all because—well—we can't pretend any more . . . you and I. It's fate—and there we are. I love you—dearly—truly. But . . ."

How could one go on?

"Oh, *Roy!*"

Her lifted gaze, her low impassioned cry told all; and before that too clear revealing his hard-won resolution quailed.

"No—not that. I don't deserve it," he broke out, lashing himself and startling her. "I've been a rank coward—letting things drift. But honestly I hadn't the conceit—we were cousins . . . it seemed natural. And now . . . *this!*"

A stupid catch in his throat arrested him. She sat motionless; never a word.

Impulsively he dropped on one knee, to be nearer, yet not too near. "Arúna—I don't know how to say it. The fact is . . . they were afraid, at Home, if I came out here, I might—it might . . . Well, just what's come to us," he blurted out in desperation. "And Mother told me frankly—it mustn't be, twice running . . . like that." Her stillness dismayed him. "Dear," he urged tenderly, "you see their difficulty—you understand?"

"I am trying—to understand." Her voice was small and contained. The courage and control of it unsteadied him more than any passionate protest. Yet he hurried on in the same low tone.

"Of course, I ought to have thought. But, as I say, it seemed natural . . . Only—on Dewáli night——"

She caught her breath. "Yes—Dewáli night. Mai Lakshmi knew. *Why* did you not say it *then?*"

"Well . . . so soon—I wasn't sure . . . I hoped going away might give us both a chance. It seemed the best I could do," he pleaded. "And—there was Dyán. I'm not vamping up excuses, Arúna. If you hate me for hurting you so——"

"Roy—you *shall* not say it!" she cried, roused at last. "Could I hate . . . the heart in my own body?"

"Better for us both perhaps if you could!" he jerked out, rising abruptly, not daring to let the full force of her confession sink in. "But—because of my father, I promised. No getting over that."

She was silent:—a silence more moving, more compelling than speech. Was she wondering—had he not promised . . .? Was he certain himself? Near enough to swear by; and the impulse to comfort her was overwhelming.

"If—if things had been different, Arúna," he added with grave tenderness, "of course I would be asking you now . . . to be my wife."

At that, the tension of her control seemed to snap; and hiding her face, she sat there shaken all through with muffled, broken-hearted sobs.

"Don't—oh, *don't!*" he cried low, his own nerves quivering with her pain.

"How can I *not?*" she wailed, battling with fresh sobs. "Because of your Indian mother—I hoped . . . But for me—England-returned—no hope anywhere: no true country now; no true belief; no true home; everything divided in two; only my heart—not divided. And that you cannot have, even if you would——"

Tears threatened again. It was all he could do not to take her in his arms.

"If—if they would only leave me alone," she went on, clenching her small hands to steady herself. "But impossible to change all the laws of our religion for one worthless me. They will insist I shall marry—even Dyán; and I cannot—I *cannot*——!"

Suddenly there sprang an inspiration, born of despair, of the chance and the hour and the grave tenderness of his assurance. No time for shrinking or doubt. Almost in speaking she was on her feet; her cloak—that had come unlinked—dropped from her shoulders, leaving her a slim strip of pallor, like a ray of light escaped from clouds.

"Roy—*Dilkusha!*" Involuntarily her hands went out to him. "If it is true . . . you are caring—and if I must not belong to you, there is a way *you* can belong to me without trouble for any one. If—if we make pledge of betrothal . . . for this one night, if you hold me this one hour . . . I am safe. For me that pledge would be sacred—as marriage, because I am still Hindu. Perhaps I am punished for far-away sins—not worthy to be wife and mother; but, by my pledge, I can remain always *Swami Bakht*—worshipper of my lord . . . a widow in my heart."

And Roy stood before her—motionless; stirred all through by the thrill of her exalted passion, of her strange appeal. The pathos—the nobility of it—swept him a little off his feet. It seemed as if, till to-night, he had scarcely known her. The Eastern in him said, 'Accept.' The Englishman demurred—'Unfair on her.'

"My dear——" he said—"I can refuse you nothing. But—is it right? You *should* marry——"

"Don't trouble your mind for me," she murmured; and her eyes never left his face. "If I keep out of purdah, becoming Brahmo Samaj . . . perhaps——" She drew in her full lower lip to steady it. "But the marriage of arrangement—I cannot. I have read too many English books, thought too many English thoughts. And I know in here"—one clenched hand smote her breast—"that now I could *not* give my body and life to any man, unless heart and mind are given too. And for me . . . Must I tell all? It is not only these few weeks. It is years and years . . ." Her voice broke.

"Arúna! Dearest one——"

He opened his arms to her—and she was on his breast. Close and tenderly he held her, putting a strong constraint on himself lest her ecstasy of surrender should bear down all his defences. To fail her like this was a bitter thing: and as her arms stole up round his neck, he instinctively tightened his hold. So yielding she was, so unsubstantial. . . .

And suddenly a rush of memory wafted him from the moonlit hillside to the drawing-room at Home. It was his mother he held against his breast:—the silken draperies, the clinging arms, the yielding softness, the unyielding courage at the core. . . .

So vivid, so poignant was the lightning gleam of illusion, that when it passed he felt dizzy, as if his body had been swept in the wake of his spirit, a thousand leagues and back: dizzy, yet, in some mysterious fashion, reinforced—assured. . . .

He knew now that his defences would hold. . . .

And Arúna, utterly at rest in his arms, knew it also. He loved her—oh yes, truly—as much as he said and more; but instinct told her there lacked . . . just something; something that would have set him—and her—on fire, and perhaps have made renunciation unthinkable. Her acute, instinctive sense of it, hurt like the edge of a knife pressed on her heart; yet just enabled her to bear the unbearable. Had it been . . . *that* way, to lose him were utter loss. This way—there would be no losing. What she had now, she would keep—whether his bodily presence were with her or no——

Next minute, she dropped from the heights. Fire ran in her veins. His lips were on her forehead.

"The seal of betrothal," he whispered. "My brave Arúna——"

Without a word she put up her face like a child; but it was very woman who yielded her lips to his. . . .

For her, in that supreme moment, the years that were past and the years that were to come seemed gathered into a burnt-offering—laid on his shrine. For her, that long kiss held much of passion—confessed yet transcended; more of sacredness, inexpressible, because it would never come again—with him or any other man. She vowed it silently to her own heart. . . .

Again far up the hillside a jackal laughed; another and another—as if in derision. She shivered; and he loosed his hold, still keeping an arm round her. To-night they were betrothed. He owed her all he had the right to give.

"Your cloak. You'll catch your death . . ." He stopped short—and flung up his head. "What was that? There—again—in those trees——"

"Some monkey perhaps," she whispered, startled by his look and tone.

"Hush—listen!" His grip tightened and they stood rigidly still, Roy straining every nerve to locate those stealthy sounds. They were almost under the arch; strong mellow light on one side, nethermost darkness on the other. And from all sides the large unheeded night seemed to close in on them—threatening, full of hidden danger.

Presently the sounds came again, unmistakably nearer; faint rustlings and creakings, then a distinct crumbling, as of loosened earth and stones. The shadowy plumes of acacia that crowned the arch stirred perceptibly, though no breeze was abroad:—and not the acacia only. To Arúna's excited fancy it seemed that the loose upper stones of the arch itself moved ever so slightly. But *was* it fancy? No—there again——!

And before the truth dawned on Roy, she had pushed him with all her force, so violently that he stumbled backward and let go of her.

Before he recovered himself, down crashed two large stones and a shower of small ones—on Arúna, not on him. With a stifled scream she tottered and fell, knocking her head against the slab of rock.

Instantly he was on his knees beside her; stanching the cut on her forehead, binding it with his handkerchief; consumed with rage and concern;—rage at himself and the dastardly intruder,—no monkey, that was certain.

His quick ear caught the stealthy rustling again, lower down; and, yes—unmistakably—a human sound, like a stifled exclamation of dismay.

"Arúna—I *must* get at that devil," he whispered. "Does your head feel better? Dare I leave you a moment?"

"Yes—oh yes," she whispered back. "Nothing will harm *me*. Only take care—please take care."

Hastily he made a pillow of his overcoat and covered her with the cloak; then, stooping down, he kissed her fervently—and was gone.

# CHAPTER XV.

> "Then was I rapt away by the impulse, one
> Immeasurable . . . wave of a need
> To abolish that detested life."
>
> —BROWNING.

LITHE and noiseless as a cat, Roy crept through the archway into outer darkness. It was hateful leaving Arúna; but rage at her hurt and the primitive instinct of pursuit were not to be denied. And she *might* have been killed. And she had done it for him:—coals of fire, indeed! Also, the others would be getting anxious. Let him only catch that mysterious skulker, and he could shout across to the Palace roof. They would hear.

Close under the wall he waited, all the scout in him alert. The cautious rustlings drew stealthily nearer; ceased, for a few tantalising seconds; then, out of the massed shadows, there crept a moving shadow.

Roy's spring was calculated to a nicety; but the thing swerved sharply and fled up the rough hillside. There followed a ghostly chase, unreal as a nightmare, lit up by the moon's deceptive brilliance; the earth, an unstable welter of light and darkness, shifting under his feet.

The fleeing shade was agile; and plainly familiar with the ground. Baulked, and lured steadily farther from Arúna, all the Rajput flamed in Roy. During those mad moments he was capable of murdering the unknown with his hands. . . .

Suddenly, blessedly, the thing stumbled and dropped to its knees. With the spring of a panther, he was on it, his fingers at its throat, pinning it to earth. The choking cry moved him not at all:—and suddenly the moonlight showed him the face of Chandranath, mingled hate and terror in the starting eyes. . . .

Amazed beyond measure, he unconsciously relaxed his grip. "*You*—is it?—you devil!"

There was no answer. Chandranath had had the wit to wriggle almost clear of him;—almost, not quite. Roy's pounce was worthy of his Rajput ancestors; and next moment they were locked in a silent, purposeful embrace. . . .

But Roy's brain was cooler now. Sanity had returned. He could still have choked the life out of the man, without compunction. But he did not choose to embroil himself, or his people, on account of anything so contemptible as the creature that was writhing and scratching in his grasp. He simply wanted to secure him and hand him over to the Jaipur authorities, who had several scores up against him.

But Chandranath, though not skilled, had the ready cunning of the lesser breeds. With a swift unexpected move, he tripped Roy up so that he nearly fell backward; and, in a supreme effort to keep his balance, unconsciously loosened his hold. This time, Chandranath slipped free of him; and, in the act, pushed him so violently that he staggered and came down among sharp broken stones with one foot twisted under him. When he would have sprung up, a stab of pain in his ankle told him he was done for. . . .

The sheer ignominy of it enraged him; and he was still further enraged by the proceedings of the victor, who sprang nimbly out of reach on to a fragment of buttressed wall, whence he let fly a string of abusive epithets nicely calculated to touch up Roy's pride and temper and goad him to helpless fury.

But if his ankle was crippled, his brain was not. While Chandranath indulged his pent-up spite, Roy was feeling stealthily, purposefully, in the semi-darkness, for the sharpest chunk of stone he could lay hands on; a chunk warranted to hurt badly, if nothing more. The strip of shadow against the sky made an admirable target; and Roy's move, when it came, was swift, his aim unerring.

Somewhere about the head or shoulders it took effect: a yell of rage and pain assured him of that, as his target vanished on the far side of the wall.

Had he jumped or fallen? And what did the damage amount to? Roy would have given a good deal to know; but he had neither time nor power to investigate. Nothing for it but to crawl back, and shout to Arúna, when he got within hail.

It was an undignified performance. His twisted ankle stabbed like a knife, and never failed to claim acquaintance with every obstacle in its path. Presently, to his immense relief, the darkness ahead was raked by a restless light, zigzagging like a giant glow-worm.

"Lance—ahoy!" he shouted.

"Righto!" Lance sang out; and the glow-worm waggled a welcome.

Another shout from the Palace roof, answered in concert; and the mad, bad dream was over. He was back in the world of realities; on his feet again—one foot, to be exact—supported by Desmond's arm; pouring out his tale.

Lance already knew part of it. He had found Arúna and was hurrying on to find Roy. "Your cousin's got the pluck of a Rajput," he concluded. "But she seems a bit damaged. The left arm's broken, I'm afraid."

Roy cursed freely. "Wish to God I could make sure if I've sent that skunk to blazes."

"Just as well you can't, perhaps. If your shot took effect, he won't be off in a hurry. The police can nip out when we get back."

"Look here—keep it dark till I've seen Dyán. If Chandranath's nabbed, he'll want to be in it. Only fair!"

Lance chuckled. "What an unholy pair you are!—By the way, I fancy Martin's pulled it off with Miss Flossie. I tumbled across them in the hanging garden. You left that door open. Gave me the tip you might be out on the loose."

Desmond's surmise proved correct. Arúna's left arm was broken above the elbow: a simple fracture, but it hurt a good deal. Thea, in charge of 'the wounded,' eased them both as best she could, during the long drive home. But Arúna, still in her exalted mood, counted mere pain a little thing, when Roy, under cover of the cloak, found her cold right hand and cherished it in his warm one nearly all the way.

No one paid much heed to Martin and Flossie, who felt privately annoyed with 'the native cousin' for putting her nose out of joint. Defrauded of her due importance, she told her complacent lover they must 'save up the news till to-morrow.' Meantime, they rode, very much at leisure, behind the barouche;—and no one troubled about them at all.

Lance and Vincent, having cantered on ahead, called in for Miss Hammond and left word at Sir Lakshman's house that Arúna had met with a slight accident; and would he and her brother come out to the Residency after dinner?

Before the meal was over, they arrived. Miss Hammond was upstairs attending to Arúna; and Sir Lakshman joined them without ceremony, leaving Dyán alone with Roy, who was nursing his ankle in an armchair near the drawing-room fire.

In ten minutes of intimate talk he heard the essential facts, with reservations; and Roy had never felt more closely akin to him than on that evening. Rajput chivalry is no mere tradition. It is vital and active as ever it was. Insult or injury to a woman is sternly avenged; and the offender is lucky if he escapes the extreme penalty. Roy frankly hoped he had inflicted it himself. But for Dyán surmise was not enough. He would not eat nor sleep till he had left his own mark on the man who had come near killing his sister—most sacred being to him, who had neither wife nor mother.

"The delicate attention *was* meant for me, you know," Roy reminded him; simply from a British impulse to give the devil his due.

"Tcha!" Dyán's thumb and finger snapped like a toy pistol. "No law-courts talk for me. You were so close together. He took the risk. By Indra, he won't take any more such risks if I get at him! You said we would not see him here. But no doubt he has been hanging round Amber, making what mischief he can. He must have heard your party was coming, and got sneaking round for a chance to score off you. Young Ramanund, priest of Kali's shrine, is one of those he has made his tool, the way he made me. If he is in

Amber, I shall find him. You can take your oath on that." He stood up, straight and virile, instinct with purpose as a drawn sword. "I am going now, Roy. But not *one word* to any soul. Grandfather and Arúna only need to know I am trying to find who toppled those stones. I shall not succeed. That is all:—except for you and me. Bijli, Son of Lightning, will take me full gallop to Amber. First thing in the morning, I will come—and make my report."

"But look here—Lance knows——"

"Well, your Lance can suppose he got away. We could trust him, I don't doubt. But what is known to more than two, will in time be known to a hundred. For myself, I don't trouble. Among Rajputs the penalty would be slight. But this thing must be kept between you and me—because of Arúna."

Roy held out his hand. Dyán's fingers closed on it like taut strips of steel. Unmistakably the real Dyán Singh had shed the husks of scholarship and politics and come into his own again.

"I wouldn't care to have those at my throat!" remarked Roy, pensively considering the streaks on his own hand.

"Some Germans didn't care for it—in France," said Dyán coolly. "But now——" He scowled at his offending left arm. "I hope—very soon . . . never mind. No more talking . . . poison gas!" And with a flash of white teeth—he was gone.

Roy, left staring into the fire, followed him in imagination, speeding through the silent city out into the region of skulls and eye-sockets—a flying shadow in the moonlight with murder in its heart. . . .

Within an hour, that flying shadow was outside the gateway of Amber, startling the doorkeepers from sleep; murder, not only in its heart, but tucked securely in its belt. No 'law-courts talk' for one of his breed; no nice adjustment of penalty to offence; no concern as to possible consequences. The Rajput, with his blood up, is daring to the point of recklessness; deaf to puerile promptings of prudence or mercy; a sword, seeking its victim; insatiate till the thrust has gone home.

And, in justice to Dyán Singh, it should be added that

there was more than Arúna in his mind. There was India—increasingly at the mercy of Chandranath and his kind. The very blindness of his earlier obsession had intensified the effect of his awakening. Roy's devoted daring, his grandfather's mellow wisdom, had worked in his fiery soul more profoundly than they knew: and his act of revenge was also, in his eyes, an act of expiation. At the bidding of Chandranath, or another, he would unhesitatingly have flung a bomb at the Commissioner of Delhi—the sane, strong man whose words and bearing had so impressed him on the few occasions they had met at the Residency. By what law of God or man, then, should he hesitate to grind the head of this snake under his heel?

One-handed though he was, he would not strike from behind. The son of a jackal should know who struck him. He should taste fear, before he tasted death. And then—the Lake, that would never give up its secret or its dead. Siri Chandranath would disappear from his world, like a stone flung into a river; and India would be a cleaner place without him.

He knew himself hampered, if it came to a struggle. But—tcha! the man was a coward. Let the gods but deliver his victim into that one purposeful hand of his—and the end was sure.

Near the Palace, he deserted Bijli, Son of Lightning; tethered him securely and spoke a few words in his ear, while the devoted creature nuzzled against him, as who should say, 'What need of speech between me and thee'? Then—following Roy's directions—he made his way cautiously up the hillside, where the arch showed clear in the moon. If Chandranath had been injured or stupefied, he would probably not have gone far.

His surmise proved correct. His stealthy approach well-timed. The guardian gods of Amber, it seemed, were on his side. For there, on the fallen slab, crouched a shadow, bowed forward; its head in its hands.

"Must have been stunned," he thought. Patently the gods were with him. Had he been an Englishman, the man's hurt would probably have baulked him of his purpose. But Dyán Singh, Rajput, was not hampered by the sportman's code of morals. He was frankly out to kill. His brain worked swiftly, instinctively: and swift action followed. . . .

Out of the sheltering shadow he leapt, as the cheetah leaps on its prey: the long knife gripped securely in his teeth. Before Chandranath came to his senses, the steel-spring grasp was on his throat, stifling the yell of terror at Roy's supposed return. . . .

The tussle was short and silent. Within three minutes Dyán had his man down; arms and body pinioned between his powerful knees, that his one available hand might be free to strike. Then, in a low fierce rush, he spoke: "Yes—it is I—Dyán Singh. You told me often —strike, for the Mother. 'Who kills the body kills naught.' I strike for the Mother *now.*"

Once—twice—the knife struck deep; and the writhing thing between his knees was still.

He did not altogether relish the weird journey down to the shore of the Lake; or the too close proximity of the limp burden slung over his shoulder. But his imagination did not run riot, like Roy's: and no qualms of conscience perturbed his soul. He had avenged, tenfold, Arúna's injury. He had expiated, in drastic fashion, his own aberration from sanity. It was enough.

The soft 'plop' and splash of the falling body, well weighted with stones, was music to his ear. Beyond that musical murmur, the Lake would utter no sound. . . .

# CHAPTER XVI.

> "So let him journey through his earthly day:
> 'Mid hustling spirits go his self-found way;
> Find torture, bliss, in every forward stride—
> He, every moment, still unsatisfied."
>
> —FAUST.

NEXT morning, very early, he was closeted with Roy, sitting on the edge of his bed; cautiously, circumstantially, telling him all. Roy, as he listened, was half repelled, half impressed by the sheer impetus of the thing; and again he felt—as once or twice in Delhi—what centuries apart they were, though related, and almost of an age.

"This will be only between you and me, Roy—for always," Dyán concluded gravely. "Not because I have any shame for killing that snake; but—as I said . . . because of Arúna——"

"Trust me," said Roy. "Amber Lake and I don't blab. There'll be a nine days' mystery over his disappearance. Then his lot will set up some other tin god—and promptly forget all about him."

"Let us follow their example, in that at least!" Grim humour flickered in Dyán's eyes, as he extracted a cigarette from the proffered case. "You gave me my chance. I have taken it—like a Rajput. Now we have other things to do."

Roy smiled. "That's about the size of it—from your sane, barbaric standpoint! I'm fairly besieged with other things to do. As soon as this blooming ankle allows me to hobble, I'm keen to get at some of the thoughtful elements in Calcutta and Bombay; educated Indian men and women, who honestly believe that India is moving towards a national unity that will transcend all antagonism of race and creed. I can't see it myself; but I've an open mind. Then, I think, Udaipur—'last, loneliest, loveliest, apart'—to knock my novel into shape before I go North. And *you*——?" He pensively took stock of his volcanic cousin. "Sure you're safe not to erupt again?"

"Safe as houses—thanks to you. That doesn't mean I can be orthodox Hindu and work for the orthodox Jaipur Raj. I would like to join 'Servants of India' Society; and work for the Mother among those who accept British connection as India's God-given destiny. In no other way will I work again—to 'make her a widow.' Also, I thought perhaps—" he hesitated, averting his eyes—"to take vows of celibacy——"

"*Dyán!*" Roy could not repress his astonishment. He had almost forgotten that side of things. Right or wrong—a tribute to Tara indeed! It jerked him uncomfortably; almost annoyed him.

"Unfair on Grandfather," he said with decision. "For every reason, you ought to marry—an enlightened wife. Think—of Arúna."

"I *do* think of her. It is *she* who ought to marry."

The emphasis was not lost on Roy:—and it hurt. Last night's poignant scene was intimately with him still. "I'm afraid you won't persuade her to," he said in a contained voice.

"I am quite aware of *that*. And the reason—even a blind man could not fail to see."

They looked straight at one another for a long moment. Roy did not swerve from the implied accusation.

"Well, it's no fault of mine, Dyán," he said, recalling Arúna's confession that tacitly freed him from blame. "*She* understands—there's a bigger thing between us than our mere selves. Whatever I'm free to do for her, I'll gladly do—always. It was chiefly to ease her poor heart that I risked the Delhi adventure. I felt I had lost the link with *you*."

"Not surprising." Dyán smoked for a few minutes in silence. He was clearly moved by the fine frankness of Roy's attitude. "All the same," he said at last, "it was not quite broken. You have given me new life; and because you did it—for her, I swear to you, as long as she needs me, I will not fail her." He held out his hand. Roy's closed on it hard.

"Later in the morning I will come back and see her," Dyán added, in a changed voice—and went out.

Later in the morning, Roy himself was allowed to see her. With the help of his stick he limped to her verandah balcony, where she lay in a long chair, with cushions and rugs, the poor arm in a sling. Thea was with her. She had heard as much of last night's doings as any one would ever know. So she felt justified in letting the poor dears have half an hour together.

Her withdrawal was tactfully achieved; but there followed an awkward silence. For the space of several minutes it seemed that neither of the 'poor dears' knew quite what to make of their privilege, though they were appreciating it from their hearts.

Roy found himself too persistently aware of the arm that had been broken to save him; of the new bond between them, signed and sealed by that one unforgettable kiss.

As for Arúna—while pain anchored her body to earth, her unstable heart swayed disconcertingly from heights of rarefied content, to depths of shyness. Things she had said and done, on that far-away hillside, seemed unbelievable, remembered in her familiar balcony with a daylight mind: and fear lest he might be 'thinking it that way too' increased shyness tenfold. Yet it was she who spoke first, after all.

"Oh, it makes me angry . . . to see you—like that," she said, indicating his ankle with a faint movement of her hand.

Roy quietly took possession of the hand and pressed it to his lips.

"How do you suppose *I* feel, seeing *you* like that!" Words and act dispelled her foolish fears. "Did you sleep? Does it hurt much?"

"Only if I forget and try to move. But what matter? Every time it hurts, I feel proud because that feeble arm was able to push you out of the way."

"You've every right to feel proud. You nearly knocked me over!"

A mischievous smile crept into her eyes. "I am afraid . . . I was very rude!"

"That's *one* way of putting it!" His grave tenderness warmed her like sunshine. He leaned nearer; his hand grasped the arm of her long chair. "You were a very wonderful Arúna last night. And—you are going to be more wonderful still. Working with Dyán, you are going to help make my dream come true—of India finding herself again by her own genius, along her own lines——"

He had struck the right note. Her face lit up as he had hoped to see it. "Oh, Roy—can I really——? Will Dyán help? Will he *let* me——"

"Of course he will. And I'll be helping too—in my own fashion. We'll never lose touch, Arúna; though India's your destiny and England's mine. Never say again you have no true country. Like me, you have two countries—one very dear; one supreme. I'm afraid there are terrible days coming out here. And in those days every one of you who honestly loves England—every one of *us* who honestly loves India—will count in the scale . . ."

He paused; and she drew a deep breath. "Oh—how you *see* things! It is you who are wonderful, Roy. I can think and feel the big things in my heart. But for doing them—I am, after all, only a woman . . ."

"An *Indian* woman," he emphasised, his eyes on hers. "I know—and you know—what that means. You have not yet bartered away your magical influence for a mess of pottage. Because of one Indian woman—supreme for me; and now . . . because of another, they all have a special claim on my heart. If India has not gone too far down the wrong road, it is by the *true* Swadeshi spirit of her women she may yet be saved. *They*, at any rate, don't reckon progress by counting factory chimneys or seats on councils. And every seed—good or bad—is sown first in the home. Get at the women, Arúna—the home ones—and tell them that. It's not only *my* dream; it was—my mother's. You don't know how she loved and believed in you all. I think she never *quite* understood the other kind. The longer she lived among them, the more she craved for all of you to remain true women—in the full sense, not the narrow one——"

He had never yet spoken so frankly and freely of that

dear lost mother; Arúna knew it for the highest compliment he could pay her. Truly his generous heart was giving her all that his jealous household gods would permit. . . .

Thea—stepping softly through the inner room—caught a sentence or two; caught a glimpse of Roy's finely-cut profile; of Arúna's eyes intent on his face; and she smiled very tenderly to herself. It was so exactly like Roy; and such constancy of devotion went straight to her mother-heart. So too—with a sharper pang—did the love hunger in Arúna's eyes.

The puzzle of these increasing race complications——! The tragedy and the pity of it . . .!

Lance travelled North that night with a mind at ease. Roy had assured him that the moment his ankle permitted he would leave Jaipur and 'give the bee in his bonnet an airing' elsewhere. That assurance proved easier to give than to act upon, when the moment came. The Jaipur Residency had come to seem almost like home. And the magnet of home drew all that was Eastern in Roy. It was the British blood in his veins that drove him afield. Though India was his objective, England was the impelling force. His true home seemed hundreds of miles away, in more senses than one. His union with Rajputana—set with the seal of that sacred and beautiful experience at Chitor—seemed, in his present mood, the more vital of the two.

And there was Lance up in the Punjab—a magnet as strong as any, when the masculine element prevailed. Yet again, some inner irresistible impulse obliged him to break away from them all. It was one of those inevitable moments when the dual forces within pulled two ways; when he felt envious exceedingly of Lance Desmond's sane and single-minded attitude towards men and things. One couldn't picture Lance a prey to the ignominious sensation that half of him wanted to go one way and half of him another way. At this juncture, half of himself felt a confounded fool for not going back to the Punjab and enjoying a friendly sociable cold weather among his father's people. The other half felt impelled to probe deeper into the complexities of changing India, to confirm and impart his belief that the destinies of England and India were one and indivisible. After all, India stood where she did to-day by virtue of what England had made her. He refused to believe that even the insidious disintegrating process of democracy could dissolve—in a brief fever of unrest—links forged and welded in the course of a hundred years.

In that case, argued his practical half, why this absurd inner sense of responsibility for great issues over which he could have no shadow of control? What was the earthly use of it—this large window in his soul, opening on to world's complexities and conflicts; not allowing him to say comfortably, 'They are not.' His opal-tinted dreams of interpreting East to West had suffered a change of complexion since Oxford days. His large vague aspirations of service had narrowed down, inevitably, to a few definite personal issues. Action involves limitation—as the picture involves the frame. Dreams must descend to earth—or remain unfruitful. It might be a little, or a great matter, that he had managed to set two human fragments of changing India on the right path—so far as he could discern it. The fruits of that modest beginning only the years could reveal. . . .

Then there was this precious novel simmering at the back of things; his increasing desire to get away alone with the ghostly company that haunted his brain. As the mother-to-be feels the new life mysteriously moving within her, so he began to feel within him the first stirrings of his own creative power. Already his poems and essays had raised expectations and secured attention for other things he wanted to say. And there seemed no end to them. He had hardly yet begun his mental adventures. Pressing forward, through sense, to the limitless regions of mind and spirit, new vistas would open, new paths lure him on. . . .

That first bewildering, intoxicating sense of power is good—while it lasts; none the less, because, in the nature of things, it is foredoomed to disillusion—greater or less, according to the authenticity of the god within.

Whatever the outcome for Roy, that passing exaltation eased appreciably the pang of parting from them all. And it was responsible for a happy inspiration.

Rummaging among his papers, on the eve of departure, he came upon the sketch of India that he had written in Delhi and refrained from sending to Arúna. Intrinsically it was hers; inspired by her. Also—intrinsically it was good: and straightway he decided she should have it for a parting gift.

Beautifully copied out, and tied up with carnation-pink ribbons, he reserved it for their last few moments together. She was still such a child in some ways. The small surprise of his gift might ease the pang of parting. It was a woman's thought. But the woman-strain of tenderness was strong in Roy, as in all true artists.

She was standing near the fire in her own sitting-room, wearing the pink dress and sari, her arm still in a sling. Last words, those desperate inanities—buffers between the heart and its own emotion—are difficult things to bring off in any case; peculiarly difficult for these two, with that unreal, yet intensely actual, bond between them; and Roy felt more than grateful to the inspiration that gave him something definite to say.

Instantly her eyes were on it—wondering . . . guessing. . . .

"It's a little thing I wrote in Delhi," he said simply. "I couldn't send it to Jeffers. It seemed—to belong to you. So I thought——" He proffered it, feeling absurdly shy of it—and of her.

"Oh—but it is too much!" Holding it with her sling hand, she opened it with the other and devoured it eagerly under his watching eyes. By the changes that flitted across her face, by the tremor of her lips and her hands, as she pressed it to her heart, he knew he could have given her no dearer treasure than that fragment of himself. And because he knew it, he felt tongue-tied; tempted beyond measure to kiss her once again.

If she divined his thought, she kept her lashes lowered and gave no sign.

He hoped she knew. . . .

But before either could break the spell of silence that held them, Thea returned; and their moment—their idyll—was over. . . .

END OF PHASE III.

# PHASE IV.

# DUST OF THE ACTUAL

## CHAPTER I.

"It's no use trying to keep out of things. The moment they want to put you in—you're in. The moment you're born, you're done for."—HUGH WALPOLE.

THE middle of March found Roy back in the Punjab, sharing a ramshackle bungalow with Lance and two of his brother officers; good fellows, both, in their diametrically opposite fashions; but superfluous—from Roy's point of view. When he wanted a quiet 'confab' with Lance, one or both were sure to come strolling in and hang round, jerking out aimless remarks. When he wanted a still quieter 'confab' with his maturing novel, their voices and footsteps echoed too clearly in the verandahs and the scantily furnished rooms. But did he venture to grumble at these minor drawbacks, Lance would declare he was demoralised by floating loose in an Earthly Paradise and becoming a mere appendage to a pencil.

There was a measure of truth in the last. As a matter of fact, after two months of uninterrupted work at Udaipur, Roy had unwarily hinted at a risk of becoming embedded in his too congenial surroundings;—and that careless admission had sealed his fate.

Lance Desmond, with his pointed phrase, had virtually dug him out of his chosen retreat; had written temptingly of the 'last of the polo,' of prime pig-sticking at Kapurthala, of the big Gymkhana that was to wind up the season:—a rare chance for Roy to exhibit his horsemanship. And again, in more serious mood, he had written of increasing anxiety over his Sikhs with that 'infernal agitation business' on the increase, and an unbridled native press shouting sedition from the house-tops. A nice state of chaos India was coming to! He hoped to goodness they wouldn't be swindled out of their leave; but Roy had better 'roll up' soon, so as to be on the spot, in case of ructions; not packed away in cotton-wool down there.

A few letters in this vein had effectually rent the veil of illusion that shielded Roy from aggressive actualities. In Udaipur there had been no hysterical press; no sedition flaunting on the house-tops. One hadn't arrived at the twentieth century, even. Except for a flourishing hospital, a few hideous modern interiors, and a Resident—who was very good friends with Vinx—one stepped straight back into the leisurely, colourful, frankly brutal life of the middle ages. And Roy had fallen a willing victim to the charms of Udaipur:—her white palaces, white temples, and white landing-stages, flanked with marble elephants, embosomed in wooded hills, and reflected in the blue untroubled depths of the Pichóla Lake. Immersed in his novel, he had not known a dull or lonely hour in that enchanted backwater of Rajasthán.

His large vague plans for getting in touch with the thoughtful elements of Calcutta and Bombay had yielded to the stronger magnetism of beauty and art. Like his father, he hated politics; and Westernised India is nothing if not political. It was a true instinct that warned him to keep clear of that muddy stream, and render his mite of service to India in the exercise of his individual gift. That would be in accord with one of his mother's wise and tender sayings: (his memory was jewelled with them) "Look always first at your own gifts. They are sign-posts, pointing the road to your true line of service." Could he but immortalise the measure of her spirit that was in him, that were true service to India—and more than India. There are men created for action. There are men created to inspire action. And the world has equal need of both.

He had things to say on paper that would take him all his time; and Udaipur had metaphorically opened her arms to him. The Resident and his wife had been more than kind. He had his books; his cool, lofty rooms in the Guest House; his own private boat on the Lake; and freedom to go his own unfettered way at all hours of the day or night. There the simmering novel had begun to move with a life of its own; and while that state of being endured, nothing else mattered much in earth or heaven.

For seven weeks he had worked at it without interruption; and for seven weeks he had been happy: companioned by the vivid creatures of his brain; and, better still, by a quickened undersense of his mother's vital share in the 'blossom and fruit of his life.' The danger of becoming embedded had been no myth: and at the back of his brain there had lurked a superstitious reluctance to break the spell.

But Lance was Lance: no one like him. Moreover, he had known well enough that anticipation of breakers ahead was no fanciful nightmare; but a sane corrective to the ostrich policy of those who had sown the evil seed and were trying to say of the fruit—'It is not.' Letters from Dyán, and spasmodic devouring of newspapers, kept him alive to the sinister activities of the larger world outside. News from Bombay grew steadily more disquieting:—strikes and riots, fomented by agitators, who lied shamelessly about the nature of the new Bills; hostile crowds and insults to Englishwomen. Dyán more than hinted that if the threatened outbreak were not resolutely crushed at the start, it might prove a far-reaching affair; and Roy had not the slightest desire to find himself 'packed away in cotton-wool,' miles from the scene of action. Clearly Lance wanted him. He might be useful on the spot. And that settled the matter.

Impossible to leave so much loveliness, such large drafts of peace and leisure, without a pang; but—the wrench over—he was well content to find himself established in this ramshackle bachelor bungalow, back again with Lance and his music—very much in evidence just now—and the two superfluous good fellows, whom he liked well enough in homœopathic doses. Especially he liked Jack Meredith, cousin of the Desmonds;—a large and simple soul, gravely absorbed in pursuing balls and tent-pegs and 'pig'; impervious to feminine lures; equally impervious to the caustic wit of his diametrical opposite, Captain James Barnard, who eased his private envy by christening him 'Don Juan.' For Meredith fatally attracted women; and Barnard—cultured, cynical, Cambridge—was as fatally susceptible to them as a trout to a May-fly; but, for some unfathomable reason they would not; and in Anglo-India a man could not hide his failures under a bushel. Lance classified him comprehensively as 'one of the War lot'; liked him, and was sorry for him, although—perhaps because—he was 'no soldier.'

Roy also liked him; and enjoyed verbal fencing-bouts with him when the mood was on. Still he would have preferred, beyond measure, the Kohat arrangement, with the Colonel for an unobtrusive third.

But the Colonel, these days, had a bungalow to himself; a bungalow in process of being furnished by no means on bachelor lines. For the unbelievable had come to pass——! And the whole affair had been carried through in his own inimitable fashion, without so much as a tell-tale ripple on the surface of things. Quite unobtrusively, at Kohat, he had made friends with the General's daughter—a dark-haired slip of a girl, with the blood of distinguished Frontier soldiers in her veins. Quite unobtrusively—during Christmas week—he had laid his heart and the Regiment at her feet. Quite unobtrusively, he proposed to marry her in April, when the leave season opened, and carry her off to Kashmir.

"*That's* the way it goes with *some* people," said Lance, the first time he spoke of it; and Roy fancied he detected a wistful note in his voice.

"That's the way it'll go with you, old man," he had retorted. "I'm the one that will have to look out for squalls!"

Lance had merely smiled and said nothing:—the reception he usually accorded to personal remarks. And, at the moment, Roy thought no more of the matter.

Their first good week of polo and riding and generally fooling round together had quickened his old allegiance to Lance, his newer allegiance to the brotherhood of action. He possessed no more enviable talent than his many-sided zest for life.

Lance himself seemed in an unusually social mood. So of course Roy must submit to being bowled round in the new dog-cart and introduced to special friends, in cantonments and Lahore, including the Deputy Commissioner's wife and good-looking eldest daughter; the best dancer in the station and an extra special friend, he gathered from Lance's best offhand manner.

Roy found her more than good-looking; beautiful, almost, with her twofold grace of carriage and feature and her low-toned harmony of colouring :—ivory-white skin, ash-blond hair and hazel eyes, clear as a Highland river; the pupils abnormally large, the short thick lashes very black, like a smudge round her lids. She was tall, in fine, and carried her beauty like a brimming chalice; very completely mistress of herself; and very completely detached from her florid, effusive, worldly-wise mother. Unquestionably, a young woman to be reckoned with.

But Roy did not feel disposed, just then, to reckon seriously with any young woman, however alluring. The memory of Arúna—the exquisite remoteness from everyday life of their whole relation—did not easily fade. And the creatures of his brain were still clamant, in spite of broken threads and drastic change of surroundings. Lance had presented him with a spacious writing-table; and most days he would stick to it for hours, sooner than drive out in pursuit of tennis or afternoon dancing in Lahore.

He was sitting at it now; flinging down a dramatic episode, roughly, rapidly, as it came. The polished surface was strewn with an untidy array of papers; the only ornaments a bit of old brass-work and two ivory elephants; a photograph of his father and a large one of his mother taken from the portrait at Jaipur. The table was set almost at right angles to his open door, and the chick rolled up. He had a weakness for being able to 'see out,' if it was only the corner of a barren 'compound' and a few dusty oleanders. He had forgotten the others; forgotten the time. All he asked, while the spate lasted, was to be left alone. . . .

He almost jumped when the latch clicked behind him and Lance strolled in, faultlessly attired in the latest suit from home; a golden-brown tie and a silk handkerchief, the same shade, emerging from his breast pocket. By nature, Lance was no dandy; but Roy had not failed to note that he was apt to be scrupulously well turned out on certain occasions. And, at sight of him, he promptly 'remembered he had forgotten' the very particular nature of to-day's occasion: the marriage of Miss Gladys Elton—step-sister of Rose—to a rising civilian some eighteen years older than his bride. It was an open secret, in the station, that the wedding was Mrs Elton's private and personal triumph, that she, not her unassuming daughter, was the acknowledged heroine of the day.

"Not ready yet—you unmitigated slacker?" Lance exclaimed with an impatient frown. "Buck up. Time we were moving."

"Awfully sorry. I clean forgot." Roy's tone was not conspicuously penitent.

"Tell us another! The whole Mess was talking of it at tiffin."

"I'm afraid I'd forgotten all about tiffin."

It was so patently the truth that Lance looked mollified. "You and your confounded novel! Now then—double. I don't want to be glaringly late."

Roy looked pathetic. "But I'm simply up to the eyes. The truth is, I can't be bothered. I'll turn up for the dancing at the Hall."

"And I'm to make your giddy excuses?"

"If any one happens to notice my absence, you can say something pretty——"

He was interrupted by the appearance of Barnard at the verandah door. "Dog-cart's ready and waiting, Major. What's the hitch?"

"Sinclair's discovered he's too busy to come!"

"What—the favoured one? The fair Rose won't relish *that* touching mark of attention. On whom she smiles, from him she expects gold, frankincense, and myrrh——"

"Drop it, Barnard," Desmond cut in imperatively; and Roy remarked almost in the same breath, "Thanks for the tip. I'll write to Bombay for the best brand of all three against another occasion."

"But this is *the* occasion! Copy—my dear chap, copy! Anglo-India in excelsis and 'Oh 'Ell' in all her glory!"

It may be mentioned that Mrs Elton's name was Olive; that she saw soldiers as trees walking. And subalterns retaliated—strictly behind her back.

But Roy remained unmoved. "If you two are in such a fluster over your precious wedding, I vote you get out—and let *me* get on."

Barnard asked nothing better. Miss Arden was his May-fly of the moment. "Come along, Major," he cried, and vanished forthwith.

As Lance moved away, Roy remarked casually: "Be a good chap and ask Miss Arden, with my best salaams, to save me a dance or two, in case I'm late turning up!"

Lance gave him a straight look. "Not I. My pockets will be bulging with your apologies. You can get some one else to do your commissions in the other line."

Sheer astonishment silenced Roy; and Desmond, from the threshold, added more seriously, "Don't let the women here give you a swelled head, Roy. They'll do their damnedest between them."

When he had gone, Roy sat staring idly at the patch of sunlight outside his door. What the devil did Lance mean by it? Moods were not in his line. To make a half-joking request, and find Lance taking it seriously, wasn't in the natural order of things. And the way he jumped on Barnard, too. Could there possibly have been a rebuff in that quarter? He couldn't picture any girl in her senses refusing Lance. Besides, they seemed on quite friendly terms. Nothing beyond that—so far as Roy could see. He would very much like to feel sure. But, for all their intimacy, he knew precisely how far one could go with Lance: and one couldn't go as far as that.

As for the remark about a swelled head, Lance must have been rotting. *He* wasn't troubling about women or girls—except for tennis and dancing; and Miss Arden was a superlative performer; in fact, rather superlative all round. As a new experience, she seemed distinctly worth cultivating, so long as that process did not seriously hamper the novel,—that was unashamedly his first consideration, at the moment.

He loved every phase of the work; from the initial thrill of inception to the nice balance of a phrase and the very look of his favourite words. His childish love of them for their own sake still prevailed. For him, they were still live things, possessing a character and charm all their own.

And now, the house being blessedly empty, his pencil sped off again on its wild career. The men and women he had loved into life were thronging his brain. Everything else was forgotten—Lance and Miss Arden and the wedding and the afternoon dancing at the Hall. . . .

## CHAPTER II.

"Which is the more perilous, to meet the temptings of Eve, or to pique her?"—GEORGE MEREDITH.

OF course he reached the Lawrence Hall egregiously late, to find the afternoon dancing, that Lahore prescribes three times a week, in full swing.

The lofty pillared Hall—an aristocrat among Station Clubs—was more crowded than usual. Half the polished floor was uncovered; the rest carpeted and furnished for lookers-on. Here Mrs Elton still diffused her exuberant air of patronage; sailing majestically from group to group of her recent guests, and looking more than life size in lavender satin besprinkled with old lace.

Roy hurried past, lest she discover him; and, from the security of an arched alcove, scanned the more interesting half of the Hall. There went little Mrs Hunter-Ranyard, a fluffy pussy-cat person, with soft eyes and soft manners—and claws. She was one of those disconnected wives whom he was beginning to recognise as a feature of the country: unobtrusively owned by a dyspeptic-looking Divisional Judge; hospitable and lively, and an infallible authority on other people's private affairs. Like too many modern Anglo-Indians, she prided herself on keeping airily apart from the country of her exile. Natives gave her 'the creeps.' Useless to argue. Her retort was unvarying and unanswerable. "East is East—and I'm *not.* It's a country of horrors, under a thin layer of tinsel. Don't talk to *me*——!" Lance Desmond had achieved fame among the subalterns by christening her the Banter-Wrangle; but he liked her well enough, on the whole, to hope she would never find him out.

She whirled past now, on the arm of Talbot Hayes, senior Assistant Commissioner; an exceedingly superior person who shared her views about 'the country.' Catching Roy's eye, she feigned exaggerated surprise and fluttered a friendly hand.

His response was automatic. He had just discovered Miss Arden—with Lance, of course—looking supreme in a moon-coloured gown with a dull gold sash carelessly knotted on one side. Her graceful hat was of gold tissue, unadorned. Near the edge of the brim lay one yellow rose; and a rope of amber beads hung well below her waist.

Roy—son of Lilámani—had an artist's eye for details of dress, for harmony of tone and line, which this girl probably achieved by mere feminine instinct. The fool he was, to have come so late. When they stopped, he would catch her and plead for an extra, at least.

Meantime, a pity to waste this one; and there was poor little Miss Delawny sitting out, as usual, in her skimpy pink frock and black hat, trying so hard not to look forlorn that he felt sorry for her. She was tacitly barred by most of the men because she was 'café au lait';—a delicate allusion to the precise amount of Indian blood in her veins.

He had not, so far, come across many specimens of these pathetic half-and-halfs, who seemed to inhabit a racial No-Man's-Land. But Lahore was full of them; minor officials in the Railway and the Post Office; living, more or less, in a substratum of their own kind. He gathered that they were regarded as a 'problem' by the thoughtful few, and simply turned down by the rest. He felt an acute sympathy for them: also—in hidden depths—a vague distaste. Most of those he had encountered were so obviously of no particular caste, in either country's estimate of the word, that he had never associated them with himself. He saw himself, rather, as of double caste; a fusion of the best in both races. The writer of that wonderful letter had said he was different; and presumably she knew. Whether the average Anglo-Indian would see any difference, he had not the remotest idea; and, so far, he had scarcely given the matter a thought.

Here, however, it was thrust upon his attention; nor

had he failed to notice that Lance never mentioned the Jaipur cousins except when they were alone :—whether by chance or design, he did not choose to ask. And if either of the other fellows had noticed his mother's photograph, or felt a glimmer of curiosity, no word had been said.

After all, what concern was it of these chance-met folk? He was nothing to them; and to him they were mainly a pleasant change from the absorbing business of his novel and the problems of India in transition.

And the poor little girl in the skimpy frock was an unconscious fragment of that problem. Too pathetic to see how she tried not to look round hopefully whenever masculine footsteps came her way. Why shouldn't he give her a pleasant surprise?

She succeeded, this time, in not looking round; so the surprise came off to his satisfaction. She was nervous and unpractised, and he constantly found her feet where they had no business to be. But sooner than hurt her feelings, he piloted her twice round the room before stopping; and found himself next to Mrs Hunter-Ranyard, who 'snuggled up' to him (the phrase was Barnard's) and proffered consolation after her kind.

"Bad boy! You missed the cream of the afternoon, but you're not *quite* too late. I'm free for the next."

Roy, fairly cornered, could only bow and smile his acceptance. And after his arduous prelude, Mrs Ranyard's dancing was an effortless delight—if only she would not spoil it by her unceasing ripple of talk. His lack of response troubled her no whit. She was bubbling over with caustic comment on Mrs Elton's latest adventure in matrimony.

"She's a mighty hunter, before the Lord! She marked down poor Hilton last cold weather," cooed the silken voice in Roy's inattentive ear. "Of course you know he's one of our coming men! And I've a shrewd idea he *was* intended for Rose. But in Miss Rose the matchmaker has met her match! She's clever—that girl; and she's reduced the tactics of non-resistance to a fine art. I don't believe she ever stands up to her mother. She smiles and smiles—and goes her own way. She likes playing with soldiers; partly because they're good company; partly, I'll swear, because she knows it keeps her mother on tenter-hooks. But when it comes to business, she'll choose as shrewdly——"

Roy stopped dancing and confronted her, half laughing, half irate. "If you're keen on talking—let's talk. I can't do both." He stated the fact politely, but with decision. "And—frankly, I hate hearing a girl pulled to pieces, just because she's charming and good-looking and——"

"Oh, my *dear* boy," she interrupted unfailingly—sweet solicitude in her lifted gaze. "*Did* I trample on your chivalrous toes? Or is it——?"

"No, it *isn't.*" He resented the barefaced implication. "Naturally—I admire her——"

"Oh, naturally! You can't help yourselves, any of you! She's 'sooner caught than the pestilence, and the taker runs presently mad.' No use looking daggers! It's a fact. I don't say she flirts outrageously—like I do! She simply expects homage—and gets it. She expects men to fall in love with her—and they topple over like ninepins. Sometimes—when I'm feeling magnanimous—I catch a ninepin as it falls! Look at her now, with that R.E. boy—plainly in the toils!"

Roy declined to look. If she was trying to put him off Miss Arden, she was on the wrong tack. Besides—he wanted to dance.

"One more turn?" he suggested, nipping a fresh outbreak in the bud. "But, please—no talking."

She laughed and shook her fan at him. "Epicure!" But after all, it was an indirect compliment to her dancing: and for the space of two minutes, she held her peace.

Throughout the brief pause, she rippled on, with negligible interludes; but not till they re-entered the Hall did she revert to the theme that had so exasperated Roy. There she espied Desmond, standing under an archway, staring straight before him, apparently lost in thought.

She indicated him, discreetly, with her fan. "The Happy Warrior (that's my private name for him) seems to have something on his mind. Can he have proposed—at last? I confess I'm curious. But of course *you* know all about it, Mr Sinclair. Don't tell *me!*"

"I won't!" said Roy gravely. "You probably know more than I do."

"But I thought you were such *intimate* friends? How superbly masculine!"

"Well—he is."

"Oh, he is! He's so firmly planted on his feet that he tacitly invites one to tilt at him! I confess I've already tried my hand—and failed. So it soothes my vanity to observe that even the Rose of Sharon isn't visibly upsetting his balance. Frankly, I'm more than a little intrigued over that affair. It seems to have reached a certain point and stuck there. At one time—I thought——"

Her thought remained unuttered. Roy was patently not attending. Miss Arden and the 'R.E. boy' had just entered the Hall.

"Don't let me keep you," she added sweetly. "It's evident *she's* the next!"

Roy collected himself with a jerk. "You're wiser than I am! I've not asked her yet."

"Then you can save yourself the trouble and go on dancing with me! She's always booked up ahead——"

Her blue eyes challenged him laughingly; but he caught the undernote of rivalry. For half a second the scales hung even between courtesy and inclination; then, from the tail of his eye, he saw Hayes bearing down upon the other pair. That decided him. He had conceived an unreasoning dislike of Talbot Hayes.

"I'm awfully sorry," he said politely. "But—I sent word I was coming in for the dancing; and——"

"Oh, go along then and get your fingers burnt, as you deserve. But never say *I* didn't try and save them!"

Roy laughed. "They aren't in any danger, thanks very much!"

Just as he reached Miss Arden, the R.E. boy left her, and Lance, forsaking his pillar, strolled casually to her side.

She greeted Roy with a faint lift of her brows.

"Was I unspeakable——? I apologise," he said impulsively; and her smile absolved him.

"You were wiser than you knew. You escaped an infliction. It was insufferably dull. We all smiled and smiled, till there were 'miles and miles of smiles'; and we were all bored to extinction! Ask Major Desmond!"

She acknowledged his presence with a sidelong glance.

He returned it with a quick look that told Roy he had been touched on the raw.

"As I spent most of the time talking to you—and as you've just recorded your sensations, I'd rather be excused," he said with a touch of stiffness. "Your innings, I suppose, old man?" And, with a friendly nod, he moved away.

Roy, watching him go, felt almost angry with the girl, and impetuously spoke his thought.

"Poor old Desmond! What did you give him a knock for? *He* couldn't be dull, if he tried."

"N-no," she agreed, without removing her eyes from his retreating figure. "But sometimes—he can be aggressive."

"I've never noticed it."

"How long have you known him?"

"A trifle of fifteen years."

"Quite a romantic friendship?"

Roy nodded. He did not choose to discuss his feeling for Lance with this cool, compelling young woman. Yet her very coolness goaded him to add: "I suppose men see more clearly than women that—he's one in a thousand."

"I'm—not so sure——"

"Yet you snub him as if he was a tin-pot 'sub.'"

His resentment would out; but the smile in her eyes disarmed him.

"Was it as bad as that? What a pair you are! Don't worry. We know each other's little ways by now."

It was scarcely convincing; but Lance would not thank him for interfering; and the band had struck up. No sign of a partner. It seemed the luck was 'in.'

"Did Desmond give you my message?" he asked.

"No—what?"

"Only—that I hoped you'd be magnanimous. . . . Is there a chance——?"

Her eyes rested deliberately on his; and the last spark of resentment flickered out. "More than you deserve! But this one does happen to be free . . ."

"Well, we won't waste any of it," said he:—and they danced without a break, without a word, till the perfect accord of their circling and swaying ceased with the last notes of the valse.

That was the real thing, thought Roy, but felt too shy for compliments; and they merely exchanged a smile. He had felt the pleasure was mutual. Now he knew it.

Out through the portico they passed into the cool green gardens, freshly watered, exhaling a smell of moist earth and the fragrance of unnumbered roses—a very whiff of Home: bushes, standards, ramblers; and everywhere—flaunting its supremacy—the Maréchal Niel; sprawling over hedges, scrambling up evergreens and falling again, in cascades of moon-yellow blossoms and glossy leaves.

Roy, keenly alive to the exquisite mingling of scent and colour and evening lights—was still more alive to the silent girl at his side, who seemed to radiate both the lure and the subtle antagonism of sex—in itself an inverted form of fascination.

They had strolled half round the empty bandstand before she remarked, in her cool, low-pitched voice: "You really are a flagrantly casual person, Mr Sinclair. I sometimes wonder—is it *quite* spontaneous? Or—do you find it effective?"

Roy frankly turned and stared at her. "Effective? *What* a question?"

Her smile puzzled and disconcerted him.

"Well, you've answered it with your usual pristine frankness! I see—it was not intentional."

"Why should it be?"

"Oh, if you don't know—I don't! I merely wondered—— You did say definitely you would come to the reception. So of course—I expected you. Then you never turned up. And—naturally——!"

A ghost of a shrug completed the sentence.

"I'm awfully sorry. I didn't flatter myself you'd notice——" Roy said simply. There were moments when she made him feel vexatiously young. "You see—it was my novel—got me by the hair. And when that happens, I'm rather apt to let things slide. Anyway, you got the better man. And if you found *him* dull, I'd have been nowhere."

She was silent a moment. Then: "I think—if you don't mind—we'll leave Major Desmond out of it," she said; adding, with a distinct change of tone: "What's the hidden charm in that common little Miss Delawny? I saw you dancing with her again to-day."

The subtle flattery of the question might have taken effect, had it not followed on her perplexing remark about Lance. As it was, he resented it.

"Why not? She's quite a nice little person."

"I daresay. But we've plenty of nice girls in our own set."

"Oh, plenty. But I rather bar set mania. I've a catholic taste in human beings!"

"And I've an ultra fastidious one!" Look and tone gave her statement a delicately personal flavour. "Besides, out here . . . there are limits——"

"And I must respect them, on penalty of your displeasure?" His tone was airily defiant. "Well—make me out a list of irreproachables, and I'll work them off in rotation—between whiles!"

The implication of that last subtly made amends: and she had a taste for the minor subtleties of intercourse.

"I shall do nothing of the kind! You're perfectly graceless this evening! I suspect all that scribbling goes to your head sometimes. Sitting on Olympian heights, controlling destinies! I suppose we earthworms down below all look pretty much alike? To discriminate between mere partners—is human. To embrace them indiscriminately—divine!"

Roy laughed. "Oh, if it came to embracing——"

"Even an Olympian might be a shade less catholic?" she queried with one of her looks, that stirred in Roy sensations far removed from Olympian. Random talk did not flourish in Miss Arden's company: delicately, insistently she steered it back to the focal point of interest—herself and the man of the moment.

From the circular drive they wandered on, unheeding; and when they re-entered the Hall a fresh dance had begun. Under the arch they paused. Miss Arden's glance scanned the room and reverted to Roy. The last ten minutes had appreciably advanced their intimacy.

"Shall we?" he asked, returning her look with interest. "Is the luck in again?"

Her eyes assented. He slipped an arm round her—and once more they danced. . . .

Roy had been Olympian indeed had he not perceived the delicate flattery implied in his apparent luck. Lance had not given his message. Yet two dances were available. The inference was not without its insidious effect on a man temperamentally incapable of conceit.

The valse was nearly half over, when the least little drag on his arm so surprised him that he stopped almost opposite the main archway ;—and caught sight of Lance, evidently looking for some one.

" Oh—there he is ! " Miss Arden's low tone was almost flurried—for her.

" D'you want him ? "

" Well — I suppose he wants me. This was his dance."

" Good Lord ! What a mean shame," Roy flashed out. " Why on earth didn't you tell me ? Wouldn't for the world . . ."

Her colour rose under his heated protest. " I never hang about for unpunctual partners. If they don't turn up in time—it's their loss."

Roy, intent on Lance, was scarcely listening. " He's seen us now. Come along. Let's explain."

It was Miss Arden who did the explaining in a manner all her own.

" Well—what became of you ? " she asked, smiling in response to Desmond's look of interrogation. " As you didn't appear, I concluded you'd either forgotten or been caught in a rubber."

" Bad shots,—both," Desmond retorted with a direct look.

" I'm awfully sorry . . . I hadn't a notion——" Roy began—and checked himself, perceiving that he could not say much without implicating his partner.

This time Desmond's smile had quite another quality. " You're very welcome. Carry on. Don't mind me. It's half over."

" A model of generosity ! " Miss Arden applauded him. " I'm free for the next—if you'd care to have it instead."

" Thanks very much ; but I'm not," Desmond answered serenely.

" The great little Banter-Wrangle—is it ? You could plead a misunderstanding and bribe Mr Sinclair to save the situation ! "

"Hard luck on Sinclair. But it's not Mrs Ranyard. I'm sorry——"

"Don't apologise. If you're satisfied, I am."

For all her careless tone, Roy had never seen her so nearly put out of countenance. Desmond said nothing; and for a moment—the briefest—there fell an awkward silence. Then with an air of marked graciousness she turned to Roy.

"We are generously permitted to go on, with a clear conscience!"

But for Roy the charm was broken. Her cavalier treatment of Lance annoyed him; and beneath the surface play of looks and words he had detected the flash of steel. It was some satisfaction that Lance had given as good as he received. But he felt troubled and curious. And he was likely to remain so. Lance, he very well knew, would say precisely nothing.

The girl, as if divining his thoughts, combated them with the delicately pointed weapons of her kind—and prevailed.

Again they wandered in the darkening garden and returned to find the Boston in full swing. Again Miss Arden's glance travelled casually round the room. And Roy saw her start; just enough to swear by . . .

Desmond was dancing with Miss Delawny——!

The frivolous comment on Roy's lips was checked by the look in his partner's eyes. Impossible not to wonder if Lance had actually been engaged; or if——?

In any case—a knock for Miss Arden's vanity. A shade too severe, perhaps; yet sympathy for her was tinged with exultation that Lance had held his own. Mrs Ranyard was right. Here was a man set firmly on his feet. . . .

Miss Arden's voice drew his wandering attention back to herself. "We may as well finish this. Or are you also—engaged?"

Her light stress on the word held a significance he did not miss.

"To you—if you will!" he answered gallantly, hand on heart. More than I deserve—as you said; but still——"

"It's just possible for a woman to be magnanimous!" she capped him, smiling. "And it's just possible for a man to be—the other thing! Remember that—when you get back to your eternal scribbling!"

An hour later he rode homeward with a fine confusion of sensations and impressions, doubts and desires seething in his brain. Miss Arden was delightful, but a trifle unsettling. She must not be allowed to distract him from the work he loved.

## CHAPTER III.

> "Shall I cool desire
> By looking at those lovely eyes of hers,
> That passionate love prefers
> To his own brand, for setting hearts on fire."
>
> —EDMUND GOSSE.

BUT neither the work he loved, nor his budding intimacy with Miss Arden, deterred him from accepting a week-end invitation from the Maharajah of Kapurthala—the friendly, hospitable ruler of a neighbouring Sikh State. The Colonel was going, and Lance, and half a dozen other good sportsmen. They set out on Thursday, the military holiday, in a state of high good-humour with themselves and their host; to return on Sunday evening, renewed in body and mind by the pursuit of pig and the spirit of Shikar, that keeps a man sane and virile, and tempers the insidious effect, on the white races, of life and work in the climate of India. It draws men away from the rather cramping station atmosphere. It sets their feet in a large room. And in this case it did not fail to dispel the light cloud that had hovered between Lance and Roy since the day of the wedding.

In the friendly rivalries of sport, it was possible to forget woman complications; even to feel it a trifle derogatory that one should be so ignominiously at the mercy of the thing. Thus Roy, indulging in a spasmodic declaration of independence; glorying in the virile excitement of pig-sticking, and the triumph of getting first spear.

But returning on Saturday, from a day after snipe and teal, he found himself instinctively allotting the pick of his 'bag' to Miss Arden; just a complimentary attention; the sort of thing she would appreciate. Having refused a ride with her because of this outing, it seemed the least he could do.

Apparently the same strikingly original idea had

occurred to Lance; and by the merest fluke they found one another out. To Roy's relief, Lance greeted the embarrassing discovery with a gust of laughter.

"I say—this won't do. You give over. It's too much of a joke. Besides—cheek on your part."

Though he spoke lightly, the hint of command in his tone promptly put Roy on the defensive.

"Rot! Why shouldn't I? But—the *two* of them . . .! A bit overwhelming!" And suddenly he remembered his declaration of independence. "After all—why should either of us? Can't we let be, just for four days? Look here, Lance. You give over too. Don't send yours. And I won't send mine."

Lance—having considered that inspired proposal—turned a speculative eye on Roy.

"Lord, what a kid you are, still!"

"Well, I mean it. Out here, we're clear of all that. Over there, the women call the tune—we dance. Sport's the God-given antidote! Though it won't be so much longer—the way things are going. We shall soon have 'em after pig and on the polo ground——"

"God forbid!" It came out with such fervour that Roy laughed.

"He doesn't—that's the trouble! He gives us all the rope we want. And the women may be trusted to take every available inch. I'm not sure there isn't a grain of wisdom in the Eastern plan; keeping them, so to speak, in a separate compartment. Once you open a chink, they flow in and swamp everything."

Up went Lance's eyebrows. "That—from you?" And Roy made haste to add: "I wasn't thinking of mothers and sisters; but the kind you play round with . . . before you marry. They've a big pull out here. Very good fun of course. And if a man's keen on marrying——"

"Aren't you keen?" Lance cut in with a quick look.

"N-no. Not just yet, anyway. It's a plunge. And I'm too full up with other things.—But what about the birds?"

"Oh, we'll let be—as you sagely suggest!"

And they did.

More pig-sticking next morning, with two tuskers for trophies; and thereafter, they travelled reluctantly back to harness, by an afternoon train, feeling—without exception—healthier, happier men.

None of them, perhaps, was more conscious of that inner renewal than Lance and Roy. The incident of the game seemed in some way to have cleared the air between them; and throughout the return journey, both were in the maddest spirits, keeping the whole carriage in an uproar. Afterwards, driving homeward, Roy registered a resolve to spend more of his time on masculine society and the novel; less of it dancing and fooling about in Lahore. . . .

A vision of his table, with its inviting disarray, and the picture of his mother for presiding genius, gave his heart a lift. He promised himself a week of uninterrupted evenings, alone with Terry and his thronging thoughts; when the whole house was still and the reading-lamp made a magic circle of light in the surrounding gloom. . . .

Meantime, there were letters: one from his father, one from Jeffers; and beneath them a too familiar envelope.

At sight of it, he felt a faint tug inside him; as it were a whispered reminder that, away at Kapurthala, he had been about as free as a bird with a string round its leg. He resented the aptness of that degrading simile. It was a new sensation; and he did not relish it. The few women he intimately loved had counted for so much in his life that he scarcely realised his abysmal ignorance of the power that is in woman—the mere opposite of man; the implicit challenge, the potent lure. Partly from temperament, partly from principle, he had kept more or less clear of 'all that.' Now, weaponless, he had rashly entered the lists.

He opened Miss Arden's note feeling antagonistic. But its friendliness disarmed him. She hoped they had enjoyed themselves immensely and slain enough creatures to satisfy their primitive instincts. And her mother hoped Mr Sinclair would dine with them on Wednesday evening: quite a small affair.

His first impulse was to refuse; but her allusion to the slain creatures touched up his conscience. To cap the omission by refusing her invitation might annoy her. No sense in that. So he decided to accept; and sat down to enjoy his home letters at leisure.

Lance, it transpired, had not been asked. He and Barnard were the favoured ones,—and, on the appointed evening, they drove in together. Roy had been writing nearly all day. He had reached a point in his chapter at which a break was distracting. Yet here he was, driving Barnard to Lahore, cursing his luck, and—yes —trying to ignore a flutter of anticipation in the region of his heart. . . .

As far as mere lust of the eye went—and it went a good way with Roy—he had his reward the moment he entered Mrs Elton's overloaded drawing-room. Rose Arden excelled herself in evening dress. The carriage of her head, the curve of her throat, and the admirable line from ear to shoulder made a picture supremely satisfying to his artist's eye.

Her negligible bodice was a filmy affair—ivory white with glints of gold. Her gauzy gold wedding-sash, swathed round her hips, fell in a fringed knot below her knee. Filmy sleeves floated from her shoulders, leaving the arms bare and unadorned, except for one gold bangle, high up—the latest note from Home. For the rest, her rope of amber beads and long earrings only a few tones lighter than her astonishing hazel eyes.

Face to face with her beauty, and her discreetly veiled pleasure at sight of him, he could not be ungracious enough to curse his luck. But his satisfaction cooled at sight of Talbot Hayes by the mantelpiece, inclining his polished angularity to catch some confidential tit-bit from little Mrs Hunter-Ranyard. Of course that fellow would take her in. He, Roy, had no official position now; and without it one was negligible in Anglo-India. Besides, Mrs Elton openly favoured Talbot Hayes. Failing Rose, there were two more prospective brides at Home—twins; and Hayes was fatally endowed with all the surface symptoms of the 'coming man': the supple alertness and self-assurance; the instinct for the right thing; and—supreme asset in these days—a studious detachment from the people and the country. In consequence, needless to say, he remained obstinately sceptical as regards the rising storm.

Very early, Roy had put out feelers to discover how much he understood or cared; and Hayes had blandly assured him: "Bengal may bluster and the D.C. may pessimise, but you can take it from me, there will be no serious upheaval in the North. If ever these people are fools enough to manœuvre us out of India, so much the worse for them; so much the better for us. It's a beastly country."

Nevertheless Roy observed that he appeared to extract out of the beastly country every available ounce of enjoyment. In affable moments, he could even manage to forget his career—and unbend. He was unbending now.

A few paces off, the dyspeptic Judge was discussing 'the situation' with his host—a large unwieldy man, so nervous of his own bulk and unready wit that only the discerning few discovered the sensitive, friendly spirit very completely hidden under a bushel. Roy, who had liked him at sight, felt vaguely sorry for him. He seemed a fish out of water in his own home; overwhelmed by the florid, assured personality of his wife.

They were the last, of course; nearly five minutes late. Trust Roy. Only four other guests; Dr Ethel Wemyss, M.B., lively and clever and new to the country; Major and Mrs Garten of the Sikhs, with a stolid good-humoured daughter, who unfailingly wore the same frock and the same disarming smile.

The Deputy Commissioner's wife permitted herself few military intimates. But she had come in touch with Mrs Garten over a *dhobi's* [1] chit and a recipe for pumelo gin. Both women were consumedly Anglo-Indian. All their values were social;—pay, promotion, prestige. All their lamentations pitched in the same key:—everything dearer, servants 'impossible,' hospitality extinct, with every one saving and scraping to get Home. Both were deeply versed in bazaar prices and the sins of native servants. Hence, in due course, a friendship (according to Mrs Ranyard) 'broad based on *jharrons* [2] and charcoal and kerosene'!

The two were lifting up their voices in unison over the mysterious shortage of kerosene (that arch-sinner Mool Chand said none was coming into the country) when dinner was announced; and Talbot Hayes—inevitably—offered his arm to Miss Arden.

[1] Washerman. [2] Dusters.

Roy, consigned to Dr Wemyss, could only pray heaven for the next best thing—Miss Arden on his left. Instead, amazedly, he found himself promoted to a seat beside her mother, who still further amazed him by treating him to a much larger share of her attention than the law of the dinner-table prescribed. Her talk, in the main, was local and personal; and Roy simply let it flow; his eyes flagrantly straying down the table towards Miss Arden and Hayes, who seemed very intimate this evening.

Suddenly he found himself talking about Home. It began with gardens. Mrs Elton had a passion for them, as her *mális*[1] knew to their cost; and the other day a friend had told her that somebody said Mr Sinclair had a lovely place at Home, with a *wonderful* old garden——?

Mr Sinclair admitted as much, with masculine brevity.

Undeterred, she drew out the sentimental stop:—the charm of a *real* old English garden! Out here, one only used the word by courtesy. Lahorites, of course, were specially favoured; but do what one would, it was never *quite* the same thing—was it . . .?

Not quite, Roy agreed amicably—and wondered what the joke was down there. He supposed Miss Arden must have had some say in the geography of the table. . . .

Her mother, meantime, had tacked sail and was probing him, indirectly, about his reasons for remaining in India. Was he going in for politics, or the life of a country gentleman in his beautiful home? Her remarks implied that she took him for the eldest son. And Roy, who had not been attending, realised with a jar that, in vulgar parlance, he was being discreetly pumped. Whereat, politely but decisively, he sheered off and stuck to his partner till the meal was over.

The men seemed to linger interminably over their wine and cigars. But he managed to engage the D.C. on the one subject that put shyness to flight—the problems of changing India. With more than twenty years of work and observation behind him, he saw the widening gulf between rulers and ruled as an almost

[1] Gardener.

equal disaster for both. He knew, none better, all that had been achieved, in his own Province alone, for the peasant and the loyal landowner. He had made many friends among the Indians of his district; and from these he had received repeated warnings of widespread, organised rebellion. Yet he was helpless; tied hand and foot in yards of red tape. . . .

It was not the first time that Roy had enjoyed a talk with him; a sense of doors opening on to larger spaces. But this evening restlessness nagged at him; and at the first hint of a move he was on his feet, determined to forestall Hayes.

He succeeded; and Miss Arden welcomed him with the lift of her brows that he was growing to watch for when they met. It seemed to imply a certain intimacy.

"Very brown and vigorous, you're looking. Was it —great fun?"

"It was topping," he answered with simple fervour. "Rare sport. Everything in style."

"And no leisure to miss partners left lamenting? I hope our stars shone the brighter, glorified by distance?"

Her eyes challenged him with smiling deliberation. His own met them full; and a little tingling shock ran through him, as at the touch of an electric needle.

"*Some* stars are dazzling enough at close quarters," he said boldly.

"But surely—'distance lends enchantment'——?"

"It depends a good deal on the view!"

At that moment, up came Hayes, with his ineffable air of giving a cachet to any one he honoured with his favour. And Miss Arden hailed him, as if they had not met for a week.

Thus encouraged, of course he clung like a limpet; and reverted to some subject they had been discussing, tacitly isolating Roy.

For a few exasperating moments, he stood his ground, counting on bridge to remove the limpet. But when Hayes refused a pressing invitation to join Mrs Ranyard's table, Roy gave it up, and deliberately walked away.

Only Mr Elton remained sitting near the fireplace. His look of undisguised pleasure, at Roy's approach, atoned for a good deal; and they renewed their talk where it had broken off. Roy almost forgot he was speaking to a senior official; freely expressed his own thoughts; and even ventured to comment on the strange detachment of Anglo-Indians, in general, from a land full of such vast and varied interests, lying at their very doors.

"Perhaps—I misjudge them," he added with the unfailing touch of modesty that was not least among his charms. "But to me it sometimes seems as if a curtain hung between their eyes and India. And—it's catching. In some subtle way this little concentrated world, within a world, seems to draw one's receptiveness away from it all. Is that very sweeping, sir?"

A smile dawned in Mr Elton's rather mournful eyes. "In a sense—it's painfully true. But the fact is—Anglo-Indian life can't be fairly judged from the outside. It has to be lived before its insidiousness can be suspected." He moistened his lips and caressed his chin with a large, sensitive hand. "Happily—there are a good many exceptions."

"If I wasn't talking to one of them, sir—I wouldn't have ventured!" said Roy; and the friendly smile deepened.

"All the same," Elton went on, "there are those who assert that it is half the secret of our success; that India conquered the conquerors, who lived *with* her and so lost their virility. Yet in our earlier days, when the personal touch was a reality, we *did* achieve a better relation all round. Of course the present state of affairs is the inevitable fruit of our whole system. By the Anglicising process, we have spread all over India a vast layer of minor officials some six million persons deep! Consider, my dear young man, the significance of those figures. We reduce the European staff. We increase the drudgery of their office work—and we wonder why the Sahib and the peasant are no longer personal friends——!"

Stirred by his subject, and warmed by Roy's intelligent interest, the man's nervous tricks disappeared. He spoke eagerly, earnestly, as to an equal in experience; a compliment Roy would have been quicker to appreciate had not half his attention been centred on that exasperating pair, who had retired to a cushioned alcove and looked like remaining there for good.

What the devil had the girl invited him for? If she wished to disillusion him, she was succeeding to admiration. If she fancied he was one of her infernal ninepins, she was very much mistaken. And all the while he found himself growing steadily more distracted, more insistently conscious of her. . . .

Voices and laughter heralded an influx of bridge players; Mrs Ranyard, with Barnard, Miss Garten, and Dr Wemyss. A table of three women and one man did not suit the little lady's taste.

"We're a very scratch lot. And we want fresh blood!" she announced carnivorously, as the pair in the alcove rose and came forward.

The two men rose also, but went on with their talk. They knew it was not their blood Mrs Ranyard was seeking. Roy kept his back turned and studiously refrained from hoping. . . .

"If you two have *quite* finished breaking up the Empire . . .?" said Miss Arden's voice at his elbow. She had approached so quietly that he started. Worse still, he knew she had seen. "I was terrified of being caught,"—she turned affectionately to her stepfather—"so I flung Mr Hayes to the wolves—and fled. You're sanctuary!"

Her fingers caressed his sleeve. Words and touch waked a smile in his mournful eyes. They seemed to understand one another, these two. To Roy she had never seemed more charming; and his own abrupt volte-face was unsteadying, to say the least of it.

"Hayes would prove a tough mouthful—even for wolves," Elton remarked pensively.

"He *would!* He's so securely lacquered over with—well—we won't be unkind. *But*—strictly between ourselves, Pater—wouldn't you love to swop him for Mr Sinclair, these days?"

"My *dear!*" Elton reproached her, nervously shifting his large hands. "Hayes is a model—of efficiency! But—well, well—if Mr Sinclair will forgive flattery to his face—I should say he has many fine qualities for an Indian career, should he be inclined that way——"

"Thank you, sir. I'd no notion——" Roy murmured,

overwhelmed, as Elton—seeing Miss Garten stranded—moved dutifully to her rescue.

Miss Arden glanced again at Roy. "*Are* you inclining that way?"

The question took him aback.

"Me? No. Of course I'd love it—for some things."

"You're well out of it, in my opinion. It'll soon be no country for a white man. He's already little more than a futile superfluity——"

"On the contrary," Roy struck in warmly, "the Englishman—of the rightest sort, is more than ever needed in India to-day."

Her slight shrug conceded the point. "I never argue! And if you start on *that* subject—I'm nowhere! You can save it all up for the Pater. He's rather a dear—don't you think?"

"He's splendid."

Her smile had its caressing quality. "That's the last adjective any one else would apply to him! But it's true. There's a fine streak in him—very carefully hidden away. People don't see it, because he's shy and clumsy and hasn't an ounce of push. But he understands the natives. Loves them. Goodness knows why. And he's got the right touch. I could tell you a tale——"

"Do!" he urged. "Tales are my pet weakness."

She subsided into the empty chair and looked up invitingly. "Sit," she commanded—and he obeyed.

He was neither saying nor doing the things he had meant to say or do. But the mere beauty of her enthralled him; the alluring grace of her pose, leaning forward a little, bare arms resting on her knees. No vivid colour anywhere except her lips. Those lips, thought Roy, were responsible for a good deal. Their flexible softness discounted more than a little the deliberation of her eyes; and to-night, her charming attitude to Elton appreciably quickened his interest in her and her tale.

"It happened out in the district. I heard it from a friend." She leaned nearer and spoke in a confidential undertone. "He got news that some neighbouring town was in a ferment. Only a handful of Europeans there; an American mission; and no troops. So the 'mish' people begged him to come in and politely wave his official wand. You must be very polite to *badmashes*[1] these days, if you're a mere Sahib; or you hear of it from some little Tin God sitting safe in his office, hundreds of miles away. Well, off he went—a twenty-mile drive; found the mission in a flutter—I don't blame them—armed with rifles and revolvers; expecting-every-moment-to-be-their-next sort of thing; and the town in an uproar. Some religious tamasha. He talked like a father to the headmen; and assured the 'mish' people it would be all right.

"They begged him to stay and see them through. So he said he would sleep at the dak bungalow. 'All alone?' they asked. 'No one to guard you?' 'Quite unnecessary,' he said:—and they were simply amazed!

"It was rather hot; so he had his bed put in the garden. Then he sent for the leading men and said: 'I hear there's a disturbance going on. I don't intimate you have anything to do with it. But you are responsible; and I expect you to keep the people in hand. I'm sleeping here to-night. If there is trouble, you can report to me. But it is for *you* to keep order in your own town.'

"They salaamed and departed. No one came near him. And he drove off next morning, leaving those Americans, with their rifles and revolvers, more amazed than ever! I was told it made a great impression on the natives, his sleeping alone in the garden, without so much as a sentry. And the cream of it is," she added—her eyes on Elton's unheroic figure—"the man who could do that is terrified of walking across a ballroom or saying polite things to a woman!"

Distinctly, to-night, she was in a new vein, more attractive to Roy than all her feminine crafts and lures. Sitting, friendly and at ease over the fire, they discussed human idiosyncrasies—a pet subject with him.

Then, suddenly, she looked him in the eyes;—and he was aware of her again, in the old disturbing way.

Yet she was merely remarking, with a small sigh, "You can't think how refreshing it is to get a little real talk sometimes with a cultivated man who is neither a soldier

[1] Bad characters.

nor a civilian. Even in a big station, we're so boxed in with 'shop' and personalities. The men are luckier. They can escape now and then; shake off the women as one shakes off burrs——!"

Another glance here; half sceptical, wholly captivating.

"It's easier said than done," admitted Roy, recalling his own partial failure.

"Charming of you to confess it! Dare I confess that I've found the Hall and the tennis rather flat these few days—without imperilling your phenomenal modesty?"

"I think you dare." It was he who looked full at her now. "My modesty badly needs bucking up—this evening."

Her feigned surprise was delicately done. "What a shame! Who's been snubbing you? Our clever M.B.?"

"Not at all. You've got the initials wrong."

"*Did* it hurt your feelings—as much as all that?" She dropped the flimsy pretence and her eyes proffered apology.

"Well—you invited me."

"And mother invited Mr Hayes! The fact is—he's been rather in evidence these few days. And one can't flick *him* off like an ordinary mortal. He's a 'coming man'!" She folded hands and lips and looked deliciously demure. "All the same—it *was* unkind. You were so unhappy at dinner. I could feel it all that way off. Be magnanimous and come for a ride to-morrow—do."

And Roy—the detached, the disillusioned—accepted with alacrity.

## CHAPTER IV.

"For every power, a man pays toll in a corresponding weakness; and probably the artist pays heaviest of all."—M. P. Willcocks.

It was the morning of the great Gymkhana, to be followed by the Bachelors' Ball. For Lahore's unfailing social energy was not yet spent; though Depot troops had gone to the Hills, and the leave season was open, releasing a fortunate few; leaving the rest to fretful or stoical endurance of the stealthy, stoking-up process of a Punjab hot-weather. And the true inwardness of those three words must be burned into body and brain, season after season, to be even remotely understood.

Already earth and air were full of whispered warnings. Roses and sweet-peas were fading. Social life was virtually suspended between twelve and two, the 'calling hours' of the cold weather; and at sunset the tree-crickets shrilled louder than ever—careless heralds of doom. Human tempers were shorter; and even the night did not now bring unfailing relief.

Roy had been sleeping badly again; partly the heat, partly the clash of sensations within him. This morning, after hours of tossing and dozing and dreaming—not the right kind of dreams at all,—he was up and out before sunrise, forsaking the bed that betrayed him for the saddle that never failed to bring a measure of respite from the fever of body and mind that was stultifying, insidiously, his reason and his will.

Still immersed in his novel, he had come up to Lahore heart-free, purpose-free; vaguely aware that virtue had gone out of him; looking forward to a few weeks of careless enjoyment, between spells of work; and above all, to the 'high old time' he and Lance would have together beyond Kashmir. Women and marriage were simply not in the picture. His attitude to that inevitable event was, on his own confession—'not yet.' Possibly, when he got Home, he might discover it was Tara, after all. It would need some courage to propose again. For the memory of that juvenile fiasco still pricked his sensitive pride. A touch of the Rajput came out there. Letters from Serbia seemed to dawdle unconscionably by the way. But, in leisurely course, he had received an answer to his screed about Dyán and the quest; a letter alive with all he loved best in her—enthusiasm, humour, vivid sympathy, deepened and enlarged by experiences that could not yet be told. But Tara was far and Miss Arden was near; and, in the mysterious workings of sex magnetism, mere propinquity too often prevails.

And all the others seemed farther still. They wrote regularly, affectionately. Yet their letters—especially his father's—seemed to tell precious little of the things he really wanted to know. Perhaps his own had been more reserved than he realised. There had been so much at Jaipur and Delhi that he could not very well enlarge upon. No use worrying the dear old man; and she, who had linked them, unfailingly, was now seldom mentioned between them.

So there grew up in Roy a disconsolate feeling that none of them cared very much whether he came Home or not. Jerry—after three years in a German prison—was a nervous wreck; still undergoing treatment; humanly lost, for the time being. Tiny was absorbed in her husband and an even Tinier baby, called Nevil Le Roy, after himself. Tara was not yet home; but coming before long, because Aunt Helen had broken down, between war work and the shock of Atholl's death.

A queer thing—separation, mused Roy, as Suráj slowed down to a walk and the glare of morning flamed along the sky. There were they—and here was he: close relations, in effect; almost strangers in fact. There was more between him and them than several hundred miles of sea. There was the bottomless gulf of the War; the gulf of his bitter grief and the slow climb up from the depths to Pisgah heights of revelation. Impossible to communicate—even had he willed—those inner, vital experiences at Chitor and Jaipur. And he had certainly neither will nor power to enlarge on his present turmoil of heart and mind.

Since his ride with Rose Arden, after the dinner-party, things seemed to have taken a new turn. Their relation was no longer tentative. She seemed tacitly to regard him as her chosen cavalier; and he, as tacitly, fell in with the arrangement. No denying he felt flattered a little; subjugated increasingly by a spell he could neither analyse nor resist, because he had known nothing quite like it before. He was, in truth, paying the penalty for those rare and beautiful years of early manhood inspired by worship of his mother. For every virtue, every gift, the gods exact a price. And he was paying it now. Deep down within him, something tugged against that potent spell. Yet increasingly it prevailed and lured him from his work. The vivid beings of his brain were fading into bloodless unrealities; in which state he could do nothing with them. Yet Broome's encouragement, and his father's critical appreciation of fragments lately sent Home, had fired him to fulfil—more than fulfil—their expectations. And now—here he was tripped up again by his all-too-human capacity for emotion—as at Jaipur.

The comparison jerked him. The two experiences, like the two women, had almost nothing in common. The charm of Arúna—with its Eastern mingling of the sensuous and spiritual—was a charm he intimately understood. It combined a touch of the earth with a rarefied touch of the stars. In Rose Arden, so far, he had discovered no touch of the stars. She suggested, rather, a day in early summer, when warmth and fragrance and colour permeate soul and body; keeping them delectably in thrall; wooing the brain from irksome queries—why, whence, whither?

By now, the sheer fascination of her had entered in and saturated his being to a degree that he vaguely resented. Always one face, one voice, intruding on him unsought. No respite from thought of her, from desire of her; the exquisite intolerable ache, at times, when she was present with him; the still more intolerable ache when she was not.

The fluidity of his own dual nature, and recoil from the Arúna temptation, inclined him peculiarly to idealise the clear-eyed, self-poised Western qualities so diversely personified in Lance and this compelling girl. Yet emphatically he did not love her. He knew the great reality too well to delude himself on that score. Were these the authentic signs of falling 'in love'? If so—in spite of rapturous moments—it was a confoundedly uncomfortable state of being. . . .

Where was she leading him—this beautiful, distracting girl, who said so little, yet whose smiles and silences implied so much? There was no forwardness or free-and-easiness about her; yet instinctively he recognised her as the active agent in the whole affair. Twice, lately, he had resolved not to go near her again; and both times he had failed ignominiously—he who prided himself on control of unruly emotions . . . !

Had Lance, he wondered, made the same resolve and managed to keep it—being Lance? Or was the Gymkhana momentarily the stronger magnet of the two? He and Paul, with a Major in the Monmouths, were chief organisers; and much practice was afoot at tent-pegging, bare-back horsemanship, and the like. For a week Lance had scarcely been into Lahore. When Roy pressed him, he said it was getting too hot for afternoon dancing. But as he still affected far more violent forms of exercise, that excuse was not particularly convincing.

By way of retort, he had rallied Roy on overdoing the tame-cat touch and neglecting the important novel. And Roy—wincing at the truth of that friendly flick—had replied no less truthfully: "Well, if it hangs fire, old chap, you're the sinner. *You* dug me out of Paradise by twitting me with becoming an appendage to a pencil! Another month at Udaipur would have nearly pulled me through it—in the rough, at least."

It was lightly spoken; but Lance had set his lips in a fashion Roy knew well; and said no more.

Altogether, he seemed to have retired into a shell out of which he refused to be drawn. They were friendly as ever, but distinctly less intimate; and Roy felt vaguely responsible, yet powerless to put things straight. For intimacy—in its essence a mutual impulse—cannot be induced to order. If one spoke of Miss Arden, or doings in Lahore, Lance would respond without enthusiasm, and unobtrusively change the subject. Roy could only infer that his interest in the girl had never gone very deep and had now fizzled out altogether. But he would have given a good deal to feel sure that the fizzling out had no connection with his own appearance on the scene. It bothered him to remember that, at first, in an odd, repressed fashion Lance had seemed unmistakably keen. But if he would persist in playing the Trappist monk, what the devil was a fellow to do?

Even over the Gymkhana programme, there had been an undercurrent of friction. Lance—in his new vein—had wanted to keep the women out of it; while Roy—in his new vein—couldn't keep at least one of them out, if he tried. In particular, both were keen about the Cockade Tournament: a glorified version of fencing on horseback: the wire masks adorned with a small coloured feather for plume. He was victor whose fencing-stick detached his opponent's feather. The prize—a Bachelor's Purse—had been well subscribed for and supplemented by Gymkhana funds. So, on all accounts, it was a popular event. There were twenty-two names down; and Roy, in a romantic impulse, had proposed making a real joust of it; each knight to wear a lady's favour; a Queen of Beauty and Love to be chosen for the prize-giving, as in the days of chivalry.

Lance had rather hotly objected; and a few inveterate bachelors had backed him up. But the bulk of men are sentimental at heart; none more than the soldier. So Roy's idea had caught on, and the matter was settled. There was little doubt who would be chosen for prize-giver; and scarcely less doubt whose favour Roy would wear.

Desmond's flash of annoyance had been brief; but he had stipulated that favours should not be compulsory. If they were, he for one would 'scratch.' This time he had a larger backing; and, amid a good deal of chaff and laughter, had carried his point.

That open clash between them—slight though it was—had jarred Roy a good deal. Lance, characteristically, had ignored the whole thing.

But not even the inner jar could blunt Roy's keen anticipation of the whole affair. Miss Arden was his partner in one of the few mixed events. He was to wear her favour for the Tournament—a Maréchal Niel rose; and, infatuated as he was, he saw it for a guarantee of victory. . . .

In view of that intoxicating possibility, nothing else mattered inordinately, at the moment: though there reposed in his pocket a letter from Dyán—with a Delhi post-mark—giving a detailed account of serious trouble caused by the recent *hartal:* [1] all shops closed; tram-cars and gharris held up by threatening crowds; helpless passengers forced to proceed on foot in the blazing heat and dust; troops and police violently assaulted; till a few rounds of buckshot cooled the ardour of ignorant masses, doubtless worked up to concert pitch by wandering agitators of the Chandranath persuasion.

"There were certain Swamis," he concluded, "trying to keep things peaceful. But they ought to know resistance cannot be passive or peaceful; and excitement without understanding is a fire difficult to quench. I believe this explosion was premature; but there is lots more gunpowder lying about, only waiting for the match. I am taking Arúna into the Hills for a pilgrimage. It is possible Grandfather may come too; we are hoping to start soon after the fifteenth, if things keep quiet. Write to me, Roy, telling all you know. Lahore is a hotbed for trouble; Amritsar, worse; but I hope your authorities are keeping well on their guard."

From all Roy heard, there seemed good reason to believe they were;—in so far as a Home policy of Government by concession would permit. But well he knew that—in the East—if the ruling power discards action for argument, and uses the sceptre for a walking-stick—things happen to men and women and children on the spot. He also knew that, to England's great good fortune, there were usually men on the spot who could be relied on, in an emergency, to think and act and dare in accordance with the high tradition of their race.

He hoped devoutly it might not come to that; but at the core of hope lurked a flicker of fear. . . .

[1] Abstention as sign of mourning.

## CHAPTER V.

"Her best is bettered with a more delight."—SHAKSPERE.

THE great Gymkhana was almost over. The last event —bareback feats of horsemanship—had been an exciting affair; a close contest between Lance and Roy and an Indian Cavalry officer. But it was Roy who had carried the day, by his daring and dexterity in the test of swooping down and snatching a handkerchief from the ground at full gallop. The ovation he received went to his head like champagne. But praise from Lance went to his heart; for Lance, like himself, had been 'dead keen' on this particular event. He had carried off a tent-pegging cup, however; and appropriately won the V.C. race. So Roy considered he had a right to his triumph; especially as the handkerchief in question had been proffered by Miss Arden. It was reposing in his breast pocket now; and he had a good mind not to part with it. He was feeling in the mood to dare, simply for the excitement of the thing. He and she had won the Gretna Green race—hands down. He further intended—for her honour and his own glory—to come off victor in the Cockade Tournament, in spite of the fact that fencing on horseback was one of Lance's specialities. He had taught Roy in Mesopotamia, during those barren, plague-ridden stretches of time when the war seemed hung up indefinitely and it took every ounce of surplus optimism to keep going at all.

Roy's hope was that some other man might knock Lance out; or—as teams would be decided by lot—that luck might cast them together. For the ache of compunction was rather pronounced this afternoon; perhaps because the good fellow's aloofness from the grand *shamiánah*[1] was also rather pronounced, considering . . .

He seemed always to be either out in the open, directing events, or very much engaged in the refreshment tent—an earthly Paradise, on this blazing day of early April, to scores of dusty, thirsty, indefatigable men.

Between events, as now, the place was thronged. Every moment, fresh arrivals shouting for 'drinks.' Every moment the swish of a syphon, the popping of corks; ginger-beer and lemonade for Indian officers, seated just outside, and permitted by caste rules to refresh themselves 'English-fashion,' provided they drank from the pure source of the bottle. Not a Sikh or Rajput of them all would have sullied his caste-purity by drinking from the tumbler used by some admired Sahib, for whom on service he would cheerfully lay down his life. Within the tent were a few—very few—more advanced beings, who had discarded all irksome restrictions and would sooner be shot than address a white man as 'Sahib.' Such is India in transition; a welter of incongruities, of shifting perilous uncertainties, of subterranean ferment beneath a surface that still appears very much as it has always been.

Roy—observant and interested as usual—saw, in the brilliant gathering, all the outward and visible signs of security, stability, power. Let those signs be shaken never so little, thought he—and the heavens would fall. But, in spite of grave news from Delhi—that might prove a prelude to eruption—not a ripple stirred on the face of the waters. The grand *shamiánah* was thronged with lively groups of women and men in the lightest of light attire. A British band was enlivening the interlude with musical comedy airs. Stewards were striding about looking important, issuing orders for the next event. And around them all—as close as boundary flags and police would allow—thronged the solid mass of onlookers: soldiers, sepoys, and sowars from every regiment in cantonments; minor officials with their families; ponies and *saises* and dogs without number; all wedged in by a sea of brown faces and bobbing turbans, thousands of them twenty or thirty deep.

[1] Marquee tent.

Roy's eyes, travelling from that vast outer ring to the crowded tent, suddenly saw the whole scene as typical of Anglo-Indian life: the little concentrated world of British men and women, pursuing their own ends, magnificently unmindful of alien eyes—watching, speculating, misunderstanding at every turn; the whole heterogeneous mass drawn and held together by the love of hazard and sport, the spirit of competition without strife that is the corner-stone of British character and the British Empire.

He had just been talking to a C.I.D.[1] man, who had things to say about subterranean rumblings that might have startled those laughing, chaffing groups of men and women. Too vividly his imagination pictured the scenes at Delhi, while his eyes scanned the formidable depths of alien humanity hemming them in, outnumbering them by thousands to one. What if all those friendly faces became suddenly hostile—if the laughter and high-pitched talk changed to the roar of an angry crowd . . . ?

He shook off the nightmare feeling, rating himself for a coward. Yet he knew it was not fantastical, not even improbable; though most of the people around him, till they saw with their own eyes, and heard with their own ears, would not believe. . . .

But thoughts so unsettling were out of place, in the midst of a Gymkhana with the grand climax imminent. So—having washed the dust out of his throat—he sauntered across to the other tent to snatch a few words with Miss Arden and secure his rose. It had been given to one of the '*kits*,' who would put it in water and produce it on demand. For the affair of the favours was to be a private affair. Miss Arden, however, in choosing a Maréchal Niel, tacitly avowed him her knight. Lance would know. All their set would know. He supposed she realised that. She was not an accidental kind of person. And she had a natural gift for flattery of the delicate, indirect order.

No easy matter to get near her again, once you left her side. As usual, she was surrounded by men; easily the Queen of Beauty and of Love. In honour of that high compliment, she wore her loveliest race gown;

[1] Criminal Investigation Department.

soft shades of blue and green skilfully blended; and a close-fitting hat bewitchingly framed her face. Nearing the tent, Roy felt a sudden twinge of apprehension. Where were they drifting to—he and she? Was he prepared to bid her good-bye in a week or ten days, and possibly not set eyes on her again? Would she let him go without a pang, and start afresh with some chance-met fellow in Simla? The idea was detestable; and yet . . .?

Half irritably he dismissed the intrusive thought. The glamour of her so dazzled him that he could see nothing else clearly.

Perhaps that was why he failed to escape Mrs Hunter-Ranyard, who skilfully annexed him in passing, and rained compliments on his embarrassed head. Fine horsemanship was common enough in India; but anything more superb——! Wide blue eyes and extravagant gesture expressively filled the blank.

"My heart was in my mouth! That handkerchief trick is *so* thrilling. You all looked as if you *must* have your brains knocked out the next moment——"

"And if we had, I suppose the thrill would have gone one better!" Roy wickedly suggested. He was annoyed at being delayed.

"You deserve 'yes' to that! But if I said what I *really* thought, your head would be turned. And it's quite sufficiently turned already!" She beamed on him with arch significance, enjoying his impatience without a tinge of malice. There was little of it in her; and the little there was, she reserved for her own sex.

"I suppose it's a *dead* secret . . . whose favour you are going to wear?"

"That's the ruling," said Roy; but he felt his blood tingling, and hoped to goodness it didn't show through.

"Well, I've got big bets on about guessing right; and the biggest bet's on yours! Major Desmond's a good second."

"Oh, he bars the whole idea."

"I'm relieved to hear it. I was angelic enough to offer him mine, thinking he might be feeling out in the cold!" (another arch look) "and—he refused. My 'Happy Warrior' doesn't seem quite so happy as he used to be——"

The light thrust struck home, but Roy ignored it. If Lance barred wearing favours, he barred discussing Lance with women. Driven into a corner, he managed somehow to escape, and hurried away in search of his rose.

Mrs Ranyard, looking after him, with frankly affectionate concern, found herself wondering—was he really quite so transparent as he seemed? That queer visionary look in his eyes, now and then, suggested spiritual depths, or heights, that might baffle even the all-appropriating Rose? Did she seriously intend to appropriate him? There were vague rumours of a title. But no one knew anything about him, really, except the two Desmonds; and she would be a brave woman who tried to squeeze family details out of them. The boy was too good for her; but still . . .

Roy, reappearing, felt idiotically convinced that every eye was on the little spot of yellow in his button-hole that linked him publicly with the girl who wore a cluster of its fellows at her belt.

Time was nearly up. She had moved to the front now, and was free of men, standing very still, gazing intently. . . .

Roy, following her gaze, saw Lance—actually in the tent—discussing some detail with the Colonel.

"What makes her look at him like that?" he wondered; and it was as if the tip of a red-hot needle touched his heart.

Next moment she saw him, and beckoned him with her eyes. He came, instinctively obedient; and her welcoming glance included the rosebud. "You found it?" she said, very low, mindful of feminine ears. "And—you deserve it, after that marvellous exhibition. You went such a pace. It—frightened me."

It frightened him, a little, the exceeding softness of her look and tone; and she added, more softly still, "My handkerchief, please."

"*My* handkerchief!" he retorted. "I won it fairly. You've admitted as much."

"But it wasn't meant—for a prize."

"I risked something to win it anyway," said he, "and now——"

The blare of the megaphone—a poor substitute for

heralds' trumpets—called the knights of the wire-mask and fencing-stick into the lists.

"Go in and win the rosebud too!" said she, when the shouting ceased. "Keep cool. Don't lose your head—or your feather!"

He had lost his head already. She had seen to that. And turning to leave her, he found Lance almost at his elbow.

"Come along, Roy," he said, an imperative note in his voice; and if *his* glance included the rosebud, it gave no sign.

As they neared the gathering group of combatants, he turned with one of his quick looks.

"You're in luck, old man. Every inducement to come out top!" he remarked, only half in joke. "I've none, except my own credit. But you'll have a tough job if you knock up against *me*."

"Right you are," Roy answered, jarred by the look and tone more than the words. "If you're so dead keen, I'll take you on."

After that, Roy hoped exceedingly that luck might cast them in the same team.

But it fell out otherwise.

Lance drew red; Roy, blue. Lance and Major Devines, of the Monmouths, were chosen as leaders. They were the only two on the ground who wore no favours: and they fronted each other with smiles of approval, their respective teams—ten a side—drawn up in two long lines; heads caged in wire-masks, tufted with curly feathers, red and blue; ponies champing and pawing the air. Not precisely a picturesque array; but if the plumes and trappings of chivalry were lacking, the spirit of it still flickered within; and will continue to flicker, just so long as modern woman will permit.

At the crack of a pistol they were off, full tilt; but there was no shock of lance on shield, no crash and clang of armour that 'could be heard at a mile's distance,' as in the days of Ivanhoe. There was only the sharp rattle of fencing-sticks against each other and the masks, the clatter of eighty-eight hooves on hard ground; a lively confusion of horses and men, advancing, backing, 'turning on a sixpence' to meet a sudden attack;

voices, Indian and English, shouting or cheering; and the intermittent call of the umpire declaring a player knocked out as his feather fluttered into the dust. Clouds of dust enveloped them in a shifting haze. They breathed dust. It gritted between their teeth. What matter? They were having at each other in furious yet friendly combat; and, being Englishmen, they were perfectly happy; keen to win, ready to lose with a good grace and cheer the better man.

In none of them, perhaps, did the desire to win burn quite so fiercely as in Lance and Roy. But more than ever, now, Roy shrank from a final tussle between them. Surely there was one man of them all good enough to put Lance out of court.

For a time Major Devines kept him occupied. While Roy accounted for two red feathers, the well-matched pair were making a fine fight of it up and down the field, to the tune of cheers and counter-cheers.

But it was the blue feather that fell; and Lance, swinging round, charged into the melée—seven reds now, to six blue.

Twice, in the scrimmage, Roy came up against him, but managed to shift ground, leaving another man to tackle him. Both times it was the blue feather that fell. Steadily the numbers thinned. Roy's wrist and arm were tiring, a trifle; but resolve to win burned fiercely as ever. By now it was clear to all who were the two best men in the field, and excitement rose as the numbers dwindled. . . .

Four to three; blues leading. Two all. And at last—an empty dusty arena; and they two alone in the midst, ringed in by thousands of faces, thousands of eyes. . . .

Till that moment, the spectators had simply not existed for Roy. Now, of a sudden, they crowded in on him—a tightly-wedged wall of humanity—expectant, terrifying. . . .

The two had drawn rein, facing each other; and for that mere moment Roy felt as if his nerve was gone. A glance at the crowded tent, the gleam of a blue-green figure leaning forward. . . .

Then Lance's voice, low and peremptory, 'Come on.'

In the same breath he himself came on, with formidable élan. Their sticks rattled sharply. Roy parried a high slicing stroke—only just in time.

Thank God, he was himself again; so much himself that he was beset by a sneaking desire to let Lance win. It was his weakness in games, just when the goal seemed in sight. Tara used to scold him fiercely. . . .

But there was Miss Arden, the rosebud. . . .

And suddenly, startlingly, Roy became aware that for Lance this was no game. He was fencing like a man inspired. There was more than mere skill in his feints and shrewd blows; more in it than a feather.

Two cuts over the arm and shoulder, a good deal sharper than need be, fairly roused Roy. Next moment they were literally fighting, at closest range, for all they were worth, to the accompaniment of yell on yell, cheer on cheer. . . .

As the issue hung doubtful and excitement intensified, it became clear that Lance was losing his temper. Roy, hurt and angry, tried to keep cool. Against an antagonist so skilled and relentless, it was his only chance. Their names were shouted. "*Shahbash*[1] *Sinkin, Sahib,*" from the men of Roy's old squadron; and from Lance's men, "*Desmin Sahib ki jai!*"[2]

Twice Roy's slicing stroke almost came off—almost, not quite. The maddening little feather still held its own; and Lance, by way of rejoinder, caught him a blow on his mask that made his head ache for an hour after.

Up went his arm to return the blow with interest. Lance, instead of parrying, lunged—and the head of a yellow bud dropped in the dust.

At that Roy saw red. His lifted hand shook visibly; and with the moment's loss of control went his last hope of victory. . . .

Next instant his feather had joined the rosebud; the crowd were roaring themselves hoarse; and Roy was riding off the ground—shorn of plume and favour, furiously disappointed, and feeling a good deal more bruised about the arms and shoulders than anything on earth would have induced him to admit.

Of course he ought to go up and congratulate Lance; but just then it seemed a physical impossibility. Merci-

[1] Well done. [2] Victory to Desmond Sahib.

fully he was surrounded and borne off to the refreshment tent; sped on his way by a rousing ovation as he passed the *shamiánah*.

Roy, following after, had his full share of praise, and a salvo of applause from the main tent.

Saluting and looking round, he dared not meet Miss Arden's eye. Had he won, she might have owned him. As it was, he had better keep his distance. But the glimpse he got of her face startled him. It looked curiously white and strained. His own imagination, perhaps. It was only a flash. But it haunted him. He felt responsible. She had been so radiantly sure. . . .

Arrived in the other tent—feeling stupidly giddy and in pain—he sank down on the first available chair. Friendly spirits ordered drinks, and soothed him with compliments. A thundering good fight. To be so narrowly beaten by Desmond was an achievement in itself; and so forth.

Lance and Paul, still surrounded, were at the other end of the long table; and a very fair wedge of thirsty, perspiring manhood filled the intervening space. Roy did not feel like stirring. He felt more like drinking half a dozen 'pegs' in succession. But soon he was aware of a move going on. The prizes, of course; and he had two to collect. By a special decree, the Tournament prize would be given first. So he need not hurry. The tent was emptying swiftly. He *must* screw himself up to congratulations. . . .

The screwing was still in process when Lance crossed the tent—nearly empty now—and stopped in front of him.

"See here, Roy—I apologise," he said hurriedly, in a low tone. "I lost my temper. Not fair play——"

Instantly Roy was on his feet, shoulders squared, the last spark of antagonism extinct.

"If it comes to that, I lost mine too," he admitted, and Lance smiled.

"You *did!* But—I began it." There was an instant of painful hesitation, then, "It—it was an accident—the favour——"

"Oh, that's all right," Roy muttered, embarrassed and overcome.

"It's not all right. It put you off." Another pause. "Will you take half the Purse?"

"Not I." Glory apart, he knew very well how badly Lance needed the money. "It's yours. And you deserve it."

They both spoke low and rapidly, as if on a matter of business, for there were still some men at the other end of the tent. But at that, to Roy's amazement, Lance held out his hand.

"Thanks, old man. Shake hands—here, where the women can see us. You bet . . . they twigged. . . . And they chatter so infernally. . . . Unfair—on Miss Arden——"

Roy felt himself reddening. It was Lance all over—that chivalrous impulse. So they shook hands publicly, to the astonishment of interested *kitmutgars*, who had been betting freely, and were marvelling afresh at the strange ways of Sahibs.

"I'll doctor your bruises to-night!" said Lance. "And I accept, gratefully, *your* share of the purse. She won't relish—giving it to the wrong 'un." The last, barely audible, came out in a rush, with a jerk of the head that Roy knew well. "Come along and see how prettily she does it."

To Roy's infatuated eyes, she did it inimitably. Standing there, tall and serene, in her pale-coloured gown and bewitching hat, instinct with the mysterious authority of beauty, she handed the prize to Desmond with a little gracious speech of congratulation, adding, "It was a close fight; but you won it—fairly."

Roy started. Did Lance notice the lightest imaginable stress on the word?

"Thanks very much," he said; and saluted, looking her straight in the eyes.

Roy, watching intently, fancied he saw a ghost of a blush stir under the even pallor of her skin. She had told him once, in joke, that she never blushed; it was not one of her accomplishments. But for half a second she came perilously near it; and although it enhanced her beauty tenfold, it troubled Roy.

Then—as the cheering died down—he saw her turn to the Colonel, who was supporting her, and heard her clear deliberate tones, that carried with so little effort:

"I think, Colonel Desmond, every one must agree that the honours are almost equally divided——"

More applause; and Roy—scarcely crediting his ears or eyes—saw her pick a rose from her cluster.

The moment speech was possible, she leaned forward, smiling frankly at him before them all.

"Mr Sinclair, will you accept a mere token by way of consolation prize? We are all agreed you put up a splendid fight; and it was no dishonour to be defeated by—such an adversary."

Fresh clapping and shouting; while Roy—elated and overwhelmed—went forward like a man walking in a dream.

It was a dream-woman who pinned the rosebud in his empty button-hole, patting it into shape with the lightest touch of her finger-tips, saying, "Well done indeed," and smiling at him again. . . .

Without a word he saluted and walked away.

She had done it prettily, past question; and in a fashion all her own.

## CHAPTER VI.

> "Blood and brain and spirit, three—
> Join for true felicity.
> Are they parted, then expect
> Someone sailing will be wrecked."
> —GEORGE MEREDITH.

ON the night after the Gymkhana the great little world of Lahore was again disporting itself, with unabated vigour, in the pillared ballroom of the Lawrence Hall. They could tell tales worth inditing, those pillars and galleries that have witnessed all the major festivities of Punjab Anglo-India—its loves and jealousies and high-hearted courage—from the day of crinolines and whiskers, to this day of the tooth-brush moustache, the retiring skirts and still more retiring bodices of after-war economy. And there are those who believe they will witness the revelry of Anglo-Indian generations yet to be.

Had Lance Desmond shared Roy's gift for visions, he might have seen, in spirit, the ghosts of his mother and father, in the pride of their youth, and that first legendary girl-wife, of whom Thea had once told him all she knew, and whose grave he had seen in Kohat cemetery with a queer mingling of pity and resentment in his heart. There should have been no one except his own splendid mother—first, last, and all the time.

But Lance, though no scoffer, had small intimacy with ghosts; and Roy's frequented other regions; nor was he in the frame of mind to induce spiritual visitations. Soul and body were enmeshed, as in a network of sunbeams, holding him close to earth.

For weeks part of him had been fighting, subconsciously, against the compelling power that is woman; now, consciously, he was alive to it, swept along by it, as by a tidal wave. Since that amazing moment at the prize-giving, all his repressed ferment had welled up and overflowed; and when an imaginative, emotional nature loses grip on the reins, the pace is apt to be headlong, the course perilous. . . .

He had dined at the Eltons'—a lively party; chaff and laughter and champagne; and Miss Arden—after yesterday's graciousness—in a tantalising, elusive mood. But he had his dances secure—six out of twenty, not to mention the cotillon, after supper, which they were to lead. She was wearing what he called her 'Undine frock'—a clinging affair, fringed profusely with silver and palest green, that suggested to his fancy Undine emerging from the stream in a dripping garment of water-weeds. Her arms and shoulders emerged from it a little too noticeably for his taste; but to-night his critical brain was in abeyance.

Look where he would, talk to whom he would, he was persistently, distractingly aware of her; and she could not elude him the whole evening long. . . .

Supper was over. The cotillon itself was almost over; the maypole figure adding a flutter of bright ribbons to the array of flags and bunting, evening dresses, and uniforms. Twice, in the earlier figures, she had chosen him; but this time, the chance issue of pairing by colours gave her to Desmond. Roy saw a curious look pass between them. Then Lance put his arm round her, and they danced without a break.

When it was over, Roy went in search of iced coffee. In a few seconds those two appeared on the same errand, and merged themselves in a lively group. Roy, irresistibly, followed suit; and when the music struck up, Lance handed her over with a formal bow.

"Your partner, I think, old man. Thanks for the loan," he said; and his smile was for Roy as he turned and walked leisurely away.

Roy looked after him, feeling pained and puzzled; the more so, because Lance clearly had the whip-hand. It was she who seemed the less assured of the two; and he caught himself wishing he possessed the power so to upset her equanimity. Was it even remotely possible that—she cared seriously, and Lance would not . . .?

"Brown studies aren't permitted in ballrooms, Mr Sinclair!" she rallied him in her gentlest voice—and Lance was forgotten. "Come and tie an extra big choc. on to my fishing-rod."

Roy disapproved of the chocolate figure, as derogatory to masculine dignity. Six brief-skirted, briefer-bodiced girls stood on chairs, each dangling a chocolate cream from a fishing-rod of bamboo and coloured ribbon. Before them, on six cushions, knelt six men; heads tilted back, bobbing this way and that, at the caprice of the angler; occasionally losing balance, and half toppling over amid shouts and cheers.

How did that kind of fooling strike the '*kits*' and the Indian bandsmen up aloft, wondered Roy. A pity they never give a thought to that side of the picture. He determined not to be drawn in. Lance, he noticed, studiously refrained. Miss Arden—having tantalised three aspirants—was looking round for a fourth victim. Their eyes met—and he was done for. . . .

Directly his knee touched the cushion, the recoil came sharply—too late. And she—as if aware of his reluctance—played him mercilessly, smiling down on him with her astonishing hazel eyes. . . .

Roy's patience and temper gave out. Tingling with mortification, he rose and walked away, to be greeted with a volley of good-natured chaff.

He was followed by Lister, 'the R.E. boy,' who at once secured the elusive bait, clearly by favour rather than skill. The rest had already paired. The band struck up; and Roy, partnerless, stood looking on, the film of the East over his face masking the clash of forces within. The fool he was to have given way! And *this*—before them all—after yesterday . . .!

His essential masculinity stood confounded; blind to the instinct of the essential coquette—allurement by flight. He resolved to take no part in the final figure —the mirror and handkerchief; would not even look at her, lest she catch his eye.

Her choice fell on Hayes; and Roy—elaborately indifferent—carried Lance off to the buffet for champagne cup. It was a thirsty evening; a relief to be quit of the ballroom and get a breath of masculine fresh air. The fencing-bout and its aftermath had consciously quickened his feeling for Lance. In the fury of that fight they seemed to have worked off the hidden friction of the past few weeks that had dimmed the steady radiance of their friendship. It was as if a storm-cloud had burst and the sun shone out again.

They said nothing intimate, nothing worthy of note. They were simply content.

Yet, when music struck up, Roy was in a fever to be with her again.

Her welcoming smile revived his reckless mood. " Ours —*this* time, anyway," he said, in an odd repressed voice.

" Yes—ours."

Her answering look vanquished him utterly. As his arm encircled her, he fancied she leaned ever so little towards him, as if admitting that she too felt the thrill of coming together again. Fancy or no, it was like a lighted match dropped in a powder magazine. . . .

For Roy that single valse, out of scores they had danced together, was an experience by itself.

While the music plays, a man encircles one woman and another, from habit, without a flicker of emotion. But to-night volcanic forces in Roy were rising like champagne when the cork begins to move. Never had he been so disturbingly aware that he was holding her in his arms; that he wanted tremendously to go on holding her when the music stopped. To this danger-point he had been brought by the unconscious effect of delicate approaches and strategic retreats. And the man who has most firmly kept the cork on his emotions is often the most unaccountable when it flies off. . . .

The music ceased. They were merely partners again. He led her out into starry darkness, velvet soft; very quiet and contained to the outer eye; inwardly, of a sudden, afraid of himself, still more afraid of the serenely beautiful girl at his side.

He knew perfectly well what he wanted to do; but not at all what he wanted to say. For him, as his mother's son, marriage had a sacredness, an apartness from random emotions, however overwhelming; and it went against the grain to approach that supreme subject in his present fine confusion of heart and body and brain.

They wandered on a little. Like himself, she seemed smitten dumb; and with every moment of silence, he became more acutely aware of her. He had discovered that this was one of her most potent spells. Never for long could a man be unaware of her, of the fact that she was before everything—a woman.

In a sense—how different!—it had been the same with Arúna. But with Arúna it was primitive, instinctive. This exotic flower of Western girlhood wielded her power with conscious, consummate skill. . . .

Near a seat well away from the Hall she stopped. "We don't want any more exercise, do we?" she said softly.

"I've had enough for the present," he answered. And they sat down.

Silence again. He didn't know what to say to her. He only craved overwhelmingly to take her in his arms. Had she a glimmering idea—sitting there, so close . . . so alluring . . .?

And suddenly, to his immense relief, she spoke.

"It was splendid. A pity it's over. That's the litany of Anglo-India. It's over. Change the scene. Shuffle the puppets—and begin again. I've been doing it for six years——"

"And—it doesn't pall?" His voice sounded quite natural, quite composed, which was also a relief.

"Pall?—You try it!" For the first time he detected a faint note of bitterness. "But still—a cotillon's a cotillon!"—She seemed to pull herself together.—"There's an exciting element in it that keeps its freshness. And I flatter myself we carried it through brilliantly—you and I." The pause before the linked pronouns gave him an odd little thrill. "But—what put you off . . at the end?"

Her amazing directness took him aback. "I—oh, well—I thought . . . one way and another, you'd been having enough of me."

"That's not true!" She glanced at him sidelong. "You were vexed because I chose the Lister boy. And he was all over himself, poor dear! As a matter of fact, I'd meant to have you. If you'd only looked at me . . .! But you stared fiercely the other way. However, perhaps we've been flagrant enough for to-night——"

"Flagrant—have we?"

Daring, passionate words thronged his brain; and

through his inner turmoil, he heard her answer lightly: "Don't ask me! Ask the Banter-Wrangle. She knows to an inch the degrees of flagrance officially permitted to the attached and the unattached! You see, in India, we're allowed . . . a certain latitude."

"Yes—I've noticed. It's a pity . . ." Words simply would not come, on this theme of all others. Was she indirectly . . . telling him . . . ?

"And you disapprove—tooth and nail?" she queried gently. "I hoped you were different. You don't know *how* tired we are of eternal disapproval from people who simply know nothing—nothing——"

"But I don't disapprove," he blurted out vehemently. "It always strikes me as a rather middle-class, puritanical attitude. I only think—it's a thousand pities to take the bloom off . . . the big thing—the real thing, by playing at it (you can see they do) like lawn tennis, just to pass the time——"

"Well, Heaven knows, we've *got* to pass the time out here—*some*how!" she retorted, with a sudden warmth that startled him: it was so unlike her. "All very fine for people at home to turn up superior noses at us; to say we live in blinkers, that we've no intellectual pursuits, no interest in 'this wonderful country.' I confess, to some of us, India and its people are holy terrors. As for art and music and theatres—where *are* they, except what we make for ourselves, in our indefatigable, amateurish way. Can't *you* see—you, with your imaginative insight—that we have virtually nothing but each other? If we spent our days bowing and scraping and dining and dancing with due decorum, there'd be a boom in suicides and the people in clover at Home would placidly wonder why——?"

"But do listen. I'm not blaming—any of you," he exclaimed, distracted by her complete misreading of his mood.

"Well, you're criticising—in your heart. And your opinion's worth something—to some of us. Even if we *do* occasionally—play at being in love, there's always the offchance it may turn out to be . . . the real thing." She drew an audible breath and added, in her lighter vein: "You know, you're a very fair hand at it yourself—in your restrained, fakirish fashion——"

"But I don't—I'm not——" he stammered desperately. "And why d'you call me a fakir? It's not the first time. And it's not true. I believe in life—and the fulness of life."

"I'm glad. I'm not keen on fakirs. But I only meant—one can't picture you playing round, the way heaps of men do with girls . . . who allow them . . ."

"No. That's true. I never——"

"What—never? Or is it 'hardly ever'?"

She leaned a shade nearer, her beautiful pale face etherealised by starshine. And that infinitesimal movement, her low tone, the sheer magnetism of her, swept him from his moorings. Words low and passionate came all in a rush.

"What *are* you doing with me? Why d'you tantalise me. Whether you're there or not there, your face haunts me—your voice. It may be play for you—it isn't for me——"

"I've never said—I've never implied—it was play . . . for *me*——"

This time perceptibly she leaned nearer, mute confession in her look, her tone; and delicate fire ran in his veins. . . .

Next moment his arms were round her; trembling, yet vehement; crushing her against him almost roughly. No mistaking the response of her lips; yet she never stirred; only the fingers of her right hand closed sharply on his arm. Having hold of her at last, after all that inner tumult and resistance, he could hardly let her go. Yet—strangely—even in the white heat of fervour, some detached fragment, at the core of him, seemed to be hating the whole thing, hating himself—and her——

Instantly he released her . . . looked at her . . . realised. . . . In those few tempestuous moments he had burnt his boats indeed . . .

She met his eyes now, found them too eloquent, and veiled her own.

"No. You are not altogether—a fakir," she said softly.

"I'd no business. I'm sorry . . ." he began, answering his own swift compunction, not her remark.

"*I'm* not—unless you really mean—*you* are?" Faint raillery gleamed in her eyes. "You did rather overwhelmingly take things for granted. But still . . . after that . . ."

"Yes—after that . . . if *you* really mean it?"

"Well . . . what do you think?"

"I simply *can't* think," he confessed, with transparent honesty. "I hardly know if I'm on my head or my heels. I only know you've bewitched me. I'm infatuated—intoxicated with you. But . . . if you *do* care enough . . . to marry me——"

"My dear—Roy—can you doubt it?"

He had never heard her voice so charged with emotion. For all answer, he held her close—with less assurance now—and kissed her again. . . .

In course of time they remembered that a pause only lasts five minutes; that there were other partners.

"If we're not to be too flagrant, even for India," she said, rising with unperturbed deliberation, "I suggest we go in. Goodness knows where they've got to by now!"

He stood up also. "It matters a good deal more . . . where *we've* got to. I'll come over to-morrow and see . . . your people . . ."

"No. You'll come over—and see me! We'll descend from the dream . . . to the business; and have everything clear to our own satisfaction before we let in all the others. I always vowed I wouldn't accept a proposal after supper! If you're . . . intoxicated, you might wake sober—disillusioned!"

"But I—I've kissed you," he stammered, suddenly overcome with shyness.

"So you have—a few times! I'm afraid we didn't keep count! I'm not really doubting either of us—Roy. But still . . . Shall we say tea and a ride?"

He hesitated. "Sorry—I'm booked. I promised Lance——"

"Very well—dinner? Mother has some bridge people. Only one table. We can escape into the garden. Now—come along."

He drew a deep breath. More and more the detached part of him was realising. . . .

They walked back rather briskly, not speaking; nor did he touch her again.

They found Lahore still dancing, sublimely unconcerned. Instinctively, Roy looked round for Lance. No sign of him in the ballroom or the card-room. And the crowded place seemed empty without him. It was queer.

Later on, he ran up against Barnard, who told him that Lance had gone home.

## CHAPTER VII.

"Of the unspoken word thou art master. The spoken word is master of thee."—*Arab Proverb.*

Roy drove home with Barnard in the small hours, still too overwrought for clear thinking, and too exhausted all through to lie awake for five minutes after his head touched the pillow. For the inner stress and combat had been sharper than he knew.

He woke late to find Terry curled up against his legs, and the bungalow empty of human sounds. The other three were up long since, and gone to early parade. His head was throbbing. He felt limp, as if all the vigour had been drained out of him. And suddenly . . . he remembered. . . .

Not in a lover's rush of exaltation, but with a sharp reaction almost amounting to fear, the truth dawned on him that he was no longer his own man. In a passionate impulse, he had virtually surrendered himself and his future into the hands of a girl whom he scarcely knew. He still saw the whole thing as mainly her doing—and it frightened him. Looking backward over the past weeks, reviewing the steps by which he had arrived at last night's involuntary culmination, he felt more frightened than ever.

And yet—there sprang a vision of her, pale and gracious in the starshine, when she leaned to him at parting. . . .

She was wonderful and beautiful—and she was his. Any man worth his salt would feel proud. And he did feel proud—in the intervals of feeling horribly afraid of himself and her. Especially her. Girls were amazing things. You seized hold of one and spoke mad words, and nearly crushed the life out of her, and she took it almost as calmly as if you had asked for an extra dance. Was it a protective layer of insensibility—or supernormal self-control? Would she, Rose, have despised him had she guessed that even at the height of his exultation he had felt ashamed of having let himself go so completely; and that before there had been any word of marriage—any clear desire of it even in the deep of his heart?

That was really the root of his trouble. The passing recoil from an ardent avowal is no uncommon experience with the finer types of men. But, to Roy, it seemed peculiarly unfitting that the son of his mother should, as it were, stumble into marriage in a headlong impulse of passion, on a superficial six weeks' acquaintance; and the shy, spiritual side of him felt alarmed, restive, even a little repelled.

In a measure, Rose was right when she dubbed him fakir. Artist though he was, and all too human, there lurked in him a nascent streak of the ascetic, accentuated by his mother's bidding, and his own strong desire to keep in touch with her and with things not seen.

And there, on his writing-table, stood her picture mutely reproaching him. With a pang he realised how completely she had been crowded out of his thoughts during these weeks of ferment. What would she think of it all? The question—what would Rose think of her simply did not arise. She was still supreme, she who had once said, "So long as you are thinking first of me, you may be sure That Other has not yet arrived."

Was Rose Arden—for all her beauty and witchery—genuinely That Other?

Beguiled by her visible perfections, he had taken her spiritually for granted. And he knew well enough that it is not through the senses a man first approaches love—if he is capable of that high and complex emotion; but rather through imagination and admiration, sympathy and humour. As it was, he had not a glimmering idea how she would consort with his very individual inner self. Yet matters were virtually settled. . . .

And suddenly, like a javelin, one word pierced his brain—Lance! Whatever there was between them, he felt sure his news would not please Lance, to say the least of it. And, as for their Kashmir plan . . .?

Why the devil was life such a confoundedly complex affair? By rights, he ought to be 'all over himself,' having won such a wife. Was it something wrong with him? Or did all accepted lovers feel like this—the morning after? A greater number, perhaps, than poets or novelists or lovers themselves are ever likely to admit. Very certainly he would not admit his present sensations to any living soul.

Springing out of bed, he shouted for *chota hazri* [1] and shaving water; drank thirstily; ate hungrily; and had just cleared his face of lather when Lance came in, booted and spurred, bringing with him his magnetic atmosphere of vitality and vigour.

Standing behind Roy, he ran his left hand lightly up the back of his hair, gripped the extra thickness at the top, and gave it a distinct tug; friendly, but sharp enough to make Roy wince.

"Slacker! Waster! You ought to have been out riding off the effects. You were jolly well going it last night. And you jolly well *look* it this morning. Good thing I'm free on the fifteenth to haul you away from all this."

Perhaps because they had first met at an age when eighteen months seemed an immense gap between them, Lance had never quite dropped the elder-brotherly attitude of St Rupert days.

"Yes—a rare good thing——" Roy echoed, and stopped with a visible jerk.

"Well, what's the hitch? Hit out, man. Don't mind me."

There was a flash of impatience, an undernote of foreknowledge, in his tone, that made confession at once easier and harder for Roy.

"I suppose it was—pretty glaring," he admitted, twitching his head away from those strong friendly fingers. "The fact is—we're . . . as good as engaged——"

Again he broke off, arrested by the mask-like stillness of Desmond's face.

"Congrats, old man," he said at last, in a level tone. "I got the impression . . . a few weeks ago. You were

[1] Early tea.

not ready for the plunge. But you've done it—in record time." A pause. Roy sat there tongue-tied—unreasonably angry with himself and Rose. "Why 'as good as . . . ?' Is it to be . . . not official ?"

"Only till to-morrow. You see, it all came . . . rather in a rush. She thought . . . we thought . . . better talk things over first between ourselves. After all . . ."

"Yes—after all," Lance took him up. "You do know a precious lot about each other! How much . . . does *she* know . . . about *you ?*"

"Oh, my dancing and riding, my temperament and the colour of my eyes—four very important items!" said Roy, affecting a lightness he was far from feeling.

Lance ignored his untimely flippancy. "Have you ever . . . happened to mention . . . your mother ?"

"Not yet. Why—— ?" The question startled him.

"It occurred to me. I merely wondered——"

"Well, of course, I shall—to-night."

Lance nodded, pensively fingered his riding-crop, and remarked, "D'you imagine now she's going to let you bury yourself up Gilgit way—with me ? Besides—you'll hardly care . . . shall we call it 'off' ?"

"Well you *are*—— ! Of course I'll care. I'm damned if we call it 'off.'"

At that the mask vanished from Desmond's face. His hand closed vigorously on Roy's shoulder. "Good man," he said in his normal voice. "I'll count on you. That's a bargain." Their eyes met in the glass, and a look of understanding passed between them. "Feeling a bit above yourself, are you ?"

Roy drew a great breath. "It's amazing. I don't yet seem to take it in."

"Oh—you *will*." The hand closed again on his shoulder. "Now I'll clear out. Time you were clothed and in your right mind."

And they had not so much as mentioned her name!

But even when clothed, Roy did not feel altogether in his right mind. He was downright thankful to be helping Lance with some sports for the men, designed to counteract the infectious state of ferment prevailing in the city, on account of to-morrow's deferred *hartal.*

For the voice of Mahatma Ghandi—saint, fanatic, revolutionary, which you will—had gone forth, proclaiming the sixth of April a day of universal mourning and non-co-operation, by way of protest against the Rowlatt Act. For that sane measure—framed to safeguard India from her wilder elements—had been twisted, by skilled weavers of words, into a plot against the liberty of the individual. And Ghandi must be obeyed.

Flamboyant posters in the city bewailed 'the mountain of calamity about to fall on the Motherland,' and consigned their souls to hell who failed, that day, to close their business and keep a fast. To spiritual threats were added terrorism and coercion, that paralysis of the city might be complete.

It was understood that, so long there was no disorder, the authorities would make no move. But, by Saturday, all emergency plans were complete: the Fort garrison strengthened; cavalry and armoured cars told off to be available.

Roy had no notion of being a mere onlooker, if things happened; and he felt sure they would. Directly he was dressed he waited on the Colonel, and had the honour to offer his services in case of need; further—unofficially—to beg that he might be attached, as extra officer, to Lance's squadron. The Colonel—also unofficially—expressed his keen appreciation; and Roy might rest assured the matter would be arranged.

So he went off in high feather to report himself to Lance, and discuss the afternoon's programme.

Lance was full of a thorough good fellow he had stumbled on, a Sikh—and a sometime revolutionary—whose eyes had been opened by three years' polite detention in Germany. The man had been speaking all over the place, showing up the Home Rule crowd, with a courage none too common in these days of intimidation. After the sports, he would address the men; talk to them, encourage them to ask questions.

It occurred to Roy that he had heard something of the sort in a former life; and—arrived on the ground—he recognised the very same man who had been howled down at Delhi.

He greeted him warmly; spoke of the meeting; listened with unmoved countenance to lurid speculations about the disappearance of Chandranath; spoke, himself, to the men, who gave him an ovation; and, by the time it was over, had almost forgotten the astounding fact that he was virtually engaged to be married. . . .

Driving out five miles to Lahore, he had leisure to remember, to realise how innately he shrank from speaking to Rose of his mother. Though in effect his promised wife, she was still almost a stranger; and the sacredness of the subject—the uncertainty of her attitude—intensified his shrinking to a painful degree.

She had asked him to come early, that they might have a few minutes to themselves; and for once he was not unpunctual. He found her alone; and, at first sight, painful shyness overwhelmed him.

She was wearing the cream-and-gold frock of the evening that had turned the scale; and she came forward almost eagerly, holding out her hands.

"Wonderful! It's not a dream?"

He took her hands and kissed her, almost awkwardly. "It still feels rather like a dream," was all he could find to say—and fancied he caught a flicker of amusement in her eyes. Was she thinking him an odd kind of lover? Even last night, he had not achieved a single term of endearment, or spoken her name.

With a graceful gesture, she indicated the sofa—and they sat down.

"Well, what have you been doing with yourself—Roy?" she asked, palpably to put him at ease. "It's a delightful name—Royal?"

"No—Le Roy. Some Norman ancestor."

"The King!" She saluted, sitting upright, laughter and tenderness in her eyes.

At that, he slipped an arm round her, and pressed her close. Then he plunged into fluent talk about the afternoon's events, and his accepted offer of service, till Mrs Elton, resplendent in flame-coloured brocade, surged into the room.

It was a purely civil dinner; not Hayes, to Roy's relief. Directly it was over the bridge players disappeared; Mr Elton was called away—an Indian gentleman to see him on urgent business; and they two, left alone again, wandered out into the verandah.

By now, her beauty and his possessive instinct had more or less righted things; and her nearness, in the rose-scented dark, rekindled his fervour of last night.

Without a word he turned and took her in his arms, kissing her again and again. "'Rose of all roses! Rose of all the world!'" he said in her ear.

Whereat, she kissed him of her own accord, at the same time lightly pressing him back.

"Have mercy—a little! If you crush roses too hard their petals drop off!"

"Darling—I'm sorry!" The great word was out at last; and he felt quaintly relieved.

"You needn't be! It's only—you're such a vehement lover. And vehemence is said—not to last!"

The words startled him. "You try me."

"How? An extra long engagement?"

"N-no. I wasn't thinking of that."

"Well, we've got to think, haven't we? To talk practical politics!"

"Rather not. I bar politics—practical or Utopian."

She laughed. There was happiness in her laugh, and tenderness and an undernote of triumph.

"You're delicious! So ardent, yet so absurdly detached from the dull plodding things that make up common life. Come—let's stroll. The verandah breathes heat like a benevolent dragon!"

They strolled in the cool darkness under drooping boughs, through which a star flickered here and there. He refrained from putting an arm round her, and was rewarded by her slipping a hand under his elbow.

"Shall it be—a Simla wedding?" she asked in her caressing voice. "About the middle of the season? June?"

"June? Yes. When I get back from Gilgit?"

"But—my dear! You're not going to disappear for two whole months?"

"I'm afraid so. I'm awfully sorry. But I can't go back on Lance."

"Oh—Lance!"

He heard her teeth click on the word. Perhaps she had merely echoed it.

"Yes; a very old engagement. And—frankly—I'm keen."

"Oh—very well." Her hand slipped from his arm. "And when you've fulfilled your *prior* engagement, you can perhaps find time—to marry me?"

"Darling—don't take it that way," he pleaded.

"Well, I *did* suppose I was going to be a shade more important to you than—your Lance. But we won't spoil things by squabbling."

Impulsively he drew her forward and kissed her; and this time he kept an arm round her as they moved on. He must speak—soon. But he wanted a natural opening, not to drag it in by the hair.

"And after the honeymoon—Home?" she asked, following up her all-absorbing train of thought.

"Yes—I think so. It's about time."

She let out a small sigh of satisfaction. "I'm glad it's not India. And yet—the life out here gets a hold, like dram-drinking. One feels as if perpetual, unadulterated England might be just a trifle—dull. But, of course, I know nothing about your home, Roy, except a vague rumour that your father is a Baronet with a lovely place in Sussex."

"No—Surrey," said Roy, and his throat contracted. Clearly the moment had come. "My father's not only a Baronet. He's a rather famous artist—Sir Nevil Sinclair. Perhaps you've heard the name?"

She wrinkled her brows. "N-no.—You see, we do live in blinkers! What's his line?"

"Mostly Indian subjects——"

"Oh, the Ramayána man? I remember—I *did* see a lovely thing of his before I came out here. But then——?" She stood still and drew away from him. "One heard he had married . . ."

"Yes. He married a beautiful high-caste Indian girl," said Roy, low and steadily. "My mother——"

"Your—*mother*——?"

He could scarcely see her face; but he felt all through him the shock of the disclosure; realised, with a sudden furious resentment, that she was seeing his adored mother simply as a stumbling-block. . . .

It was as if a chasm had opened between them—a chasm as wide as the East is from the West.

Those few seconds of eloquent silence seemed interminable. It was she who spoke.

"Didn't it strike you that I had—the right to know this . . before . . ?"

The implied reproach smote him sharply; but how could he confess to her—standing there in her queenly assurance—the impromptu nature of last night's proceedings?

"Well I—I'm telling you now," he stammered. "Last night I simply—didn't think. And before . . . the fact is . . . I *can't* talk of her, except to those who knew her . . who understand . . ."

"You mean—is she—not alive?"

"No. The War killed her—instead of killing *me*."

Her hand closed on his with a mute assurance of sympathy. If they could only leave it so! But—her people . . . ?

"You must try and talk of her—to me, Roy," she urged, gently but inexorably. "Was it—out here?"

"No. In France. They came out for a visit, when I was six. I've known nothing of India till now—except through her."

"But—since you came out . . . hasn't it struck you that . . Anglo-Indians feel rather strongly . . . ?"

"I don't know—and I didn't care a rap what they felt," he flung out with sudden warmth. "Now, of course—I do care. But . . . to suppose *she* could . . . stand in my way, seems an insult to her. If *you*'re one of the people who feel strongly, of course . . . there's an end of it. You're free."

"*Free?* Roy—don't you realise . . . I care. You've made me care."

"I—made you?"

"Yes; simply by being what you are—so gifted, so detached . . . so different from the others . . . the service pattern . . ."

"Oh yes—in a way . . . I'm different."—Strange, how little it moved him, just then, her frank avowal, her praise.—"And now you know—why. I'm sorry if it upsets you. But I can't have . . . that side of me accepted . . . on sufferance——"

To his greater amazement, she leaned forward and kissed him, deliberately, on the mouth.

"Will *that* stop you—saying such things?" There was repressed passion in her low tone. "I'm not accepting . . . any of you on sufferance. And, really, you're not a bit like . . . not the same . . ."

"*No!*" She smiled at the fierce monosyllable. "All that lot—the poor devils you despise—are mostly made from the wrong sort of both races—in point of breeding, I mean. And that's a supreme point, in spite of the twaddle that's talked about equality. Women of good family, East or West, don't intermarry much. And quite right too. I'm proud of my share of India. But I think, on principle, it's a great mistake . . ."

"Yes—yes. That's how *I* feel. I'm not rabid. It's not my way. But . . . I suppose you know, Roy, that . . . on this subject, many Anglo-Indians are."

"You mean—your people?"

"Well—I don't know about Pater. He's built on large lines, outside and in. But mother's only large to the naked eye; and she's Anglo-Indian to the bone."

"You think . . . she'll raise objections?"

"She won't get the chance. It's my affair—not hers. There'd be arguments, at the very least. She tramples tactlessly. And it's plain you're abnormally sensitive; and rather fierce under your gentleness——!"

"But, Rose—I must speak. I refuse to treat—my mother as if she was—a family skeleton——"

"No—not that," she soothed him with voice and gesture. "Of course they shall know—later on. It's only . . . I couldn't bear any jar at the start. You might, Roy—out of consideration for me. It would be quite simple. You need only say, just now, that your father is a widower. It isn't as if—she was alive——"

The words staggered him like a blow. With an incoherent exclamation, he swung round and walked quickly away from her towards the house, his blood tingling in a manner altogether different from last night. Had she not been a woman, he could have knocked her down.

Dismayed and startled, she hurried after him. "Roy, my dear—dearest," she called softly. But he did not heed.

She overtook him, however, and caught his arm with both hands, forcing him to stop.

"Darling—forgive me," she murmured, her face appealingly close to his. "I didn't mean—I was only trying to ease things for you, a little—you quiver-full of sensibilities."

He had been a fakir, past saving, could he have withstood her in that vein. Her nearness, her tenderness, revived the mood of sheer bewitchment, when he could think of nothing, desire nothing but her. She had a genius for inducing that mood in men; and Roy's virginal passion, once roused, was stronger than he knew. With his arms round her, his heart against hers, it was humanly impossible to wish her other than she was—other than his own.

Words failed. He simply clung to her, in a kind of dumb desperation to which she had not the key.

"To-morrow," he said at last, "I'll tell you more—show you her picture."

And, unlike Arúna, she had no inkling of all that those few words implied.

## CHAPTER VIII.

"The patience of the British is as long as a summer's day; but the arm of the British is as long as a winter's night."—*Pathan Saying.*

THEY parted on the understanding that Roy would come in to tiffin on Sunday. Instead, to his shameless relief, he found the squadron detailed to bivouac all day in the Gol Bagh, and be available at short notice.

It gave him a curious thrill to open his camphor-drenched uniform case—left behind with Lance—and unearth the familiar khaki of Kohat and Mespot days; to ride out with his men in the cool of early morning to the gardens at the far end of Lahore. The familiar words of commands, the rhythmic clatter of hoofs, were music in his ears. A thousand pities he was not free to join the Indian Army. But, in any case, there was Rose. There would always be Rose now. And he had an inkling that their angle of vision was by no means identical. . . .

The voice of Lance, shouting an order, dispelled his brown study; and Rose—beautiful, desirable, but profoundly disturbing—did not intrude again.

Arrived in the gardens, they picketed the horses, and disposed themselves under the trees to await events. The heat increased and the flies, and the eternal clamour of crows; and it was nearing noon before their ears caught a far-off sound—an unmistakable hum rising to a roar.

"Thought so," said Lance, and flung a word of command to his men.

A clatter of hoofs heralded arrivals—Elton and the Superintendent of Police with orders for an immediate advance. A huge mob, headed by students, was pouring along the Circular Road. The police were powerless to hold them; and at all costs they must be prevented from debouching on to the Mall. It was brisk work; but the squadron reached the critical corner just in time.

A sight to catch the breath and quicken the pulses—that surging sea of black heads, uncovered in token of mourning; that forest of arms beating the air to a deafening chorus of orthodox lamentation; while a portrait of Ghandi, on a black banner, swayed uncertainly in the midst.

A handful of police, shouting and struggling with the foremost ranks, were being swept resistlessly back towards the Mall—the main artery of Lahore; and a British police officer on horseback was sharing the same fate. Clearly nothing would check them save that formidable barrier of cavalry and armoured cars.

At sight of it they halted; but disperse and return they would not. They haggled; they imposed impossible conditions; they drowned official parleyings in shouts and yells.

For close on two hours, in the blazing sun, Lance Desmond and his men sat patiently in their saddles—machine-guns ready in the cars behind them—while the Civil Arm, derided and defied, peacefully persuaded those passively resisting thousands that the Mall was not deemed a suitable promenade for Lahore citizens in a highly processional mood.

For two hours the human tide swayed to and fro; the clamour rose and fell; till a local leader, after much vain speaking, begged the loan of a horse, and headed them off to a mass meeting at the Bradlaugh Hall.

The cavalry, dismissed, trotted back to the gardens, to remain at hand in case of need.

What the Indian officers and men thought of it all, who shall guess? What Lance Desmond thought, he frankly imparted to Roy.

"A fine exhibition of the masterly inactivity touch!" said he, with a twitch of his humorous lips. "But not exactly an edifying show for our men. Wonder what my old Dad would think of it all? You bet there'll be a holy rumpus in the city to-night."

"And then——?" mused Roy, his imagination leaping ahead. "This isn't the last of it."

"The last of it—will be bullets, not buckshot," said

Lance in his soldierly wisdom. "It's the only argument for crowds. The soft-sawder lot may howl 'militarism.' But they're jolly grateful for a dash of it when their skins are touched. It takes a soldier of the right sort to know just when a dash of cruelty is kindness—and the reverse—in dealing with backward peoples; and crowds, of any colour, are the backwardest peoples going! It would be just as well to get the women safely off the scene."

He looked very straight at Roy, whose sensitive soul winced, at the impact of his thought. Since their brief talk, the fact of the engagement had been tacitly accepted—tacitly ignored. Lance had a positive genius for that sort of thing; and in this case it was a godsend to Roy.

"Quite so," he agreed, returning the look.

"Well—you're in a position to suggest it."

"I'm not sure if it would be exactly appreciated. But I'll have a shot at it to-morrow."

The city, that night, duly enjoyed its 'holy rumpus.' But on Monday morning shops were open again; everything as normal as you please; and the cheerful prophets congratulated themselves that the explosion had proved a damp squib after all.

Foremost among these was Mr Talbot Hayes, whose ineffable air of being in the confidence of the Almighty—not to mention the whole Hindu Pantheon—was balm to Mrs Elton at this terrifying juncture. For her mountain of flesh hid a mouse of a soul, and her childhood had been shadowed by tales of Mutiny horrors. With her it was almost an obsession. The least unusual uproar at a railway station, or holiday excitement in the bazaar, sufficed to convince her that the hour had struck for which, subconsciously, she had been waiting all her life.

So, throughout Sunday morning, she had been a quivering jelly of fear; positively annoyed with Rose for her serene assurance that 'the Pater would pull it off all right.' She had never quite fathomed her daughter's faith in the shy, undistinguished man for whom she cherished an affection secretly tinged with contempt. In this case it was justified. He had returned to tiffin quite unruffled; had vouchsafed no details; simply assured her she need not worry. Thank God, they had a strong L.G. That was all.

But authority, in the person of Talbot Hayes, was more communicative—in a flatteringly confidential undertone. A long talk with him had cheered her considerably; and on Monday she was still further cheered by a piece of news her daughter casually let fall at breakfast, between the poached eggs and the marmalade.

Rose—at last! And even Gladys' achievement thrown into the shade! Here was compensation for all she had suffered from the girl's distracting habit of going just so far with the wrong man as to give her palpitations. She had felt downright nervous about Major Desmond. For Rose never gave one her confidence. And she had suffered qualms about this new unknown young man. But what matter now? To your right-minded mother, all's well that ends in the Wedding March—and Debrett! Most satisfactory to find that the father *was* a Baronet; and Mr Sinclair *was* the eldest son! Could anything be more gratifying to her maternal pride in this beautiful, difficult daughter of hers?

Consequently, when the eldest son came in to report himself, all that inner complacency welled up and flowed over him in a volume of maternal effusion, trying enough in any case; and to Roy intolerable, almost, in view of that enforced reservation that might altogether change her tone.

After nearly an hour of it, he felt so battered internally that he reached the haven of his own room feeling thoroughly out of tune with the whole affair. Yet —there it was. And no man could lightly break with a girl of that quality. Besides, his feeling for her—infatuation apart—had received a distinct stimulus from their talk about his mother and the impression made on her by the photograph he had brought with him, as promised. And if Mrs Elton was a Brobdingnagian thorn on the stem of his Rose, the D.C.'s patent pleasure and affectionate allusions to the girl atoned for a good deal.

So, instead of executing a 'wobble' of the first magnitude, he proceeded to clinch matters by writing first to his father, then to a Calcutta firm of jewellers for a selection of rings.

But he wavered badly over facing the ordeal of wholesale congratulations—the chaff of the men, the reiterate inanities of the women.

On Tuesday, Rose warned him that her mother was dying to give a dinner, to invite certain rival mothers, and announce her news with due éclat.

"Hand us round, in fact," she added serenely, "with the chocs and Elvas plums!—No! Don't flare up!" Her fingers caressed the back of his hand. "In mercy to you, I diplomatically sat down upon the idea, and remained seated till it was extinct. So you're saved—by your affianced wife, whom you don't seem in a frantic hurry to acknowledge . . . !"

He caught her to him, and kissed her passionately. "You *know* it's not that——"

"Yes, *I* know . . . you're just terror-struck of all those women. But if you will do these things, you must stand up to the consequences—like a man."

He jerked up his head. "No fear. We'll say to-morrow, or Thursday."

"I'll be merciful, and say Thursday. It's to be announced this afternoon. Have you mentioned it—to any one?"

"Only to Lance."

A small sound between her teeth made him turn quickly.

"Anything hurt you?"

"You've quick ears! Only a pin-prick." She explored her blouse for the offending pin. "Do you tell each other everything—you two?"

"Pretty well—as men go."

"You're a wonderful pair."

She sighed and was silent a moment. Then, "Shall it be a ride on Thursday?" she asked, giving his arm a small squeeze.

"Rather. There are Brigade Sports; but I could cry off. We'll take our tea out to Shadera, have a peaceful time there, and finish up at the Hall."

So it was arranged, and so it befell, though not exactly according to design.

On Thursday they rode leisurely out through the heat and dusty haze, away from bungalows and the watered Mall, through a village alive with shrill women, naked babies, and officious pariahs, who kept Terry furiously occupied: on past the city, over the bridge of boats that spans the Ravi, till they came to the green secluded garden where the Emperor Jehangir sleeps, heedless of infidels who, generation after generation, have picnicked and made love in the sacred precincts of his tomb.

Arrived at the gardens, they tethered the horses, drank thermos tea and ate sugared cakes, sitting on the wide wall that looked across the river and the plain to the dim huddled city beyond. And Roy talked of Bramleigh Beeches in April, till he felt home-sick for primroses and the cuckoo and the smell of mown grass; while, before his actual eyes, the terrible sun of India hung suspended in the haze, like a platter of molten brass, till the turning earth, settling to sleep, shouldered it almost out of sight.

That brought them back to realities.

"We must scoot," said Roy. "It'll be dark, and there's only a slip of a moon."

"It's been delicious!" she sighed; and they kissed mutually—a lingering kiss.

Then they were off, racing the swift-footed dusk. . . .

Skirting the city, they noticed scurrying groups of figures, shouting to each other as they ran; and the next instant, Roy's ear caught the ominous hum of Sunday morning.

"Good God! They're out again. Hi—You! What's the *tamasha?*" he called to the nearest group.

They responded with wild gestures, and fled on. But one lagged a little, being fat and scant of breath; and Roy shouted again. This time the note of command took effect.

"Where are you all running? Is there trouble?" he asked.

"Big trouble, Sahib—Amritsar," answered the fleshly one, wiping the dusty sweat from his forehead, and shaking it unceremoniously from his finger-tips. "Word comes that our leaders are taken. Mahatma Ghandi, also. The people are burning and looting; Bank-*ghar*,[1] Town Hall-*ghar;* killing many Sahibs and one Mem-sahib. *Hai! hai!* Now there will be *hartal* again; Committee *ki ráj*. No food; no work. *Hai! hai!*[2] Ghandi *ki jai!*"

[1] House. [2] Alas, alas!

"Confound the man!" muttered Roy, not referring to the woebegone one. "Look here, Rose, if they're wedged up near Anarkali, we must change our route. I expect the squadron's out; and I ought to be with it——"

"Thank God, you're *not*. It's quite bad enough——" She set her teeth. "Oh, *come* on."

Back they sped, at a hand-gallop, past the Fort and the Badshahi Mosque; then, neck and neck down the long straight road, that vibrant roar growing louder with every stride.

Near the Church they slackened speed. The noise had become terrific, like a hundred electric engines; and there was more than excitement in it—there was fury.

"Sunday was a treat to this," remarked Roy. "We shan't get on to the Mall."

"We can go through Mozung," said Rose coolly. "But I want to *see*—as far as one can. The Pater's bound to be there."

Roy, while admiring her coolness, detected beneath it a repressed intensity, very unlike her. But his own urgent sensations left no room for curiosity; and round the next swerve they drew rein in full view of a sight that neither would forget while they lived.

The wide road, stretching away to the Lahori gate, was thronged with a shouting, gesticulating human barrier; bobbing heads and lifted arms, hurling any missile that came to hand—stones, bricks, lumps of refuse—at the courageous few who held them in check.

Cavalry and police, as on Sunday, blocked the turning into the Mall; and Roy instantly recognised the silhouette of Lance, sitting erect and rigid, doubtless thinking unutterable things.

Low roofs of buildings, near the road, were alive with shadowy figures, running, yelling, hurling bricks and mud from a half-demolished shop near by. Two mounted police officers made abortive attempts to get a hearing; and a solitary Indian, perched on an electric standard, well above the congested mass, vainly harangued and fluttered a white scarf as signal of pacific intentions. Doubtless one of their 'leaders,' again making frantic, belated efforts to stem the torrent that he and his kind had let loose.

And the nightmare effect of the scene was intensified

by the oncoming dusk, by the flare of a single torch hoisted on a pole. It waved purposefully; and its objective was clear to Roy—the electric supply wires.

"That brute there's trying to cut off the light!" he exclaimed, turning sharply in the saddle, only to find that Rose had not even heard him.

She sat stone-still, her face set and strained, as he had seen it after the tournament. "*There* he is," she murmured—the words a mere movement of her lips.

He hated to see her look like that; and putting out a hand, he touched her arm.

"I don't see him," he said, answering her murmur. "He'll be coming, though. Not nervous, are you?"

She started at his touch—shrank from it almost; or so he fancied. "Nervous? No—furious!" Her low tone was as tense as her whole attitude. "Mud and stones! Good heavens! Why don't they *shoot?*"

"They will—at a pinch," Roy assured her, feeling oddly rebuffed, and as if he were addressing a stranger. "Stay here. Don't stir. I'll glean a few details from one of our outlying sowars."

The nearest man available happened to be a Pathan. Recognising Roy, he saluted, a fighting gleam in his eyes.

"*Wah, wah!* Sahib! This is not man's work, to sit staring while these throw words to a pack of mad jackals. On the Border we say, *páili láth; pechi bhát.*[1] That would soon make an end of this devil's noise."

"True talk," said Roy, secretly approving the man's rough wisdom. "How long has it been going on?"

"We came late, Sahib, because of the sports; but these have been nearly one hour. Once the police-*lóg* gave buckshot to those on the roofs. How much use—the Sahib can see. Now they have sent a sowar for the Dep'ty Sahib. But these would not hear the Lát Sahib himself. One match will light such a bonfire; but a hundred buckets will not put it out."

Roy assented, ruefully enough. "Is it true there has been big trouble at Amritsar—burning and killing?"

"*Wah, wah! Shurrum ki bhát.*[2] Because he who made all the trouble may not come into the Punjab, Sahibs who have no concern—are killed——"

[1] First a blow, then a word.

[2] True talk. Shameful talk.

An intensified uproar drew their eyes back to the mob. It was swaying ominously forward, with yellings and prancings, with renewed showers of bricks and stones.

"Thus they welcome the Dep'ty Sahib," remarked Sher Khan with grim irony.

It was true. No mistaking the bulky figure on horseback, alone in the forefront of the throng, trying vainly to make himself heard. Still he pressed forward, urging, commanding; missiles hurtling round him. Luckily the aim was poor; and only one took effect.

A voice shouted, "You had better come back, sir."

He halted. There was a fierce forward rush. Large groups of people sat down in flat defiance.

Again Rose broke out with her repressed intensity, "It's madness! Why on *earth* don't they shoot?"

"The notion is—to give the beggars every chance," urged Roy. "After all, they've been artificially worked up. It's the men behind—pulling the strings—who are to blame——"

"I don't care *who's* to blame. They're as dangerous as wild beasts." She did not even look at him. Her eyes, her mind were centred on that weird, unforgettable scene. "And *our* people simply sitting there being pelted with bricks and stones . . . the Pater . . . Lance . . ."

She drew in her lip. Roy gave her a quick look. That was the second time; and she did not even seem aware of it.

"Yes. It's a detestable position, but it's not of their making," he agreed; adding briskly: "Come along, now, Rose. It's getting dark; and I ought to be in Cantonments. There'll be pickets all over the place—after this. I'll see you safe to the Hall, then gallop on."

Her lips twitched in a half-smile. "Shirking congrats again?"

"Oh, drop it! I'd clean forgotten. I'll conduct you *right in*—and chance congrats. But they'll be too full of other things to-night. Scared to death, some of them."

"Mother, for one. I never thought of her. We must hurry."

For new-made lovers, their tone and bearing was oddly detached, almost brusque. They had gone some distance before they heard shots behind them.

"Thank goodness! At last! I hope it hurt some of them badly," Rose broke out with unusual warmth. She was rather unusual altogether this evening. "Really, it would serve them right—as Mr Hayes says—if we *did* clear out, lock, stock, and barrel, and leave their precious country to be scrambled for by others of a very different *ját*[1] from the stupid, splendid British. I'm glad *I'm* going, anyway. I've never felt in sympathy. And now, after all this . . . and Amritsar . . . I simply couldn't . . ."

She broke off in mid-career, flicked her pony's flanks, and set off at a brisk canter.

Pause and action could have but one meaning. "She's realising," thought Roy, cantering after, pain and anger mingled in his heart. At such a moment, he admitted, her outburst was not unnatural. But to him it was, none the less, intolerable. The trouble was, he could say nothing, lest he say too much.

At the Lawrence Hall they found half a company of British soldiers on guard,—producing, by their mere presence, that sense of security which radiates from the policeman and the soldier when the solid ground fails underfoot.

Within doors, the atmosphere was electrical with excitement and uncertainty. Orders had been received that, in case of matters taking a serious turn, the hundred or so of English women and children gathered at the Club would be removed under escort to Government House. No one was dancing. Every one was talking. The wildest rumours were current.

At a crisis the curtains of convention are rent and the inner self peers through, sometimes revealing the face of a stranger. While the imposing Mrs Elton quivered inwardly, Mrs Ranyard—for all her 'creeps' and her fluffiness—knew no flicker of fear. In any case, there were few who would confess to it, though it gnawed at their vitals; and Roy's quick eye noted that, among the women, as a whole, the light-hearted courage of Anglo-India prevailed. It gave him a sharp inner tweak to look at them all and remember that nightmare of seething, yelling rebels at Anarkalli. He wished to God Rose had not seen it too. It was the kind of thing that would stick in the memory.

[1] Caste.

On their appearance in the Hall, Mrs Elton deserted a voluble group and bore down upon them, flustered and perspiring.

"My darling girl — thank God! I've been in a fever!" she cried, and would have engulfed her stately daughter before them all, but that Rose put out a deterring hand.

"I was afraid you'd be upset—so we hurried," she said serenely; not the Rose of Anarkalli, by any means. "But we were all right along the Mozung road."

That 'we,' and a possessive glance—the merest—at her lover, brought down upon the pair a small shower of congratulations. Every one had foreseen it, of course, but it was so delightful to *know*. . . .

After the sixth infliction, Roy whispered in her ear, "I say, I can't stand any more. And it's high time I was off."

"Poor dear! 'When duty calls . . . ?'" Her cool tone was not unsympathetic. "I'll let you off the rest."

She came out with him, and they stood together a moment in the darkness under the portico.

"I shall dream to-night, Roy," she said gravely. "And we may not even see the Pater. He's taken up his abode in the Telegraph Office. Mother will want to bolt. I can see it in her eye!"

"Well, she's right. You ought all to be cleared out of this, instanter."

"Are you—so keen?"

"Of course not." His tone was more impatient than loverly. "I'm only keen to feel—you're safe."

"Oh—safe!" she sighed. "*Is* one—anywhere—ever?"

"No," he countered with unexpected vigour, "or life wouldn't be worth living. There are degrees of unsafeness, that's all. It's natural—isn't it, darling?—I should want to feel you're out of reach of that crowd. If it had pushed on here, and to Government House, Amritsar doings would have been thrown into the shade."

She shivered. "It's horrible—incredible! I suppose one has to be a lifelong Anglo-Indian to realise quite *how* incredible it feels—to us."

He put his arms round her, as if to shield her from the memory of it all.

"I'll see you to-morrow?" she asked.

"Of course. If I can square it. But we shall be snowed under with emergency orders. I'll send a note in any case."

"Take care of yourself—on my account," she commanded softly; and they kissed.

But—whether fancy or fact—Roy had an under sense of mutual constraint. It was not the same thing at all as that last kiss at Shadara.

There they had come closer, in spirit, than ever yet. Now—not two hours later—the thin end of an unseen wedge seemed to be stealthily pressing them apart.

# CHAPTER IX.

"It has long been a grave question whether any Government not too strong for the liberties of the people, can be strong enough to maintain its existence in great emergencies."—Abraham Lincoln.

Back in Cantonmnets, Roy found strong detachments being rushed to all vital points, and Brigade Headquarters moving into Lahore.

It was late before Lance returned, tired and monosyllabic. He admitted they had mopped things up a bit — outside; and left a detachment, in support of the police, guarding the Mall. But—the city was in open rebellion. No white man could safely show his face there. The anti-British poison, instilled without let or hindrance, was taking violent effect. He'd seen enough of it for one day. He wanted things to eat and drink—especially drink. 'Things' were produced; and afterwards—alone with Roy in their bungalow—he talked more freely, in no optimistic vein, sworn foe of pessimism though he was.

"Sporadic trouble? Not a bit of it! Look at the way they're going for lines of communication. And look at these choice fragments from one of their posters I pinched off a police inspector. 'The English are the worst lot and are like monkeys, whose deceit and cunning are obvious to high and low. . . . Do not lose courage, but try your utmost to turn these men away from your holy country.' Pretty sentiments—eh? Fact is, we're up against organised rebellion."

Roy nodded. "I had that from Dyán, long ago. Paralysis of movement and Government is their game. We may have a job to regain control of the city."

"Not if we declare Martial Law," said the son of Theo Desmond with a kindling eye. "Of course, I'm only a soldier—and proud of it! But I've more than a nodding acquaintance with the Punjabi. He's no word-monger; handier with his *láthi* than his tongue. If you stir him up, he hits out. And I don't blame him. The voluble gentlemen from the South don't realise the inflammable stuff they're playing with——"

"Perhaps they do," hazarded Roy.

"M-yes—perhaps. But the one on the electric standard this evening didn't exactly achieve a star turn!—You saw him, eh?" He looked very straight at Roy. "I noticed you—hanging round on the edge of things. You ought to have gone straight on."

Roy winced. "We'd heard wild rumours. She was anxious about the D.C."

Lance nodded, staring at the bowl of his pipe. "When does—Mrs Elton make a move?"

"The first possible instant I should say, from the look of her."

"Good. She's on the right tack, for once! The D.C. deserves a first-class Birthday Honour—and may possibly wangle an O.B.E.! I'm told that he and the D.I.G., with a handful of police, pretty well saved the station before we came on the scene. It's been a nearer shave than one cares to think about. And it's not over."

They sat up till after midnight discussing the general situation, that looked blacker every hour. And, till long after midnight, an uproarious mob raged through the city and Anarkalli, only kept from breaking all bounds by the tact and good-humour of a handful of cavalry and police; men of their own race, unshaken by open or covert attempts to suborn their loyalty—a minor detail worth putting on record.

Friday was a day of rumours. While the city continued furiously to rage, reports of fresh trouble flowed in from all sides: further terrible details from Amritsar; rumours that the Army and the police were being tampered with and expected to join the mob; serious trouble at Ahmedabad and Lyallpur, where seventy British women and children were herded, in one bungalow, till they could safely be removed. Everywhere the same tale: stations burned, railways wrecked, wires cut.

Fresh stories constantly to hand; some true, some wildly exaggerated; anger in the blood of the men; terror in the hearts of the women, longing to get away, yet suddenly afraid of trains packed with natives, manned by natives, who might be perfectly harmless; but, on the other hand, might not. . . .

It was as Rose had said; to realise the significance of these things, one needed to have spent half a lifetime in that other India, in the good days when peaceful loyal masses had not been galvanised into disaffection; when an Englishwoman, of average nerve, thought nothing of travelling alone up and down the country, or spending a week alone in camp—if needs must—secure in the knowledge that—even in a disturbed Frontier district—no woman would ever be touched or treated with other than unfailing respect.

Yet a good many were preparing to flit: and to the men their departure would spell relief; not least, to Roy—the new-made lover. Parting would be a wrench; but at this critical moment—for England and India—the tug two ways was distinctly a strain; and the less she saw of it all, the better for their future chance of happiness. He felt by no means sure it had not been imperilled already.

But the exigencies of the hour left no room for vague forebodings. Emergency orders, that morning, detailed Lance with a detachment for the Railway Workshops, where passive resisters were actively on the warpath. Roy, after early stables, was despatched with another party, to strengthen a cavalry picket near the Badshahi Mosque, on the outskirts of the city, where things might be lively in the course of the day.

Passing through Lahore, he sent his *sais* with a note to Rose; and, on reaching the Mosque, he found things lively enough already. The iron railings, round the main gate of the Fort, were besieged by a hooting, roaring mob, belabouring the air with *láthis* and axes on bamboo poles; rending it with shouts of abuse and one reiterate cry, "Kill the white pigs, brothers! Kill! Kill!"

Again and again they stormed the railings, frantically trying to bear them down by sheer weight of numbers—yelling ceaselessly the while.

"How the devil can they keep it up?" thought Roy; and sickened to think how few of his own kind there were to stand between the English women and children in Lahore and those hostile thousands. Thank God, there remained loyal Indians, hundreds of them—as in Mutiny days; but surely a few rounds from the Fort just then would have heartened them and been distinctly comforting into the bargain.

The walls were manned with rifles and Lewis guns, and at times things looked distinctly alarming; but not a shot was fired. The mob was left to exhaust itself with its own fury. Part melted away, and part was drawn away by the attraction of a mass meeting in the Mosque, where thirty-five thousand citizens were gathered to hear Hindu agitators preaching open rebellion from Mahommedan pulpits; and a handful of British police officers—present on duty—were being hissed and hooted, amid shouts of "*Hindu-Mussalman ki jai!*"

From the city all police pickets had been withdrawn, since their presence would only provoke disturbance and bloodshed. And the bazaar people were parading the streets, headed by an impromptu army of young hotheads, carrying *láthis*, crying their eternal '*Hai!*' and '*Jai!*' with extra special '*Jai's*' for the 'King of Germany' and the Afghan Amir.

Portraits of Their Majesties were battered down and trampled in the mud; and over the fragments the crowd swept on, shouting: '*Hai! hai! Jarge Margya!*'[1] And the air was full of the craziest rumours, passed on, with embellishments, from mouth to mouth. . . .

Roy, on reaching Cantonments, was relieved to find that the decision had already been taken to regain control of the city by a military demonstration in force; eight hundred troops and police, under the officer commanding Lahore civil area. Desmond's squadron was included; and, sitting down straightway, Roy dashed off a note to Rose.

"My Darling,—

"I'm sorry, but it looks like 'no go' to-morrow. You'll hear all from the Pater. I might look in for

[1] "Hai! Hai! George is dead."

tiffin, if things go smoothly, and if *you*'ll put up with me all dusty and dishevelled from the fray! From what I saw and heard to-day, we're not likely to be greeted with marigold wreaths and benedictions! Of course hundreds will be thankful to see us. But I doubt if they'll dare betray the fact. I needn't tell you to keep cool. You're simply splendid.

"Your loving and admiring,

ROY."

It was after ten next morning, the heat already intense, when that mixed force, British and Indian, and the four aeroplanes acting in concert with them, halted outside the Delhi Gate of Lahore City, while an order was read out to the assembled leaders that, if shots were fired or bombs flung, those aeroplanes would make things unpleasant. Then—at last they were on the move; through the Gate, inside the City, aeroplanes flying low, cavalry bringing up the rear.

Here normal life and activity were completely suspended—hence more than half the trouble. Groups of idlers, sauntering about, stared, spat, or shook clenched fists, shouting, "Give us Ghandi—and we will open!" "Repeal Rowlatt Bill and we will open."

And, at every turn, posters exhorted true patriots —in terms often as ludicrous as they were hostile—to leave off all dealings with the 'English monkeys,' to 'kill and be killed.'

And as they advanced, leaving pickets at stated points —pausing that Mr Elton might exhort the people to resume work—mere groups swelled to crowds, increasing in number and virulence; their cries and contortions more savage than anything Roy had yet seen.

But it was not till they reached the Hira Mundi vegetable market, fronting the plain and river, that the real trouble began. Here were large excited crowds streaming to and fro between the Mosque and the Mundi—material inflammable as gunpowder. Here, too, were the hotheads armed with leaded sticks, hostile and defiant, shouting their eternal cries. And to-day, as yesterday, the Badshahi Mosque was clearly the centre of trouble. Exhortations to disperse peacefully were unheeded or unheard. All over the open space they swarmed like locusts. Their wearisome clamour ceased not for a moment. And the mosque acted as a stronghold. Crowds packed away in there could neither be dealt with nor dispersed. So an order was given that it should be cleared and the doors guarded.

Meantime, to loosen the congested mass, it was cavalry to the front—thankful for movement at last.

There was a rush and a scuffle. Scattered groups bolted into the city. Others broke away and streamed down from the high ground into the open plain, sowars in pursuit; rounding them up, shepherding them back to their by-lanes and rabbit-warrens.

"How does it feel to be a sheep-dog?" Lance asked Roy, as he cantered up, dusty and perspiring. "A word from the aeroplanes would do the trick. Good God! *Look* at them——!"

Roy looked—and swore under his breath. For the half-dispersed thousands were flowing together again like quicksilver. The whole Hira Mundi region was packed with a seething dangerous mob, completely out of hand, amenable to nothing but force.

And now from the doors of the Mosque fresh thousands, inflamed by fanatical speeches, were swarming across the open plain to join them, flourishing their *láthis* with threatening gestures and cries. . . .

It was a sight to shake the stoutest heart. Armed, they were not; but the *láthi* is a deadly weapon at close quarters; and their mere numbers were overwhelming. Roy, by this time, was sick of their everlasting yells; their distorted faces full of hate and fury; their senseless abuse of 'tyrants,' who were exercising a patience almost superhuman.

An order was shouted for the troops to turn and hold them. Carnegie, of the police, dashed off to the head of the column that was nearing the gate of exit; and the cavalry lined up in support of Mr Elton, who still exhorted, still tried to make himself heard by those who were determined not to hear.

Directly they moved forward, there was a fierce, concerted rush; *láthis* in the forefront, bricks and stones hurtling, as at Anarkalli, but with fiercer intent.

A large stone whizzed past the ear of an impassive Sikh Ressaldar; half a brick caught Roy on the shoulder;

another struck Suráj on the flank and slightly disturbed his equanimity.

While Roy was soothing him, came a renewed rush, the crowd pushing boldly in on all sides with evident intent to cut them off from the rest.

The line broke. There was a moment of sickening confusion. A howling man, brandishing a *láthi*, made a dash at Roy, a grab at his charger's rein. . . .

One instant his heart stood still; the next, Lance dashed in between, riding-crop lifted, unceremoniously hustling Roy, and nearly oversetting his assailant—but not quite——

Down came the leaded stick on the back of his bridle hand, cutting it open, grazing and bruising the flesh. With an oath he dropped the reins and seized them in his right hand.

"Rather neatly done!" he remarked, smiling at the dismay in Roy's eyes. "Ought to have floored him, though—the murdering brute!"

"Lance, you'd no business——"

"Oh, drop it. This isn't polo. It's a game of Aunt Sally. No charge for a shy——!" As he spoke, a sharp fragment of brick struck his cheek and drew blood. "Damn them. Getting above themselves. If it rested with me I'd charge. We can hold 'em, though. Straighten the line."

"But your hand——"

"My hand can wait. I've got another." And he rode on leaving Roy with a burning inner sense as of actual coals of fire heaped on his unworthy self.

But urgent need for action left no leisure for thought. Somehow the line was straightened; somehow they extricated themselves from the embarrassing attentions of the mob. Carnegie returned with armed police; and four files were lined up in front of the troops; the warning clearly given; the response—fresh uproar, fresh showers of stones. . . .

Then eight shots rang out—and it sufficed.

At the voice of the rifle, the sting of buckshot, valour and fury evaporated like smoke. And directly the crowd broke, firing ceased. A few were wounded; one was killed—and carried off with loud lamentations. An ordered advance, with fixed bayonets, completed the effect that nothing else on earth could have produced:—and the Grand Processional was over.

It emerged from the Báthi Gate a shadow of itself, having left more than half its numbers on guard at vital points along the route.

"Scotched—not killed," was Lance's pithy verdict on the proceedings. "As a bit of mere police work—excellent. As to the result—we shall see. The C.O. must have been thankful his force wasn't a shade weaker."

This, unofficially, to Roy, who had secured leave off for tiffin at the Eltons', and had ridden forward to report his departure and inquire after the damaged hand, that concerned him more than anything else just then—not even excepting Rose.

It had been roughly wrapped in a silk handkerchief; and Lance pooh-poohed concern.

"Hurts a bit, of course. But it's no harm. I'll have it scientifically cleaned up by Collins. Don't look pathetic about nothing, old man. My silly fault for failing to ride the beggar down. Just as well it isn't your hand, you know. Unpleasant—for the women."

"Oh, it's all very well," Roy muttered awkwardly. Lance in that vein had him at a disadvantage, always.

"Don't be too late," he added, as Roy turned to go. "We may be needed. Those operatic performers in the City aren't going to sit twiddling their thumbs by the look of them. When's . . . the departure?"

"To-morrow or next day, I think."

"Good job." A pause. "Give them my regards. And don't make a tale over my hand."

"I shall tell the truth," said Roy with decision. "And I'll be back about six."

He saluted and rode off; the prospective thrill of making love to Rose damped by the fact that he had not been able to look Lance in the eyes.

Things couldn't go on like this. And yet . . .? Impossible to ask Rose outright whether there had been anything definite between them. If she said "No," he would not believe her:—detestable, but true. If she—well . . . if in any way he found she had treated Lance shabbily, he might find it hard to control himself—or forgive her: equally detestable and equally true. But uncertainty was more intolerable still. . . .

He found the household ready for immediate flitting, and Mrs Elton in a fluster of wrath and palpitation over startling news from Kasur.

"The station burnt and looted. The Ferozepur train held up! Two of our officers wounded and two warrant officers *beaten* to *death* with those horrible láthis!" She poured it all out in a breathless rush before Roy could even get near Rose. "It's official. Mr Haynes has just been telling us. An English woman and three tiny children—miraculously saved by two N.C.O.'s and a friendly native Inspector. Did you *ever*——! And I hear they poured kerosene over the buildings they burnt, and the bodies of those poor men at Amritsar. So *now* we know why the price ran up and why 'none was coming into the country!' Yet they say this isn't another Mutiny,—don't tell *me!* I was so thankful to be getting away; and now I'm terrified to stir. Fancy if it happened to *us*—to-morrow!"

"My dear Mother, it won't happen to us." Her daughter's cool tones had a tinge of contempt. "They're guarding the trains. And Fakir Ali wouldn't let any one lay a finger on us."

Mrs Elton's sigh had the effect of a small cyclone. "Well, *I* don't believe we shall reach Simla without having our throats cut—or worse," she declared with settled conviction.

"You'll be almost disappointed if we do!" Rose quizzed her cruelly, but sweetly. "And now *perhaps* I may get at Roy, who's probably tired and thirsty after all those hours in the sun."

The Jeremiad revived, at intervals, throughout tiffin; but directly it was over Rose carried Roy off to her boudoir—her own corner; its atmosphere as cool and restful as the girl herself, after all the strife and heat and noise of the city.

They spent a peaceful two hours together. Roy detected no shadow of constraint in her; and hoped the effect of Thursday had passed off. For himself—all inner perturbations were charmed away by her tender concern for the bruised shoulder—a big bruise; she could feel it under his coat—and the look in her eyes while he told the story of Lance; not colouring it up, because of what he had said; yet not concealing its effect on himself.

"He's quite a splendid sort of person," she said, with a little tug at the string of her circular fan. "But *you* know all about that."

"Rather."

She drew in her lip and was silent. If he could speak now. In this mood, he might believe her—might even forgive her. . . .

But it was she who spoke.

"What about—the Kashmir plan?"

"God knows. It's all in abeyance. The Colonel's wedding too."

"Will you be *allowed*—I wonder—to pay me a little visit first?" Her smile and the manner of her request were irresistible.

"It's just possible!" he returned, in the same vein. "I fancy Lance would understand."

"Oh—he *would*. And to-morrow—the night train? Can you be there?"

He looked doubtful. "It depends—how things go. And—I rather bar station partings."

"So do I. But still . . . Mother's been clamouring for you to come up with us and guard the hairs of our heads! But I deftly squashed the idea."

"Bless you, darling!" He drew her close, and she leaned her cheek against him with a sigh, in which present content and prospective sadness were strangely mingled. It was in these gentle, pensive moods that Roy came near to loving her as he had dreamed of loving the girl he would make his wife.

"I'm still jealous of the Gilgit plan," she murmured. "And, of course, I wish you were coming up to-morrow—even more than Mother does! But at least I've the grace to be glad you're not—which is rather an advance for me!"

Their parting, if less passionate, was more tender than usual; and Roy rode away with a distinct ache in his heart at thought of losing her; a nascent reluctance to make mountains out of molehills in respect of her and Lance. . . .

Riding back along the Mall, he noticed absently an approaching horsewoman, and recognised—too late for escape—Mrs Hunter-Ranyard. By timely flight on Thursday, he had evaded her congratulations. Intuition told him she would say things that jarred. Now he flicked Suráj with the base intent of merely greeting her as he passed.

But she was a woman of experience and resource. She beckoned him airily with her riding-crop.

"Mr Sinclair? What luck! I'm dying to hear how the 'March Past' went off. Did you get thunders of applause?"

"Oh, thunders. The Monsoon variety!"

"I saw you all in the distance, coming in from my early ride. You looked very imposing with your attendant aeroplanes!—May I?" She turned her pony's head without awaiting permission, and rode beside him at a foot's pace, clamouring for details.

He supplied them fluently, in the hope of heading her off personalities. A vain hope: for personalities were her daily bread.

She took advantage of the first pause to ask, with an ineffable look: "Are you still feeling *very* shy of being engaged? You bolted on Thursday. I hadn't a chance. And I'm rather *specially* interested." The look became almost caressing. "Did it ever occur to your exquisite modesty, I wonder, that I rather wanted you for *my* cavalier. You seemed so young—in experience, that I thought a little innocuous education might be an advantage before you plunged. But she snatched—oh, she did!—without seeming to lift an eyebrow, in her inimitable way. Very clever. In fact, she's been distinctly clever all round. She's eluded her 'coming man' on one side; and ructions over her soldier man on the other——"

"Look here—I'm engaged to her," Roy protested, trying not to be aware of a sick sensation inside. "And you know I hate that sort of talk——"

"I ought to, by this time!" She made tenderly apologetic eyes at him. "But I'm afraid I'm incurable. Don't be angry, Sir Galahad! You've won the Kohinoor; and although you seem to live in the clouds, you've had the sense to make things *pukka* straightaway. 'Understandings' and private engagements are the root of all evil!"

"I'm blest if I know what you're driving at!" he flashed out, his temper rising.

But she only laughed her tinkling laugh and shook her riding-whip at him.

"*Souvent femme varie!* Have you ever heard that, you blessed innocent? And the general impression is —there's already been one private engagement—if not more. I was trying to tell you that afternoon to save your poor fingers——"

"It's all rot—spiteful rot!" The pain of increasing conviction made Roy careless of his manners. "The women are jealous of her beauty, so they invent any tale that's likely to be swallowed——"

"Possibly, my dear boy. But I can't tell my neighbours to their faces that they lie! After all, if you win a beautiful girl of six-and-twenty you've got to swallow the fact, with a good grace, that there must have been others; and thank God you're IT—if not the only IT that ever was on land or sea!—After that maternal homily, allow me to congratulate you. I've already congratulated her, *de mon plein cœur!*"

"Thanks very much. More than I deserve!" said Roy, only half mollified. "But I'm afraid I must hurry on now. Desmond asked me not to be late."

"Confound the women!" was his ungallant reflection, as he rode away.

Mrs Ranyard's tongue had virtually undone the effect of his peaceful two hours with Rose. After that—clash or no clash—he must have the thing out with Lance, at the first available moment.

# CHAPTER X.

> "In you I most discern, in your brave spirit,
> Erect and certain, flashing deeds of light,
> A pure jet from the fountain of all Being;
> A scripture clearer than all else to read."
>
> —J. C. Squire.

Roy returned to an empty bungalow.

On inquiry, he learnt that the Major Sahib had gone over to see the Colonel Sahib; and Wazir Khan—Desmond's bearer—abused, in lurid terms, the bastard son of a pig who had dared to assault the first Sahib in creation.

Roy, sitting down at his table, pushed aside a half-written page of his novel, and his pen raced over the paper in a headlong letter to Jeffers:—an outlet, merely, for his pent-up sensations; and a salve to his conscience. He had neglected Jeffers lately, as well as his novel. He had been demoralised, utterly, these last few weeks: and to-day, by way of crowning demoralisation, he felt by no means certain what the end would be—for himself; still less, for India.

The damaged Major Sahib—untroubled by animosity—appeared only just in time to change for Mess; his cheek unbecomingly plastered, his hand in a sling.

"Beastly nuisance; *Hukm hai*,"[1] he explained in response to Roy's glance of inquiry. "Collins says it's a bit inflamed. I've been confabbing with Paul over the deferred wedding. But, of course, there's no chance of things settling down, unless we declare martial law. The police are played out; and as for the impression we made this morning—the D.C.'s just telephoned in for a hundred British troops and armoured cars to

[1] It is an order.

picket and patrol bungalows in Lahore. Seems he's received an authentic report that the city people are planning to rush civil lines, loot the bungalows, and assault our women—damn them. So, by way of precaution, he has very wisely asked for troops.—Are they off—those two?"

"To-morrow night," said Roy, feeling so horribly constrained that the influx of Barnard and Meredith was, for once, almost a relief.

Then there was Mess; fresh speculations, fresh tales, and a certain amount of chaff over Desmond having 'stopped a brick'; Barnard, in satirical vein, regretting to report a bloody encounter: one casualty: enemy sprinkled with buckshot, retired according to plan.

Before the meal was over, Roy fancied he detected a change in Lance; his talk and laughter seemed a trifle strained; his lips set, now and then, as if he were in pain.

Later on he came up and remarked casually: "I'm not feeling very bright. I think I'll turn in. Perhaps the sun touched me up a bit." Clearly Roy's face betrayed him; for Lance added in an imperative undertone: "*Don't* look at me like that. I'm going to slip off quietly—not to worry Paul."

"Well, I'm going to slip off too," Roy retorted with decision. "I feel used up; and my beast of a bruise hurts like blazes."

"Drive me home, then," said Lance; and his changed tone, no less than the surprising request, told Roy he would be glad of his company.

They said little during the drive; Roy, because he felt vaguely anxious, and knew it would annoy Lance if he betrayed concern, or inquired after symptoms. It seemed a shame to worry the poor fellow in this state; but silence had now become impossible.

"Are you for bed, old man?" he asked when they got in.

"Rather not. I just felt a bit queer. Wanted to get away from them all and be quiet."

His normal manner eased Roy's anxiety a little. Without more ado, they settled into long verandah chairs and called for 'pegs.' The night was utterly still. A red distorted moon hung just above the tree-tops. Yelling and spitting crowds seemed to belong to another world.

Lance leaned back in the shadow, the tip of his cigar glowing like a fierce planet. Roy sat forward, tense and purposeful: hating what he had to say; yet goaded by the knowledge that he could have no peace of mind till it was said.

He was silent a few moments, pulling at his cigar: then, "Look here, Lance," he said. "I've got a question to ask. You won't like it. I don't either. But the truth is . . . I'm bothered to know what is . . . or has been . . . between you and . . ."

"Drop it, Roy." There was pain and impatience in Desmond's tone. "I'm not going to talk about *that*."

Flat opposition gave Roy precisely the spur he needed.

"I'm afraid *I*'ve got to, though." The statement was placable but decisive. "I can't go on this way. It's getting on my nerves——"

"Devil take your nerves," said Lance politely. Then—with an obvious effort—"Has she—said anything?"

"No."

"Then why the hell can't you let be?"

"I *shall* let be—altogether, if this goes on;—this infernal awkwardness between us; and the things she says—the way she looks . . . almost as if she cares."

"Well, I give you my oath—she doesn't. I suppose *I* ought to know?"

"That depends how things were before I came up. She's twice let your name slip out, unawares. And at Anarkalli she was extraordinarily upset. And to-day—about your hand. Then, riding home, I met Mrs Ranyard. And she started talking . . . hinting at a private engagement——"

"Mrs Ranyard deserves to have her tongue removed. She'd tell any lie about another woman."

"Quite so. But *is* it a lie? It fits in too neatly with—the other things——"

Lance gave him a sidelong look. Their faces were just visible in the moonlight.

"Jealous—are you?"—His tone was almost tender. —"You damned lucky devil—you've no cause to be."

That natural inference startlingly revealed to Roy that jealousy had little or nothing to do with his trouble;

and so great was the relief of open speech between them, that instinctively he told truth.

"N-no. I'm bothered about *you*."

"Good God!" Desmond's abrupt laugh had no mirth in it. "*Me?*"

"Yes—naturally. If it amounted to . . . an engagement, and I charged in and upset everything . . . I can't forgive myself . . . or her——"

At that Desmond sat forward, obstructive no longer. "If you're going so badly off the rails, you must have it straight. And . . . confound you! . . . it hurts——"

"I can see that. And it's more or less my doing——"

"On the contrary . . . it was primarily *my* doing . . . as you justly pointed out to me a week or two ago."

Roy groaned. The irony of the situation stung like a whip-lash. "*Did* it amount to an engagement?" he persisted.

"There or thereabouts." Lance paused and took a long pull at his cigar. "*But*—it was quite between ourselves—in fact, conditional on . . . the headway I could manage to make. She—cared, in a way. Not—as I do. That was one hitch. The other was Oh 'Ell's antipathy to soldiers, as husbands for her precious family. She—Rose—knew there would be ructions; a downright tussle, in fact. Well—she'll go almost any length to avoid ructions; specially with her mother. I don't blame her. The woman's a caution. So—she shirked facing the music . . . till she felt quite sure of herself . . ."

"*Till* she felt sure of herself, there should have been *no* engagement," Roy decreed, amazed at his own rising anger. "Unfair on you."

Desmond's smile was the ghost of its normal self. "You always were a bit of a purist, Roy! Besides—it was my doing again. I pressed the point. And I think . . . she liked me . . . loving her. She really seemed to be coming my way—till *you* turned up——" He clenched his hand and leaned back again, drawing a deep breath. "I'm forcing myself to tell you all this—since you've asked for it—because I won't have you blaming *her*——"

Roy said nothing. Remembering how, throughout, the initiative had been hers, how hard he had striven against being ensnared, he did blame her, a good deal more than he could very well admit to this friend, whose single-hearted devotion made his own mere mingling of infatuation and passion seem artificial as gaslight in the blaze of dawn.—But knowing so much, he must know all.

"How long—was it on?"

"Oh, about three weeks before you came. *I* was on a long while. Before Christmas."

"Since when has it been—off?"

Lance hesitated. "Well—things became shaky after Kapurthala. That day—the wedding, you remember? —I spoke rather straight . . . about you. I saw you were getting keen. And I didn't want you to come a cropper——"

"Why the devil didn't you tell me the *truth?*"

Lance set his lips. "Of course I wanted to. But—it was difficult. She said—not any one. Made a point of it. Not even Paul. And I was keen for her to feel quite free; no slur on her—if things fell through. So—as I couldn't warn you, I spoke to her. Perhaps I was a fool. Women are queer. You can never be sure . . . and it seemed to have quite the wrong effect. Then I saw she was really losing her head over you—— Natural enough. So I simply stood by. If she really wanted *you*—not me, that was another affair. And it's plain . . . she did."

"But when—did she *make* it plain?" Roy insisted, feeling more and more as if the ground were giving way under his feet.

"Just before the Gym. That . . . was why. . . ." He looked full at Roy now. His eyes darkened with pain. "I felt like murdering you that day, Roy. Afterwards . . . well—one managed to carry on somehow. One always can—at a pinch . . . *you* know."

"My God! It's the bitterest, ironical tangle!" Roy burst out with a smothered vehemence that told its own tale. "You *ought* to have insisted about me, Lance. I wouldn't for fifty worlds . . ."

"Of course you wouldn't. Don't fret, old man. And don't blame *her*."

"Blame or no, I can't pretend it doesn't alter things . . . spoil things, badly . . ."

He broke off, startled by the change in Desmond. His face was drawn. He was shivering violently.

"Lance—*what* is it? Fever? Have you been feeling bad?"

Desmond set his lips to steady them. "On and off—at Mess. Touch of the sun, perhaps. I'll get to bed and souse myself with quinine."

But he was so obviously ill that Roy paid no heed. "Well, I'm going to send for Collins instanter."

"Don't make an ass of yourself, Roy," Lance flashed out: but his hands were shaking: his lips were shaking. He was no longer in command of affairs. . . .

While the message sped on its way, Roy got him to bed somehow; eased things a little with hot bottles and brandy; nameless terrors knocking at his heart. . . .

In less than no time Collins appeared, with the Colonel; and their faces told Roy that his terror was only too well founded. . . .

Within an hour he knew the worst—acute blood-poisoning from the *láthi* wound.

"Any hope——?" he asked the genial doctor, while Paul Desmond knelt by the bed speaking to his brother in low tones.

"Too early to give an opinion," was the cautious answer. But the caution and the man's whole manner told Roy the incredible, unbearable truth.

Something inside him seemed to snap. In that moment of bewildered agony, he felt like a murderer. . . .

Looking back afterwards, Roy marvelled how he had lived through the waking nightmare of those two days—while the doctor did all that was humanly possible, and Lance pitted all the clean strength of his manhood against the swift deadly progress of the poison in his veins. It was simply a question of hours; of fighting the devil to the last on principle, rather than from any likelihood of victory. With heart and hope broken, superhumanly they struggled on.

For Roy, the world outside that dim whitewashed bedroom ceased to exist. The loss of his mother had been anguish unalloyed; but he had not *seen* her go. . . .

Now, he saw—and heard, which was worse than all.

For Lance, towards the end, was constantly delirious;

and, in delirium, he raved of Rose—always of Rose. He, the soul of reserve, poured out incontinently his passion, his worship, his fury of jealousy—till Roy grew almost to hate the sound of her name.

Worse—he was constrained to tell the Colonel the meaning of it all: to see anger flash through the haunting pain in his eyes.

Only twice, during the final struggle, the real Lance emerged; and on the second occasion they happened to be alone. Their eyes met in the old intimate understanding. Lance flung out his undamaged hand, and grasped Roy's with all the force still left him.

"Don't fret your heart out, Roy . . . if I can't pull through," he said in his normal voice. "Carry on. And—*don't* blame Rose. It'll hurt her—a bit. Don't hurt her more—because of me. And—look here, stand by Paul for a time. He'll need you."

Roy's "Trust me, dear old man," applied, mentally, to the last. Even at that supreme moment he was dimly thankful it came last.

Then the Colonel returned; and they could say no more; nor could Roy find it in his heart to grudge him a moment of that brief blessed interlude of real contact with the man they loved. . . .

There could be no question of going to Lahore station on Sunday evening. He was ill himself, though he did not know it; and his soul was centred on Lance—the gallant spirit inwoven with almost every act and thought and inspiration of his life. By comparison, Rose was nothing to him; less than nothing; a mushroom growth—sudden and violent—with no deep roots; only fibres.

So he sent her, by an orderly, a few hurried lines of explanation and farewell.

"My Dear,—

"I'm sorry, but I *can't* come to-night. We are all in dreadful grief. Lance down with acute blood-poisoning. Collins evidently fears the worst. I can't write of it. I do trust you get up safely. I'll write again, when it's possible.

"Yours,

Roy."

Yes, he was still hers—so far. More than that he could not honestly add. Beyond this awful hour he could not look. It was as if one stood on the edge of a precipice, and the next step would be a drop into black darkness. . . .

By Monday night it was over. After forty-eight hours of fever and struggle and pain, Lance Desmond lay at rest—serene and noble in death, as he had been in life. And Roy—having achieved one long, slow climb out of the depths—was flung back again, deeper than ever. . . .

It was near midnight when the end came. Utterly weary and broken, he had sunk into Lance's chair, leaning forward, his face hidden, his frame shaken all through with hard dry sobs that would not be stilled.

Through the fog of his misery, he felt the Colonel's hand on his shoulder; heard the familiar voice, deep and kindly: "My dear Boy, get to bed. We can't have you on the sick-list. There's work to do; a great gap to be filled—somehow. I'll stay—with him."

At that, he pulled himself together and stood up. "I'll do my best, Colonel," was all he could say. The face he had so rarely seen perturbed was haggard with grief. They looked straight at one another; and the thought flashed on Roy, 'I must tell him.' Not easy; but it had to be done.

"There's something, sir," he began, "I feel you ought to know. By rights, it—it should have been *me.* That brute with the *láthi* was right on me; and he—Lance—dashed in between . . . rode him off—and got the knock intended for me. It—it haunts me."

Paul Desmond was silent a moment. Pain and exaltation contended strangely in his tired eyes. Then: "I—don't wonder," he said slowly. "It—was like him. Thank you for telling me. It will be—some small comfort . . . to all of them. Now—try and get a little sleep."

Roy shook his head. "Impossible.—Good-night, Colonel. It's a relief to feel you know. For God's sake, let me do any mortal thing I can for any of you."

There was another moment of silence, of palpable

hesitation; then once again Paul Desmond put his hand on Roy's shoulder.

"Look here, Roy," he said. "Drop calling me Colonel. You two—were like brothers. And—as Thea's included, why should I be out of it. Let me—be 'Paul.'"

It was hard to do. It was inimitably done. It gave Roy the very lift he needed in that hour when he felt as if they must almost hate him, and never wish to set eyes on him again.

"I—I shall be proud," he said; and, turning away to hide his emotion, went back to the bed that drew him like a magnet.

There he knelt a long while, in a torment of mute, passionate protest against the power of so trivial an injury to rob the world of so much gallantry and charm. Resignation was far from him. With all the vehemence that was in him, he raged against his loss. . . .

Next morning, they awoke, as from a prolonged and terrible dream, to find Lahore practically isolated; all wires down, but one; the *hartal* continuing in defiance of orders and exhortations; more stations demolished; more trains derailed and looted; all available British troops recalled from the Hills. But for five sets of wireless plant, urgently asked for, isolation would have been complete.

By the fourteenth, the position was desperate. Civil authority flatly defied; the police—lacking reserves—fairly played out; the temperature chart of rebellion at its highest point. The inference was plain.

Organised revolt is amenable only to the ultimate argument of force. Nothing, now, would serve but strong action, and the compelling power of Martial Law.

Happily for India, the men who had striven their utmost to avoid both did not falter in that critical hour.

At Amritsar strong action had already been taken; and the sobering effect of it spread, in widening circles, bringing relief to thousands of both races; not least to men whose nerve and resource had been strained almost to the limit of endurance.

In Lahore, notices of Martial Law were issued. The

suspended life of the city tentatively revived. Law-abiding men of all ranks breathed more freely; and for the moment it seemed tho worst was over. . . .

Roy, having slept off a measure of his utter fatigue, took up the dead weight of life again, with the old sick sensation, of three years ago, that nothing mattered in earth or heaven. But then, there had been Lance to uphold and cheer him. Now there was only the hard unfailing mercy of work to be pulled through somehow.

There was also Rose—and the problem of letting her know that he knew. And—their marriage? All that seemed to have suffered shipwreck with the rest of him. He was still too dazed and blinded with grief to see an inch ahead. He only knew he could not bear to see her, who had made Lance suffer so, till the first anguish had been dulled a little—on the surface at least.

## CHAPTER XI.

> "Why did'st thou promise such a beauteous day,
>
> . . . . . . . .
>
> To let base clouds o'ertake me in my way,
> Hiding thy bravery in their rotten smoke?"

AND away up in Simla, Rose Arden was enduring her own minor form of purgatory. The news of Lance Desmond's sudden death had startled and saddened her; had pierced through her surface serenity to the deep places of a nature that was not altogether shallow under its veneer of egotism and coquetry.

On a morning, near the end of April, she sat alone in the garden under deodar boughs tasselled with tips of young green. In a border, beyond the lawn, spring flowers were awake; the bank was starred with white violets and wild-strawberry blossoms; and through a gap in the ilex trees beyond, she had a vision of far hills and flashing snow-peaks, blue-white in the sun, cobalt in shadow. Overhead, among the higher branches, a bird was trilling out an ecstatic love-song.

But the year's renewal, the familiar flutter of Simla's awakening, sharpened, rather, that new ache at her heart; the haunting, incredible thought that down there, in the stifling dusty plains, Lance Desmond lay dead in the springtime of his splendid manhood; dead of his own generous impulse to save Roy from hurt.

Since the news came, she had avoided sociabilities and, unobtrusively, worn no colours. Foolish and fatuous, was it? Perhaps. She only knew that—Lance being gone—she could not make *no* difference in her daily round, whatever others might think or say.

And the mere fact of his being gone seemed strangely to revive the memory of his love for her, of her own genuine, if inadequate, response. For she had been more nearly in love with him than with any of his predecessors (and there had been several), who had been admitted to the privileged intimacies of the half-accepted lover. More: he had commanded her admiration; and she had not been woman could she have held out indefinitely against his passionate, whole-hearted devotion.

After months of patient wooing—and he by nature impatient—he had insisted that matters be settled, one way or the other, before he went on leave; and she had almost reached the point of decision, when Roy, with his careless charm and challenging detachment, appeared on the scene. . . .

And now—Lance was gone; Roy was hers; Bramleigh Beeches and a prospective title were hers; but still . . .

The shock of Roy's revelation had upset her a good deal more than she dared let him guess. And the effect did not pass—in spite of determined efforts to be unaware of it. She knew, now, that her vaunted tolerance sprang chiefly from having ignored the whole subject. Half-castes she instinctively despised. For India and the Indians she had little real sympathy; and the rising tide of unrest, the increasing antagonism, had sharpened her negative attitude to a positive dislike and distrust, acutely intensified since that evening at Anarkalli, when the sight of Lance and her stepfather, sitting there at the mercy of any chance-flung missile, had stirred the slumbering passion in her to fury. For one bewildering moment she had scarcely been able to endure Roy's touch or look, because he was even remotely linked with those creatures, who mouthed and yelled and would have murdered them all without compunction.

The impression of those few nerve-wracking days had struck deep. Yet, in spite of all, Roy's hold on her was strong; the stronger perhaps because she had been aware of his inner resistance, and had never felt quite sure of him. She did not feel fundamentally sure of him, even now. His letters had been few and brief; heart-broken, naturally; yet scarcely the letters of an ardent lover. The longest of the four had given her a poignant picture of Lance's funeral; almost as if he knew, and had written with intent to hurt her. In addition to half the British officers of the station, the cemetery had been thronged with the men of his squadron, Sikhs and Pathans—a form of homage very rare in India. Many of them had cried like children; and for himself, Roy confessed, it had broken him all to bits. He hardly knew how to write of it; but he felt she would care to know.

She cared so intensely that, for the moment, she had almost hated him for probing so deep, for stamping on her memory a picture that would not fade.

His next letter had been no more than half a sheet. That was three days ago. Another was overdue; and the post was overdue also.

Ah—at last! A flash of scarlet in the verandah and Fazl Ali presenting an envelope on a salver, as though she were a goddess and the letter an offering at her shrine.

It was a shade thicker than usual. Well, it ought to be. She had been very patient with his brevity. This time it seemed he had something to say.

Her heart stirred perceptibly as she opened it and read:—

"Dearest Girl,—

"I'm afraid my letters have been very poor things. Part of the reason you know and understand—as far as any one can. I'm still dazed. Everything's out of perspective. I suppose I shall take it in some day.

"But there's another reason—connected with *him*. Perhaps you can guess. I've been puzzled all along about you two. And now I *know*. I wonder—does that hurt you? It hurts me horribly. I need hardly say *he* didn't give you away. It was things you said—and Mrs Ranyard. Anyhow, that last evening, I insisted on having the truth. But I couldn't write about it sooner—for fear of saying things I'd regret afterwards.

"Rose—what *possessed* you? A man worth fifty of me! Of course, I know loving doesn't go by merit. But to keep him on tenterhooks, eating his heart out with jealousy, while you frankly encouraged me—you *know* you did. And I—never dreaming; only puzzled at the way he sheered off after the first. Between us, we made his last month of life a torment, though he never let me guess it. I don't know how to forgive myself. And, to be honest, it's no easy job forgiving you. If that makes you angry, if you think me a prig, I can't help it. If *you'd* heard him—all those hours of delirium—you might understand.

"When he wasn't raving, he had only one thought—I mustn't blame *you*, or hurt you, on account of him. I'm trying not to. But if I know you at all, *that* will hurt more than anything *I* could say. And it's only right I should tell it you.

"My dearest Girl, you can't think how difficult—how strange it feels writing to you like this. I meant to wait till I came up. But I couldn't write naturally, and I was afraid you mightn't understand.

"I'm coming, after all, sooner than I thought, for my fool of a body has given out, and Collins won't let me hang on, though *I* feel the work just keeps me going. It must be Kohat first, because of Paul. Now things are calming down, he is getting away to be married. The quietest possible affair, of course; but he's keen I should be best man in place of Lance. And I needn't say how I value the compliment.

"No more trouble here or Amritsar, thank God—and a few courageous men. Martial Law arrangements are being carried through to admiration. The Lahore C.O. seems to get the right side of every one. He has a gift for the personal touch that is everything out here; and in no time the poor deluded beggars in the City were shouting 'Martial Law *ki jai*' as fervently as ever they shouted for Ghandi and Co.

"One of my fellows said to me: 'Our people don't understand this new talk of "Committee Ki Raj" and "Dyarchy Raj." Too many orders make confusion. But they understand "*Hukm Ki raj.*"'[1] In fact, it's the general opinion that prompt action in the Punjab has fairly well steadied India—for the present at least.

"Well, I won't write more. We'll meet soon; and I don't doubt you'll explain a good deal that still puzzles and hurts me. If I seem changed, you must make

[1] Government by order.

allowances. I can't yet see my way in a world empty of Lance. But we must help each other, Rose—not pull two ways. Don't bother to write long explanations. Things will be easier face to face.

"Yours ever,

Roy."

"Yours ever," . . . Did he mean that? He certainly meant the rest. Her hands dropped in her lap; and she sat there, staring before her—startled, angry, more profoundly disturbed and unsure of herself than she had felt in all her days. Though Roy had tried to write with moderation, there were sentences that struck at her vanity, her conscience, her heart. Her first overwhelming impulse was to write back at once telling him he need not trouble to come up, as the engagement was off. Accustomed to unquestioning homage, she took criticism badly; also—undeniably—she was jealous of his absorption in Lance. The impulse to dismiss him was mere hurt vanity.

And the queer thing was, that deep down under the vanity and the jealousy, her old feeling for Lance seemed again to be stirring in its sleep.

The love of such a man leaves no light impress on any woman; and Lance had unwittingly achieved two master-strokes calculated to deepen that impress on one of her nature. In the first place, he had fronted squarely the shock of her defection—patently on account of Roy. She could see him now—standing near her mantelpiece, his eyes sombre with passion and pain; no word of reproach or pleading, though there smouldered beneath his silence the fire of his formidable temper. And just because he had neither pleaded nor stormed, she had come perilously near to an ignominious *volte-face*, from which she had only been saved by something in him, not in herself. If she did not know it then, she knew it now. In the second place, he had died gallantly—again on account of Roy. Snatched utterly out of reach, out of sight, his value was enhanced tenfold; and now, to crown all, came Roy's revelation of his amazing magnanimity. . . .

Strange, what a complicated affair it was, for some people, this simple natural business of getting married.

Was it part of the price one had to pay for being beautiful? Half the girls one knew slipped into it with much the same sort of thrill as they slipped into a new frock. But those were mostly the nice plain little things, who subsided gratefully into the first pair of arms held out to them. And probably they had their reward.

In chastened moods, Rose did not quite care to remember how many times she had succumbed, experimentally, to that supreme temptation. Good heavens! What would her precious pair think of her—if they knew! At least, she had the grace to feel proud that the tale of her conquests included two such men.

But Lance was gone—on account of Roy—where no spell of hers could touch him any more; and Roy—was he going too . . . on account of Lance . . . ? Not if she could prevent him; and yet . . . goodness knew!

The sigh that shivered through her sprang from a deeper source than mere self-pity.

Rattle of rickshaw wheels, puffing and grunting of *jhampannis*, heralded the return of her mother, who had been out paying a round of preliminary calls. It took eight stalwart men and a rickshaw of special dimensions to convey her formidable bulk up and down Simla roads; and affectionate friends hinted that the men demanded extra pay for extra weight!

A glance at her florid face warned Rose there was trouble in the air.

"Oh, Rose—*there* you are. I've had the shock of my life!" Waving away her *jhampannis*, she sank into an adjacent cane chair that creaked and swayed ominously under the assault. "It was at Mrs Tait's. My dear—would you *believe* it? That fine fiancé of yours—after worming himself into our good graces—turns out to be practically a *half-caste.* A superior one, it seems. But still—the deceitfulness of the man! Going about looking like everybody else too! And grey-blue eyes into the bargain!"

At that Rose fatally smiled—in spite of genuine dismay.

"I can't see anything *funny* in it!" snapped her mother. "I thought you'd be furious. Did you ever notice—— ? Had you the least suspicion?"

"Not the least," Rose answered, with unruffled calm. "I knew."

"You *knew?* Yet you were fool enough to accept him—and wilfully deceive your own mother! I suppose he insisted, and you——"

"No. *I* insisted. I knew my own mind. And I wasn't going to have him upset——"

"But if *I'm* upset it doesn't matter a brass farthing?"

"It does matter. I'm very sorry you've had such a jar." Rose had some ado to maintain her coolness; but she knew it for her one unfailing weapon. "Of course, I meant to tell you later; in fact, as soon as he came up to settle things finally——"

"Most con*sider*ate of you! And when he *does* come up, *I* propose to settle things finally——" She choked, gulped, and glared. She was realising . . . "The *position* you've put me in! It's detestable!"

Rose sighed. It struck her that her own position was not exactly enviable. "I've said I'm sorry. And really—it didn't seem the least likely. . . . Who *was* the officious instrument of Fate?"

"Young Joe Bradley, of the Forests. We were talking of the riots and poor Major Desmond, and Mrs Tait happened to mention Roy Sinclair. Mr Bradley asked—was he the artist's son; and told how he once went to tea there—when his mother was staying with Lady Despard—and had a stand-up fight with Roy. He said Roy's mother was rather a swell native woman—a *pucca* native; and Roy went for him like a wild thing, because he called her an ayah——"

Again Rose smiled in spite of herself. "He would!"

"Would he, indeed! That's all *you* think of—though you know I've got a weak heart. And I nearly fainted—if *that's* any interest to you! The Bradley boy doesn't know—about us. But Mrs Tait's a perfect little sieve. It'll be all over Simla to-morrow. And I was so pleased and proud——" Her voice shook. Tears threatened. "And it's so awkward—so undignified . . . backing out——"

"My dear mother, I've no intention whatever of backing out."

"And I've no intention what*ever* of having a half-caste for a son-in-law."

Rose winced at that, and drew in a steadying breath. For now, at last, the cards were on the table. She was committed to flat opposition or retreat—an impasse she had skilfully avoided hitherto. But for Roy's sake she stood her ground.

"It was—rather a jar when he told me," she admitted, by way of concession. "But truly, he *is* different—if you'll only listen, without fuming! His mother's a Rajput of the highest caste. Her father educated her almost like an English girl. She was only seventeen when she married Sir Nevil; and she lived altogether in England after that. In everything but being her son, Roy is practically an Englishman. You can't class him with the kind of people we associate with—the other word out here——"

Very patiently and tactfully she put forward every redeeming argument in his favour—without avail. Mrs Elton—broadly—had the right on her side; and the gods had denied her the gift of discrimination. She saw India as a vast, confused jumble of Rajahs and *bunnias* and servants and coolies—all steeped in varying depths of dirt and dishonesty, greed and shameless ingratitude. It did not occur to her that sharp distinctions of character, tradition, and culture underlay the more or less uniform tint of skin. And beneath her instinctive antipathy, burned furious anger with Roy for placing her, by his deceitfulness (it *must* have been his) in the ironic position of having to repudiate the engagement she had announced with such éclat only three weeks ago. . . .

The moment she had recovered her breath, she returned unshaken to the charge.

"That's very fine talk, my dear, for two people in love. But Roy's a half-caste: that's flat. You can't wriggle away from the damning fact by splitting hairs about education and breeding. Besides—*you* only think of the man. But are you prepared for your precious first baby to be as dark as a native? It's more than likely. I know it for a fact——"

"Really, Mother! You're a trifle previous." Rose was cool no longer; a slow, unwilling blush flooded her face. Her mother had struck at her more shrewdly than she knew.

"Well, if you *will* be obstinate, it's my duty to open your eyes; or, of course, I wouldn't talk so to an unmarried girl. There's another thing—any doctor will tell you—a particular form of consumption carries off half the wretched children of these mixed marriages. A mercy, perhaps; but think of it——! Your own! And you know perfectly well the moral deterioration——"

"There's none of that about *Roy*." Rose grew warmer still. "And *you* know perfectly well most of it comes from the circumstances, the stigma, the type of parent. But you can say what you please. I'm of age. I love him. I intend to marry him."

"Well, you won't do it from *my* house. I wash my hands of the whole affair."

She rose, upon her ultimatum, a-quiver with righteous anger, even to the realistic cherries in her hat. The girl rose also, outwardly composed, inwardly dismayed.

"Thank you. Now I know where I stand. And *you* won't say a word to Roy. You *mustn't*—really——" She almost pleaded. "He worships his mother in quite the old-fashioned way. He simply couldn't see—the other point of view. Besides—he's ill . . . unhappy. Whatever *your* attitude forces one to say, can only be said by me."

"I don't take orders from my own daughter," Mrs Elton retorted ungraciously. She was in no humour for bargaining or dictation. "But I'm sure *I've* no wish to talk to him. I'll give you a week or ten days to make your plans. But whenever you have him here, I shall be out. And if you come to your senses—you can let me know."

On that she departed, leaving Rose feeling battered and shaken, and horribly uncertain what—in the face of that bombshell—she intended to do: she, who had made Lance suffer cruelly, and evoked a tragic situation between him and Roy, largely in order to avoid a clash that would have been as nothing compared with this . . .!

Her sensations were in a whirl. But somehow—she *must* pull it through. Home life was becoming intolerable. And—for several cogent reasons—she wanted Roy. If need be, she would tell him, diplomatically; dissociating herself from her mother's attitude.

And yet—her mother had said things that would stick; hateful things, that might be true. . . .

Decidedly, she could not write him a long letter: only enough to bring him back to her in a relenting mood. Sitting down again, she unearthed from her black-and-silver bag a fountain pen and half a sheet of paper.

"MY DARLING ROY" (she wrote),—

"Your letter *did* hurt—badly. Perhaps I deserved it. All I can say till we meet, is—forgive me, if you can, because of Lance. It's rather odd—though you *are* my lover, and I suppose you do care still—I can think of no stronger appeal than that. He cared so for us both, in his big splendid way. Can't we stand by each other?

"You ask me to make allowances. Will you be generous, and do the same on a larger scale for your sincerely loving (and not altogether worthless)

ROSE?"

## CHAPTER XII.

"She had a step that walked unheard,
It made the stones like grass;
Yet that light step had crushed a heart
As light as that step was."
—W. H. Davies.

At last, Roy was actually coming. The critical moment was upon them; and Rose sat alone in the drawing-room awaiting him.

Her mother was out; had arranged to be out for the evening also. The strain between them still continued; and it told most on Rose. The cat-like element in her loved comfort; and an undercurrent of clash was peculiarly irritating in her present sore, uncertain state of heart. Weeks of it, she knew, would scarcely leave a dent on her mother's leathern temperament. When it came to a tug the tougher nature scored, which was one reason why she had so skilfully avoided tugs hitherto.

True, she was of age; and her father's small legacy gave her a measure of independence. But how could one set about getting married in the face of open opposition? And—how keep the truth from Roy? Or tone it down, so that he would not go off at a tangent straightaway?

Assuredly the Fates had conspired to strip her headlong romance of its gilded trappings. But her moment for marriage had come. She was sick to death of the Anglo-Indian round—from the unattached standpoint, at least. Roy fascinated her as few men had done; and she had been deliberately trying to ignore the effect of her mother's brutal frankness. Their coming together again, in these changed conditions, would be the ultimate test. Such a chasm of distance seemed to yawn between that tender parting in her boudoir and this critical reunion—in another world. . . .

Sounds of arrival brought her to her feet; but she checked the natural impulse to welcome him in the verandah. Her innate sense of drama shrank from possible awkwardness, a false step, at the start.

And now he appeared in the doorway—very straight and slim in his grey suit, with the sorrowful black band on his arm.

"Rose!" he cried—and stood gazing at her, pulses hammering, brain dizzy. The mere sight of her brought back too vividly the memory of those April days that he had been resolutely shutting out of his mind.

His pause—the shock of his changed aspect—held her motionless also. He looked older, more sallow; his sensitive mouth compressed; no lurking gleam in his eyes. He seemed actually less good-looking than she remembered; for anguish is no beautifier.

So standing, they mutely confronted the change in themselves—in each other; then Rose swept forward, both hands held out.

"Roy—my darling—*what* you must have been through! Can you—will you—in spite of all——?"

Next moment, in his silent, vehement fashion, he was straining her to him; kissing her eyes, her hair, her lips; not in simple lover's ecstasy, but in a fervour of repressed passion, touched with tragedy, with pain. . . .

Then he held her from him, to refresh his tired eyes with the sheer beauty of her; and was struck at once by the absence of colour; the wide black sash, the black velvet round her throat and hair.

He touched the velvet, looking his question. She nodded, drawing in her lip to steady it.

"I felt—I must. You don't mind?"

"*Mind*——?—Sometimes I wonder if I shall ever really *mind* things any more."

His face worked. That queer dizziness took him again. With an incoherent apology, he sat down rather abruptly, and leaned forward, his head between his hands, hiding the emotion he could not altogether control.

Rose stood beside him, feeling helpless and vaguely aggrieved. He had just got back to her, after a two weeks' parting, and he sat there lost in an access of grief that left her quite out of account. Inadvertently there flashed the thought, "Whatever Lance might have suffered, he would not succumb." It startled her. She had never so compared them before. . . .

Then, looking down at his bowed head, compunction seized her, and tenderness, that rarely entered into her feeling for men. She could think of nothing to say that would not sound idiotically commonplace. So she laid her hand on his hair, and moved it caressingly now and then.

She felt a tremor go through him. He half withdrew his head, checked himself, and capturing her hand, pressed it to his lips, that were hot and feverish.

"Roy—what is it? What went wrong?" she asked softly.

He looked up now with a fair imitation of a smile. "Just—an old memory. It was dear of you. Ungracious of me."—Pain and perplexity went from her. She slipped to her knees beside him, and his arm enclosed her. "Sorry to behave like this. But I'm not very fit. And—seeing you, brought it all back so sharply! It's been—a bit of a strain, this last week. A letter from Thea—brave, of course; but broken utterly. The wedding too: and that beast of a journey fairly finished me."

She leaned closer, comforting him by the feel of her nearness. Then her practical brain suggested needs more pedestrian, none the less essential.

"Dearest—you're simply exhausted. How about tea—or a peg?"

He pleaded for a peg, if permissible. She fetched it herself; made tea; plied him with sandwiches and sugared cakes, for which he still retained his boyish weakness.

But talking proved difficult. There were uncomfortable gaps. In their first uplifted moment all had seemed well. Love-making was simple, elemental, satisfying. Beyond the initial glamour and passion of courtship they had scarcely adventured, when the fabric of their world was shattered by the startling events of those four days. Both were realising—as they stepped cautiously among the fragments—that, for all their surface intimacy, they were still strangers underneath.

Roy took refuge in talk about Lahore; the high tribute paid to the conduct of all troops—British and Indian—and police, under peculiarly exasperating circumstances, the C.O.'s conviction that unless sterner measures were taken—and adhered to—there would be more outbreaks, at shorter intervals, better organised. . . .

He hoped her charming air of interest was genuine, but felt by no means sure. And all the while, he was craving to know what she had to say for herself; yet doubting whether he could stand the lightest touch on his open wound. Lance had begged him not to hurt her. Had it ever occurred to that devout lover how sharply she might hurt him?

Tea and a restful hour in an arm-chair eased the strain a little. Then Rose suggested the garden, knowing him susceptible to the large healing influences of earth and sky; also with diplomatic intent to draw him away from the house before her mother's meteoric visitation.

And she was only just in time. The rattle of rickshaw wheels came up the main path two minutes after they had turned out of it towards a favourite nook, which she had strangely grown to love in the last two weeks.

"Poor darling! You've just missed Mother!" She condoled with him, smiling sidelong under her lashes; and she almost blessed her maternal enemy for bringing back the familiar gleam into his eyes.

"Bad luck! Ought we to go in again?"

"Gracious, no. She's only tearing home to change for an early dinner at Penshurst and the theatre. Anyway, please note, you're immune from the formalities. We're going to have a peaceful time, quite independent of Simla rushings. Just ourselves to ourselves."

"Good."

It was an asset with men—second only to her beauty—this gift for creating a restful atmosphere.

Her nook, in an angle above the narrow path, was a grassy bank, looking across crumpled ranges—velvet-soft in the level light—to the still purity of the snows.

"Rather nice, isn't it?" she said. "I'm not given to mooning out of doors; but I've spent several evenings here . . . lately."

"It's sanctuary," Roy murmured; but his sigh was

tinged with apprehension. Flinging off his hat, he reclined full length on the gentle slope, hands under his head, and let the healing rays flow into the deeps of his troubled being.

Rose sat upright beside him, her fingers locked loosely round one raised knee. She was troubled too, and quite at a loss how to begin.

"So you've not been going out much?" he asked, after a prolonged pause.

"No—how could I—with you, so unhappy, down there—and . . ."—She deliberately met his eyes; and the look in them impelled her to ask: "*What* is it, Roy—lurking in your mind?"

"Am I—to be frank?"

She shivered. "It sounds—rather chilly. But I suppose we'd better take our cold plunge—and get it over!"

"Well"—he hesitated palpably. "It was only a natural wonder—if you care . . . all that . . . now he's gone, how could you deliberately hurt him so—while he lived?"

She drew in her lip. It was going to be more unsteadying than she had foreseen.

"How *can* a woman explain to a man the simple fact that she is incurably—perhaps unforgivably—a woman?"

"I don't know. I hoped you could—up to a point," said Roy, looking away to the snows and remembering, suddenly, *that* was where he ought to be now—with Lance—always Lance: no other thought or presence seemed vital to him, these days. Yet Rose remained beautiful and desirable—and clearly she loved him.

"It doesn't make things easier, you know," she was saying, in her cool, low voice, "to feel you are patently regretting events that, unhappily, did hurt—him; but also—gave me to you . . ."

Her beauty, her evident pain, penetrated the settled misery that enveloped him like an atmosphere.

"Darling—forgive me!" He reached out, pulling her hands apart, and his fingers closed hard on hers. "I'm only trying—clumsily—to understand . . ."

"And goodness knows I'm willing to help you," she sighed, returning his pressure. "But—I'm afraid the little I can say for myself won't do much to regild my halo—if there's any of it left! I gather you aren't very well up in women, or girls, Roy?"

"No—I'm not. Perhaps it makes me seem to you a bit of a fool?"

"Quite the reverse. It's all along been a part of your charm."

"My—charm?"

There was more of tenderness than amusement in her low laugh. "Precisely! If you didn't possess—*some* magnetic quality, could I have been drawn away from a man—like Lance, when I'd nearly made up my mind—to face the music."

For answer, he kissed her captured hand.

Then: "Roy, if it doesn't hurt too much," she urged, "will you tell me first—just—what Lance said?"

It would hurt, horridly. But it was as well she should know; and not a word need he withhold. Could there be a finer tribute to his friend? It was his own share in their last unforgettable talk that could not be reproduced.

"Yes—I'll tell you," he said. And, his half-closed eyes resting on the sunlit hills, he told her, in a voice from which all feeling was carefully expunged. Only so could he achieve the telling; and she listened without interruption, for which he felt grateful, exceedingly. . . .

When it was over he merely moved his head and looked up at her; and she returned his look, her eyes heavy with tears. Mutually their fingers tightened.

"Thank you," she said. "It makes me . . ashamed, but it makes me proud."

"It made *me* angry and bewildered," said Roy. "If you really were . . . coming his way, what the devil did *I* do to upset it all? Of course I admired you; and I was interested—on his account. But—I had no thought—I was absorbed in other things——"

She nodded slowly, not looking at him. "Quite so. And I suppose—being me—I didn't choose that a man should dance with me, ride with me, obviously admire me, and yet remain absorbed in other things. And—being you—of course it never struck you that, for my kind of girl, your provocatively casual attitude almost amounted to a challenge. Besides—as I said—you were charming; you were different. Perhaps—if I'd felt a shade less sure—of Lance, if he'd had the wit even to *seem* keen on some one else . . . he might have saved himself. As it was—you were irresistible."

She heard him grit his teeth; and turned with swift compunction.

"My poor Roy! Am I jarring you badly? I suppose, if I talked till midnight, I'd never succeed in making a man like you understand how purely instinctive it all is. Analysed, like this, it sounds cold-blooded. But, it's just—second nature. He—Lance—understood up to a point. That's why he was aggressive that day: oh—furiously angry; all because of you. The pair you are! He said if I fooled you, and didn't play fair, he'd back out, or insist on a *pucca* engagement. And—yes—it did have the wrong effect. It made me wonder—if I *could* marry a man, however splendid, who owned such exacting standards and such a hot temper. And there were you—an unknown quantity, with the Banter-Wrangle discreetly in pursuit. A supreme inducement in itself!—Yes, distinctly, that afternoon was a turning-point. Just Lance losing his temper, and you coolly forgetting an arrangement with me——"

She paused, looking back over it all; felt Roy's hold slacken and unobtrusively withdrew her hand.

"Soon after Kapurthala, he was angry again. And that time, I'm afraid I reminded him that our engagement was only 'on' conditionally; that if he started worrying at me, it would soon be unconditionally off——"

"So it *should* have been!" Roy jerked up on to his elbow, and confronted her with challenging directness. "Once you could speak like that, feel like that, you'd no *right* to keep him hanging on—hoping when there was practically no hope. It wasn't playing the game——"

This time she kept her eyes averted, and a slow colour invaded her face. There was a point beyond which feminine frankness could not go. She could not—would not—tell this unflatteringly critical lover of hers that it was not in her nature to let the one man go till she felt morally sure of the other.

Roy had only a profile view of her warm cheek, her sensitive nostril a-quiver, her lip drawn in. And when she spoke, it was in the tense, passionate tone of that evening at Anarkalli.

"Oh yes—it's easy work sitting in judgment on other people. I told you I hadn't much of a case—I asked you to make allowances. You clearly can't. *He* asked you—not to hurt me. You clearly feel you must. Yet—in justice to you both—I'm doing what I can. I've never before condescended to explain myself—almost excuse myself—to *any* man; and I certainly never shall again. It strikes me you'd better apply your own indictment . . to your own case. If *you* can think and feel . . as you seem to do, better face the fact and be done with it——"

But Roy, startled and penitent, was sitting upright by now; and, when she would have risen, he seized her, crushing her to him, would she or no. In her pain and anger she more than ever drew him. In his utter heart-loneliness, he more than ever needed her. And the reminder of Lance crowned all.

"My darling—don't go off at a tangent, that way," he implored her, his lips against her hair. "For me—it's a sacred bond. It can't be snapped in a fit of temper—like a bit of knotted thread. I'll accept . . what I can't see clear. We'll stand by each other, as you said. Learn one another—Rose . . . ! My dearest girl—*don't*——!"

He strained her closer, in mingled bewilderment and distress. For Rose—who trod lightly on the hearts of men, Rose—the serene and self-assured—was sobbing brokenly in his arms. . . .

Before the end of the evening, they were more or less themselves again; the threatened storm averted; the trouble patched up and summarily dismissed, as only lovers can dismiss a cloud that intrudes upon their heaven of blue.

# CHAPTER XIII.

"Le pire douleur est de ne pas, pleurer ce qu'on a perdu."—De Coulevain.

But as days passed, both grew increasingly aware of the patch; and both very carefully concealed the fact. They spent a week of peaceful seclusion from Simla and her restless activities. Roy scarcely set eyes on Mrs Elton; but—Rose having skilfully prepared the ground—he merely gave her credit for her mother's unusual display of tact.

Neither was in the vein for dances or tennis parties. They rode out to Mashobra and Fagu. They spent long days, picnicking in the Glen. Roy discovered, with satisfaction, that Rose had a weakness for being read to and a fair taste in literature, so long as it was not poetry. He also discovered—with a twinge of dismay—that if they were many hours together, he found reading easier than talking.

On the whole, they spent a week that should, by rights, have been ideal for new-made lovers; yet, at heart, both felt vaguely troubled and disillusioned.

Pain and parting and harsh realities seemed to have rubbed the bloom off their exotic romance. And for Rose the trouble struck deep. She had deliberately willed to put aside her own innate shrinking from the Indian strain in Roy. But she reckoned without the haunting effect of her mother's plain speaking. At first she had flatly ignored it; then she fortified her secret qualms by devising a practical plan for getting away to a friend in Kashmir. There was a sister in Simla going to join her. They could travel together. Roy could follow on. And there they two could be quietly married without fuss or audible comment from their talkative little world.

It was not precisely her idea of the manner in which she—Rose Arden—should be given in marriage. But the main point was that—if she could help it—her mother should not score in the matter of Roy. *Could* she help it? That was the question persistently knocking at her heart.

And she was only a degree less troubled by the perverse revival of her feeling for Lance. Vanished—his hold on her deeper nature seemed mysteriously to strengthen. Memories crowded in, unbidden, of their golden time together just before Roy appeared on the scene; till she almost arrived at blaming her deliberately chosen lover for having come between them and landed her in her present distracting position. For now it was the ghost of Lance that threatened to come between her and Roy; and the irony of it cut her to the quick. If she had dealt unfairly by these two men, whose standards were leagues above her own, she was not, it seemed, to escape her share of suffering. . . .

For Roy's heart also knew the chill of secret disillusion. The ardour and thrill of his courtship seemed fatally to have suffered eclipse. When they were together, the lure of her was potent still. It was in the gaps between that he felt irked, more and more, by incipient criticism. In the course of that first talk, she had unwittingly stripped herself of the glamour that was more than half her charm; and at bottom his Eastern subconsciousness was jarred by her casual attitude to the sanctities of the man and woman relation, as instilled into him by his mother. When he quarrelled with her treatment of Lance, she saw it merely as a rather exaggerated concern for his friend. There was that in it, of course; but there was more.

Yet undeniably Desmond's urgent plea influenced his own effort to ignore the still small voice within him, that protested against the whole affair. At another time he would have taken it for a clear intimation from his mother; but she seemed to have lost, or deserted him, these days. All he could firmly hold on to, at present, was his loyalty to Lance, his duty to Rose; and both seemed to point in the same direction.

It struck him as strange that she did not mention the wedding; and she had been so full of it that very first evening. Once, when he casually asked if any fixtures were decided on yet, she had smiled and answered, "No; not yet." And some other topic had intervened.

It was only a degree less strange that she spoke so often of Lance, without attempting to disguise her admiration—and something more. And in himself—strangest of all—this surprising manifestation stirred no flicker of jealousy. It seemed a link, rather, drawing them nearer together. She frankly encouraged talk of their school-days that involved fresh revealings of Lance at every turn: talk that was anodyne or anguish according to his mood.

She also encouraged him to unearth his deserted novel and read her the opening chapters. In Lahore, he had longed for that moment; now he feared lest it too sharply emphasise their inner apartness. For the Indian atmosphere was strong in the book; and the Indian atmosphere jarred. The effect of the riots had merely been repressed. It still simmered underneath.

Only once she had broken out on the subject; and had been distinctly restive when he demurred at the injustice of sweeping indictments against the whole country, because a handful of extremists were trying to wreck the ship. Personally he blamed England for virtually assisting in the process. It had come near to an altercation—a very rare event with Rose; and it had left Roy feeling more unsettled than ever.

A few readings of his novel made him feel more uncomfortable still. Like all true artists, he listened, as he read, with the mind of his audience; and intuitively, he felt her antagonism to the Indian element in his characters, his writing, his theme.

For three days he persisted. Then he gave it up.

They were sitting in their nook; Rose leaning back, her eyes half closed, gazing across the valley. In the middle of a flagrantly Indian chapter, he broke off: determined to take it lightly; not to make a grievance of it: equally determined she should hear no more.

For a few seconds she did not realise. Then she turned and looked up at him. "Well——? Is that all?"

"Yes. That's all—so far as you're concerned!"

Her brows went up in the old beguiling way. He felt her trying to hide her thought, and held up a warning finger.

"Now, don't put it on! Frankly—isn't she relieved? Hasn't she borne the infliction like a saint?"

The blood stirred visibly under her pallor. "It was *not* an infliction. Your writing's wonderful. Quite uncanny—the way you get inside people and things. If there's more—go on."

"There's a lot more. But I'm not going on—even at her Majesty's express command!—Look here, Rose . . . let be." He suddenly changed his tone. "I can feel how it bothers you. So—why pretend . . .?"

She looked down; twisting her opal ring, making the delicate colours flash and change.

"It's a pity—isn't it?"—she seemed to muse aloud—"that more than half of life is made up of pretending. It becomes rather a delicate problem—fixing boundary lines. I *do* admire your gift, Roy. And you're so intensely human. But I confess, I—I *am* jerked by parts of your theme. Doesn't all this animosity and open vilification affect your own feeling about—things, the least bit?"

"Yes. It does. Only—not in your way. It makes me unhappy, because the real India—snowed under with specious talk and bitter invective—has less chance now than ever of being understood by those who can't see below the surface."

"Me—for instance?"

He sighed. "Oh, scores and scores of you, here and at Home. And scores of others, who have far less excuse. That's why one feels bound to do what one can . . ."

His thoughts on that score went too deep for utterance. But Rose was engaged in her own purely personal deliberations.

"You might want to come out again . . . afterwards?"

"Yes—I should hope to. Besides . . . there are my cousins . . ."

"Indian ones——?"

"Yes. Very clever. Very charming. Rose . . . you've been six years in India. Have you ever met, in a friendly way, a cultivated, well-born Indian—man or woman?"

"N-no. Not worth mentioning."

"And . . . you haven't wanted to?"

He felt her shrink from the direct question.

"Why press the point, Roy? It needn't make any real difference—need it—between you and me?"

Her counter-question was still more direct, more searching.

"Perhaps not—now," he said. "It might . . . make a lot . . . afterwards——"

At that critical juncture their talk was interrupted by a peon with a note that required immediate attention: and Roy, left alone, felt increasingly disillusioned and dismayed.

Later on, to his relief, Rose suggested a ride. She seemed suddenly in a more elusive mood than he had experienced since their engagement. She did not refer again to his novel, or to the thorny topic of India; and their parting embrace was chilled by a shadow of constraint.

"*How* would it be—afterwards?" he wondered, riding back to the Club, at a foot's pace, feeling tired and feverish and gravely puzzled as to whether it might not—on all counts—be the greater wrong to make a fetish of a bond so rashly forged.

To-day, very distinctly he was aware of the inner tug he had been trying to ignore. And to-day it was more imperative; less easily stilled. Could it be . . . veritably, his mother, trying to reach him—and failing, for the first time?

That thought prompted the test question—if *she* were alive, how would he feel about bringing Rose home as daughter-in-law, as mother of her grandson . . . the gift of gifts? If she were alive, could Rose herself have faced the conjunction? And to him she was still verily alive—or had been, till his infatuate passion had blinded him to everything but one face, one form, one desire.

That night there came to him—on the verge of sleep—the old thrilling sensation that she was there—yearning to him across an impassable barrier. And this time he knew—with a bitter certainty—that the barrier was within himself. Every nerve in him craved—as he had not craved this long while—the unmistakable *sense* of her that seemed gone past recall. Desperately, he strained every faculty to penetrate the resistant medium that withheld her from him—in vain.

Wearied out, with disappointment and futile effort, he fell asleep—praying for a dream visitation to revive his shaken faith. None came; and conviction seized him that none would come, until . . .

One could not, simultaneously, live on intimate terms with earth and heaven. And Rose was earth in its most alluring guise. More: she had awakened in him sensations and needs that, at the moment, she alone could satisfy. But if it amounted to a choice; for him, there could be no question. . . .

Next day and the day after, a sharp return of fever kept him in bed: and a touch of his father in him tempted him to write, sooner than face the strain of a final scene. But moral cowardice was not among his failings; also unquestionably—if irrationally—he wanted to see her, to hold her in his arms once again. . . .

On the third morning he sent her a note saying he was better; he would be round for tea; and received a verbal answer. Miss Sahib sent her salaam. She would be at home.

So, about half-past three, he rode out to the house on Elysium Hill, wondering how—and, at moments, whether—he was going to pull it through. . . .

Her smile of welcome almost unmanned him. He simply did not feel fit for the strain. It would be so much easier and more restful to yield to her spell.

"I'm so sorry. Idiotic of me," was all he said; and went forward to take her in his arms.

But she, without a word, laid both hands on him, holding him back.

"*Rose!* What's the matter?" he cried, genuinely upset. Nothing undermines a resolve like finding it forestalled.

"Simply—it's all over. We're beaten, Roy," she said in a queer, repressed voice. "We can't go on with this. And—you know it."

"But—darling!" He took her by the arms.

"No . . . *no!*" The passionate protest was addressed to herself as much as to him. "Listen, Roy. I've never hated saying anything more—but it's true. You said, last time,—'Why pretend?' And that struck home. I knew I had been pretending hard—because I wanted to—for more than a week. You made me realise . . . one couldn't go on at it all one's married life.—But, my dear, what a wretch I am! You're not fit . . ."

"Oh, I'm just wobbly . . . stupid," he muttered, half dazed, as she pressed him down into a corner of the Chesterfield.

"Poor old boy. When you've had some tea, you'll be able to face things."

He said nothing; merely leaned back against the cushion and closed his eyes—part of him rebelling furiously against her quiet yet summary proceedings—while she attended to the sputtering kettle.

How prosaic, after all, are even the great moments of life! They had been ardent lovers. They had come to the parting of the ways. But a kettle on the boil would wait for no man; and, till the body was served, the troubles of the heart must wait.

She drew the table nearer to him; carefully poured out tea; carefully avoided his eyes. And—in the intervals between her mechanical occupations—she told him as much of the truth as she felt he could bear to hear, or she to speak. Among other things, unavoidably, she explained how—and through whom—her mother had come to know about their reservation——

"*That* young sweep!" Roy muttered, so suddenly half-alert and fierce that amused tenderness tripped up her studied composure.

"You'd go for him now, just the same, I believe!"

"I would—and a bit extra. Because—of you."

She sighed. "Oh yes, it was a *mauvais quart d'heure* of the first order. And coming on the top of your crushing letter——"

He captured her hand. Their eyes met—and softened.

"No, Roy," she said, gently but inexorably releasing her fingers. "We've got to keep our heads to-day, somehow."

"Has yours so completely taken command of affairs?"

"I'm afraid—it has."

"Yet—you stood up to your mother?"

"Oh, I did—as I've never done yet. But afterwards I realised—it was only skin deep. She said . . . things I can't repeat; but equally . . . I can't forget; things about . . . possible children . . ."

The blood flamed in Roy's sallow face. "Confound her! What does *she* know about possible children?"

"More than I do, I suppose," Rose admitted, with a pathetic half smile. "Anyway, after that, she refused to countenance the engagement—the wedding——"

Roy sat suddenly forward, scorn and anger in his eyes.

"*Refused*——! After the infernal fuss she made over me, because my father happened to have a title and a garden. And now——" his hand closed on the edge of the table. "I'm considered a pariah—am I?—simply on account of my lovely little mother—the guardian angel of us all!"

His blaze of wrath, his low passionate tone, startled her to silence. He had spoken so seldom of his mother since the first occasion, that—although she knew—she had far from plumbed the height and depth of his worship. And instinctively she thought, 'I should have been jealous into the bargain.'

But Roy had room just then for one consideration only.

"Here have I been coming to her house on sufferance . . . polluting her precious drawing-room, while she's been avoiding me as if I was a leper, all because I'm the son of a sainted woman, whose shoe she wouldn't have been worthy . . oh, I beg your pardon——" He checked himself sharply. "After all—she's *your* mother."

Rose felt her cheeks growing uncomfortably warm. "I did warn you, in Lahore, some people felt . . . that way."

"Well, I never dreamed they would *behave* that way. It's not as if I'd been born and reared in India and might claim relations in her compound."

"My dear—one can't make her see the difference," Rose urged desperately.

"Well, I *won't* stay any longer in her house. I won't eat her food——"

He pushed aside his plate so impatiently that Rose felt almost angry. But she saw his hand tremble; and covered it with her own.

"Roy—my dear! You're ill; and you're being rather exaggerated over things——"

"Well, you put me in such a false position. You ought to have told me."

She winced at that and let fall her hand.

"That's all one's reward for trying to save you from jars when you were knocked up and unhappy. And I told you . . . I defied her . . I . . I would have married you . . ."

He looked at her, and his heart contracted sharply.

"Poor Rose—poor darling!" He was his normal self again. "What a beast of a time you must have had! But—how *did* you propose to accomplish it——?"

She told him, haltingly, of the Kashmir plan; and he listened, half incredulous, leaning back again; thinking: "She's plucky; but still, all she troubled about really was to save her face."

And she, noting his impatient frown, was thinking: "He's like a sensitive plant charged with gunpowder. Is it the touchiness of——?"

"I'm afraid I'd have kicked at that." His voice broke in upon her thought. "Such a hole-and-corner business. Hardly fair on my father . . ."

"Well, there's no question of it now," she reminded him, with a touch of asperity. "I've told you—the whole thing's defunct. Later—we'll be glad, perhaps, that I discovered in time that part of me could not be coerced—by the other part, which still wants you as much as ever. We should have been landed in disaster—soon or late. Better soon—before the roots have struck too deep. But you're so furiously angry with the *reason*—that you seem almost to forget . . . the fact."

His eyes brooded on her, full of pain and the old, half-unwilling infatuation. He could not so hurt her pride as to confess that their discovery had been mutual. Let her glean what satisfaction she could from having taken the lead—first and last. Part of him, also, still wanted her; though in the depths, he felt a glimmer of relief that the thing was done—and by her.

"No," he said, "I don't forget the fact. But—the reason cuts deep. I want to know——" he hesitated—"is all this . . . antipathy you can't get over—you and your mother—the ordinary average attitude? Or is it . . . exceptionally acute?"

She drew in her lip. Why *would* he force her to hurt him more? For they had got beyond polite evasion. Clearly he wanted the truth.

"Mother's is acute," she said, not looking at him. "Mine—I'm afraid—is . . . the ordinary average feeling against it. The exception would be to find a girl—especially out here—who could honestly . . . get over it——"

"*Unless*—she cared in the real big way," Roy interposed; his own pain goading him to an unfair hit at her. "To be blunt, I suppose it's the case—of Lance over again. You've found . . . you don't love me enough——?"

"And *you*——?" she struck back, turning on him the cool deliberate look of early days. "Do *you* love me enough? Do you care—as he did?"

"No—not as he did. I've cared blindly, passionately—somehow we didn't seem to meet on any other plane. In fact, it . . . it was realising how magnificently Lance cared . . and how little you seemed able to appreciate the fact, that made me feel—as I did, down there. In a sense, he's been barring the way . . . ever since . . ."

"*Roy!* How strange!" She faced him now, the mask of repression flung aside. "It's been the same—with me!"

"With *you?*"

"Yes. Ever since I heard . . . he was gone, he has haunted me to distraction. I've seemed to see him and feel him in quite a different way."

"Good Lord!" Roy murmured—incredulous, amazed. "Human beings *are* the queerest things. If only . . . you'd felt like that . . . sooner——?"

"Yes—if only I had——!" she lamented frankly, looking straight before her.

"I'm glad—you told me," said her unaccountable lover.

"I nearly—didn't. But when you said that, I felt it might—ease things. And that was his great wish—wasn't it?—to ease things . . . for us both. Oh—was there ever any one . . . *quite* like him?"

Tears stood in her eyes, and Roy contemplating her—

seeing, for the first time, something beyond her beauty—felt drawn to her in an altogether new way; and sitting there they talked of him quietly, like friends, rather than lovers on the verge of parting for good.

As real to them, almost, as themselves, was the spirit of the man who had loved both more greatly than they were capable of loving one another; who, in life, had refused to stand between them; yet, in death, had subtly thrust them apart. . . .

Then there came a pause. They remembered. . . .

"We're rather a strange pair—of lovers," she murmured shakily. "I feel, now, as if I can't bear letting you go. And yet . . . it wouldn't last.—Dearest, *will* you be sensible . . . and finish your tea?"

"No. It would choke me," he said with smothered passion. "If I've got to go—I'm going."

He stood up, bracing his shoulders. She stood up also, confronting him. Neither could see the other's face quite clear.

Then: "Only six weeks!" she said very low. "Roy—we ought to be ashamed of ourselves."

"I am—heartily," he confessed. "I was never more so."

She was looking down now, twisting her ring. "I'm afraid . . . I'm not talented in that line. Somehow . . . except for Lance, I can't regret it." She slid the ring over her knuckle.

"Oh, *keep* the beastly thing!" he flung out in an access of pain. "Or throw it down the khud. I said it would bring bad luck."

She sighed. "All the same—poor thing! It's too lovely . . ."

"Well then, don't wear it; but keep it"—his tone changed—"as a reminder. We have been something to one another . . . if it couldn't be everything."

Her eyes were still lowered, her lips not quite steady. "You've been . . . very near it to me. Yet—it seemed, the more . . . I cared, the less I could get over . . . that. And I felt as if you—wouldn't get over . . Lance."

"My God! It's been a bitter, contrary business all round! I can't bear hurting you. And—the talk and all that——" She nodded. For her that was not the least bitter part of it all. "And you——? Oh, Lord—will it be Hayes to the fore again?"

"*No!*" Reproach underlay her vehemence. "Mother may rage. I shall go with Dolly Smyth to Kashmir.—And you——?"

"Oh, I'll go out to Narkhanda."

"Alone? But you're ill. You want looking after."

"Can't be helped. Azim Khan's a treasure. And really I don't care a damn what comes to me."

"Oh, but *I* do——!"

It was a cry from her heart. The strain of repression snapped. She swayed, just perceptibly——

In a moment his arms were round her; and they clung together a long while, in the only complete form of nearness they had known. . . .

For Roy, that last passionate kiss was dead-sea fruit. For Rose, it was her moment of completest surrender to an elemental force she had deliberately played with only to find herself the sport of it at last. . . .

When it was over—all was over. Words were impertinent. He held her hands close, a moment, looking into her tear-filled eyes. Then he took up hat and stick and stumbled blindly down the verandah steps. . . .

Back in his bachelor room at the Club, he realised that fever was on him again: his eyeballs burning; little hammers beating all over his head. Mechanically, he picked up two letters that lay awaiting him: one from his father, one from Jeffers, congratulating him, in rather guarded phrases, on his engagement to Miss Arden.

It was the last straw.

END OF PHASE IV.

# PHASE V.

# A STAR IN DARKNESS

# CHAPTER I.

> "Thou art with life
> Too closely woven, nerve with nerve intwined;
> Service still craving service, love for love . . .
> Nor yet thy human task is done."
>
> —R. L. S.

In the verandah of Narkhanda dák bungalow Roy lay alone, languidly at ease, assisted by rugs and pillows and a Madeira cane lounge at an invalid angle; walls and arches splashed with sunshine; and a table beside him littered with convalescent accessories. There were home papers; there were books; there was fruit and a syphon, cut lemons and crushed ice—everything thoughtfulness could suggest set within easy reach. But the nameless depression of convalescence hung heavy on his spirit and his limbs.

He was thirsty; he was lonely; he was mentally hungry in a negative kind of way. Yet it simply did not seem worth the trivial effort of will to decide whether he wanted to pick up a book or an orange or to press the syphon handle. So he lay there, inert, impassive, staring across the valley at the snows—peak beyond soaring peak, ethereal in the level light.

The beauty of them, the pellucid clearness and stillness of early evening, stirred no answering echo within him. His brain was travelling back over a timeless interval; wandering uncertainly among sensations, apparitions, and dreams, presumably of semi-delirium: for Lance was in them and his mother and Rose and Dyán, saying and doing impossible things. . . .

And in clearer intervals, there hovered the bearded face of Azim Khan, pressing upon his refractory Sahib this infallible medicine, that 'chikken bráth' or jelly. And occasionally there was another bearded face:

vaguely familiar, though he could not put a name to it.

Between them the two had brought out a doctor from Simla. He remembered a sharp altercation over that. He wanted no confounded doctor messing round. But Azim Khan, for love of his master, had flatly defied orders: and the forbidden doctor had appeared—involving further exhausting argument. For on no account would Roy be moved back to Simla. Azim Khan understood his ways and his needs. He was damned if he would have any one else near him.

And this time he had prevailed. For the doctor, who happened to be a wise man, knew when acquiescence was medically sounder than insistence. There had, however, been a brief intrusion of a strange woman, in cap and apron, who had made a nuisance of herself over food and washing, and was infernally in the way. When the fever abated, she melted into the landscape; and Roy had just enough of his old spirit left in him to murmur, '*Shahbash!*' in a husky voice: and Azim Khan, inflated with pride, became more autocratic than ever.

The other bearded face had resolved itself into the Delhi Sikh, Jiwán Singh. He had been on a tramp among the Hills, combating insidious Home-Rule fairy-tales among the villagers: and finding the Sahib very ill, had stayed on to help.

This morning they had told him it was the third of June:—barely three weeks since that strange, poignant parting with Rose. Not seven weeks since the infinitely more poignant and terrible parting with Lance. Yet, as his mind stirred unwillingly, picking up threads, he seemed to be looking back across a measureless gulf into another life. . . .

"The Sahib has slept? His countenance has been more favourable since these few days?"

It was the voice of Jiwán Singh; and the man himself followed it—taut and wiry, instinct with a degree of energy and purpose almost irritating to one who was feeling emptied of both; aimless as a jelly-fish stranded by the tide.

"Not smoking, *Hazúr?* Has that scoundrel Azim Khan forgotten the cigarettes?"

Roy unearthed his case, and held it up, smiling.

"The scoundrel forgets nothing," said he, knowing very well how the two of them had vied with one another in forestalling his needs. "Sit down, my friend—and tell me news. I am too lazy to read." He touched an unopened 'Civil and Military Gazette.' "Too lazy even to cast out the devil of laziness. But very ready to listen. Are things all quiet now? Any more tamashas?"

"Only a very little one across the frontier," said the Sikh with his grim smile: and proceeded to explain that the Indian Government had lately become entangled in a sort of a war with Afghanistan; a rather '*kutcha bandobast*'[1] in Jiwán Singh's estimation; and not quite up to time; but a war, for all that.

"You mean——" asked Roy, his numbed interest faintly astir, "that it was to have been part of the same game as the trouble down there?"

"God has given me ears—and wits, *Hazúr*," was the cautious answer. "*That* would be *pukka bundobast*,[2] for war and trouble to come at one stroke in the hot season, when so many of the white soldier-*lóg* are in the Hills. Does your Honour suppose that merely by *chance* the Amir read in his paper of riots in India, and said in his heart, 'Wah! Now is the time for lighting little fires along the Border'?"

"N-no—I don't suppose——"

"Does your Honour suppose Hindus and Moslems—outside a highly educated few—are truly falling on each other's necks, without one thought of political motive?"

"No, my friend—I do not suppose."

"Yet these things are said openly among our people: and too few, now, have courage to speak their thought. For it is the loyal who suffer—*shurrum ki bhát!*[3] Is it surprising, *Hazúr*, if we, who distrust this new madness, begin to ask ourselves, 'Has the British Raj lost the will—or the power—of former days to protect friends and smite enemies'? If the noisy few clamouring for *Swaráj* make India once more a battlefield, *your* people can go. We Sikhs must remain, with Pathans and Afghans—as of old—hammering at our doors——"

At sight of the young Englishman's pained frown, he

[1] Crude arrangement. [2] Sound arrangement.
[3] Shameful talk.

checked his expansive mood. "To the Sahib I can freely speak the thoughts of my heart; but this is not talk to make a sick man well. God is merciful. Before all is lost—the British Raj may yet arise with power, as in the great days . . ."

But his talk, if unpalatable, was more tonic than he knew; because Roy's love for India went deeper than he knew. The justice of Jiwán Singh's reproach; the hint at tragic severance of the two countries mingled within him, waked him effectually from semi-torpor; and the process was as painful as the tingling renewal of life in a frozen limb. By timely courage, on the spot, the threat to India had been staved off: but it was there still—sinister, unsleeping, virtually unchecked.

'Scotched—not killed.' The voice of Lance sounded too clearly in Roy's brain; and the more intimate pain, deadened a little by illness, struck at his heart like a sword. . . .

Within a week, care and feeding and inimitable air, straight from the snowfields, had made him, physically, a new man. Mentally, it had brought him face to face with actualities, and the staggering question, 'What next'?

At the back of his mind he had been dreading it, evading it, because it would force him to look deep into his own heart; and to make decisions, when the effort of making them was anathema, beclouded as he was by the depression that still brooded over him like a fog. The doctor had prescribed a tonic and a whiff of Simla frivolity; but Roy paid no heed. He knew his malady was mainly of the heart and the spirit. The true curative touch could only come from some arrowy shaft that would pierce to the core of one or the other.

This morning, by way of reasserting his normal self, he had risen very early with intent to walk out and spend the day at Baghi dák bungalow, ten miles on. Taking things easily, he believed it could be done. He would look through his manuscript; try and pick up threads. Suráj could follow later; and he would ride home over the pass in the cool of the evening.

He set out under a clear heaven, misted with the promise of heat: the air rather ominously still. But the thread of a path winding through the dimness and vastness of Narkhanda Forest was ice-cool with the breath of night. Pines, ilex, and deodars clung miraculously to a hillside of massive rock, that jutted above him at intervals—threatening, immense; and often, on the *khud* side, dropped abruptly into nothingness. When the road curved outward, splashes of sunlight patterned it; and intermittent gaps revealed the flash of snow-peaks, incredibly serene and far.

Normally the scene—the desolate grandeur of it—would have intoxicated Roy. But the stranger he was carrying about with him, and called by his own name, reacted in quite another fashion to the shadowed majesty of looming rocks and forest aisles. The immensity of it dwarfed one mere suffering man to the dimensions of a pebble on the path. And the pebble had the advantage of insensibility. The stillness and chillness made him feel overwhelmingly alone. A sudden craving for Lance grew almost intolerable. . . .

But Lance was gone. Paul, with his bride, had vanished from human ken; Rose, a shattered illusion, gone too. Better so—of course; though, intermittently, the man she had roused in him still ached for the sight and feel of her. She gave a distinct thrill to life: and, if he could not forgive her, neither could he instantly forget her.

Still less could he forget the significance of the shock she had dealt him on their day of parting. Patently she loved him, in her passionate, egotistical fashion—as he had never loved her; patently she had combated her shrinking in defiance of her mother: and yet . . . !

Rage as he might, his Rajput pride, and pride in his Rajput heritage, were wounded to the quick. If all English girls felt that way, he would see them further, before he would propose to another one, or 'confess' to his adored Mother, as if she were a family skeleton or a secret vice. Instantly there sprang the thought of Arúna—her adoration, her exalted passion; Arúna, whom he might have loved, yet was constrained to put aside because of his English heritage; only to find himself put aside by an English girl on account of his Indian blood. A pleasant predicament for a man who must needs marry in common duty to his father and himself.

And what of Tara? Was it possible . . .? Could that be the meaning of her final desperate, 'I *can't* do it, Roy—even for you'? Was it conceivable—she who loved his mother to the point of worship? Still smarting from his recent rebuff, he simply could not tell. Thea and Lance loved her too; yet, in Lance especially, he had been aware of a tacit tendency to ignore the Indian connection.

The whole complication touched him too nearly, hurt and bewildered him too bitterly, for cool consideration. He only saw that which had been his pride converted into a reproach, a two-edged sword barring the way to marriage: and in the bitterness of his heart he found it hard to forgive his parents—mainly his father—for putting him in so cruel a position, with no word of warning to soften the blow.

Perhaps people felt differently in England. If so, India was no place for him. How blatantly juvenile—to his clouded, tormented brain—seemed his arrogant dreams of Oxford days! What could such as he do for her, in this time of tragic upheaval. And how could all the Indias he had seen—not to mention the many he had not seen—be jumbled together under that one misleading name? That was the root fallacy of dreamers and 'reformers.' They spoke of her as one, when in truth she was many—bewilderingly many. The semblance of unity sprang mainly from England's unparalleled achievement—her Pax Britannica, that held the scales even between rival chiefs and races and creeds; that had wrought, in miniature, the very inter-racial stability which Europe had vainly fought and striven to achieve. Yet now, some malign power seemed constraining her, in the name of progress, to undo the work of her own hands. . . .

All his thronging thoughts were tinged with the gloom of his unhopeful mood; and his body flagged with his flagging spirit. Before he had walked four miles, his legs refused to carry him any farther.

He had emerged into the open, into full view of the vastness beyond. Naked rock and stone, jewelled with moss and young green, fell straight from the path's edge; and one ragged pine, springing from a group of boulders, was roughly stencilled on blue distances empurpled with shadows of thunderous cloud.

A flattened boulder proved irresistible; and Roy sat down, leaning his head against the trunk, sniffing luxuriously—whiffs of resin and sun-warmed pine-needles. Oh, to be at home, in his own beech-wood! But the journey in this weather would be purgatorial. Meantime, there was his walk; and he decided, prosaically, to fortify himself with a slab of chocolate. Instead—still more prosaically, he fell sound asleep. . . .

But sleep, in an unnatural position, begets dreams. And Roy dreamed of Lance; of that last awful day when he raved incessantly of Rose. But in the dream he was conscious; and before his distracted gaze Roy held Rose in his arms; craving her, yet hating her; because she clung to him, heedless of entreaties from Lance, and would not be shaken off. . . .

In a frantic effort to free himself, he woke—with the anguish of his loss fresh upon him—to find the sky heavily overcast, the breathlessness of imminent storm in the air. Away to the North there were blue spaces, sun-splashed leagues of snow. But from the South and West rolled up the big battalions—heralds of the monsoon.

He concluded apathetically that Baghi was 'off.' He was in for a drenching. Lucky he had brought his burberry. . . .

Yet he did not stir. A ton weight seemed to hang on his limbs, his spirit, his heart. He simply sat there, in a carven stillness, staring down, down, into abysmal depths. . . .

And startlingly, sharply, the temptation assailed him. The tug of it was almost physical. . . . How simple to yield—to cut his many tangles at one stroke!

In that jaundiced moment he saw himself a failure foreordained; debarred from marriage by evils supposed to spring from the dual strain in him; his cherished hopes of closer union between the two countries he loved threatened with shipwreck by an England complacently experimental, an India at war with the British connection and with her many selves. He seemed fated to bring unhappiness on those he cared for—Arúna, Lance, even Rose. And what of his father—if he failed to marry? He hadn't even the grit to finish his wretched novel. . . .

He rose at last, mechanically, and moved forward to the unrailed edge of all things. The magnetism of the depths drew him. The fatalistic strain in his blood drew him. . . .

He stood—though he did not know it—as his mother had once stood, hovering on the verge; his own life—that she bore within her—hanging in the balance. From the fatal tilt, she had been saved by the voice of her husband—the voice of the West. And now, at Roy's critical moment, it was the voice of the West—of Lance—that sounded in his brain: "Don't fret your heart out, Roy. Carry on."

Having carried on, somehow, through four years of war, he knew precisely how much of casual, dogged pluck was enshrined in that soldierly phrase. It struck the note of courage and command. It was Lance incarnate. It steadied him, automatically, at a crisis when his shaken nerves might not have responded to any abstract ethical appeal. He closed his eyes a moment to collect himself; swayed, the merest fraction—then deliberately stepped back a pace. . . .

The danger had passed.

Through his lids he felt the glare of lightning: the first flash of the storm.

And as the heel of his retreating boot came firmly down on the path behind, there rose an injured yelp that jerked him very completely out of the clouds.

"Poor Terry—poor old man!" he murmured, caressing the faithful creature; always too close by, always getting trodden on—the common guerdon of the faithful. And the whimsical thought intruded, "If I'd gone over, the good little beggar would have jumped after me. Not fair play."

The fact that Terry had been saved from involuntary suicide seemed somehow the more important consideration of the two.

A rumbling growl overhead reminded him that there were other considerations—urgent ones.

"You're not hurt, you little hypocrite. Come on. We must leg it."

And they legged it to some purpose; Terry—idiotically vociferous—leaping on before. . . .

## CHAPTER II.

"I seek what I cannot get;
I get what I do not seek."
—Rabindranath Tagore.

Then the storm broke in earnest. . . .

Crash on flash, crash on flash—at ever-lessening intervals—the tearless heavens raged and clattered round his unprotected head. Thunder toppled about him like falling timber stacks. Fiery serpents darted all ways at once among black boughs that swayed and moaned funereally. The gloom of the forest enhanced the weird magnificence of it all: and Roy—who had just been within an ace of flinging away his life—felt irrationally anxious on account of thronging trees and the absence of rain.

He had recovered sufficiently to chuckle at the ignominious anti-climax. But, as usual, it was the creepsomeness rather than the danger that got on his nerves and forced his legs to hurry of their own accord. . . .

In the deep of a gloomy indent, the thought assailed him—"Why do I know it all so well? Where . . .? When . . .?"

An inner flash lit the dim recesses of memory. Of course—it was that other day of summer, in the far beginning of things; the day of the Golden Tusks and the gloom and the growling thunder; his legs, as now, in a fearful hurry of their own accord; and Tara waiting for him—his High-Tower Princess. With a pang he recalled how she had seemed the point of safety—because she was never afraid.

No Tara waiting now. No point of safety, except a very prosaic dák bungalow and good old Azim, who would fuss like the devil if rain came on and he got a wetting.

Ah—here it was, at last! Buckets of it. Lashing his face, running down his neck, saturating him below his flapping burberry. Buffeted mercilessly, he broke into a trot. Thunder and lightning were less virulent now; and he found himself actually enjoying it all.

Tired——? Not a bit. The miasma of depression seemed blown clean away by the horseplay of the elements. He had been within an ace of taking unwarranted liberties with Nature. Now she retaliated by taking liberties with him; and her buffeting proved a finer restorative than all the drugs in creation. Electricity, her 'fierce angel of the air,' set every nerve tingling. A queer sensation: but it was *life.* And he had been feeling more than half dead. . . .

Azim Khan, however—being innocent of 'nerves' —took quite another view of the matter.

Arrived at the point of safety, Roy found a log fire burning; and a brazier alight under a contrivance like a huge cane hen-coop, for drying his clothes. Vainly protesting, he was made to change every garment; was installed by the fire, with steaming brandy-and-water at his elbow, and lemons and sugar—and letters . . . quite a little pile of them.

"*Belaiti dák, Hazúr,*" [1] Azim Khan superfluously informed him, with an air of personal pride in the whole *bundobast*—including the timely arrival of the English mail.

There were parcels also—a biggish one, from his father; another from Jeffers, obviously a book. And suddenly it dawned on him—this must be the tenth of June. Yesterday was his twenty-sixth birthday; and he had never thought of it; never realised the date! But *they* had thought of it weeks ahead: while he—graceless and ungrateful—had deemed himself half forgotten.

He ran the envelopes through his fingers—Tiny, Tara. (His heart jerked. Was it congratulations? He had never felt he could write of it to her.) Arúna; a black-edged one from Thea; and—his heart jerked in quite another fashion—Rose!

Amazing! What did it mean? She wasn't—going back on things . . .?

[1] English mail.

Curiosity—sharpened by a prick of fear—impelled him to open her letter first. And the moment he had read the opening line, compunction smote him.

"Roy—my Dear, I couldn't help remembering the ninth. So I feel I must write and wish you 'many happy returns' of it—happier than this one—with all my heart. I have worried over you a good deal. For I'm sure you must have been ill. Do go home soon and be properly taken care of, by your own people. I'm going in the autumn with my friend, Mrs Hilton. Some day you will surely find a wife worthier of you than I would have been. When your good day comes, let me know—and I'll do the same by you. Good luck to you always.—Rose."

Roy slipped the note into his pocket and sat staring at the fire, deeply moved. A vision of her—too alluring for comfort—was flashed upon his brain. She was confoundedly attractive. She had no end of good points: but . . . with a very big B. . . .

His gaze rested absently on the parcel from his father. What the deuce could it be? To the imaginative, an unopened parcel never quite loses its intriguing air of mystery. The shape suggested a picture. His mother . . .?

With a luxury of deliberation he cut the strings; removed wrapper after wrapper to the last layer of tissue. . . .

Then he drew a great breath—and sat spellbound; gazing—endlessly gazing—at Tara's face:—the wild roses in her cheeks faded a little; the glory of her hair undimmed; the familiar way it rippled back from her low, wide brow; a hint of hidden pain about the sensitive lips and in the hyacinth blue of her eyes. Only his father could have wrought a vision so appealingly alive. And the effect on Roy was instantaneous . . . overwhelming. . . .

Tara—dearest and loveliest! Of course it was her—always had been, down in the uttermost depths. The treasure he had been far to seek had blossomed beside him since the beginning of things: and he, with his eyes always on the horizon, had missed the one incomparable flower at his feet. . . .

*Had* he missed it? Had there ever been a chance? What, precisely, had she meant by her young, vehement refusal of him? And—if it were not the dreaded reason —was there still hope? Would she ever understand . . . ever forgive . . . the inglorious episode of Rose? If, at heart, he could plead the excuse of Adam, he could not plead it to her.

Reverently he took that miracle of a picture between his hands and set it on the broad mantelpiece, that distance might quicken the illusion of life.

Then the spell was on him again. Her sweetness and light seemed to illumine the unbeautiful room. Of a truth he knew, now, what it meant to love and be in love with every faculty of soul and body; knew it for a miracle of renewal, the elixir of life. And—the light of that knowledge revealed how secondary a part of it was the craving with which he had craved possession of Rose. Steeped in poetry as he was, there stole into his mind a fragment of Tagore—'She who had ever remained in the depths of my being, in the twilight of gleams and glimpses . . . I have roamed from country to country, keeping her in the core of my heart.'

All the jangle of jarred nerves and shaken faith; all the confusion of shattered hopes and ideals would resolve itself into coherence at last—if only . . . if only——!

And dropping suddenly from the clouds, he remembered his letters . . . *her* letter.

A sealed envelope had fallen unheeded from his father's parcel: but it was hers he seized—and half hesitated to open. What if she were announcing her own engagement to some infernal fellow at home? There must be scores and scores of them. . . .

His hand was not quite steady as he unfolded the two sheets that bore his father's crest and the home stamp, 'Bramleigh Beeches.'

"MY DEAR ROY (he read),

"*Many* happy returns of June the Ninth. It was one of our great days—wasn't it?—once upon a time. All your best and dearest wishes we are wishing for you—over here. And of course I've heard your tremendous news; though you never wrote and told me

—why? You say she is beautiful. I hope she is a lot more besides. You would need a lot more, Roy, unless you've changed very much from the boy I used to know.

"It is *cruel* having to write—in the same breath—about Lance. From the splendid boy he was, one can guess the man he became. To me it seems almost like half of you gone. And I'm sure it must seem so to you—my *poor* Roy. I don't wonder you felt bad about the way of it; but it was the essence of him—that kind of thing. A verse of Charles Sorley keeps on in my head ever since I heard it:—

'Surely we knew it long before;
Knew all along that he was made
For a swift radiant morning; for
A sacrificing swift night shade.'

"I *can't* write all I feel about it. Besides, I'm hoping your pain may be eased a little now; and I don't want to wake it up again.

"But not even these two big things—not even your Birthday—are my reallest reason for writing this particular letter to my Bracelet-Bound Brother. *Do* you remember? Have you kept it, Roy? Does it still mean anything to you? It does to me—though I've never mentioned it and never asked any service of you. *But*—I'm going to, now. Not for myself. Don't be afraid! It's for Uncle Nevil—and I ask it in Aunt Lilámani's name.

"Roy, when I came home, the change in him made me miserable. He's never really got over losing her. And you've been sort of lost too—for the time being. I can see how he's wearing his heart out with wanting you: though I don't suppose he has ever said so. And you—out there, probably thinking he doesn't miss you a mite. I *know* you—and your ways. Also I know him—which is my ragged shred of excuse for rushing in where an angel would probably think better of it!

"He has been an angel to me ever since I got back; and it seems to cheer him up when I run round here. So I do—pretty often. But I'm not Roy! And perhaps you'll forgive my bold demand, when I tell you Aunt Jane's looming—positively *looming!* She's becoming a perfect ogre of sisterly solicitude. As he won't go to

London, she's threatening to cheer him up by making the dear Beeches her headquarters after the season! And he—poor darling—with not enough spirit in him to kick against the pricks. If *you* were coming, he would have an excuse. Alone—he's helpless in her conscientious talons!

"If *that* won't bring you, nothing will—not even my bracelet command.

"I *know* the journey in June will be a nightmare. And you won't like leaving Indian friends or Miss Arden. But think—here he is alone, wanting what only you can give him. And the bangle I sent you That Day—*if* you've kept it—gives me the right to say 'Come—*quickly*.' It may be a wrench. But I promise you won't regret it. Wire, if you can.

"Always your loving

TARA."

By the time he had finished reading that so characteristic and endearing letter his plans were cut and dried. Her irresistible appeal—and the no less irresistible urge within him—left no room for the deliberations of his sensitive complex nature. It flung open all the floodgates of memory; set every nerve aching for Home—and Tara, late discovered; but not too late, he passionately prayed. . . .

The nightmare journey had no terrors for him now. In every sense he was 'hers to command.'

He drew out his old, old letter-case—her gift—and opened it. There lay the bracelet, folded inside her quaint, childish note; the 'ribbin' from her 'petticote' and the gleaming strands of her hair. The sight of it brought tears of which he felt not the least ashamed.

It also brought a vision of himself standing before his mother, demurring at possible obligations involved in their 'game of play.' And across the years came back to him her very words, her very look and tone: 'Remember, Roy, it is for always. If she shall ask from you any service, you must not refuse—ever. . . . By keeping the bracelet you are bound . . .'

Wire? Of course he would.

Before the day was out his message was speeding to her: "Engagement off. Coming first possible boat. Yours to command—ROY."

## CHAPTER III.

"Did you not know that people hide their love,
Like a flower that seems too precious to be picked?"
—WU-TI.

SANCTUARY—at last! The garden of his dreams—of the world before the deluge—in the quiet-coloured end of a July evening; the garden vitally inwoven with his fate—since it was responsible for the coming of Joe Bradley and his 'beaky mother.'

Such gardens bear more than trees and flowers and fruit. Human lives and characters are growth of their soil. With the wholesale demolishing of boundaries and hedges, their influence may wane; and it is an influence—like the unobtrusive influence of the gentleman—that human nature, especially English nature, can ill afford to fling away.

Roy, poet and fighter—with the lure of the desert and the horizon in his blood—knew himself, also, for a spiritual product of this particular garden—of the vast lawn (not quite so vast as he remembered), the rose-beds and the beeches in the full glory of their incomparable leafage; all steeped in the delicate clarity of rain-washed air—the very aura of England, as dust was the aura of Jaipur.

Dinner was over. They were sitting out on the lawn, he and his father; a small table beside them, with glass coffee-machine and chocolates in a silver dish; the smoke of their cigars hovering, drifting, unstirred by any breeze. No Terry at his feet. The faithful creature—a vision of abject misery—had been carried off to eat his heart out in quarantine. Tangled among tree-tops hung the ghost of a moon, almost full. Somewhere, in the far quiet of the shrubberies, a nightingale was communing with its own heart in liquid undertones;

and in Roy's heart there dwelt an iridescence of peace and pain and longing shot through with hope——

That very morning, at an unearthly hour, he had landed in England, after an absence of three and a half years: and precisely what that means in the way of complex emotions, only they know who have been there. The purgatorial journey had eclipsed expectation. Between recurrent fever and sea-sickness, there had been days when it seemed doubtful if he would ever reach Home at all. But a wiry constitution and the will to live had triumphed: and, in spite of the early hour, his father had not failed to be on the quay.

The first sight of him had given Roy a shock for which—in spite of Tara's letter—he was unprepared. This was not the father he remembered—humorous, unruffled, perennially young; but a man so changed and tired-looking that he seemed almost a stranger, with his empty coat-sleeve and hair touched with silver at the temples.

The actual moment of meeting had been difficult; the joy of it so deeply tinged with pain that they had clung desperately to surface commonplaces, because they were Englishmen, and could not relieve the inner stress by falling on one another's necks.

And there had been a secret pang (for which Roy sharply reproached himself) that Tara was not there too. Idiotic to expect it, when he knew Sir James had gone to Scotland for fishing. But to be idiotic is the lover's privilege; and his not phenomenal gift of patience had been unduly strained by the letter awaiting him at Port Said.

They were coming back to-night; but he would not see her till to-morrow. . . .

In his pocket reposed a brief Tara-like note, bidding her 'faithful Knight of the Bracelet' welcome Home. Vainly he delved between the lines of her sisterly affection. Nothing could still the doubt that consumed him, but contact with her hands, her eyes.

For that, and other reasons, the difficult meeting had been followed by a difficult day. They had wandered through the house and garden, very carefully veiling their emotions. They had lounged and smoked in the studio, looking through his father's latest pictures.

They had talked of the family. Jeffers would be down to-morrow night, for the week-end; Tiny on Tuesday with the precious Baby; Jerry, distinctly coming round, and eager to see Roy. Even Aunt Jane sounded a shade keen. And he, undeserving, had scarcely expected them to 'turn a hair.' Then they discussed the Indian situation; and Roy—forgetting to be shy—raged at finding how little those at Home had been allowed to realise, to understand.

Not a question, so far, about his rapid on-and-off engagement, for which mercy he was duly grateful. And of her, who dwelt in the foreground and background of their thoughts—not a word.

It would take a little time, Roy supposed, to build their bridge across the chasm of three and a half eventful years. You couldn't hustle a lapsed intimacy. To-morrow things would go better, especially if . . .

Yet, throughout, he had been touched inexpressibly by his father's unobtrusive tokens of pleasure and affection: and now—sitting together with their cigars, in the last of the daylight—things felt easier.

"Dad," he said suddenly, turning his eyes from the garden to the man beside him, who was also its spiritual product. "If I seem a bit stupefied, it's because I'm still walking and talking in a dream; terrified I may wake up and find it's not true! I can't, in a twinkling, adjust the beautiful, incredible *sameness* of all this, with the staggering changes inside me."

His father's smile had its friendly, understanding quality.

"No hurry, Boy. All your deep roots are here. Change as much as you please, you still remain—her son."

"Yes—that's it. The place is full of her," Roy said very low; and at present they could not trust themselves to say more.

It had not escaped Sir Nevil's notice that the boy had avoided the drawing-room, and had not once been under the twin beeches, his favourite summer retreat. No hammock was slung there now.

After a considerable gap, Roy remarked carelessly: "I suppose they must have got home by now?"

"About an hour ago, to be exact," said Sir Nevil; and Roy's involuntary start moved him to add: "You're not running round there to-night, old man. They'll be tired. So are you. And it's only fair I should have first innings. I've waited a long time for it, Roy."

"*Dads!*" Roy looked at once penitent and reproachful—an engaging trick of schoolroom days, when he felt a scolding in the air. "You never said—you never gave me an idea."

"*You* never sounded as if the idea would be acceptable."

"Didn't I? Letters are the devil," murmured Roy —all penitence now. "And if it hadn't been for Tara——" He stopped awkwardly. Their eyes met, and they smiled. "Did you know . . . she wrote? And that's why I'm here?"

"Well done, Tara! I didn't know. I had dim suspicions. I also had a dim hope that—my picture might tempt you——"

"Oh, it *would* have—letter or no. It's an inspired thing."—He had already written at length on that score. —"You were mightily clever—the two of you!"

His father twinkled. "That as may be. We had the trifling advantage of knowing our Roy!"

They sat on till all the light had ebbed from the sky and the moon had come into her own. It was still early; but time is the least ingredient of such a day; and Sir Nevil rose on the stroke of ten.

"You look fagged out, old boy. And the sooner you're asleep—the sooner it will be to-morrow! A pet axiom of yours. D'you remember?"

Did he not remember?

They went upstairs together; the great house seemed oppressively empty and silent. On the threshold of Roy's room they said good-night. There was an instant of palpable awkwardness; then Roy—overcoming it—leaned forward and kissed the patch of white hair on his father's temple.

"God bless you," Sir Nevil said rather huskily. "You ought to sleep sound in there. Don't dream."

"But I love to dream," said Roy; and his father laughed.

"You're not so staggeringly changed inside! As sure as a gun, you'll be late for breakfast!"

And he did dream. The moment his lids fell—she

was there with him, under the beeches, their sanctuary—she who all day had hovered on the confines of his spirit, like a light, felt not seen. There were no words between them, nor any need of words; only the ineffable peace of understanding, of reunion. . . .

Dream—or visitation—who could say? To him it seemed that only afterwards sleep came—the dreamless sleep of renewal. . . .

He woke egregiously early: such an awakening as he had not known for months on end. And out there in the garden it was a miracle of a morning: divinely clear, with the mellow clearness of England; massed trees, brooding darkly; the lawn all silver-grey with dew; everywhere blurred outlines and tender shadows; pure balm to eye and spirit after the hard brilliance and contrasts of the East.

Madness to get up; yet impossible to lie there waiting. He tried it, for what seemed an endless age: then succumbed to the inevitable.

While he was dressing, clouds drifted across the blue. A spurt of rain whipped his open casement; threatening him in playful mood. But before he had crept down and let himself out through one of the drawing-room windows, the sky was clear again, with the tremulous radiance of happiness struck sharp on months of sorrow and stress.

Striding, hatless, across the drenched lawn, and resisting the pull of his beech-wood, he pressed on and up to the open moor; craving its sweeps of space and colour unbosomed to the friendly sky that seemed so much nearer earth than the passionate blue vault of India.

It was five years since he had seen heather in bloom—or was it five decades? The sight of it recalled that other July day, when he had tramped the length of the ridge with his head full of dreams and the ache of parting in his heart.

To him, that far-off being seemed almost another Roy in another life. Only—as his father had feelingly reminded him—the first Roy and the last were alike informed by the spirit of one woman; visible then, invisible now; yet sensibly present in every haunt she had made her own. The house was full of her; the wood was full of her. But the pangs of reminder he had so dreaded resolved themselves, rather, into a sense of indescribable, ethereal reunion. He asked nothing better than that his life and work should be fulfilled with her always: her and Tara—if she so decreed. . . .

Thought of Tara revived impatience, and drew his steps homeward again.

Strolling back through the wood, he came suddenly upon the open space where he had found the Golden Tusks, and lingered there a little—remembering the storm and the terror and the fight; Tara and her bracelet; and the deep unrealised significance of that childish impulse, inspired by *her*, whose was the source of all their inspirations. And now—seventeen years afterwards, the bracelet had drawn him back to them both; saved him, perhaps, from the unforgiveable sin of throwing up the game.

On he walked, along the same mossy path, almost in a dream. He had found the Tusks. His High-Tower Princess was waiting—his 'Star far-seen.'

Again, as on that day—he came unexpectedly in view of their tree: and—wonder of wonders (or was it the most natural thing on earth?), there was Tara herself, approaching it by another path that linked the wood with the grounds of the black-and-white house, which was part of the estate.

Instantly he stepped back a pace and stood still, that he might realise her before she became aware of him:—her remembered loveliness, her new dearness.

Loveliness was the quintessence of her. With his innate feeling for words, he had never—even accidentally—applied it to Rose. Had she, too, felt impatient? Was she coming over to breakfast for a 'surprise'?

At this distance, she looked not a day older than on that critical occasion, when he had realised her for the first time; only more fragile—a shade too fragile. It hurt him. He felt responsible. And again, to-day—very clever of her—she was wearing a delphinium blue frock; a shady hat that drooped half over her face. No pink rose, however—and he was thankful. Roses had still a too baleful association. He doubted if he could ever tolerate a Maréchal Niel again—as much on account of Lance, as on account of the other.

Tara was wearing *his* flower—sweet-peas, palest pink and lavender. And, at sight of her, every shred of doubt seemed burnt up in the clear flame of his love for her:—no heady confusion of heart and senses, but a rarefied intensity of both, touched with a coal from the altar of creative life. The knowledge was like a light hand reining in his impatience. Poet, no less than lover, he wanted to go slowly through the golden mist. . . .

But the moment he stirred, she heard him; saw him. . . .

No imperious gesture, as before; but a lightning gleam of recognition, of welcome and — something more——?

He hurried now. . . .

Next instant, they were together, hands locked, eyes deep in eyes. The surface sense of strangeness between them, the undersense of intimate nearness—thrilling as it was—made speech astonishingly difficult.

"Tara," he said, just above his breath.

Her senstive lips parted, trembled—and closed again.

"*Tara!*" he repeated, dizzily incredulous, where a moment earlier he had been arrogantly certain. "*Is* it true . . . what your eyes are telling me? Can you forgive . . . my madness out there? Half across the world you called to me; and I've come home to *you* . . . with every atom of me . . . I'm loving you; and I'm still . . . bracelet-bound . . ."

This time her lips trembled into a smile. "And it's not one of the Prayer-book affinities!" she reminded him, a gleam of that other Tara in her eyes.

"No, thank God—it's not! But you haven't answered me, you know . . ."

"Roy, what a story! When you know I really said it first!" Her eyes were saying it again now; and he, bereft of words, mutely held out his arms.

If she paused an instant, it was because she felt even dizzier than he. But the power of his longing drew her like a physical force—and, as his lips claimed hers, the terror of love and its truth caught her and swept her from known shores into uncharted seas. . . .

This was a Roy she scarcely knew. But her heart knew; every pulse of her awakened womanhood knew. . . .

Presently it became possible to think. Very gently she pushed him back a little.

"O-oh—I never knew . . . you were . . . like *that!* And you've crushed my poor sweet-peas to smithereens! Now—behave! Let me *look* at you . . . properly, and see what India's done to you. Give me a chance!"

He gave her a chance, still keeping hold of her—to make sure she was real.

"High-Tower Princess, are we truly US? Or is it a 'bewitchery'?" he asked, only half in joke. "Will you go turning into a butterfly presently——?"

"Promise I won't!" Her low laugh was not quite steady. "We're US—truly. And we've got to Farthest-End, where your dreams come true. D'you remember—I always said they couldn't. They were too crazy. So I don't deserve——"

"It's *I* that don't deserve," he broke out with sudden passion. "And to find you under our very own tree! Have you forgotten—that day? Of course *you* went to the 'tipmost top'; and I didn't. It's queer—isn't it?—how *bits* of life get printed so sharply on your brain; and great spaces, on either side, utterly blotted out. That day's one of my bits. Is it so clear—to you?"

"To *me*——?" She could scarcely believe he did not know. . . . Unashamedly, she wanted him to know. But part of him was strange to her—thrillingly strange: which made things not quite so simple.

"Roy," she went on, after a luminous pause, twisting the top button of his coat. "I'm going to tell you a secret. A big one. For me that Day was . . . the beginning of everything.—Hush—listen!"—Her fingers just touched his lips. "I'm feeling—rather shy. And if you don't keep quiet, I can't tell. Of course I always . . . loved you, next to Atholl. But after that . . . after the fight, I simply . . . adored you. And . . . and . . . it's never left off since . . ."

"Tara! My loveliest!" he cried, between ecstasy and dismay; and gathering her close again, he kissed her softly, repeatedly, murmuring broken endearments. "And there was *I* . . . !"

"Yes. There were you . . . with your poems and Aunt Lila and your dreams about India—always with your head among the stars . . ."

"In plain English, a spoilt boy—as you once told me—wrapped up in myself."

"No, you weren't. I won't *have* it!" she contradicted him in her old imperious way. "You were wrapped up in all kinds of wonderful things. So you just . . . didn't see me. You looked clean over my head. Of course it often made me unhappy. But—it made me love you more. That's the way we women are. It's not the men who run after us; it's the other kind . . .! I expect you looked clean over poor Arúna's head. And if I asked her, privately, she'd confess that was partly why . . . and the other girl too . . . if . . ."

"Darling—*don't!*" he pleaded. "I'm ashamed, beyond words. I'll tell you every atom of it truthfully . . . my Tara. But this is *our* moment. I want more—about you.—Sit. It's full early. Then we'll go in (of course you're coming to breakfast) and give Dad the surprise of his life. . . . Bother your old hat! It gets in the way. And I want to see your hair."

With a shyness new to him—and to Tara, poignantly dear—he drew out her pins; discarded the offending hat, and took her head between his hands, lightly caressing the thick coils that shaded from true gold to warm delicate tones of brown.

Then he set her on the mossy seat near the trunk; and flung himself down before her in the old way, propped on his elbows—rapt, lost in love; divinely without self-consciousness.

"I'm *not* looking over your head now," he said, his eyes deep in hers:—deep and deeper, till the wild-rose flush invaded the delicate hollows of her temples; and leaning forward she laid a hand across those too eloquent eyes.

"Don't blind me altogether—darling. When people have been shut away from the sun a long time——"

"But, Tara—why *were* you . . .?" He removed the hand and kept hold of it. "I begged you to come. I wanted you. Why *did* you . . .?"

She shook her head, smiling half wistfully. "That's a bit of my old Roy! But you're man enough to know—now, without telling. And I was woman enough to know—then. At least, by instinct, I knew . . ."

"Then it wasn't because . . . because—I'm half . . . Rajput?"

"*Roy!*" But for all her surprise and reproach, intuition told him the idea was not altogether new to her. "What made you think—of *that?*"

"Well—because it partly . . . broke things off—out there. That startled me. And when Dad's miracle of a picture woke me up with a vengeance . . . it terrified me. I began wondering. . . . Beloved, are you *quite* sure about Aunt Helen . . . Sir James . . .?"

She paused—a mere breathing-space; her free hand caressed his hair. (This time, he did not shift his head.) "I'm utterly sure about Mother. You see . . . she knows . . . we've talked about it. We're like sisters, almost. As for Father . . . well, we're less intimate. I did fancy he seemed the wee-est bit relieved when . . . your news came . . ." The pain in his eyes checked her. "My blessed one, I won't have you *daring* to worry about it. I'm feeling simply beyond myself with happiness and pride. Mother will be overjoyed. She realises . . . a *little* . . . what I've been through. Of course—in our talks, she has told me frankly what tragedies often come from mixing such 'mighty opposites.' But she said all of you were quite exceptional. And she knows about such things. And *she's* the point. She can always square Father if—there's any need. So just be quiet—inside!"

"But . . . that day," he persisted, Roy-like, "*you* didn't think of it——?"

"Faithfully, I didn't. I only felt your heart was too full up with Aunt Lila and India to have room enough for me. And I wanted *all* the room—or nothing. Vaguely, I knew it was *her* dream. But my wicked pride insisted it should be *your* dream. It wasn't till long after, that Mother told me how—from the very first—Aunt Lila had planned and prayed, because she knew marriage might be your one big difficulty; and she could only speak of it to Mummy. It was their great link; the idea behind everything—the lessons and all. So you see, all the time, she was sort of creating me . . . for you. And the bitter disappointment it must have been to her! If I'd had a glimmering . . . of all that—I don't believe I could have held out against you——"

"Then I wish to heaven you'd had a glimmering—because of her and because of *us*. Look at all the good years we've wasted——"

"We've not—we've *not!*" she protested vehemently. "If it had happened then, it wouldn't have come within miles—of this. You simply hadn't it *in* you, Roy, to give me . . . all I can feel you giving me now. As for me—well, that's for you to find out! Of course, the minute I'd done it, I was miserable: furious with myself. For I couldn't stop . . . loving you. My heart had no shame, in spite of my important pride. Only . . . after *she* went—and Mother told me all—something in me seemed to know her free spirit would be near you—and bring you back to me . . . somehow: *till* . . . your news came. And—*look!* The Bracelet! I hesitated a long time. If you hadn't been engaged, I'm not sure if I would have ventured. But I did—and you're here. It's all been her doing, Roy, first and last. Don't let's spoil any of it with regrets."

He could only bow his head upon her hand in mute adoration. The courage, the crystal-clear wisdom of her—his eager Tara, who could never wait five minutes for the particular sweet or the particular tale she craved. Yet she had waited five years for him—and counted it a little thing. Of a truth his mother had builded better than she knew.

"You see," Tara added softly. "There wouldn't have been . . . the deeps. And it takes the deeps to make you realise the heights——"

Lost in one another—in the wonder of mutual self-revealing—they were lost, no less, to impertinent trivialities of place and time; till the very trivial pang of hunger reminded Roy that he had been wandering for hours without food.

"Tara—it's a come down—but I'm fairly starving!" he cried suddenly—and consulted his watch. "Nine o'clock. The wretch I am! Dad's final remark was, 'Sure as a gun, you'll be late for breakfast.' And it seemed impossible. But sure as guns we *will* be! Put on the precious hat. We must jolly well run for it."

And taking hands, like a pair of children, they ran. . .

# CHAPTER THE LAST.

"Who shall allot the praise, and guess
What part is yours—what part is ours?"
—ALICE MEYNELL.

"Perhaps a dreamer's day will come . . . when judgment will be pronounced on all the wise men, who always prophesied evil—and were always right."—JOHAN BOJER.

Two hours later Roy and his father sat together in the cushioned window seat of the studio, smoking industriously; not troubling to say much—though there was much to be said—because the mist of constraint that brooded between them yesterday had been blown clean away by Roy's news.

If it had not given Sir Nevil 'the surprise of his life,' it had given him the deepest, most abiding gratification he had known since his inner light had gone out, with the passing of her who had been his inspiration and his all. Dear though his children were to him, they had remained secondary, always. Roy came nearest—as his heir, and as the one in whom her spirit most clearly lived again. Since she went, he had longed for the boy; but remembering her plea on that summer day of decision—her mountain-top of philosophy, 'to take by leaving, to hold by letting go'—he had studiously refrained from pressing Roy's return. Now, at a word from Tara, he had sped home in the hot season; and—hard on the heels of a mysteriously broken engagement—had claimed her at sight.

Yesterday their sense of strangeness had made silence feel uncomfortable. Now that they slipped back into the old intimacy, it felt companionable. Yet neither was thinking directly of the other. Each was thinking of the woman he loved.

By chance their eyes encountered in a friendly smile, and Roy spoke.

"Daddums—you've come alive! I believe you're *almost* as happy over it—as I am?"

"You're not far out. You see"—his eyes grew graver—"I'm feeling . . . Mother's share, too. Did you ever realise . . .?"

"Partly. Not all—till just now. Tara told me."

There was a pause. Then Sir Nevil looked full at his son.

"Roy—*I've* got something to tell you—to show you . . . if you can detach your mind for an hour——?"

"Why, of course. *What* is it—where?"

He looked round the room. Instinctively, he knew it concerned his mother.

"Not here. Upstairs—in her House of Gods." He saw Roy flinch. "If *I* can bear it, old boy, you can. And there's a reason—you'll understand."

The little room above the studio had been sacred to Lilámani ever since her home-coming as a bride of eighteen; sacred to her prayers and meditations; to the sandalwood casket that held her 'private god'; for the Indian wife has always one god chosen for special worship —not to be named to any one, even her husband. And although a Christian Lilámani had discontinued that form of devotion, the tiny blue image of the Baby-god, Krishna, had been a sacred treasure always, shown, on rare occasions only, to Roy. To enter that room was to enter her soul. And Roy, shrinking apart, felt himself unworthy—because of Rose.

On the threshold there met him the faint scent of sandalwood that pervaded her. For there, in an alcove, stood Krishna's casket. In larger boxes, lined with sandalwood, her many-tinted silks and saris lay lovingly folded. Another casket held her jewels, and arranged on a row of shelves stood her dainty array of shoes—gold and silver and pale brocades: an intimate touch that pierced his heart.

Near the Krishna alcove, hung a portrait he had not seen: a thing of fragile, almost unearthly beauty, painted when her husband came home—and realised . . .

An aching lump in Roy's throat cut like a knife; but his father's remark put him on his mettle. And, the next instant, he saw. . . .

"*Dad!*" he breathed, in awed amazement.

For there, on the small round table, stood a model in

dull red clay: unmistakably, unbelievably — the rock fortress of Chitor: the walls scarped and bastioned; Khumba Rána's tower; and the City itself—no ruin, but a miniature presentment of Chitor, as she might have been in her day of ancient glory, as Roy had been dimly aware of her in the course of his own amazing ride. Temples, palaces, huddled houses—not detailed, but skilfully suggested—stirred the old thrill in his veins, the old certainty that he knew. . . .

"Well——?" asked Sir Nevil, whose eyes had not left his face.

"*Well!*" echoed Roy, emerging from his trance of wonder. "I'm dumfounded. A few mistakes, here and there; but—as a whole . . . Dad—how in the world . . . could you know?"

"I don't know. I hoped you would. I . . . saw it clearly, just like that——"

"How? In a dream?"

"I suppose so. I couldn't swear, in a court of law, that I was awake. It happened—one evening, as I lay there, on her couch—remembering . . . going back over things. And suddenly, out of the darkness, blossomed —that. Asleep or awake, my mind was alert enough to seize and hold the impression, without a glimmer of surprise . . . *till* I came to, or woke up—which you will. Then my normal, sceptical self didn't know what to make of it. I've always dismissed that sort of thing as mere brain-trickery. But—a vivid, personal experience makes it . . . not so easy. Of course, from reading and a few old photographs, I knew it was Chitor: and my chief concern was to record the vision in its first freshness. For three days I worked at it: only emerging now and then to snatch a meal. I began with those and that——"

He indicated a set of rough sketches and an impression in oils; a ghost of a city full of suggested beauty and mystery. "No joke, trying to model with one hand; but you wouldn't believe . . . the swiftness . . . the sureness . . . as if my fingers knew . . ."

Roy could believe. Occasionally his own fingers behaved so.

"When it was done, I put it in here," his father went on, masking, with studied quietness, his elation at the effect on Roy. "I've shown it to no one—not even Aunt

Helen. I couldn't write of it. I felt it would sound crazy——"

"Not to me," said Roy.

"Well, I couldn't tell that. And I've been waiting—for *you*."

"Since—when ?"

"Since the third of March, this year."

Roy drew an audible breath. It was the anniversary of her passing. "All that time! How could you——? Why didn't you——?"

"Well—*you* know. You were obviously submerged—your novel, Udaipur, Lance. . . . You wouldn't have forgone all that . . . if I know you, for a mere father. But you're here, at last, thank God. And—I want to know. You've seen Chitor, as it is to-day . . ."

"I've seen more than that," said Roy. "I can tell you, now. I couldn't—before. Let's sit."

And sitting there, on her couch, in her House of Gods, he told the story of his moonlit ride and its culmination; told it in low tones, in swift vivid phrases that came of themselves. . . .

Throughout the telling—and for many minutes afterwards—his father sat motionless; his head on his hand, half shielding his face from view. . . .

"I've only spoken of it to Grandfather," Roy said at last. "And with all my heart, I wish he could see . . . that."

Sir Nevil looked up now, and the subdued exaltation in his eyes was wholly new to Roy.

"*I've* gone a good way beyond wishing," he said. "But again—I was waiting for you. I want to go out there, Roy—with you two, when you're married—and see it all for myself. With care, one could take the thing along, to verify and improve it on the spot. Then—what do you say?—you and I might achieve a larger reproduction—for Grandfather: a gift to Rajputana—my source of inspiration; a tribute . . . to her memory, who still lights our lives . . . with the inextinguishable lamp of her spirit——"

The last words—almost inaudible—were a revelation to Roy; an illumining glimpse of the true self, that a man hides very carefully from his fellows; and shows—at supreme moments only—to 'a woman when he loves her.'

Shy of their mutual emotion, he laid a hand on his father's arm.

"You can count on me, Dad," he said in the same low tone. "Who knows—one day it might inspire the Rajputs to rebuild their Queen of Cities, in white marble, that she may rise again, immortal through the ages . . ."

When they stood up to leave the shrine their eyes met in a steadfast look; and there was the same thought behind it. She had given them to each other in a new way; in a fashion all her own.

For that brief space, Roy had almost forgotten Tara. Now the wonder of her flashed back on him like a dazzle of sunlight after the dim sanctity of cathedral aisles.

And down in the studio it was possible to discuss practical issues of his father's inspiration—or rather his mother's; for they both felt it as such.

Roy would marry Tara in September; and in November they three would go out together. There were bad days coming out there; but, as Roy had once said, every man and woman of goodwill—British or Indian—would count in the scale, were it only a grain here, a grain there. The insignificance of the human unit—a mere fragment of star-dust on sidereal shores—is off-set by the incalculable significance of the individual in the history of man's efforts to be more than man. In that faith these two could not be found wanting; debtors as they were to the genius, devotion, and high courage of one fragile woman, who had lived little more than half her allotted span.

They at least would not give up hope of the lasting unity vital to both races, because political errors and poisonous influences and tragic events had roused a mutual spirit of bitterness difficult to quell. . . .

Conceivably, it *might* touch the imagination of their India—Rajputana (Roy was chary, now, of the all-embracing word), that an Englishman should so love an Indian woman as to immortalise her memory in a form peculiar to the East. For a Christian Lilámani, neither temple, nor tomb, but the vision of a waste city rebuilded—the city whose name was written on her heart. In their uplifted moment, it seemed not quite unthinkable.

"And it's India's imagination we have most of us

signally failed to touch—if not done a good deal to quench," said Roy, his eyes brooding on a bank of purple-grey cloud, his own imagination astir. . . .

It was his turn now to catch a flitting inspiration on the wing.

Would it be utterly impossible——? Could they spend a wander-year in Rajputana—the cities, the desert, the Aravallis: his father painting—he writing? The result—a combined book, dedicated to her memory; an attempt to achieve something in the nature of interpretation—his arrogant dream of Oxford days; a vindication of his young faith in the arts as the true medium of mutual understanding. In any case, it would be a unique achievement. And they would feel they had contributed their mite of goodwill, had followed 'the gleam.' . . .

"Besides—out there, other chances might crop up. Thea, Grandfather, Dyán. . . . And Tara would be in it all, heart and soul," he concluded—remembering, with a twinge, a certain talk with Rose. "And it would do *you* all the good on earth—which isn't the least of its virtues, in my eyes!"

The look on his father's face was reward enough—for the moment.

"Well done, Roy," said Sir Nevil very quietly. "That year in Rajputana shall be my wedding present—to you two——"

Later on the 'inspired plan' was expounded to Tara—with amplifications. She had merely run home—escorted, of course, through the perils of the wood—to impart her great news and bring her mother back to lunch, which Roy persistently called 'tiffin.' Food disposed of, they stepped straight out of the house into a world of their own—the world of their 'Game-without-an-End'; the rose garden, the wood, the regal splendours of the moor, gleaming and glooming under shadows of drifting cloud: on and on, in a golden haze of content, talking, endlessly talking. . . .

The reserve and infrequency of their letters had left whole tracts, outer and inner, unexplored. Here, thought Roy—in his mother's beautiful phrase—was 'the comrade of body and spirit' that his subconsciousness had been seeking all along; while he looked over the heads of one and another, lured by the far, yet emotionally susceptible to the near. Once—unbidden —the thought intruded: "How different! How unutterably different!"

Reading aloud to Tara would seem pure waste of her; except when it came to the novel, of which he had told her next to nothing, so far. . . .

And Tara carried her happiness proudly, like a banner. The deliciousness of being loved; the intoxication of it, after the last spark of hope had been quenched by that excruciating engagement! Her volcanic heart held a capacity for happiness as tremendous as her capacity for daring and suffering. But the first had so long eluded her, that now she dared scarcely let herself go.

She listened half incredulous, wholly entranced, while Roy drew rapid word-pictures of the cities they would see together—Udaipur, Chitor, Ajmir; and, not least, Komulmir, the hill fortress crowned with the 'cloud-palace' of Prithvi Raj and that distant Tara, her namesake. Together, they would seek out the little shrine —Roy knew all about it—near the Temple of the Mother of the Gods, that held the mingled ashes of those great lovers who were pleasant in their lives and in death were not divided. . . .

It was much later on, in the evening, when they sat alone near the twin beeches, under a new-lighted moon, that Roy at last managed to speak of Rose. In the dimness it was easier, though difficult at best. But all day he had been aware of Tara longing to hear; unable to ask; too sensitive on his account; too proud on her own.

Sir James and Lady Despard were dining, to honour the event: and if Sir James had needed 'squaring' no one heard of it. Jeffers had arrived, large and genial —his thatch of hair thinned a little and white as driven snow. Healths had been drunk. It was long since the Beeches had known so hilarious a meal. Yet the graceless pair had made haste to escape, and blessed Lady Despard for remaining with the men.

Tara was leaning back in a low chair; Roy on a floor cushion, very close; a hand slipped behind her, his cheek against her arm; yet, in a deeper sense, she wanted him closer still. Surely he knew. . . .

He did know.

"Tara—my loveliest—shall I tell you?" he asked suddenly. "Are you badly wanting to hear?"

"Craving to," she confessed. "It's like a bit of blank space inside me. And I don't want blank spaces—about you. It's the house swept and garnished that attracts the seven devils. And one of my devils is jealousy! I've hated her *so*, poor thing. I can't hate her more, whatever you tell——"

"Try hating her less," suggested Roy.

"Try and make me!" she challenged him. "Are you—half afraid? Were you . . . fearfully smitten?"

"Wonderful Tara! 'Smitten' is the very word." He looked up at her moonlit face, its appealing charm, its mingling of delicacy and strength. "I would never dream of saying I was 'smitten'—with *you*."

For reward, her lips caressed his hair. "What a Roy you are—with your words! Tell me—tell from the beginning."

And from the beginning he told her: first in broken, spasmodic sentences, with breaks and jars; then more fluently, more unreservedly, as he felt her leaning closer—more and more understanding; more and more forgiving, where understanding faltered, where gaps came—on account of Lance, and of pain that went too deep for words. She had endured her own share of that. She knew. . . .

When all had been said, it was she who could not speak; and he gathered her to him, kissing with a passion of tenderness her wet lashes, her trembling lips——

At last: "Beloved—*has* the blank space gone?" he asked. "Are you content now?"

"Content! I'm lifted to the skies."

"To the tipmost top of them?" he queried in her ear; and mutely she clung to him, returning his kisses, with the confidence of a child, with the intensity of a woman. . . .

All too soon it was over—their one mere day: the walk back through the wood—never more enchanted than on a night of full moon: Tara, dropped from the skies, lost to everything but the sound of Roy's voice in the darkness, deep and soft, like the voice of her own heart heard in a dream. It seemed incredible that there would be to-morrow—and to-morrow—and to-morrow, world without end. . . .

Back in the garden, Jeffers—a miracle of tact—wandered away to commune with an idea, leaving father and son alone together.

Sir Nevil offered Roy a cigarette, and they sat down in two of the six empty chairs near the beeches and smoked steadily without exchanging a remark.

But this time they were thinking of one woman. For at parting Tara had said again, "It's all been her doing—first and last." And Roy—with every faculty sensitised to catch ethereal vibrations above and below the human octave—divined that identical thought in his father's silence. Her doing indeed! None of them —not even his father—knew it better than himself.

And now, while he sat there utterly still in the midst of stillness—no stir in the tree-tops, no movement anywhere but the restless glow of Broome's cigar—the inexpressible sense of her stole in upon him, flooding his spirit like a distillation from the summer night. Moment by moment the impression deepened and glowed within him. Never, since that morning at Chitor, had it so uplifted and fulfilled him. . . .

Surely, now, his father could feel it too? Deliberately he set himself to transmit, if might be, the thrill of her nearness—the intimacy, the intensity of it.

Then, craving certainty, he put out a hand and touched his father's knee.

"Dad," the word was a mere breath. "Can you feel . . .? She is here."

His father's hand closed sharply on his own.

For one measureless moment they sat so. Then the sense of her presence faded as a light dies out. The garden was empty. The restless red planet was moving towards them.

On a mutual impulse they rose. Once again, as in her shrine, they exchanged a steadfast look. And Roy had his answer.

He slipped a possessive hand through his father's arm; and without a word, they walked back into the house. . . .

*Parkstone, February* 1920.
*Parkstone, March* 27, 1921.

THE END.